A
River
out
of
Eden

Also by John Hockenberry

MOVING VIOLATIONS

John

Hockenberry

Doubleday

New York London Toronto

Sydney Auckland

A River out of Eden

a novel

PUBLISHED BY DOUBLEDAY
a division of Random House, Inc.
1540 Broadway, New York, New York 10036

DOUBLEDAY and the portrayal of an anchor with a dolphin are
trademarks of Doubleday, a division of Random House, Inc.

All of the characters in this book are fictitious, and any resemblance
to actual persons, living or dead, is purely coincidental.

Book design by Maria Carella

"Castles Made of Sand" and "Machine Gun" by Jimi Hendrix,
© Experience Hendrix, LLC. Used by permission. All rights reserved.

Photograph of Celilo Falls on endpapers
and title page by Benjamin Gifford, circa 1899.
Courtesy of the Oregon Historical Society.

Library of Congress Cataloging-in-Publication Data
Hockenberry, John.
    A river out of Eden : a novel / John Hockenberry.—1st ed.
        p. cm.
      1. Northwest, Pacific—Fiction. 2. Dams—Design and
construction—Fiction. 3. Indians of North America—Fiction.
4. Salmon fisheries—Fiction. 5. Columbia River—Fiction. I. Title.
PS3558.O34182 R5 2001
813'.54—dc21

                                            00-055476

ISBN 0-385-49425-4

To

Alison,

Zoë,

and Olivia

And he shewed me a pure river of water of life, clear as crystal, proceeding from the throne of God and of the Lamb.

Revelation 22:1

So the Skookums had all the fish, but the people had none. Coyote was very angry. "Before many suns, fish shall come up the river. . . ." Then Coyote picked up the key and went to the dam. Coyote opened the dam and let the fish through.

"Coyote and the Salmon," myth of the Klamath

And so castles made of sand melt into the sea, eventually.

Jimi Hendrix

Historical Note

Like all works of fiction, this story is drawn from some very real places and events that need no embellishment from the pens of novelists. Chief among these, are the Columbia River, its native salmon, and the astonishing dams of the Columbia/Snake River system, which include Grand Coulee, Bonneville, Chief Joseph, Mica, and the lesser dams. References to them in this book are factual with one glaring exception: The Dalles Dam was built in 1957, not 1967. I altered the time frame to fit my character's needs. I trust it will not interfere with anyone's enjoyment of the story. Celilo Falls, Maryhill Mansion, and the Hanford Nuclear Reservation are also real, although only the latter two can actually be seen and visited now. But one can still view with the same clarity today, as people have for thousands of years, the face of Tsagaglalal, who watches the Columbia from the rocks overlooking the Dalles.

The many references to the practices of the Pacific Northwest tribes in these pages are as accurate as I could make them. It is my hope that readers might find themselves awakened to interest in people whose stories lie outside the popularized details of American history. Any inaccuracies or offense are my responsibility alone and not the fault of the numerous and superb historical sources I have relied upon.

In this book, the prophetic and the inevitable are indistinguishable. It is a feeling I first got walking the banks of the Columbia, seeing always at the same moment what was and what had once been. Such is the character of the Pacific Northwest. It is a place both ancient and in its infancy. This story is inspired by the Pacific Northwest's heroic and tragic histories. They all hover close by, just out of view, like the loamy breath of its oldest trees. While this is entirely a work of fiction, the convergence of those histories is real, and waits patiently for some future generation.

Pronunciation Guide

For reasons that are both frustrating and hard not to respect, native tribes are loath to engage in the distribution of cultural information when the purpose does not clearly reflect tribal interests. As such, no tribal official would agree to assist with the pronunciation of important words, names, and places that appear frequently in this book. In preparing a guide for non-native speakers, I have had to rely on my own memory of words spoken to me in numerous conversations, some helpful but unofficial sources, and texts that offer pronunciation guidance. Tribal languages are always transliterated into English phonetically, as they represent oral traditions, yet certain words represent a unique challenge to non-native speakers. Herewith a pronunciation guide for some frequent references in this book that are hardly obscure to people of the region but, it is fair to say, rarely used in conversation.

Celilo = *Sa 'lie-low*

Smohalla = *Smaw 'hah-lah*
(Accent on the second syllable, the h is mildly guttural, all the vowels are short.)

Nch'i-Wana = *N* (hard *n*) *chee 'wah-nah*

Tsagaglalal = *Te 'sahg-gahg 'lahl-lahl*
(This word is so challenging for most non-natives that rather than butchering the name of a sacred spirit, out of respect most simply use the English translation: She Who Watches.)

Jokulhlaup = 'Yo-*kool hlawp*
(This word may be challenging, but it is not Indian. Rather, it comes from Icelandic, a language in which people have been describing nature's more violent acts for all of their history.)

A River out of Eden

A baptism

It had rained hard. At both ends of the Columbia River, Pacific Northwest gray gave way to skies of slate, urgent with chill and downpours that for weeks had drained the color from the world. At the headwaters in northern Canada, the rain had its way with the forest, slap-punching the trees and ferns into submission. Rain had compelled the rocks and plants and animals of the valley into service for the moving waters. Each leaf was a funnel, each hoof-print of elk and deer a link in a primeval bucket brigade, each slab of granite a God-given spillway, the rich, fertile mud a sieve, all of it channeling every drop, every lump of snow ever downward into the ancient path of the river. The water paused only long enough to fill each obstruction and move on to the next temporary catch basin in an inexorable thousand-mile march to the Pacific.

In the shadows the warrior stood invisible, motionless, his heart pounding with the anticipation of action. His wide hat kept him dry and his eyes clear. He watched the rain cascading off the truck in front of him and thought of the souls of nusuh within, thousands of them trapped, their sacred life promise withdrawn by the hands of men who cared nothing for the Creator's promises. It had been a long time since he had even touched machinery. He watched, intently orienting and remembering what it took to operate a large vehicle. It was idling. He would not have to figure out how to start it. That was good.

An Indian stood near the truck in the parking lot of a liquor store. The warrior wished this Indian gone. It enraged him to see a man so completely drunk that it was apparent in every move: another defeated soul among his people. He wanted to lunge at him now, but the voice of Smohalla quieted him *within'. Smohalla had commanded him. The warrior knew only what he was to do at that moment. Beyond this he understood only that prophecy was about to be fulfilled, and he was its agent. He waited for his moment, knowing it would come.*

The Indian was soaking wet, but his mouth was still dry, his tongue heavy with the taste of Montana Gin, thick and numb. When real drink could not be obtained, every Indian schoolboy knew you could suck Lysol cleaner through a folded-over slice of Wonder bread. He'd been doing it all night; a piece of rain-soaked bread still hung from his shirt pocket. Now, squatting half-awake in the parking lot of a liquor store near the town of Celilo, he was hoping for something better. Only real drink could clean out a head full of cleaning fluid, but he was a broke, sorry sight for begging. He looked around at the large truck idling in a deep puddle. He could barely see the truck's blinking lights: It was a chore just keeping his eyes open. He was wet enough that he could not even feel the rain. His sweatshirt, which said Shoulder Moon Casino, Celilo, Washington: Good Luck Is Sacred Ground, *was drenched. Steam rose from his feverish body.* Only a dry man can feel the raindrop's sting, *he thought.* Only a drunk could love being waterlogged like a rat. *The thought made him laugh out loud. He opened his eyes.*

"When do they collect the human garbage around here?"

A tall man in a raincoat who had nearly tripped over him on the way into the store emerged holding a paper bag containing two bottles of whiskey.

"No garage around here," the Indian said, standing up, hoping for a handout. "You'll have to go up to Hood River. I could ride along and show you."

"Hood River?" The man with the bag reached out and poked at the Indian's shoulder with his finger. Water rolled off it onto the man's arm. "I said, 'When do they pick up the human garbage around here?' " The drunken Indian stood his ground, trying to keep from weaving. He was thinking about the bottles the man was holding and how one good swallow would clear the taste of Lysol from his mouth.

"Climb back into your fucking Dumpster, Tonto. Get out of my way."

The Indian stared at the paper bag and tried to imagine what the man with the bottles would do if he grabbed one of them.

"What's the matter?" The man held up one of the bottles. "Won't your casino-owning brothers give you any more free drinks?"

The weaving Indian reached out to take the bottle, but the man had gripped it by the neck and brought the heavy end around to connect solidly with his jaw and ear. The thud of the bottle made a sickening sound inside his skull. Water showered off his head, but he remained standing. Behind him the lights went off in the liquor store, and he could hear the door being latched.

"That's for the one hundred bucks I lost at craps the other day. Tell you what, medicine man, if you can stay standing, I'll let you have the bottle."

The Indian brightened. He watched as the bottle came around again. "That's for the five hundred I lost at the roulette table." The pain exploded through the Indian's teeth and up into his eyes and hair. He tasted blood. The sensation cleared his head, but the impact stirred up his stomach, where he had less control. He bit his lip hard and remained standing.

"You're one of those wooden Indians, Tonto, sturdier than a fucking totem pole," the man in the raincoat said. The Indian reached out again for the bottle but the man pulled it away. The Indian stumbled, but still he did not fall. He would have liked to kill this man now, but he wanted the bottle more. The need for drink brought on a wave of nausea. He retched into the puddle where he was standing. Foam bobbed on the surface. He coughed.

The man had pulled a small camera from a box on the seat of his truck. "I always wanted a real Indian souvenir. There's a spot for you on the wall in my bathroom. Now hold still and say cheese, medicine man. This is for all the money I ever lost to you fucking Indians."

The flash blinded him. He reached out to receive the bottle he'd been promised and abruptly doubled over in agony. It was thrown with enough force to shatter, if it had been a wall that stopped it instead of his groin. When he fell, his face hit the puddle and he began to retch all over again. He struggled to his hands and knees and emptied his stomach in a half dozen violent spasms. He heard laughter.

"Too bad, Tonto. I said you had to stay on your feet."

On the side of the man's truck the Indian could read the words Salmon Program. *Bobbing in the puddle in front of him was the bottle, the cap gone. The smell of spilled whiskey and the Lysol from his stomach filled his nostrils. He drank from the bottle, hoping the contents were not too diluted. His mouth, still deadened, couldn't taste a thing. He retched again. Angry, he staggered to his feet, pulled up his pants, and ran through the puddle trying to pull a blade from his pocket.*

"Motherfucking cosho," *he said, using the Chinook word for "pig."*

The driver stood on the running board, staring into the darkness. The Indian was surprised at the man's lack of response to his threat until he noticed that the man was dying. A long wooden pole with a large barbed point on the end had been driven into his chest just to the right of his sternum.

A man with long dark hair had stepped from the gray darkness. He was wearing old things: a large silver necklace; around his waist a traditional cloth, woven of goat wool; on his head a tall, round, straw hat that came to a point at the top.

"Nusuh," he said. The Chinook word for "salmon."

The driver stood frozen against the side of his truck. His attacker then took hold of the pole and leaned into it, lifting the driver off his feet. Blood gurgled from his mouth, ran down the white door of the truck and onto its shiny fender. As though he were placing a mop into a bucket, the man with the hat stuffed the limp, lifeless driver into the truck's cab. The driver's wallet, stuffed with money, fell from a raincoat pocket and landed in a rain puddle. The attacker ignored it, and with both arms he snapped the pole, severing it from the embedded harpoon point. He climbed up into the truck and started to put it into gear.

The drunken Indian, amazed at his sudden good fortune, stumbled to the truck and fished the wallet out of the puddle. "You'd better not stay around here. I know the back roads through these parts. I could ride with you to Hood River."

Under the brim of his wide hat, two fiery eyes beamed with rage from the face of a warrior. He shouted the words: "Kahkwa man cultus iktas." *Chinook words for "human garbage."*

The Indian recognized the face. "Charley," *he said, as he backed away in terror.*

"Tamala! Tamala!" *The warrior shrieked in the words of a more ancient tongue, and with a swift movement brought the broken wooden pole crashing down on the wet and sore head of the Indian, who crumpled to the ground as the truck turned out onto the highway along the river. Before he blacked out, he noticed that the rain had washed all the blood away.*

1

They swam like creatures of a single mind, their eyes inclined upward together, finding a point in common somewhere above the surface of the river. In perfect synchrony, they turned in the morning light, their motion confident and curious in equal measure, yet as indecipherable as the secret language of a storm. Their skin stretched taut beneath a coating of glassy scales as thin as frost; it rippled with muscle, tiny and perfect, as its web of nerves channeled sign and signal from the water. As long as they had existed as a species, the salmon had read the water, matching hints of seasons and patterns they had no need to comprehend in order to reach their destination.

For tens of thousands of years, the salmon had decoded their river's songs and stirrings. They had inhaled its breath. Down the long canyon between its banks, time was told and foretold, and from great distances upstream it was possible for each fingertip-sized brain to hear the faraway voice of the ocean. In the same way, and two years hence as fully grown chinooks and sockeyes, they would sense the river's call from thousands of miles out to sea. The water gave them everything. In their lives they would take much and eventually give it all back. At this moment their offerings were speckles of color, jeweled signatures adorning each slender body like the daggers of a genie.

Yet this water told them nothing. In precise formation the baby salmon probed for direction, seeking the current only to end up in the place where they had begun. All around them nourishment was hanging in translucent spirals off a floating mass in the center of the water, casting a faint, inert shadow below. The bits of torn flesh were reassuring. Salmon were born in water filled with the floating, shredded remains of parents who spawned and died, exhausted and broken from the effort. The pungent gravy of putrefaction and rot was, for these infants, a life force that had ushered them into the world. But they understood that the body floating amongst them was not of their lineage. They fed anyway.

Through their skin they could hear the steady humming of machines pumping and circulating the water. This place matched nothing they were bred to understand. Only bits and pieces of their river could be deciphered from this water through the blood-gorged muslin of their gills and the nerves of their skin. The hatchlings swam forward, wary of predators, feeding gently off the body that bled slowly into the water around them. They puzzled together. Like tightly wound springs they were eager to take expected cues and hurl themselves back the way their long dead parents had come. But there were no cues, only the gnawing hunger as they circled; each time they encountered the walls of the tank they were surprised.

Located about an hour's drive east of Portland and an equal distance west of Francine Smohalla's home along the Columbia River, the U.S. Army Corps of Engineers salmon hatchery was her responsibility and her passion. It was nestled next to the Bonneville Dam complex, thirteen dams away from Mica Dam upstream in Canada and the last dam on the Columbia before the river made its final turn to the Pacific. Francine walked by the six tanks without a glance, and locating a panel on the wall, she tripped the automatic dimmers that manufactured daylight for two hundred thousand hatchlings. Out the open window she could see the river from where she stood.

Francine pretended that the baby salmon she took care of at the hatchery were family. She pretended when she packed her bag lunch every day that it was for someone besides her, that she would hand it to him on his way to some office and spend the day waiting for his return. Each afternoon when she ate lunch, she pretended that it had been packed not by her, but by someone that she would be going home to. It almost worked. Her emptiness remained at bay for as long as it took to pack and then eat each day. But since looking after someone and being looked after were conditions she had never known in her own life, she couldn't tell for sure how much she yearned for them, and the emptiness always returned.

Bonneville was the largest of five federal dams between here and the Snake River junction. Its hatchery was the largest of four on the river. It adjoined the Bonneville locks, and Francine could watch the ships and barges from all over the world as she worked. The vast concrete arch of the dam stretched like a bridge to the Oregon side of the river. The halogen lights of the powerhouse cast arcs of white over the precipice, reflecting off clouds of spray rising up from the turbine penstocks. The wind teased Bonneville's clouds into wisps and ringlets. The whole effect was of a boiling cauldron, another spectacle credited to the unseasonably heavy rain. Like every other dam on the Columbia, Bonneville was at high water, and she was the last gatekeeper draining the interior of a continent into the Pacific Ocean.

Bonneville allowed more than water through its various gates. Unlike the Grand Coulee Dam upstream, Bonneville had not completely sealed the river to migrating fish and commerce. It was a busy outpost and had actually been built with salmon in mind. Besides the hatchery there was a fish ladder, a series of concrete steps up which salmon could swim much more easily than they could jump the old falls that used to churn the river during ancient times. The craggy, treacherous falls that had bedeviled the white settlers for hundreds of years and were named for ancient characters in the creation myths of the river's Indians had also been the salmon's path into the interior. With the building of the dams, those falls had all been replaced, leveled into ladders, or more precisely riverine escalators more suited to the modern age.

Francine was a marine biologist and half Chinook Indian from a town to the east, Celilo, Washington. Both of these facts qualified her to understand the predicament of the salmon around her, to understand that unfortunately, fish ladders didn't really work. Each year she cataloged the increasingly pitiful return of the sockeyes, the pinks, the chums, and *Oncorhynchus tshawytscha*—literally "King Hooknose"—the species name for the chinook salmon, grandest of them all. When they returned, only the hardiest or luckiest of fish ever managed to make their way past the dams to the untamed spawning waters of Hanford Reach and beyond. The hatchery was an attempt to keep the dams from wiping out the fish entirely. A few males and females would be intercepted by the hatchery workers, to breed a new generation of hatchery fish whose spawning home would, according to theory, become these concrete tanks, the imprinted man-made birthplaces that the salmon, as adults, would dream of returning to in a few years to start the cycle all over again.

Francine couldn't believe that even a creature as primitive as a fish could be made to yearn for some wretched concrete spawning tanks with the same primeval passion that had driven their ancestors back to the clear streams and tributaries of the old Columbia. Hatchery-spawned salmon had no streams to return to. They needed the white man's help to propagate. The salmon ranchers, as hatchery workers were called, nabbed fertile males and females on their way upstream, mixed their sperm and roe in big plastic buckets, and left the surrogate lovers to die. It always reminded Francine of her own forlorn and soulless couplings with men. Disappointments punctuated with quick showers and loads of laundry, catching breakfast during the spin cycle, trying not to be late for work. Random, tinged with regret, her romantic experiences were, in biological terms, experimental results too inconclusive to publish.

Francine watched the hatchlings grow accustomed to the manufactured daylight. Unlike wild fish, the youngsters in these tanks were descended from a few pairs of parents. She stared at tank number one, slowly working her way through the morning checklist: temperature, salinity. . . . Each time she saw the hatchlings turn abruptly in precise unison just shy of the tank wall she thought they were looking up at her. Francine wondered if they blamed her for the wall. She knew enough neuroscience to understand that salmon had insufficient memory in their brains to retain the dimensions of the tank they lived in. By the time they made it to the other side they had already forgotten about the barrier they encountered a few moments before. The salmon had no need for this kind of memory. They navigated by comparing what was familiar to what was not, through a complex strand of genetic coding that recorded the river's temperature, salinity, smell, and sound into a vast archive of permanent and shared memory accumulated one generation at a time. New truth could be added, but nothing was ever taken away.

Such a memory would constitute the entire history of Western culture crammed into a space a fiftieth the size of the human brain. Shared memory made sense to Francine. It was close to the manner in which Indians kept track of their history. If white men even had such shared memory stored away in their cells and available to them, they never used it; perhaps this was why they spent so much energy on museums. Shared memory was of no importance in the atomized modern world, just as it was no use to fish in a tank. Each traversal, each unexpected encounter with the tank wall, was a completely new and uniquely rude awakening, like the white man's world. Rude awakenings—fish cycling endlessly, each piscine Columbus endlessly seeking passage to India and condemned to discover America instead, finding and losing the unknown, trying to fix its position, failing, trying again, failing again.

Francine wondered if, after a number of generations of hatchery life, this experience would finally, somehow, imprint itself on their brains. Perhaps the salmon would grow to expect the blank wall, even to feel reassured by its presence. But with their maddening tank crossings, the hatchlings seemed to be holding out, through pure stubborn ignorance, against the biological theory that predicted their enslavement. Perhaps the impish spirit Coyote was whispering to them, encouraging them to tease Francine as she had always suspected he did whenever her carefully laid plans were foiled. Francine walked from tank to tank holding a small dip net for removing the dead hatchlings that could be found near the drain filters every morning.

She threw the switch to the feeding tubes. Fans scattered pellets of carefully manufactured fish food in precise quantities uniformly out over the water. The surface instantly became a furious foam of silver and white as each hatchling jumped for a pellet. The synchronized swimmers became a mob. The sound of the electric motor that sprayed the pellets over the water was drowned out by the din of thousands of splashing hatchlings. Francine didn't have to touch the switch to start the feeding. The entire operation was timed and controlled automatically by computers, but she always felt better doing it herself.

Francine treasured these early morning moments alone at the hatchery. It wasn't just giving food to the baby salmon that appealed to her. It was something else, something deeper. It thrilled and terrified her to watch the way the hatchlings took over the surface, crowding out the water itself. Francine hated crowds. She had nearly always been alone in her life. The fish densely packed together in the tanks often brought on her own claustrophobia. The hatchlings also reminded her of an old legend of the Columbia River that her uncle, Joe Moses, used to tell when she was a little girl: "You could cross the river by walking on the backs of *nusuh*."

When Francine was small, her uncle spoke often of the abundant fish that were born by the untold millions in the farthest upstream reaches of the Columbia and Snake Rivers and lived in the mighty Pacific Ocean far from the tribes whose lives had once depended on the hatchlings' safe departure and the adults' return. Here in a rectangular tank, that image of abundance was reconstituted in miniature. Francine imagined her Indian ancestors as tiny apparitions walking on the backs of the jumping and churning hatchlings. Among the ancestors would be her father's people, the people who had given her the name of a crazy holy man without ever explaining why. The past before her birth was as perplexing to her as the high-tech aquarium was to the fish before her, another blank wall.

The controlled feeding lasted a minute or so, and then the fish slipped back beneath the surface to resume their graceful squadrons. Francine was left alone listening to the electric motor of the empty feed-

ing tube echoing in the tank room. In one of the tanks, hatchlings continued to feed. She could hear the little frenzied splashes and took a few steps along the tile-covered floor to investigate. Near the open window
she noticed a dark mass shadowing the last tank in the row.

Francine stepped to the edge of the water and stopped. The light from the ceiling illuminated the bleeding, partially clothed body of an adult white male floating facedown in the middle of the tank. Hatchlings darted around and below the head of the corpse, feeding on the soft tissue of the face. A single eye floated by itself in a dull haze of blood, pushed and pulled by frenzied hatchlings, each of which tried to claim it for their own. The lifelessness of the body, unmistakably human, wore a uniform she recognized. The sight made her uneasy and sick: The human was powerless to fend off the tiny predators. Death distributed life's uncataloged remains on a strictly first-come, first-served basis. Francine watched as her fish seemed to acquire the taste for human flesh. Her fish.

With a biologist's eye she observed the hatchlings feed. The salmon darted at the body, growing bolder and more savage in the light—silvery and swordlike. What was most chilling to Francine was that the image of salmon killing and eating their human destroyers was something she had fantasized about herself on many occasions. In her dream she was the murderer.

Francine grabbed a long aluminum pole used to adjust equipment in the tank and aimed it toward the pale lifeless body. The blue sheen of the skin emptied it of personality. For a moment Francine regarded it simply as an island of unsorted biomass. The body moved in response to the pole and then without warning floated upright, its face eyeless. The salmon had stripped the soft tissue, but around the eyes were sharp lines like those on the face of a raccoon. She couldn't tell if they were painted or scratched in. The lips had been pulled back off of the teeth, forming a ferocious smile that for a moment seemed familiar to Francine. Four of the front teeth, two top and two bottom, had been removed, leaving a black square in the center of the mouth.

The mutilated face now looked more like a terrifying mask with empty black holes for eyes. The mask's gaze took away whatever compassion she might have had for the man who had once been behind it, but she recognized him as one of the truck drivers who made the regular run from the upstream hatcheries to the release point just below Bonneville. *Dave,* the cheerful red letters on his work coveralls named him.

A thin object, something Francine had not noticed before, fell from the back of the body and sank to the bottom of the tank. The hatchlings swam for the corner, instinctively finding the thickest place in the opaque silt to hide. The tank seemed suddenly empty of fish. Francine pulled the body toward her. It was stiff and blue, nearly bloodless. When she looked around her for some clue of how it had gotten there, all she saw was the open window.

With her net she scooped the fallen object from the bottom of the tank. A thick metal barb wrapped between two pieces of deer antler to make a triangle shape; she recognized this object more readily than the body. It was a traditional harpoon point, although the barbed metal betrayed its modern construction. An original tribal object would have been made of deer bone. It was not far off: The harpoon point was unmistakably of Chinook design. It took no effort to insert and would tear the rib cage from even a full-grown elk before being dislodged. It appeared that the last moments of the human whose remains were floating at her feet were spent experiencing the sensation of being disemboweled from within.

In one of the drawers of her desk she rummaged until she found a beautiful nickel-plated revolver. Francine was surprised to find it, even though she had placed it there years ago. It was a memento of the grandfather she had never known, but it was not the object she was looking for. Next to the firearm was the two-way radio she was after.

"We got a situation down here. There's a dead body in the hatchery." She called the central security office for the dam.

"What's the problem? Drowned fish?" The voice was expressionless, weary with third shift.

"There's a dead body floating in hatchery tank number six, and he's wearing a U.S. Army Corps of Engineers uniform."

There was a pause. Francine watched the floating body rotate slowly in the tank.

"Ten-four. Security's on the way over. We'll need to call the cops, too. Leave everything as it is for the report." The voice was breathless. "Are you okay?"

Francine ignored the question. She put down her radio and went back to watching the tank.

Outside, there was no sign of the dead man's truck. It was nowhere to be seen. In a morning light of full Pacific Northwest gray, Francine could see cars beginning to fill the parking lot for the day shift at the dam. She could see security and the police pulling up to the hatchery. She wondered what they would ask her, if they would assume that she was a terrified woman in shock over the discovery of a body. More likely they would just ignore the Indian woman in their midst. She quietly placed the harpoon tip in her pocket and looked down again at the driver's torn-up face. The only thing she knew about him was that he wasn't an Indian, which matched her fish dream as well.

As she walked over to unlock the door to the hatchery, she looked at the hatchlings and said, "Let's just keep this between us." Francine was sure they heard her.

2

"Lapidus philosophorum."

Under an eerie blue light, the stooped, almost bald man spoke to a row of chalkboards covered with symbols. Above the chalkboard, near the ceiling, hung a face in a black-and-white photograph. The man wore a thick plastic security badge that clumsily weighed down the pocket of his otherwise neat and clean white shirt. He rarely talked to himself, but he liked the sound of his voice speaking Latin. It made him feel that he was bringing the dead to life, repeating the wisdom of the alchemists in their discarded language.

Jack Charnock wore a metal welding hood as he stood before a thick granite pedestal that looked as though it could withstand a nuclear explosion. He had been coming to work in this drafty lab room for the past twenty years and to another one for twenty years before that. The lab was as much an archive now as it was a place for research. The archive of a single life was spread out before him. Evidence of all the various projects, large and small, that he had worked on was neatly cataloged. Stacks of boxes and binders lined the shelves. Small-scale mock-ups and prototypes of devices recognizable only to him littered the countertops and desk space—the nuclear knickknacks of a cold war–weapons designer.

Jack Charnock was himself something of an artifact of the nuclear age, but what he sat working on was more than this. He had worked on nothing for as long. He cared about nothing more passionately. He paused in mid-assembly to realize with a deep sense of satisfaction that this was no prototype; it was the real thing.

On the radio, country music played.

Charnock looked up at the photo on the wall. "We haven't heard from you in a while, Kisty. It would be a good time to speak." George Kistiakovsky, one of the original scientists at Los Alamos, a chemist, not an alchemist, although Charnock had the same sort of reverence for the bony, toothy-looking Polish émigré as he had for the ancients. Kisty had unlocked the secret energy of plutonium with his theory of controlled implosion, of focusing the chemical forces of high explosives to compress plutonium atoms rapidly and trigger a more violent nuclear reaction. Working with his hands, Kisty had shaped and assembled the delicately fabricated chunks of high explosive until they became a precise chemical force focused on a single point.

This was what Charnock was doing in his laboratory at the FFTF reactor facility on the Hanford Nuclear Reservation. He hovered over an elaborate wire frame in which pieces of curved triangular TATB explosive were to be laid like fine tile. Geodesics, Charnock called them. The wire was thin and sparse, no more than was needed to hold the tiles in place. As each tile was laid, this creator admired his precision. So closely did they match the dimensions of the frame, the curved surfaces looked to be suspended in midair. Bluish light emanating from below poured from every hole and crack in the surface. But as each tile was snapped into place, the light was replaced by the blackness of the opaque and neatly fashioned shapes. The cracks vanished. Charnock was visible only in outline, a hovering shadow whose arms and fingers were tinged with sparkles of blue as they moved over the structure. The black geodesics hovered in the light as though manipulated by unseen forces; slowly the tiles were being assembled into the surface of a sphere.

In the center of each tile was a threaded hole. As Charnock placed each piece, he inserted and screwed into place what looked to be an ordinary engine spark plug. From each spark plug a wire emerged. From a distance it looked like nothing so much as a skull on the pedestal constructed from layers of pink granite that had been carved elaborately into the shape of a basin. This was Charnock's intention—a suggestion from the ancients—and given what would eventually go inside the globe at the center of the focused wave of explosive energy, a skull could not have been more appropriate. Fully assembled, the globe would fit into the granite basin perfectly.

When he placed the last tile he stood back. Beams of light shone from unfilled holes and illuminated the cluttered shelves and chalkboards on every wall, chalkboards covered with numbers and hastily sketched diagrams, and shelves full of sealed glass vessels full of floating dead rats. In the flat blue glow they resembled a ghostly procession, floating sentinels from some watery purgatory of multiple limbs and wrathful mutations. The line began with nearly normal-looking, ratlike creatures; toward the end of the row they became distorted bodies festooned with vestigial heads and large misshapen growths protruding from their abdomens until the last jar, which contained a floating raft of tumors upon which only a pair of eyes suggested that a creature might once have inhabited the ravaged corpus. The country music on the radio ended. A voice replaced it.

"Tommy Liberty here, friends, with a message about the United Nations. We invited this anti-American, anti-Christian army onto our sovereign territory. Its sole purpose is to imprison and enslave the free people of the United States of America. This is not just what your friend Tommy Liberty is telling you. This is what it says in the Bible. The Bible knows all about the United Nations."

Perched on a wooden stool, the old vacuum-tube radio was always on in the lab. Its yellow illuminated dial pulsed to the howling voice through a worn speaker that made every voice sound phlegmy and indistinct. It was tuned to the only station that could be picked up out here.

"The United Nations was created by the abortionists at the end of the war. No one was looking, no one was paying attention. The Japanese had to bomb America to arouse our fighting spirit. But we have let the allies of Satan onto our soil. . . . We invited them here."

Charnock paid no attention to the voice. The old radio was simply comforting in the background. Like many of the older items in the lab, including the ghoulish jars of dead rats, the radio had belonged to his father, Harold Charnock, who had worked at Hanford as a nuclear chemist long ago in the original "100 area." His son, Jack, was in the 400 area. The Fast Flux Test Facility reactor was the only place where weapons research still went on. Back in the old days all of Hanford was about weapons. Harold was working in the 100 area when he had the accident that made him immortal in nuclear history.

Harold had taken what was believed to be three hundred times a lethal dose of the transuranic isotope americium back in 1961 in the worst on-the-job nuclear accident in U.S. history up to that time. An electrical spark had ignited a reactor vessel of tritium—hydrogen gas heavy with extra neutrons. It exploded like the *Hindenburg*, spraying Harold with a hot concoction of radioactive isotopes, enough gamma radiation to mutate a head of lettuce into a catfish, and impregnating his body with thousands of tiny, hot black pieces of alpha-emitting shrapnel.

Although no one could ever explain it, Harold survived and went on to become one of the lesser milestones of the Atomic Age, a research project unto himself. With a handsome pension for life, his job was to get regular medical checkups and submit to endless biopsies, rectal exams, and urine tests. From the day of the accident, every gram of fluid and human waste he excreted was classified. His medical condition was evoked in military papers estimating civilian casualties from a nuclear strike. The Charnock Constant was a measure of minimum liver function, coined by Pentagon doctors when they discovered how the human body seemed to have a built-in capacity to absorb enormous amounts of radiation.

Charnock's accident revealed some hidden biological contingency, as though the body were actually prepared, as if foretold, to live in some uncontemplated nuclear winter. The accident explained why Charnock's son, Jack, was unafraid of the subatomic world. As he stared at his partially assembled device and the place at the center where every bit of wire and geometry converged, where the plutonium would be placed, he felt only joy.

"Nature doth first beget the imperfect, then proceeds she to the perfect."

Jack Charnock took a deep breath. He lived for these moments; a vision was coalescing into a physical test of properties in the real world, a fusion of the wisdom of the ancients and the technology of the modern world. Plutonium was magical to Charnock, his *lapidus philosophorum,* the philosopher's stone, the most perfect element of the ancient alchemists.

In a ritual that stretched back to the first instant of the nuclear age, every notion was tested. With each detonation, the known universe blinked. At these times Charnock always felt that he was peering through a window at a time before the universe came to be. One by one he inserted the remaining spark plugs into the holes, affixing wires to each, which he harnessed together like electronic dreadlocks and let dangle off the pedestal. The wires led to the hood of a small pickup truck parked inside the cavernous hangarlike shed. More wires led from the truck to a table on which a computer screen emitted its own dull glow. The creator sat down at the keyboard.

Responding to keystrokes, the screen displayed the image of a sphere like the one on the pedestal. More keystrokes. The engine of the truck came to life. More keystrokes and the engine began to race. On the computer display, two colored bars of unequal height appeared. As the engine revved higher, one bar inched upward until it matched the other bar. The screen flashed the letters *SYNC.*

Charnock walked over to the pedestal where the assembled sphere/skull rested and reached into one of the deep pockets of his lab coat. In his hand was a baseball. Opening the front of the skull where the face would have been, he placed the baseball inside, where it was bathed in blue light. He closed the sphere and walked back to the keyboard. He smiled as he pulled the welding helmet down over his face and placed sound-absorbing ear protectors on his head. Glancing once at the sphere and once at the display, he reached over to an industrial push switch and pressed it.

The flash lit up the dark shed and made the rats in the jars appear to jump. The steel walls and aluminum ceiling of the work building roared with the sound of the explosion, as if a gun had been fired off in a tunnel. Smoke poured from the sphere. The truck engine died at the moment of the explosion but was otherwise unaffected. The computer displayed an error message. Charnock ignored it. Fragile modern computers and their whiny error laments bore no resemblance to the older machines from the dawn of the nuclear age, which only the largest trucks could carry. He began to inspect the smoking sphere. It had maintained its shape as it imploded. Wearing a big fireproof mitt, Charnock reached through the smoke to grab the baseball, which was charred on the surface, its burn marks in a distinct pattern equally spaced, as though the ball had been carefully drilled all the way around.

He held the ball up to the light and with his gloved thumb began to peel away the surface. Chunks of the ball crumbled away and dropped to the floor as matted embers of calfskin and twine. The explosion appeared to have compressed the remaining ball into a smaller solid sphere, which its creator dusted off and smoothed with a stiff brush. Between thumb and forefinger he examined the ball. From his pocket he took another ball, a golf ball. He placed it next to his creation and saw that they were virtually identical in size and shape, if not coloration.

He smiled and stepped back to the granite pedestal he had carved. Meticulously fitted pieces that were the products of his mind had formed a sphere that had exploded so precisely that all of the energy contained by itself, by geometry, concentrated and absorbed by the imploded baseball, was now compressed into the dimensions of a golf ball. This was what it meant to be a scientist. To imagine, to predict, to act, and then to see the signature he had carved upon the world.

"We're on the fairway," Charnock said, looking at a ratio marked on the chalkboard and underlined. The charred result he held perfectly matched the theoretical properties described by the chalk markings. Releasing the energy in plutonium required a critical mass, which in turn required an implosion that would compress a sphere of Pu-239 into a much smaller sphere of the same mass—the difference, it turned out, between the size of a baseball and a golf ball. The truth of this proposition was first demonstrated by George Kistiakovsky at Los Alamos in 1945, and shortly thereafter, it was demonstrated again over Nagasaki, Japan. Kisty was Jack Charnock's hero, a fact that smoldered out of the past like the mutilated baseball in his hands.

Charnock's heroes, his father included, all came from the world before 1945, but he was cursed to live after it. Jack Charnock came of age in the cold-war sixties, a world that had gradually been given over to the theorists in every sphere of endeavor. The Kistiakovskys and the Oppenheimers, scientists who had actually made things, passed the torch to the grand wizards of the cold war who preached fear, concocted theories using dominoes to explain the new world, dividing it up from their offices in Washington, D.C.

When the cold war ended, they in turn had passed the torch to people who couldn't actually make anything anymore, the puzzlers and manipulators of technology, whose preferred tool was the computer, who considered everything to be a form of information. Technologists relegated real science to the status of hobby, or worse, a get-rich-quick scheme. They stared into screens, looked for trends, imagined deals, calculated who could be laid off and when, sold stock in their own hot air, and abandoned truth to the unsung armies of real scientists such as Charnock who still worked with materials, elements, molecules, and atoms. To Charnock, information was antimatter and the Information Age, science's Antichrist. He was more like the alchemists, preferring to seek the truth in the substances made by God, not in pictures and symbols made by man.

Charnock's contribution to the world, although no one knew it yet, was that he had taken Kisty's implosion device and made it as small and portable as it could be. No one at Hanford could remember who had given Jack Charnock this project, but he'd been working on it for decades. He had named it Hobby Horse. It had begun as a cold-war effort to miniaturize nuclear detonations for a variety of applications—some for war, others for peace—but the project had been slowed and finally mothballed. But Charnock had never stopped working on it, and to honor Kisty, his father, and his family, he had carried on. Ultimately his work honored the old-fashioned spirit of making something other than a splash in the world, and for that Jack Charnock now allowed the tears to roll down his face.

The tears were for his son. Sam. Jack had lived to see Hanford make casualties of his son as well as his father. Sammy's death was without mystery or any scientific interest. He had been killed during construction of one of the many nuclear power plants at Hanford. He had fallen into liquid concrete and become part of one of the cooling towers that formed Hanford's sparse and menacing skyline. Sammy had been dead for many years now. Jack couldn't remember how many. On his work desk Charnock kept the only picture of Harold, Jack, and Sam together—smiling, arms around one another, proud soldiers of the Nuclear Age. His wife, Rebecca, had taken the picture. She had endured all of her husband's failures and setbacks. She had stood by as her son was taken from her. She had stayed with him through it all. He was never quite sure why. He looked around at the smoke from the perfect test of his implosion device. This would be the reward for all they had endured, a sweet triumph together. He had always thought of science as something to liberate the world. It saddened him to think that instead, it had turned out to be his prison.

Jack Charnock thought of the physical world as a long hallway of locked doors ushering humanity in one dreary direction like cattle.

Chemists picked locks and opened doors and made new passageways. He wanted Sammy and Rebecca to see what he could see. He calmly tossed the former baseball, now a golf ball, in one hand and looked back at the pedestal, still smoldering. It was more than a laboratory test now: It was an altar, a sculpture. With the addition of plutonium, Pu-239, his device would be operational.

The morning would break soon. Behind the shed where he had been working was the yellow dome of the FFTF reactor, the most highly classified operational facility at Hanford, a sodium-cooled fast-breeder reactor. It was a real beauty, the most advanced piece of equipment he had ever worked on, and it was losing its futuristic luster. These days it looked more like a mosque left over from some long dead caliph. Charnock shook his head. Like him, FFTF was getting old. He breathed deeply. It was the arid spice of the eastern Washington desert mixed with the watery hint of hydrogen ions from the river. He couldn't see the Columbia from this far inside the Hanford Nuclear Reservation, but he knew she was out there.

He could clearly see the fluted conical cooling tower for WPPSS Number Three. He stared at it, and as he thought of the crushed and suffocated bones of Sam buried there in the concrete, he wished he could free them in a single grand explosion that would pulverize everything into tiny anonymous particles, pieces of atoms riding the wind forever. The ion-tinged air off the water made him think of neutrons and electrons. Baseballs and golf balls, each with its own rules, its own game. Charnock sought passage between the states of matter through which one thing could become another. It was his passion as a nuclear-chemical engineer and as a heartbroken father. To the brightening sky he mumbled words of the first alchemist, Plato, which were never far from his mind:

Hence the god set water and air between fire and earth, and made them as proportionate to one another as was possible, so that what fire is to air, air is to water, and what air is to water, water is to earth.

Charnock hurled both balls across the dusty Hanford soil toward the horizon. He dreamed of all the unseen balls rattling through the universe, waiting to be played with by conscious little-boy creatures like himself. He would make the rules. It was surely a grand game.

A communion . . .

The warrior stepped from under the arch of the old concrete ruin and emerged from the shadows. He was tired. He had paddled his kayak from far downriver for the past three days. His arms were limp and sore when he reached the center of the free-running river to the particular spot of shoreline where the barbed wire was rusted and crumbled, and the chain link could be bent below the surface of the high water. Here he could paddle over the barriers and reach the sheltered lagoon. His body answered with pain the commands of its spirit-host who offered only anger as a salve, and whose demands could not be ignored or appealed. The pain was visible only in the taut cords beneath the skin of his neck. He made no sound.

He had hauled the body trailing behind his kayak until it floated alongside him. He rolled it over and when he was satisfied that it was prepared for the journey, he picked up his paddle and stroked swiftly out into the center of the current. His destination was where the water was deepest and the channel clear of obstructions. When he cut the body free and gave it a shove downward, the current took it firmly so that it did not even bob to the surface. By the time he saw it again, it was far downstream, almost reaching the place where the river bends to the south. He turned and paddled back upstream.

Here at the water's edge his river lived, but no people were permitted. This was Hanford, his perfect hiding place that hinted at the abundance of the old river. Here he could see salmon rippling the river surface, but standing tall to spear or net a tikwinat swimming upstream would invite discovery. He would have to fish another way. He left his lances and harpoons in the kayak *and instead removed a rawhide sack from his belt. He was deeply hungry. His hands trembled.*

Inside the rawhide sack was a handful of lincomium roots collected from the lush woodlands downstream. On a flat rock he removed the dried clods of dirt and pounded the roots into a pulp, expertly scraping and smashing them until they were the consistency of thick paste. He added drops of water to thin the mixture until it was closer to mud. Then he sat still and watched the water in the sheltered pool until he could see one or two good-sized ripples cross the surface. When he was satisfied, he leaned toward the pool and without making a sound, placed some of the pulped roots into the water and gently swirled his hand to dissolve it. He repeated the action once, then sat back to wait for the herb to have its effect.

After about a minute the ripples on the surface became more pronounced, followed by splashes of tails breaking the surface. Then a large salmon could clearly be seen struggling to stay upright. Another swam around in dazed circles nearby until suddenly it swam full tilt toward the muddy shore, propelling itself out of the water where it lay heaving and helpless. The larger fish was floating on its side a few feet out, its mouth opening and closing, otherwise unable to move. The warrior waded into the water and gently picked up the salmon, a silvery chinook, and laid it next to the other on the shore.

For a moment they looked at each other. The man was praying. On the faces of the fish was tranquility: the bond of hunter and hunted. When he was fully satisfied that the fish understood their fate, the man took an old long knife, and holding them gently and lovingly, he sliced them behind the eyes with powerful clean strokes, rendering them headless in an instant. Moments later he had gutted them. They barely struggled. The flesh of the salmon twitched, still alive, as he washed the two silver-and-pink bodies with river water. He gathered the heads and guts, and with equally clean motions, he buried them in wet sand, removing all traces of the fish and the roots that had immobilized them.

He stood and observed every detail that announced his presence and went about methodically erasing every one of them, down to the kayak that he slid quietly into a slot between two beams of a rusted dock until it was invisible. His footprints gone, the rock where he had crushed the roots returned to its spot, cleaned with river water. He knew many things, but mostly he knew how to disappear. He then gathered the fish, and before tying them to a long stick, he sliced a chunk of flesh from the belly of the larger of the two and placed it in his mouth. With his eyes closed he chewed slowly. His body was overdue this nourishment, yet he was restrained, focused on the sensations, as if conscious of needing to give something in return for what he was taking.

In his mouth was the taste of the river. As his stomach warmed and he lost the sensation of hunger, he felt a profound shame for fishing in this way. He longed to stand amidst the river's torrent, clinging to the wooden platforms over Celilo Falls, contesting the river's bounty rather than engaging in this trickery. It made him angry. He looked out at the calm surface. Even here there were only hints of the river's proud white mane and nothing of its old-time roar. The face and voice of the water had been stolen. They could be found downstream where the dams hoarded both, releasing them only at the whim of the river's new masters.

Into the whirlpools below the dams his life had also gone. His future sacrificed to duty, while the only woman he had ever loved drifted away like the spray that hovered above the spillways, slave to the passing winds. He dreamed of her. What had been their last moments together were also the last moments of his beloved Celilo.

■

On the morning of the dedication of the last downstream dam on the Columbia, Mary Hale was up well before dawn. The Dalles Dam was nothing much to look at, but it would raise the river level the last ninety feet, completing the shipping corridor from Idaho to the Pacific and wringing the last bit of electricity from the falling water.

She looked out the window for signs. She saw nothing. The Columbia looked the way it always did. The smooth wide flats on the Washington side took a bend to the south and emptied over the falls at Celilo, which under the bluish light of the setting moon still looked like a white horseshoe stamped into the dark river. The new dam was just out of view, beyond the rise of the gorge at the edge of her land. Maryhill Mansion marked the farthest reach of the coastal rains and the edge of eastern desert. To the west the land became dense with shrubs and then tall trees. To the east and north it was the alluvial dust mixed with volcanic ash covering thick granite and lava rock that stretched for thousands of square miles.

Mary wore only a silk chemise as she stood before the tall window. Her breasts rose and fell silently. Thick velvet curtains surrounded her and moved slowly in the morning breeze. Her body hung like the curves of mist in the canyons below. The wrought iron balcony railing made a filigree border around her navel and hips as she leaned rhythmically forward and back. Mary hungered for the river and the life that seemed to pour from it outside the windows. Inside was prison. Out there was the land, the river, and every sensation she worshiped to distraction. It would have nothing to do with her, however. Mary's round white face with high cheekbones, born of the northern Europe she had never seen, was fringed with blond hair she kept unfashionably long. It was the look of a child and an inmate, which is what she was, the only child whose laughter had ever echoed in the halls of her castle home.

She turned back to the bed where Charley Shen-oh-way lay naked above the blankets. His body was hard and dark, his hair long and black. He was a full-blooded Chinook. He always preferred that as little as possible be between him and the air. Maryhill Mansion with its high ceilings and three floors, its carpets and tapestries, already felt like a form of burial. She knew him well enough to know that he was awake. She knew all of the shades of his stillness. She could feel him aware of her, listening for her, smelling her, taking her in with a hunter's intensity.

"You must choose, me or Nch'i-Wana." Mary whispered the Indian name for the river.

"I have chosen already. The river is crying out."

"Rivers don't cry," she said, but she knew it was a silly thing to say.

"Perhaps it is only Coyote laughing."

Mary sighed. Anything without a reasonable explanation was credited to Coyote. "What is there to laugh about?"

"Coyote loves a good joke, and these dams are the best joke Coyote has ever seen. The last time Coyote freed Nch'i-Wana he only had to trick five old women and snap a piece of wood to topple the dam. It won't be so easy for him this time."

"There have been dams before, and there will be dams again." Mary had seen many dams dedicated, from the time when, as a little girl, she had accompanied her father to the opening of the Grand Coulee. President Roosevelt had been there that day in 1941.

Charley sat up on his elbows and punched one of the frilly velveteen pillows behind his head. His smile was gone. "Maybe Indian people are finished with the old ways. The prophecies are complete. Finally we have lost all that we were given."

He sat upright. He'd also been watching the dam builders since he was a wide-eyed toddler and had been seduced, as were all little Indian boys, by the power of the white man. No matter that it had made him feel cheap and small, like the thrill of paying the girls at school to show him their toy breasts and ballpoint nipples. Still he had looked. Each of the dams had anchored him to the ripe flesh and cold stone of manhood. No longer was he amazed or outraged by what the machines could do: He was only ashamed. He felt the river's wounds. But Charley could not simply watch as Celilo disappeared.

Mary turned toward the window. "Why can't we simply go away from here?" Raised in a castle without a kingdom, Mary Hale had never really come to live in the place where she was born. As a child, she used to imagine that Maryhill Mansion had once been dropped by one of the army helicopters she had watched fly up and down the Columbia gorge. For the war they flew, people told her, but Mary had seen no war out here.

She came away from the window and climbed up onto Charley's thick, smooth legs. She gripped his taut skin and pushed her own warmth against his thigh. "Here we belong, Charley," she whispered. "I choose you."

Mary eased forward to the sad man before her. She was too tired to admit that she also understood something was ending. With his hands Charley placed her hips over him and plunged inside her. Mary moaned and climbed down on top of him until their bodies locked together. Charley let himself be held, postponing his own body's crash into Mary's rhythms. He stared at her breasts, wide and contoured against her ribs. He pulled her down with his arms, and she seemed to shrink into him, clinging like a nursing child.

"Coyote can't take my father's dams away," Mary said. It was still dark. Only the moon illuminated the granite faces of the gorge.

"Maybe not. But I think Coyote gets a lot of laughs over how your father gave birth to his own worst enemy." Charley sat up and brushed his hair off Mary's shoulders, tied it behind his head, and walked over to the window. The river was different. "The dams are here now. All I can do is warn the salmon that Celilo is no more. Coyote will free the fishes. There is nothing more for us to do."

"Nothing can free the fishes now." Mary walked over to Charley, placed her head against his back and held him close. *"Jokulhlaup,"* she said, the most ancient word for the most ancient of floods. "My father said this river was made by the world's biggest flood. Only a *jokulhlaup* could bring that river back."

"From the days when ice was stone," Charley said. He watched the moon set behind Mount Hood to the west. Morning would soon arrive.

"I will pray for those days."

"I love you, Boston woman." He spoke the Chinook name for all Americans.

"Boston is one place I've never been, Charley."

Charley walked out of the room and down the vaulted staircase into the arched atrium of Maryhill Mansion. He opened the huge front door and walked out onto the promenade, feeling the morning air on his skin. Behind him, Mary had quickly dressed and hurried down, arriving as he was starting to descend the steep trail that led down to the river. In one hand Charley carried two intricately carved bones for playing *tlukuma*, the "hand game." A small wooden bowl, shiny and worn from age, hung from a leather thong, which held a small pouch and was fastened loosely around his waist. Otherwise, he was naked.

Charley took Mary's hand and climbed down to the edge of the water and onto the top of an enormous rock. They sat watching the river. From here you could only hear, not see, Celilo. The smell of still-burning campfires gave the air a rancid taint that was erased with each breeze. The morning was still. Strong winds through the gorge would come later with the sun. Charley closed his eyes and sat for a long time lost in thought. Powerful muscles rippled beneath his olive skin, his arms and shoulders like great timbers. The thick black hair hanging down his back was dark as the river. Yet Charley seemed fragile and feminine to Mary. His deep-set eyes with their long lashes and arched thick brows made him more voluptuous than fearsome. Aside from these features he was hairless. He made no motion, though his skin was marked with bumps raised against the chilled air. When he was aware that the sun was about to wash the rounded peaks of the gorge with pink, he opened his eyes and let go of her hand.

He stood and stepped toward the river. Indians knew every square inch of this area around Celilo. Charley had been coming to this spot all his life, binding together the wooden platforms of his family's ancestral fishing camp, repairing the nets, and carving the tools for catching salmon as they jumped the falls. He stopped to select a long, slender, double-pointed spear leaning against a rock with other various lances and dip nets. The spear was elaborately carved in the style of the Chinook people and was as shiny as the little bowl Shen-oh-way carried. The tips were sharp and barbed, their metal lashed tightly to the wood as if it had flowered a lethal thorn for hunting. Charley turned back and smiled warmly at Mary. He waded into the water and, twenty feet out from the bank, stepped up onto another large rock. On one side there was shallow water; on the other, the deep channel of the river came right to its edge. From the top of the rock Charley could see the river's bottom slipping away into the darkness.

His attention drawn to the edge of the falls, Charley could hear a sharp slap that sounded like hands clapping in the middle of a roll of thunder. He cocked his head and studied the surface of the river on the deep side of the rock.

"They've come," Charley spoke. His voice startled Mary. She stepped out from the trees.

"Sockeyes," Charley said to her without turning around. "But the chinooks are behind them. Their tails make the wind. Soon we will say good-bye."

Mary stood looking at the back of his head as the tears came. Charley's tears would come later. Mary Hale would never see them.

■

He had no more tears for these memories. They were simply companions in the darkness now. It was time to find shelter. He looked out over the desert and saw the scattered lights. When he was satisfied that the remains of the fish were secure to the stick he carried, he took off running swiftly across the desert toward the large concrete tower a short distance away, his longhouse. But it was more tall than long. His steps were noiseless. His breath was not. The effort of much killing and age had weakened him, but he could not slacken his pace. In the darkness, Hanford was a sanctuary for all of the river's refugees. Full light and it was sanctuary for the white man's atomic secrets. Light would reveal his presence, and inside this place Indians could be shot on sight. It was like the old times, he thought, and smiled as he ran. The cooling tower rose before him like the mouth of time itself, greedy to swallow up the present for the past.

3

From where he stood, Duke McCurdy saw only forces that were lined up against him: It was how he felt most comfortable. From the bridge of his boat, Duke imagined he could see every drop of water that had ever made it into the river. At the mouth of the Columbia, turbulent whirlpools and pounding surf tossed seven-foot-wide trunks of Douglas fir trees around like toothpicks. Gorged and teeming with weather drained from half a continent, here the river was a boil of raw physics, one more hyperemic cataclysm of the natural world. Each droplet of dew along the course of the Columbia had a role to play in the confrontation between river and ocean at Astoria Bay. Here the Columbia was an unmuted torrent at the edge of America, and Duke plowed his boat straight for it.

Through the windshield of the dual-inboard launch with the name *Queequeg,* the horizon bobbed like a cork and then vanished entirely. High tide was meeting a river. Waves formed and broke all around. The craft rolled like an otter, and Duke struggled for his footing. He gunned the throttle, and the boat skidded around on its prop in front of two towering waves—one just off the port bow, the other aimed starboard for broadside. Duke flipped a coin in his mind and turned sharply to the left, easing up on the throttle to let his nose down and anchor the hull into the water at the base of the wave.

The port of Astoria at the mouth of the Columbia was named by New York businessman and fur trader John Jacob Astor, whose records for losing money in the 1800s would stand as the region's monument to wealth and power until the dam builders arrived a century later. The Columbia's wide channel reached its greatest depth here. At Astoria the river became a gray fist that dumped its offering of North American silt onto the slender rim of continental shelf and hurled itself with biblical force into the Pacific.

"Let's climb Niagara," Duke shouted at no one, then shoved the throttle all the way forward. And as the *Queequeg*'s nose rose toward the vertical, it headed into and over the wave. This was the most turbulent bit of coastline on the Pacific, or the Atlantic for that matter. Unlike the desolate reaches of the Aleutian Islands, where the water was often this bad, here there were people: A boat went down regular as clockwork once a week off Astoria. The water was cold and fast. It took just seconds to be sucked offshore by the Columbia's icy currents, frozen like a fish stick, next stop Japan. More than a few times skipper Duke McCurdy had been an angel of mercy to anyone stupid enough or unlucky enough to end up spilled in these waters. Right now he thought he saw something in the surf.

The place where the Columbia met the Pacific was a watery barrier that had actually hidden the river for centuries from coastal navigators searching for the elusive Northwest Passage. If the sandbars, which reached impossibly far out to sea, didn't wreck a curious craft, the tricky, perilous current would slingshot even the largest man-of-wars out and down the desolate rocky coastline perimeter. Back then, the mouth of the Columbia was never far from those eager reckless explorers, but it was always concealed by walls of pounding surf that kept it just out of view of an explorer's spyglass. Duke reached up and attached his climber's carabiner hook to the formidable steel bracket above the helm, lashing himself to the cabin.

The *Queequeg* powered up the front of the wave. At the top Duke could see just how much of a pounding the shipping channel was taking. Most of the jetty was submerged. High tide was at its peak. Only the row of red lights along the top of the stone wall was visible through the thick spray. The hidden jetty added to Duke's headaches. It was deadlier than a sandbar underwater. The wall was bristling with radio beacons. Any boat getting too near was amply warned, but there was something about four miles of jagged rock placed in a shipping channel by the Army Corps of Engineers that seemed like a sick joke on all the skippers who had to steer around it.

A side wave hit hard and rolled the boat a good fifteen degrees. Duke grabbed one of the many handholds above his head and powered forward. The bow needled over the front wave, escaping into another deep trough. The horizon vanished the moment the body appeared, gripping the wave as though it were a picture hung on a wall of water. The steep curvature of the wave made the body appear only a few yards from Duke, but in reality more like one hundred yards of water surface separated them. In these waters the shortest distance was never a straight line.

The trick on a pickup in this surf was to gauge where the waves would leave you. Going directly at something generally tossed you farther away. It was a puzzle, like driving on a twisted ribbon, a Möbius strip flapping in a stiff wind. Duke's instincts told him the floater would be just on the other side of the trough if he let the wave pass underneath him. He wanted the wave to do the work. If he could keep the *Queequeg*'s bow in front of the leading edge of the wave, the floater would come to him.

Duke saw every day on the river as a battle between the forces of nature and the fortunes of men. Like no other place on earth, here the two were evenly matched. Duke respected the majestic Columbia dams, but he always rooted for the river, which is why he loved Astoria Bay. It was the one place the Columbia broke free of its constraints, roaring out of her channel into the ocean and in that moment of her freedom, sinking anonymously into the infinite Pacific, where the voices of thousands of rivers sobbed the rhythm of the tides, echoing from the beginning of time.

"You're not free just yet," Duke snarled and quickly backed off the throttle. The maneuver plunged the bow into the wave. The *Queequeg* nearly flipped, but something about the angle caused it to surf backward down the wave rather than roll in it. Duke scanned the water out the window, held the throttle, and waited for his moment. Hanging on the wave, the craft was frozen in a complex equilibrium, a single motionless moment that vanished like foam when McCurdy inched back up on the throttle. The boat righted itself violently and spun out facing the direction of the wave, taking the crest like a climber's summit. Rising to meet it was the floater.

Duke idled the boat, putting it at the mercy of the surf, removed his Cleveland Indians cap, and quickly stepped out on deck. The body floated even with the deck and Duke sank a hook into a clump of fabric. With his other hand, he held the railing, struggling to keep his balance while he hauled the body aboard and dragged it into the cabin as waves crashed over the deck.

Duke ran back to the helm, screaming as he shook the water from his hair and gunned the throttle once more just as it seemed the boat would come apart. The throaty engine sound filled the cabin. He aimed the *Queequeg* into the waves and slammed the boat over the bar until it landed in the shipping channel like a head hitting a pillow. In only a few seconds the cliffs of water were gone. The river was flat. He headed upriver where the banks rose gently, gaining vegetation and buildings until quiet lawns surrounded what had been a perilous chaos of whirlpool and surf.

Duke always wondered what had been in the minds of the captains who tried this crossing with their square-rigged ships built out of wood, in search of the Northwest Passage two centuries earlier. He would often shut down his engine and wait for those few moments when every sound of the modern world paused and he could hear what they had heard as they plied these coasts so long ago. Duke's own craft was built with the knowledge of what these waters could do to a boat. He had obtained it as a rusting hulk from the Coast Guard years ago and had rebuilt and repainted every square inch of the craft, restoring it to perfect working order.

Duke assumed the square-rig captains had to be lunatics to sail these waters. But he didn't need to understand the old things to love them. Those men had been brave beyond imagining, wagering their lives to be able to say they had been the first to see some dreary, lethal stretch of coastline before anyone else. Many of them ended their days as floaters. Duke looked down at the body, waterlogged, misshapen, anonymous, a puddle of seawater spreading beneath it on the floor of the cabin. Unlike this poor fucker, Duke thought, at least the square-riggers had a reason for seeking the Northwest Passage.

He had seen floaters before. They were barely recognizable as human, just the jellified protein and fat of land animals, a faded IOU to the waters from whence all life came. This was clearly the body of a white male, freshly killed, violently in the worst way. The face was horribly mutilated, and there appeared to be a wound of some kind on the back of the khaki U.S. Army Corps of Engineers shirt. The trousers bulged below the belt as though they were inflated. The body was largely untouched by river predators and could not have been in the water for more than a few days. To make it to the mouth of the river in such a short time, someone must have deliberately cast it adrift in the swiftest part of the shipping channel.

With close to a full tank of fuel, McCurdy proceeded upstream at top speed. The effect of the high tide would soon begin to wear off and make progress against the current more difficult. The surf hog was made for bobbing in the waves, but like any boat it loved a straight line. The skipper sipped a large mug of coffee with too much milk and sugar and followed a path well out of the main shipping channel. Upriver always seemed like a different country than the perpetually stormy and frigid river mouth.

It would take more than five hours at top speed to make it to the Bonneville Dam, which was the first big Army Corps of Engineers facility on the river. It would be late morning by then. He hoped the Bonneville locks were clear and that the clouds stayed around. Waiting for barge traffic to pass in the noontime sun would warm the body on deck and attract every seagull and nasty scavenger for miles. He pushed the throttle, poured himself another mug of coffee, and watched the river go by.

The river was Duke's first love, the only neutral zone in his embattled life, and the only reliable escape from his father, Roy. Duke McCurdy had been taught, from the moment he had first been made aware of the outside world, that enemies were everywhere. Duke had been raised by the Aryan Nation, the Christian Identity movement, and other more anonymous zealots dedicated to the destruction of anyone not like them. He had spent time in dozens of wilderness compounds from Idaho to Kansas. They had changed their public names so many times, Duke rarely recognized the mail that came to the places they lived. He had forgotten the aliases and was thankful his parents had always used their real names with him.

Brought up to hate for no reason, from the first time he set his course in the world, Duke McCurdy's landmarks were all the people not of his tribe, people not white like him and his family. Such people were called the children of Ham, Satan, Killers of Christ, and other biblical euphemisms. Or they were called by simpler, more hate-filled names in the casual conversations of the people he grew up with: niggers, kikes, spics, and gooks were the points on Duke McCurdy's peculiar compass. Steer around them and be safe. He didn't know why. He didn't know any different. Blacks were easiest to avoid, and they seemed already to have plenty against his kind. Later, others added to the roster took some explaining, especially the Jews. On the river there were no such enemies. The battles in nature he much preferred to those of his father and mother on land.

Duke loved being on the river. While his father and mother preached of race wars and Armageddon beneath the Northwest's stubborn tranquil prosperity, he had preferred to imagine the wild river that flowed beneath the big powerboats he watched racing the waters outside Richland, Washington—the only place his parents had spent any significant time during Duke's childhood years. The races were the closest thing Richland and Duke had to a tradition. They had begun as part of "Atomic Frontier Days," named for the Nagasaki bomb that carried Richland's proudest product, plutonium. Every schoolchild was taught about the bomb each August 9, during the weeklong festival of barbecues and concerts and carnivals where you could buy pins and bumper stickers that reflected Richland's uncompromising clarity about the nuclear age.

Nuclear Plants Are Built Better Than Jane Fonda was the slogan of a sticker Duke had on the door to his bedroom next to his high-school team letters and his Farrah Fawcett poster. The high-school team in Richland carried the name of "the Bombers." When Duke was in school the town was an unabashed nuclear booster, preaching the coming nuclear utopia. By the time he graduated, reactors were shutting down. Arms-control talks had slowed down production at Hanford so that the city fathers, sensing that tourists might not want to drive out of their way to eat Mushroom Cloud Burgers, or Spicy Multiple Warhead MIRV Chili-dogs, changed the name of the festival to Inland Empire Days. Richland High School would not relinquish the name Bombers, however. That and the powerboat races on the wide, flat water of the river each August were the only things that remained from the old Atomic Frontier Days.

While Duke had never raced, he had used every penny of his odd-job income to keep a fast boat running on the water. The *Queequeg* wasn't much to look at, but it was nearly all engine belowdecks. Duke liked that. His boat became a second home in the years after his mother was killed, a place to escape his father, who now lived only for the dream of reversing the clock and himself taking the bullet that cut down his wife. He ran a radio station up on the driest of land in the high desert, where Duke worked alongside him.

The *Queequeg* sped past Portland and its kayakers and windsurfers who gave the finger to any inlander's motor launch. Duke once enjoyed swamping the Gortex-clad river-bugs with his powerful wake, but these days the sympathies of the authorities were squarely with the small fry.

Spilling a kayaker could get you in some serious trouble. Duke left them alone now, but they still gave him the finger as he motored by.

There was no delay going through the locks. It took just a half hour to get above the dam. Duke always marveled at the powerful simplicity of the locks. The energy of the water flowing down through the electric turbines drove the heavy pumps that filled the sealed locks and allowed boats to float uphill, ninety-eight feet in the case of Bonneville Dam. As he emerged from the upstream lock, passing through the giant metal doors, there was a tug and a line of freight barges filled with wheat and potatoes setting up to go downriver, where their cargo would be off-loaded in Portland and shipped to destinations all over the world.

Below the dam Duke could see another vessel, a stray barge float-ing helplessly and tethered to an iron stay near the entrance to the locks. On the side of the boat in big letters were the words *Anadromous Fish Transport* and the Army Corps logo. It was a standard gasoline tanker but had been adapted to some other use. There were three bow-to-stern tanks and a whole lot of unfamiliar equipment on deck, including what looked like a wheelhouse for a pilot. At both ends of the deck was yel-low police tape indicating that this was a crime scene. He could see no one on the tanker, so he aimed his boat toward shore and the series of concrete ponds near the edge of the dam compound. Duke closed his eyes and smelled the wind off the high desert. It was here that the dis-tinct ocean smell from downriver ended and the sweet desert air began. He breathed in deeply and opened his eyes.

Her back was to him at first. He couldn't quite tell if it was a man or woman that the sun had surrounded with jeweled halos of yellow and white. The sun seemed to have found a hole in the clouds for her illu-mination. When she turned, Duke followed the lines of her chin and then down her strong arms holding the long handle of the dip net. He watched the rhythm of her body as she stirred and pulled the net from the water, the way she handled the tiny fish, and the way in which she tossed her head to fling thick hair off her face. Duke was struck by her tenderness.

He had been looking for uniformed police, some kind of official-looking guard post to unload the body. He forgot about all that. He forgot about the body lying on the deck of his boat. He was in the middle of a concrete fortress surrounded by the same federal workers his father had taught him to hate, yet he did not see the uniform she was wearing. Something about her stately posture, the intensity of her work, and some union he sensed between her and the fish made him think about the old river and pictures he had seen of Indians with their dip nets who had fished here long before the dams. It was enough for him to overlook that this was a modern hatchery for artificially spawned salmon.

Francine stood in the mottled gray morning light, jet-black hair catching the yellow flashes of sunlight. Her cotton work shirt, with its official patches, was unbuttoned at the collar, and a film of rainwater coated the dark skin on her neck. Steam misted off her forehead. She was working the net hard, dipping it deep into the tank, bringing it up, inspecting the chinook hatchlings, tossing them back, removing sluggish or dead fish, and repeating the operation. Murder had thrown everything into confusion, she brooded. Two drivers had been found dead and one barge skipper was missing. Francine didn't hear the voice calling to her.

"Are you with the Army Corps?" Duke had to say it twice.

"Maybe." Francine stood up and looked at the man with red hair and the baseball cap on the deck of the powerboat behind her. She hated the way the vessels coming through the locks could just appear out of nowhere. "Who wants to know?"

The tenderness Duke had noted a moment before was gone. Francine stood there, defiant, the wondrous light still on her. "Is there something like a head of security around here?" he said, anticipating a lecture on the evils of powerboats.

"I'll do."

"How long do these fish have to stay in prison like this?" Duke offered this observation to break the ice.

"They're salmon. If you want to take the Bonneville tour, there's a line inside you can stand in."

"Maybe some other time. This is an official visit."

"What do you want with security?"

"The body I found seems to be somebody you folks might know. But it's not a dead fish."

Francine looked up. Duke noted that it was not a look of surprise.

"When did you find it?"

"This morning, at the mouth of the river."

"What made you bring it here?"

"It's wearing the same uniform you've got on. I figured it would save time bringing it to you rather than deal with the Astoria police or the Coast Guard."

"You're right." Francine put down her net and walked up toward the small dock used for loading and off-loading salmon. "But the cops will be here soon enough. Mind if I come on board?"

"Not at all." Duke maneuvered his boat next to where Francine was standing and, with a single motion, tossed a line over the pier and tied up to the dock. He stepped up on deck and offered his hand to Francine. She declined it and hopped aboard on her own. "Francine Smohalla, U.S. Army Corps Salmon Hatchery, pleased to meet you." She pointed back at the salmon ponds where she had been standing a moment before. Duke rarely had anyone aboard his boat, let alone a woman.

"I'm Duke McCurdy, skipper of the *Queequeg,* happy to have you aboard." He grabbed her hand all at once and began pumping it awkwardly. "You're a rancher on a federal fish farm. You don't seem like one though."

"I need to see the body." Francine looked around and then brought her eyes back to Duke's face. She glanced up somewhat skeptically at his baseball cap with the smiling Cleveland Indians face on it.

"Of course. This way." Duke turned to lead her into the cabin above deck.

"I figure he's been dead for two days at most." In the presence of the body and Francine, all at once his voice cracked in an awkward, ugly squawk. "I found him floating out near the Astoria jetty."

Francine heard the voice squeak. "If you need a drink of water to settle you down, I can talk over here."

"I'm okay."

"He's pretty dead, I'd say." Francine started to examine the body. She recognized the man as a recent hire, a barge pilot. The other victim was a truck driver.

Francine shook her head, knelt down, and felt the place where she could see something stuffed inside the man's trousers. She pulled at the zipper and revealed a piece of blue fabric cut from a government-issue flotation collar. "I guess it's pretty clear why he was floating," Duke said as Francine took a knife, sliced neatly through the man's trousers and belt to remove a small pillow-sized piece of flotation collar that had been cut crudely to fit inside the man's pants.

"He wasn't swimming." Francine looked at the face of the dead man. The eyes were gone, as they had been with the other body she had seen. "That's for sure."

"Friend of yours?" Duke asked.

"Didn't have time to know this one." A spot of compassion warmed Francine's face. "He was only on the job for a week."

"What was his job?"

"He was one of our transport people. He moved salmon smolts downriver and around the dams. He belonged to that abandoned barge up there and the one hundred fifty thousand missing baby fish that were released when he was killed."

"You make it sound like the fish murdered him."

"It's as good an explanation as any right now." Francine looked up at Duke. "Could you help me turn him over?"

"Sure." He stepped down to her. He didn't even look at the body, only at Francine's deep blue eyes. "I get the idea that you aren't exactly the police," he said. "But you don't act much like a biologist."

"You don't seem much like a detective, either." Francine lifted the shirt and examined the skin underneath a large bloodstain on the man's back. "Any more questions?"

"Probably." Duke smiled. Francine looked back down at the body, concealing her reaction.

"Let's see if there is a weapon anywhere back here."

"Why would the weapon still be around?"

"Whoever killed this guy wanted the body to float and someone to find it. Maybe the weapon is a part of the package."

Francine pulled up what was left of the shirt. It was torn and had wrapped itself around something on its trip downstream. The grayish black skin with its leathery texture made her wince. The fishy signature of the river, reclaiming all that lived and died in its waters, made her cough.

"Here, hand me the knife." Duke knelt down next to Francine. "I see something."

He cut the shirt away from the body.

"There." Francine saw a harpoon point, deeply embedded in the man's back between horribly bruised shoulder blades.

"Well, I'll be damned." With his hand Duke grabbed the end of the harpoon point and gave it a slight twist, lifting the torso of the corpse as he did. "No give there," Duke said as he looked at the hole where the steel had entered the skin. The point was sunk in below the skin a good three inches. "This looks like it was shot out of a cannon."

"A skilled hunter would need no cannon to kill with an *ik'ik*." Francine just stared at the weed-encrusted object sticking out of the man's back, thinking out loud. "I don't recognize this design. The other one was Wasco."

Duke leaned down to scrape away some of the seaweed. "It's Indian all right. This is from a sturgeon harpoon. They use them up north along the Fraser River. I'd say its Salish. You probably know that already, though."

"How do you know that?" Francine was startled. "Who are you?" she asked, suddenly drawn to the red-haired boatman.

"I've been collecting things like this ever since I was a kid exploring the river. There's Indian stuff lying everywhere around here, probably a hundred thousand of these buried under the water and silt behind the dams."

"They belong to my people. I think I know where they came from." The reference to "Indian stuff" was a sensitive point with Francine, as the term traditionally included objects like the heads and bones of people she might be related to. "My people call this an *ik'ik*. Whalers use harpoons."

"Now if I'm not mistaken a lot of the *siwash* occasionally hunt for *ekkoli*." Duke used the Chinook words for "Indian" and "whale." Francine's eyes widened. Duke continued gently, "I don't know what people you're talking about as your people, but you're the first Indian I ever saw to have such big blue eyes."

Francine narrowed her eyes as if to hide them. "So you think all Indians look like that smiling idiot on your hat?"

"He's not one of your people." Duke thought he was being reassuring. "He's from Cleveland. Do you follow baseball?"

"I'm afraid not."

"You should."

Both of them realized at once that they had forgotten about the dead body at their feet. After an awkward pause, Francine looked down as though she were intent on the murder weapon. She wondered how much time had passed and if anyone else had noticed them. When she was satisfied that no other employees at Bonneville were paying attention to the boat, she began to tug at the harpoon point, trying to dislodge it.

"Isn't that something the police ought to be taking care of?" Duke could see she wanted very much to separate this body from the ugly object protruding from its back.

"So call the police or help me get this thing out of him, since you know so much about *ik'ik*s."

Duke carefully took the knife and slid it into the wound using the edge of the deer antler hilt of the harpoon to pry with; with his other hand he pushed the point forward at first, then rotated it, and began to bring it slowly out of the body.

"These are nasty. The Salish use them in pairs, but you probably know that."

"I didn't. Let's hurry, okay?"

"The sturgeon is a big dumb fish that has to be hauled up from the bottom. It can feed a family for a week. You don't ever want to lose a sturgeon."

"I've never lost a sturgeon." Francine couldn't tell if this man was making fun of her or trying to impress her. It was a disconcerting thought amidst the gruesome business before them. With a last tug Duke pulled the hook, its horrible barb emerged from the body where it was more recognizable. Francine grabbed it immediately.

"Is it yours?" he said.

Francine didn't answer right away as she searched the object for any marks that might identify it. It was similar to the hook she had pulled from the other body. "Of course it's not mine." She handed it back to Duke.

"That's good because I was beginning to think you were one of those fish terrorists working right under the dam people's noses."

"You have a vivid imagination. The people who work in the transport program are my friends and coworkers. The people who make these harpoon points are my blood."

"An Indian who works for the dams. That's a good one. You are a real *sitkum siwash* then."

"I think it's quite charming that you know some Chinook words, Dick, Duke, Zeke, whatever your name is, but I'll thank you not to call me a half-breed before you know anything about me."

"I didn't mean to offend you," he said. "I think just about everyone is a half-breed."

Francine looked at Duke. There was something tender in his face and voice even though Francine felt she was being accused of something.

She was sensitive about working for the dams and always conscious of
being one of a very few Indians at Bonneville. "It's not just your kind

who built these dams. There are plenty of full-blood and half-blood
bones down in the concrete along with your beloved whites." Francine
held out her hand and demanded that Duke return the harpoon point.
"You're not going to the police, are you?"

"Aren't you?" Duke said as he handed it back to her. He felt a chill
about the body. Had he found it or had it found him? It had led him to
this woman who seemed to have as big a chorus of demons as he did. She
was not white, something which would have repelled his father but
which he found unexpectedly alluring. Destiny, his father would say,
but Duke suddenly wished he hadn't tried to sound like he knew so
much about the body of the federal worker who had once worn the torn
uniform that lay in pieces on his deck—or about the weapon that killed
him.

"Eventually, of course," she said.

"So someone is killing your fish drivers. Is that the mystery?"

"It's part of it." Francine seemed to be pleading. "We can just report the body like this. We'll say we found the flotation collar stuffed
down in his pants; that's all. There's no need to speak about the *ik'ik*."

"Why, because an Indian might have done the killing?"

"I have no idea who is doing the killing."

"How do you know that Indians didn't do it?" Duke asked.

"I don't."

"You think you can protect every Indian along the river? That's a
rough crowd. Are you sure it isn't better to hand everything over to the
police?"

"If we take this to the police, they'll start arresting Indian fishermen all up and down the river." Francine looked away. "The cops barely
need an excuse to do that, anyway. I want to get to the bottom of these
killings before I give up what I know."

"Look," Duke said with the voice of someone who was used to being under suspicion for things that he hadn't done. "I don't like the po-

lice any more than you do, but we shouldn't hold on to this body any longer than we have to; otherwise they're going to think we both killed him."

Duke was being drawn into a mystery with a woman. He had rarely encountered either in his life. Francine placed the harpoon point into a plastic bag for fish feed, picked up her radio, and called for security. Duke rearranged the shirt on the corpse's back and hauled it over to the edge of the deck. With a gentle heave, he rolled it onto the concrete. Aside from the torn flotation collar still sitting there on the deck, the body looked just the same as when Duke pulled it aboard. It crossed his mind that the same force that had directed him to the floating body had directed him here as well, that he was already an accomplice to a crime he knew nothing about and to a woman he suddenly wanted to know much more about.

"Who came up with this fish-transport scheme?" Duke asked when Francine put the radio down. "And why would anyone want to kill people who drive fish around?"

"It's a federal program," Francine replied. "Bonneville Power and the Army Corps."

"Federal workers have a lot of enemies, you know, more than just Indians," Duke said darkly.

Curious remark, Francine thought. "You say the strangest things, Mr. McCurdy."

He laughed. "Never mind. So tell me. The Army Corps builds the dams that block the fish, and their solution is a fish taxi service? That's a good one."

"I'm a biologist at heart, not a soldier, and this is my first experience with the Army Corps," Francine said as she shook her head. " 'Nature's Motherfucker' is the Corps' unofficial motto. Hiring biologists is kind of a new thing for them."

"Biologist on a dead river. Gotta love that." Duke sneered at the irony. "The Feds spend decades killing it, and they finally call an Indian lady doctor."

"The Columbia River is anything but dead, and the loss of one hundred thousand salmon smolts is a serious matter." Francine was used to justifying her work. Every aspect of the river had its passionate critics. "As for the drivers, it's not a federal thing. People don't like the salmon program, period. Farmers think the money would be better spent on irrigation; fishermen think it's a scheme to transplant the Columbia's chinooks down to California where the money is; Indians just hate the idea of fish being driven around by the same people who built the dams that are killing them."

"Do you like the idea?"

"Not really. But there is no other option as long as the dams block the way upriver."

A sudden suspicion floated through Duke's head. "If I were you, I'd try to be a little more concerned about what happened to your friend here and forget the fish for now. I'm sure the salmon are content to find their own way to the ocean."

"What are you saying?" Francine walked up and put her face close to him. In the distance, security personnel from the dam office were already on their way over to the dock. Francine whispered, "Do you think I had something to do with this?"

"The thought never crossed my mind," Duke lied, and inhaled the mix of body and soap that came from Francine's tawny skin. He breathed in, unable to conceal his interest and added, "Do you think I did?"

"The thought never crossed my mind," Francine lied, and looked into this man's eyes. They both thought about all the things that had crossed their minds up until that point. It was Francine who broke the silence. "What kind of a name for a boat is 'Queequeg'?"

Talking about his boats put Duke at ease and lowered his guard. He pointed to the nameplate on the hull of his boat. In as quiet and friendly a voice as he had ever managed he said, "It's an old nigger name from the book *Moby-Dick*."

Francine winced visibly and moved away from him. "Is that some kind of joke?"

"No, it's true."

"What's true? That you talk like someone at a lynching?"

"Look, Queequeg was no lynching nigger," Duke said, anxious to pursue the conversation. "He was a whaler from Tahiti, the paradise in the Pacific."

"Mr. McCurdy, are you telling me that besides knowing something about Indians, you know who should and should not be lynched?" Francine gave Duke a look of disgust and disappointment. "What's your real name for my people?"

"Indians aren't black, and even if they were, with those eyes, you have more than enough white blood." Duke searched his mind for words that would help him to clarify things. His face was full of pain and embarrassment. The attempt at recovery had only made matters worse.

"So how much white blood is enough for you? That's a useful piece of information for a half-breed Chinook bitch." Francine had heard about people such as Duke living up in the hills of Washington and Idaho, but she had never actually met one. "I'd be interested to know where you learned all about white blood."

"I'm truly sorry. It's my people talking now." Duke was angry and frustrated. "I should never speak about these things, but where I come from, who is white and who is a nigger is a big deal."

"Maybe you should go back there."

"I never left. Please excuse me. I'm sorry, truly sorry. I have really enjoyed speaking with you. Try not to be angry with me. Your secret is safe. Now here's one for you to keep. There are people in this world who would happily kill anyone in a federal uniform." Duke handed her a business card from a radio station; the name Tommy Liberty was written at the bottom. "And they're not all Indians." Francine looked over her shoulder to see official vehicles approaching the dam complex.

Duke walked back into the cabin of the *Queequeg*. He grabbed the remaining debris from the body and tossed it over onto the dock. A police cruiser with a federal insignia and a flasher slowly idled up to the hatchery office, and two plainclothesmen got out.

"So what do I tell the Feds about you?" Francine asked. "They'll want to know how to reach you."

"Will you want to reach me?"

"Maybe."

"There's a lot of anger out there in all the pretty little homesteads and pickups. There's a lot more behind these dams than just water. We could talk sometime." Duke's heart was pounding as he said this. He spoke softly, almost a whisper. "I can tell you things."

"You said you think everybody is a half-breed. What did you mean?"

Duke took a breath and looked at Francine. He saw, once again, the person who had reminded him of the old river. "Everyone is a piece of who they are and who they might be. That's all I meant."

Intrigued and still outraged, she pulled a card out of her shirt pocket and scribbled a number on the back. "Call me here if you're ever not being an asshole. Do you know where Maryhill is?"

"The old mansion near Celilo?"

"That's right. Mornings are best; just leave your burning crosses at home."

Duke pointed to the card Francine was still holding. "This is the only number where you can leave a message for me. Don't worry about the Feds. They're responsible for the death of my mother a long time ago. They know who I am and can reach me anytime."

Duke untied his boat and shoved off. He gently increased the throttle and glided off onto the smooth water above Bonneville. His face was hot with embarrassment. He was reminded again that he lived in a place where he was lost, spoke a strange language, and had no map. The world he had been raised to see was not the world as others knew it.

Francine watched Duke go until the officers reached her and began firing questions at her about the body lying on the dock. She identified with him: Unlike other whites she had known in her life, he spoke like a member of his own tribe. It drew her to him. She could be disgusted by him and curious at the same time. It was the first time she had ever

52

thought of a white person in this way, the way she nearly always thought of her Indian friends, as people trapped and defined by their traditions.

Francine had never thought of her white ancestors as a tribe. She looked down at the body of the man at her feet. He had died carrying her baby salmon. He was one of her people. To her great surprise she realized she was sad that he was dead.

4

The truck was all lit up in the steady, misting rain. The droplets reflected Duane Madison's headlights into thousands of points of white light, which seemed to rush at him as he drove toward the abandoned truck in his official Department of Energy four-by-four. The truck lights and the rain were giving him a good case of the creeps. There were so many variations of vertigo out here. In the unearthly desolation of the Hanford Nuclear Reservation, the only way to keep from going crazy was to have a sound track. Hendrix blasted from Madison's dashboard speakers. Duane didn't like desert silence and out here sound, particularly Hendrix, was his only blanket.

Duane pounded the dashboard and sang along as he approached the truck. There was a Department of Energy car parked behind it, and Duane could see one of his officers with a flashlight walking slowly around the vehicle. He turned down his music and stared at the truck, now a crime scene. It had all the usual running lights plus a few more, because of the electric equipment running from one end of the tanker to the other. Trucks allowed this deep onto Hanford, Madison could count on the fingers of his hands, and this tanker definitely wasn't one of them. Madison was the head of security at Hanford, but the job didn't generally involve police work. The fugitives and killers roaming around Madison's domain were the chemicals and radioactive isotopes produced by a half century of making weapons.

The vehicle was plainly visible in the early morning darkness along the gentle rise of road that traced the path of Columbia in the shadow of Rattlesnake Mountain. As Madison got closer, he could see that both the truck's blinkers were flashing and that the headlights, fog lights, and high beams were on. The cab interior was fully lit, and both its doors were open.

Adorned with a razor-thin mustache and acne that stayed well past his teens, Madison was a black man who had grown up in the obscure military neighborhoods of Seattle's Fort Lewis. Like Hendrix, he was an exile from the city of his birth. Hendrix had left Seattle promising to make himself a legend and to return only in a pine box. He'd made good on both. Madison had hated Seattle as much as Hendrix, but chasing a legend proved to be harder than police work. In the end he had become a waste-disposal technician because chasing nasty isotopes around the desert paid a lot better than chasing criminals around the streets of Seattle. He was a well-paid specialist in chemical and nuclear waste now and had no plan to return to Seattle—in a pine box or otherwise. He still loved Hendrix's music though.

The body was lying facedown in the dust in front of the truck headlights, wearing a raincoat. Duane noticed that underneath the man's face, black blood had soaked into the normally yellowish soil. He shook his head; this was normally his day off. This call had robbed him of his usual day and night at the roulette tables.

"I figure there's got to be some small-caliber entrance wound to the back of the head." The officer on the scene was wearing a name tag that said *Westcott*. He had called in the body on the radio. "Classic execution style, I figure. He fell forward bleeding from the mouth and nose." Westcott said the words *execution style* with particular pride. He was one of the younger federal security guards around Hanford who all acted like mall cops, everything equally matter-of-fact. He swaggered back over to the body. "Least he didn't suffer much."

Duane bent down. The body was unusually stiff. The hands were bent forward and both thumbs jutted out to the side. His limbs seemed crumpled, not like someone struggling to crawl, or even falling onto his hands and knees after being shot. The grainy soil around the body, moist from the rain but still loose, was undisturbed. On the back of the head Duane found no sign of an entrance wound.

"Shouldn't we wait to turn him over? We don't want to disturb the crime scene." The combination of the smell and the condition of the body was beginning to get to Westcott. "Maybe he was trying to get to the river."

Duane shook his head. "Look carefully. There's no disturbed soil around here. He landed in this spot and didn't move. I don't think he was trying to get anywhere. He'd already arrived at the pearly gates."

Grabbing a shoulder with one hand, Duane flipped the body over onto its side. "Or maybe it was hell instead. Not even a plutonium waste pool over in area two hundred will do this to a person." The face was nearly torn from the skull, and both eyes had been gouged out. The sockets were both ringed with purplish lines, the lips carved away to reveal teeth that had been smashed in the center, making a dark square opening into the mouth. The faceless skull with its black eyes had a look that yearned simply to be dead. Duane hoped the man was long gone by the time this work had been done.

"There was no shooting here," Duane said. A four-inch piece of wood, snapped off at one end and soaked with blood, protruded from the man's chest. When Duane pulled on it, the whole body moved. Whatever was inside was not coming out easily. It was hardwood, perfectly round and finely crafted, like a javelin.

"Look here, the tongue is gone."

An ugly slash above the neck made enough of a hole that light from the truck headlights shone clean through, causing the skull to glow from within. Something had slashed through the skin between the jawbones, carving away the tongue neatly as though it had never been there. There had been plenty of gruesome nuclear and industrial-style accidents at Hanford, but this was making even Duane queasy. "Its like those animal bodies the buzzards get to. They always go for the soft bits first, eyes and tongue."

"You don't think a buzzard did this?" Westcott was completely ashen. Duane was thinking about whether he had to call the local Richland police department. "Not a buzzard," Duane said, carefully placing the body back in the position he found it. "But somebody who's done this kind of thing a lot, maybe somebody who hunts and dresses his own game." Westcott opened the door to the truck. The seat was covered with blood on the passenger side.

"The guy sure didn't drive here," Duane said. "There's still a lot of him up in the truck."

On the side of the tanker in big letters were the words *Salmon Program: Juvenile Fish Transportation.* The body was wearing a uniform with a sewn-on name tag: *Dave Whillers.* He was U.S. Army Corps of Engineers, one of the grunts who maintained the Columbia dams.

"This is a truck for hauling fish?" Westcott was used to nuclear cargo. "Are they for bait or what?"

"These are some million-dollar bait," Duane said. "This truck hauls salmon babies for the Feds." Madison had never seen one of the trucks at Hanford, but he'd heard of them. At the rear was a large hose, a pumping unit, and some kind of computer panel that monitored the temperature inside where thirty-five hundred gallons of baby salmon swam around in the dark. "Each one of these baby fish would go for eight bucks a pound as a grown-up off the boat in Seattle, and twenty times that on your plate next to some steamed escarole and shallots." Duane had a cold half sandwich from Arby's on the seat of his truck. After this corpse, it would take more than dreaming of high-class restaurants to revive his appetite.

The truck was one of a fleet of seven or so that made the regular run from Priest Rapids down to Bonneville, part of a salmon-protection program the federal government had put together when it realized that swimming downstream through dams killed more salmon than any amount of overfishing ever could. After sixty years the federal government had finally concluded what the Indians had been saying all along: that one of the most abundant species of game fish on earth was on its way to extinction. The trucks got the baby fish downstream, but scientists could not say if the trucking and barging of baby fish had really done anything to stop the decline of the ancient salmon runs.

"The Army Corps thinks it can do anything with trucks and dozers." Duane took a whiff of the wide hose connected to the pumping unit and scratched his head. "Looks like this truck pumped out its load last night." When he flicked a toggle switch, the panel of digital lights went dark, and the hum of the pump motor halted.

"Whoever did this went to a lot of trouble to empty the fish into the river and see to it that the body was discovered right away." Duane could see the truck had been backed down the ramp into the water because the rear tires still had a dusting of wet sand. He looked out onto the river. The driver wasn't the only casualty: The riverbank was lined with mutilated fish bodies and engorged seagulls. A dozen or so silvery fish floated in a clump of green muck.

"Where are the rest of them?" Westcott was still having trouble putting it together.

"Let's hope they swam away. This truck was supposed to keep them alive." Duane picked up one of the dead fish. "Didn't work for these poor fuckers, though." Looking on the floor of the cab, Madison found a paper bag in a half-congealed puddle of blood. Inside there was a bottle of whiskey and a receipt from a liquor store about ninety miles downstream.

"This must have been one of the last things he did, buy some cheap whiskey." Duane looked closely at the receipt. "Westcott, look around for another bottle. It says here he bought two."

This section of the reservation was part of the Washington Public Power Supply System compound, something of a local joke as well as a nuclear ghost town. The consortium of little local utilities called itself WPPSS, pronounced "whoops," and in a celebrated and quickly outdone financial fiasco of the 1980s, it had gone bankrupt trying to build five gigantic nuclear power plants with federal bonds sold to millions of un-lucky pensioners in Arizona and Florida.

In a single month back in the 1980s, WPPSS went from being the largest construction site in the Western Hemisphere to an abandoned padlocked ruin: All that was left were the eerie cooling towers of unfin-ished reactors and rusted debris. Years ago everything that could be re-moved and rescued had been stripped and trucked away. Only one of the reactors, WPPSS Number Two, actually functioned, generating some of the costliest electricity ever made. WPPSS Number Three looked fin-ished but was in fact a spectacularly expensive home for bats and birds. Blended in with the cheap power from the Columbia River dams, WPPSS was a quietly forgotten failure. The lights from Number Two could be seen a half mile away; here on the Number Three site there was only darkness.

Duane jogged up an earth berm to view where this truck might have been heading. The river swallowed the horizon, stretching out dark and bubbling for miles in both directions. He took a deep breath. The fifty-two miles of unobstructed water here had acquired the name Han-ford Reach. Beneath warnings that trespassers would be shot on sight and the brightly colored logo of the U.S. Department of Energy, there was real white water. Fish swam free. The last natural spawning ground for salmon was inside a top-secret facility where each cubic yard of silt along the riverbank contained enough radioactive iodine to give the en-tire city of Seattle a dose of chemotherapy.

The riverbank was also a museum of artifacts from the forties when the whole reservation had been part of the Manhattan Project. On a rusting concrete-and-steel pumping station that backed right up to the water, the river lapped at the still-visible Hanford Engineering Works sign dating from the days when the fate of the world depended on build-ing bombs to drop on Hitler, Stalin, or Hirohito. Back then, no one at Hanford was ever sure. They didn't care. They made plutonium. Gener-als in Washington picked the targets.

The abundant power from the Columbia River dams made this an ideal place to produce nuclear materials for the war effort. DOE signs had replaced those of the now-defunct Atomic Energy Commission, and occasionally the even older MED signs could be seen littering the dusty ground. The Manhattan Engineering District of the Army Corps of Engineers had built the first buildings here. Long before the Atomic Age, an army of concrete trucks and earthmovers fought a war against the river and had obtained its unconditional surrender.

No dam had ever been built near Hanford. As a top-secret nuclear reservation, it had its own use for the river. During the forties and for twenty years thereafter, Hanford had diverted the Columbia into streams that cooled the Pentagon's reactors, heating the river by an estimated two degrees and adding a nasty brew of radioactive substances to the downstream water supply. All but one of the Pentagon's reactors were shut down now, but the seasoning of the river from tons of accumulated waste continued, especially when it rained. But there was no longer much of anything secret about Hanford. Its cover was blown the day a bomb packed with a grapefruit-sized sphere of Hanford's plutonium was dropped on Nagasaki. More than fifty years later, out of habit or fear of radiation, few people not wearing a uniform ever came to see the longest and last remaining free run of the Columbia.

"You better come look at this." Westcott's voice barked on the radio from over by the truck. Madison jogged back to the truck. On the side facing the river, etched into its painted metal was a wide-eyed face ringed with circles. The mouth was a broad grimace with a dark square at the center where the teeth should have been.

"This is some Indian thing," Westcott said. "It's got to be." The image had been scratched into the metal, but a closer look showed that it had been gone over in blood.

"Looks like one of those paintings downriver." Duane had seen such paintings for years on the rocks above the Columbia. There were thousands of them scattered across the region, mostly of elk and stick-figured animals. There were only a few faces and Duane Madison knew this one.

"It's the face on that rock over near the Dalles," Duane said. "You know which one I'm talking about?"

"I can't say as I do," Westcott replied. "But I think I've seen that face before. It's on that poor driver over there."

Madison walked back to the body and turned it over and carefully examined what was left of the man's face.

"You're an observant man, Westcott. I'd say someone is trying to scare the shit out of more people than just us. That's some radioactivity we can't do nothing about around here." Duane felt a chill. He took his flashlight and beamed it into the blood-filled eye sockets.

"Hand me that handkerchief you got in your mouth."

Westcott did as he was told reluctantly, wiping a string of drool from his lips. Duane laid the handkerchief out on the ground and leaned down close to the face of the body as though he were fixing a clock radio. He carefully stuck his paper clip into one of the eye sockets.

"Well, lookee here," said Duane. In the spaces where the body's eyeballs used to be, two pieces of bone were nearly floating, one in each socket. They were rounded, with carving on them like the scrimshaw pieces in trinket shops up and down the Oregon coast. "These bones certainly weren't in his head when he met the person who killed him."

Westcott was fully spooked. Duane stood up and pulled him to his feet. "You know, son, I don't know what style you were talking about a few minutes ago, but this murder was definitely an execution."

The young officer was breathing deeply. "Do we have to stay out here with him?"

"I'll stay here." Duane opened the door to his four-by-four; the reduced volume of the sound from his stereo system still shattered the silence. Westcott jumped back toward his vehicle. Duane chuckled. "Settle down, go put in a call to the coroner and DOE, then head back to base."

"What about the sheriff?"

"This looks like terrorism, so technically it's still a federal matter." Duane didn't want the locals involved just yet. "I'll call the sheriff in the morning."

Westcott looked back at Duane. "I guess I wouldn't have figured you for being into heavy metal."

"Hendrix is acid, not metal. You're showing your age. Now get going."

On the riverbank there was only the disturbed soil where the dead man had been dropped and the tire tracks from his truck. The fish were gone. So who did this and where were they now? If the murderer or murderers had escaped into the swift current of Hanford Reach, dead or alive, they would be well beyond the federal reservation by morning. This was just as true of the many nuclear toxins that leached into the river and had to be tracked, but usually vanished without a trace.

The echo-heavy voice of Hendrix rang out into the night. Duane Madison reached in and switched off the stereo when Westcott was finally gone. He looked away from the river. Just visible in the moist sandy soil was a faint trail of footsteps leading away from the truck and into the desert scrubland of Hanford toward Rattlesnake Mountain and then vanishing under the windblown sands of the interior. Out here, the morning desert winds would erase any recent trail by noon, despite the rainfall.

Duane's job was to oversee thousands of tons of the most terrifying substances known to humanity that were stored or bubbling about at Hanford. He'd never so much as gotten a goose bump before this. But now, Duane was thinking that whatever poisons man creates and world-ending weapons he uses, man himself is the most terrifying. For a moment he was back on Sixth and Pike looking at the mutilated body of a dead Indian, the typical victim of a drive-by. Finding such random brutality over and over again in a place that had no business being anything but peaceful was why he'd left Seattle.

Grabbing a blanket from inside the cab of the truck to cover the body, he noticed something he hadn't seen before. In the compartment between the seats was a small camera with film in it. A few shots had been taken. He put the camera in his pocket and took the blanket over to the body. Covering it made him feel better. He got into his car to warm up and peered out through the windshield at the river lit from above by a half-moon. The Columbia bubbled in the moonlight. He could feel the tranquility taunting him. He demolished it with a twist of his stereo knob. A guitar screamed. The river had all the answers for now.

5

"Stanley, Idaho, line three."

Steam from a coffee mug spiraled into the air around the microphone. The flashing lights from the five callers on hold provided all the light there was in the room.

"Hello, Tommy?" The caller's voice was slow. Duke McCurdy shook his head and mouthed the word *asshole*. "Am I on the air?"

"It's a free country, now what's on your mind?" Duke looked into the glass as he spoke. His voice did not match his face. The face was soft and young, while the voice coming through the radio was shrill and hard.

"Yeah, Tommy. First-time caller and I want to tell you how much my family and I appreciate having a place to hear the truth about America."

"Just doing our jobs." Duke had no patience with callers who couldn't get their brains out of the box. He punched the phone. "We give you the news, not all those Jews. It's eleven before the hour. The Tommy Liberty Show on KGOG radio, voice of the free people of the high-desert country. We'll be right back, and maybe we'll talk to some callers who have something to say."

This was Duke's real job, the only employment he'd ever had, working for the family-owned radio station, playing Tommy Liberty, a voice that embodied everything his father and mother had ever taught him about the world. In his real life Duke fell far short of Tommy, a fact that keenly disappointed Duke's father, Roy. In his real life Duke feared that anyone might find out he was the voice of Tommy, that anyone would detect the peculiar way he had been taught to think about the outside world. But on the air he was free. He was accepted. He was exactly who he was supposed to be.

Since he was a little boy, with the exception of the numerous scrapes in which he'd had to save Roy, Duke McCurdy had managed to avoid meeting anyone who wasn't white. He wanted to keep it that way, not out of hatred, but because he was certain getting too close would just foul everything up with his father. Roy always said the great enemy of hatred was curiosity, and Duke understood he was born with a lot more of the latter than the former.

Even for a doubter, Duke had his own anger to draw on. There was the little-boy anger over the death of his mother long ago. There was the more grown-up anger he felt each time he had to intervene to keep some murderously provoked black man from killing or injuring his father in a racially inspired brawl. It wasn't just blacks. Every time his father had taken his peculiar notion of patriotism beyond the flag and turned a peaceable crowd of Hispanics or Jews into a near-riot, Duke could always find within him the anger and the strength he needed to whisk his father away. As humiliating as it was to be continually drawn into these altercations, he had never known anything different.

Protecting Roy was something Duke had always done without thinking, and every time it rekindled his hatred for the role he had been born to play. Hatred brought clarity. But it would never last. So Duke McCurdy, aka Tommy Liberty, avoided most of the people in the world not because he hated them, but because he feared he didn't hate them enough. A lifetime of this had left him with a lingering curiosity. The longer he tried to hate people, the more he wanted to know who they all were. It was this curiosity that led him into radio.

The station was located in a cramped Airstream trailer next to a lean-to structure that served as additional office space and living quarters. It was cozy and flimsy. The radio station had been Roy McCurdy's idea, one of the few Roy brought home that Duke's mother had thought were any good. Ignored by the authorities for years, the tiny AM transmitter set up long ago to provide information on weather and pork-belly futures had found an audience and was now a small industry issuing books and leaflets, sponsoring conferences and lectures, gun shows and constant fund-raising events.

KGOG had become the voice of discontent on the airwaves from the Rockies to the Pacific coast. Duke had also liked the idea of radio, even if he felt his father's station could benefit from a change of formats. With the Tommy Liberty character, Duke found a perfect cross between his father and mother. From the moment he went on the radio to fill in for his father, he found a sanctuary behind the microphone and glass where people could imagine who he was and no one could actually see him.

Roy liked the station more for the clout it gave him among the like-minded fanatics that populated eastern Washington, Oregon, and Idaho. Roy spent long hours dreaming up new ventures and composing E-mail on various subjects of interest, usually Jewish-conspiracy warnings and state-of-emergency declarations for the New Israelite Nation, which in Roy's leaflets was always under attack by federal armies. In Roy McCurdy's pronouncements, the New Israelite Nation, the most serious military enemy of America since Red China, was always poised on the verge of total victory.

Duke could tell his father had returned home. The slamming of the trailer front door went out over the air. In the commercial breaks, Duke went back to cleaning and polishing his collection of stones, ranging from the size of toy marbles to one that was as large as a grapefruit. The stones were part of his obsession with the river. Whenever he could, he turned his mind back to it. He was especially fascinated by its geology.

The stones in Duke's collection were naturally smooth river rock but polished to a glassy gemlike finish. The smaller ones were brightly colored, while the larger ones swirled with patterns of crystal and veins of color, as though they were pieces of exotic wood. One of the stones was deeply pitted, and Duke used a thin paintbrush to remove sediment packed within. It took about the length of the final commercial in the break for him to empty the hole in the stone, gather the sediment into a neat pile on a white paper surface, put his tools aside, and return to the microphone.

"Line four, Wenatchee, Washington. What have you done for white America today?"

"Been out shootin' Martians, Tommy." The caller laughed. Duke picked up a tape cartridge that had the letters *INV* scrawled on an old label. He tossed it into the old machine and pressed Play. Immediately the sound of gunfire filled the studio over the theme music from the sixties television show *The Invaders*.

"Invaders," Duke shouted down the microphone. In his headset he could hear the caller laughing. "How many Martians did you get for us, Mr. Wenatchee?"

"Maybe two. I wasn't using a scope."

"Sounds like a good day. What color were they?"

"Well, Tommy, that's my question." The caller's tone was serious. "Do Indians count as Martians?"

"Is the Indian a Martian? Do we think we might have shot an Indian, Mr. Wenatchee?"

"I'm not sayin' that exactly."

"You don't want to say anything exactly on this program. The federal jackboots are listening. But please continue, sir."

"If you look closely at the face of the average Indian, you got what my friends and I think is your gook face, which would make Indians a form of gook, right?"

"Except for one thing. The gook brain is large. Everybody knows what crafty bastards the gooks are. But your Indian, see, is as dumb as a rusted-out Dodge up on blocks."

"So that would make them more like Mexicans, I guess?"

"Well, they're not gooks."

"Is that right?"

"And they're not Mexicans, either."

"I'm stumped, Tommy."

"No reason to be. The Mexican is a product of polluted blood between the Aztec Indians and your Spaniards who gave syphilis to the Indians and went insane. Indians in North America stayed pure-blooded for much longer." What Duke liked best about radio was how it made everything he said true. Even the most outlandish stuff he said sounded like Socrates coming back through his headphones.

"But they're not white." The caller continued. "You can't tell me that your Indian is a white man."

"I'm not saying that. But your Indian has something that we have to respect even though most of the time we're dealing with a drunken lowlife. Unlike your Martians, Indians have their own land. Reservation land is sovereign land the U.S. government can't touch. Indians have fought wars with the U.S. government down through history. I'm not saying they did very well, but at least these are people who have actually taken up arms against ZOG. So technically we don't put your Indian in there with the Martians."

"Is that right?"

"That's right." The caller paused, and Duke punched the phone to get rid of him. "Three minutes in front of the hour here on the *Tommy Liberty Show*, and I'm about out of here. I'll see you again tomorrow night. Be sure to stay right here for the *Mount Carmel Christian Soldier Hour* and after that, *Overnight Oldies*. I'm going to leave you with the last hit Hank Williams ever recorded: 'I'll Not Leave This World Alive.' This is Tommy Liberty advising you to buy your ammo now; you won't be able to later. Good night, all. This is KGOG, fifty thousand clear-channel watts for the free American people of the high-desert country."

Duke McCurdy, the voice of Tommy Liberty, pressed Play on the old reel-to-reel that contained the *Christian Soldier Hour*. The plastic reels began to turn and a distorted organ-music theme lurched through the speakers while the machine struggled to reach the proper speed. Duke went back to being the person he was away from his father's microphones. He picked up his box of stones, grabbed a small bag of tools and his Cleveland Indians baseball cap, and walked through the small door at the end of the trailer.

Duke's mother, Ida, had died years ago in a shoot-out with federal officers at a place called Maccabee Pond near Walla Walla where he and his father narrowly escaped the same fate. Duke had been tethered to Roy from the moment he had seen his mother fall. When he had innocently asked his father where she had gone, Roy had grabbed the little boy's hand and scolded him. "She died for you; now we're all going to have to live for her." Duke had taken this to mean that he was somehow responsible for her death. Roy had explained that now his mother would be watching over him every minute, making sure he was the fighter she had wanted to raise. Most cruelly, Roy had warned Duke that his mother would know if he began to forget her. The thought filled him with terror, and each day as his memory faded, he felt his dead mother's disappointment, until Roy's suffocating, scolding voice completely filled the void.

From that time, Duke could never separate the hatred of all the people his father counted as enemies from a deeper hatred of self. Duke found that he hated anyone in a uniform but secretly coveted the power such people seemed to have. Duke had none of the certainty of his parents except about his own inadequacies. His dead mother's legendary passion for the white race and his father's pure crystalline contempt for nearly everyone on the planet, a zealous loathing that never wavered, were sentiments their son could only marvel at.

"Not too bad tonight."

Roy McCurdy greeted his son gruffly as he stepped into the cramped office that served as the place he ran all of his activities with messianic fervor. His main claim to fame was now being the widower of the woman martyred by the federal jackboots. Roy's other memorable achievement was having been the defendant in a lawsuit that established his free-speech right to say the word *nigger* on the air. The case had gone all the way to the Supreme Court. A book he wrote about his struggle was an underground best-seller, so were his cassettes and various "end of the world" newsletters. A large stack of cassette orders was ready for mailing and teetering precariously on the desk. There was his Nazi Internet site—Idacrusade.com—up and running, which he was now updating with a tirade against the United Nations, one of Roy's favorite targets.

"I'm sure the Feds were paying attention to that guy talking about shooting Martians," Roy said, laughing.

The New Israelite Nation was another project of his father's. It had its own bank and printed its own promissory notes, which Roy always insisted were legal tender just as legitimate as worthless paper dollars from the U.S. Treasury. The New Israelites claimed sovereignty over a territory that consisted of the half-acre lot occupied by Roy's dented-up Airstream. The New Israelites considered local authorities, including the man who tried each month to read the electric meter, to be agents of invading armies. There were only two citizens of the New Israelite Nation. Duke's responsibility was to play along, which he did as long as his father didn't threaten to do something that would get them arrested. Being a New Israelite also meant he had to listen to criticism about his performance on the radio.

"But what was that horseshit about Indians and Spaniards you were giving that fellah?"

"Just the usual," Duke answered. A lecture was coming. "I was filling time with a few tall tales."

"You're too smart on the air, boy. Just say *nigger*. That's why people tune in. They don't want smart, they want hate. If I've learned anything in all these years, it's that."

"The caller seemed to buy it."

"I don't care. It makes you sound like a friend of these millionaire Indian bastards who are more coddled than a bunch of welfare niggers, son. Don't forget it. The casino down at Celilo clears three hundred million a year. And we let them get by with it. Our courts say Indians can fish where they want, live where they want, take any land that they want, do things any real American would be in jail for trying."

"I just made the stuff up. It's the only fun left in this job." Duke set his box of stones down on the table and started to pack up his bag of tools. Roy picked up one of the stones.

"Nice one. Where is it from?"

"It's a piece of granite from up near Lake Roosevelt, an erratic. Look how smooth it is. I haven't even started polishing."

"How much money could you get for that?"

"None, but this stone is rarer than gold, I'll guarantee that."

"And worth nothing."

"It's only worth something to another rock hound or a geologist, a perfectly preserved erratic from a twenty-thousand-year-old flood. This rock began its life way up in Canada. It was ground into this shape in the biggest, deepest flood this planet has ever known."

"If you could find a piece of Noah's ark in those rocks you'd have some serious money coming."

"If Noah found himself in this flood, he and the ark would have been fish food and sawdust in a matter of seconds. Nothing survived this flood. It's why they call rocks like these erratics. From Idaho to the coast, strange-looking, round, pitted rocks and boulders were dropped and scattered randomly by the floodwaters."

"I wish a flood could explain the behavior of my goddamned son."

Duke ignored his father and stared at the rock in his hand. "Each rock like this sits at the bottom of a pit. The flood's giant whirlpools take rocks and churn them around, carving smooth round bowls in the granite. When the waters receded, the stone that did the carving, rounded from all the abuse, is just sitting there in the bottom of the pit."

"Waiting for my son to put them in his shoe box. If there's something that's worth nothing, I can count on you having a real hankering for it."

"People have been asking how the big rocks got here for thousands of years. The Indians used to say that Coyote dropped them to trip up the gods who were chasing him."

"Today Indians are too busy counting their money to worry about coyotes. I think we should plan a little visit to that casino, what do you think?"

"What are you talking about?"

"Nothing big, just go down there, take a look around. Maybe we can find a way to remind the Indians that it's a favor we did them that they're not all dead, and wake up the people who give all their money away to people who hate white America probably more than even niggers do."

"What is the point of that?" Duke said. "Besides, the place is full of bouncers and bodyguards."

"It's a target just sitting there along the river, a wounded elk waiting for someone to put it out of its misery. I want to help is all."

"What are you saying, Daddy?"

"If you and I go down there we could have some fun while we look around."

"But no scenes, no fighting?" Duke knew what the word *target* meant to his father.

"I'm legit, completely legit. I even have a shiny new credit card from the Jewish bankers that I picked up in town. I've already used it. It works." Roy flashed his wallet at his son. "Come on boy, do you feel lucky?"

"You went to the gun show today?"

"Sure enough. A lot of our friends were there. They always ask about you."

"What do you tell them?"

"I tell them you can't hold down a job, spend all your time out in that damn boat of yours, and that you have a rock collection. That ends the conversation."

At the gun show you could always find someone with a false ID to sell. If you pestered people enough, you might get ahold of a stolen or counterfeit bank card, strictly under the table. Roy had been under every table at every gun show in three states for years. When Duke's mother was alive they went as a family. The boy would have a hot dog while his parents talked with friends about bombs and survival basements full of provisions and the best ammo for dealing with attacking federal agents. It had all seemed exciting to Duke then. Since his mother had been killed, he stayed away and let his father go alone. He was not going to get in trouble among friends. But if he were going down to Celilo, his father would need supervision. "The casino is a place for people to have fun," Duke said. "Nobody is going to want to talk about the United Nations and ZOG and the rest of it."

"A casino's no place for talking, boy. You're right. We're going to have fun like anyone else. With this card we can walk right up to the window and play any game we want. Destiny picked the location, and destiny is going to give us a big jackpot. Are you in, or do you want to stay home and play with your worthless rocks?"

"I'm in."

"Day after tomorrow. This credit card won't be good very long."

"I'll be there." Duke stepped outside. The desert air was moist and chilled. The Indian casino had changed a lot of things out on the high desert. Its success angered and disgusted Roy and lots of other people who liked to grumble about all the brand-new Indian millionaires strutting about. But Duke had noticed that anger and jealousy did not keep people from clogging the highways through the Columbia gorge seven nights a week to try their luck. In just a few short years, the casino had become the most successful enterprise along the river, exploding without warning out of the desert like the flashing signs with their colored neon that rudely pierced the river's tranquil darkness. From his boat, its lights reminded Duke of one of those cheap incandescent necklaces you might buy at a summer fair that would flash for a time at night and then burn out. But the casino never stopped flashing. Duke wondered what his father had planned. He would play his role. He would make sure his father came home safe. He would not feel lucky.

6

Headlights from the oncoming car caught the raindrops scurrying across his windshield like insects in a suddenly lit room. Deep in northern Canada, near the headwaters of the Columbia, Jeff Markel, chief engineer for BC Hydro Operations Division, knew where each droplet was headed as surely as he knew the words of the prophet Isaiah:

> Who hath measured the waters in the hollow of his hand,
> and meted out heaven with the span, and comprehended the
> dust of the earth in a measure, and weighed the mountains
> in scales, and the hills in a balance?

It was just before dawn. The hills were out of balance; the heavens had stayed hidden behind rain clouds for weeks now; and as for measuring the waters of the world, Markel would have the numbers for his little corner of the world as soon as he got to the office. He was pretty sure what they would say. Kinbasket Reservoir was slowly rising behind Mica Dam, the first in the Columbia chain. He drove past the security gate for Mica, waved to the guard who knew him by face and by his beat-up truck, parked, and walked in the pouring rain the hundred yards or so to the powerhouse. The rains had flooded the employee parking lot days before, and workers had to use the old visitors' center lot. Markel believed the swampy employee lot was some architect's afterthought, anyway. The visitors' center lot never flooded. Neatly paved, and decorated with cheerful signs, it was located right next to the lip of the dam, with a spectacular view 650 feet above the riverbed.

The visitors' center had been built for the admiring tourists who dam builders were certain would come to see what they had done to the river. *A Technical Marvel to Rival the Pyramids* was the title of the loud black-and-white short film that told the story of how the trucks came and mowed down the forest, brought in earthmoving equipment the size of dinosaurs to scoop out the soil, divert the river, and fill in the ancient riverbed. When the river had been allowed back along its familiar path, there was Mica Dam: "Blocking the Columbia for all time in the service of mankind."

Children unlucky enough to be brought here by parents still under the impression that there was something high-tech and magical about a dam, thought it bad TV. Mica's four turbine generators produced more than enough electricity to run every television, video game, and VCR that had ever been built, but all the kids ever saw here was a lake and a big wall. They used the nice clean rest rooms and waited impatiently for their parents. The visitors' center had closed a few years after it opened. Only the rest rooms stayed operational.

The rain soaked Markel through his jacket as he walked from his car to the elevator that took him down into the depths of the power-house where more than two million kilowatts of energy were channeled out across Canada and North America. Markel was probably the only soul awake at that hour who knew that compared to the energy of the river muscled up and pressing like a giant shoulder against the dam, the electricity produced here barely amounted to the sizzle on an iron.

From the edge of the dam the rain and gray washed all color out of the landscape. The reservoir receded into a wedge of black against the forest. There were no lights along the edge of the 140-mile-long Kinbas-ket Lake. It made Markel uneasy that in a cathedral devoted to the production of electricity, there was only darkness around Mica Dam and the reservoir it held back.

In his knees he could feel the vibration of the spillway as he walked. The hint of moonlight through the clouds barely illuminated the white spray that boiled up from the four massive spillway doors. They had been open for a week now, and even more of the river was being drained off through all of the generators, which were now running at full tilt. The hum of the excess power and the constant hammering of the gas-operated switches echoed through the powerhouse as he shivered in the narrow corridors on the way to his office.

Glancing at the main control-room panel, Markel could see that the reservoir had gained a few more inches overnight. The roar of the river penetrated all the way through to his bones. Markel knew what kind of force Mica could take, yet he could never get used to the unearthly sound of the open spillway concrete as it absorbed the millions of tons of water pounding down on it each second, letting the river pass through. The sound was the river trying to coax the earthen dam downstream, just as the water had carved countless other channels and eventually leveled every obstruction it had ever encountered from here to the sea.

Sometimes Markel thought that the concrete emitted a whine, a low-frequency shriek that seemed to well up from the atoms themselves. The spillway's concrete shafts were large enough to contain the skyline of a small city, with plenty of room left over to slosh the buildings around like a half-empty toy chest. They shook and wailed. *Concrete shouldn't make such sounds,* Markel thought. But he also understood that compared to the surrounding mountain rock, hewn by ancient glaciers, the spillways were as flimsy as Popsicle sticks. As he sat in the control room looking at the gauges and computer-display numbers on the wall, he could still feel the rain through his soaked clothes.

It shouldn't rain like this, he thought. *Not even here.* They called it a one-hundred-year flood, and there had already been two of them in the twenty-one years since Mica Dam started operation. *One-hundred-year flood* didn't really mean anything. It was just a discreet way of acknowledging that there was no human scale for measuring what dams did. They were in another league altogether; like earthquakes and typhoons, dams were among the planetary events in climatology. Certainly nothing on the wall of the power station control room gave Markel any indication when this rain would end.

"He disappointeth the devices of the crafty, so that their hands cannot perform their enterprise." Markel's Bible was a more meaningful gauge. "Yet man is born unto trouble, as the sparks fly upward."

No one had planned for this water.

∎

Nine hundred and fifty miles to the south and west, in the basement of the Dittmer Control Center in Vancouver, Washington, an error message filled the screen on the computer of Colonel Bud Hermiston, U.S. Army Corps of Engineers.

"Don't tell me I'm wrong." Hermiston talked to the screen. "I am your only goddamned truth."

Hermiston had written the error message and nearly every other line of code in the Columbia River simulation that allowed him to play with water levels before he pulled the actual levers that opened and closed the dams and controlled the river. The terminal was asking if he was sure about the water-level data that he was downloading into the HYDROSIM computer before it would start the daily runoff model.

"Of course I'm sure." Hermiston had been using computers of one kind or another since the 1960s, but he had never gotten used to them. Only humans would create a machine that questions its maker's intelligence. He preferred something real that moved the earth.

The computer was programmed not to believe the weather data Hermiston had been loading for a week now. Looking at this error message all this time had begun to make him irritable. The computer didn't believe the rain; even he didn't believe the amount of rain that had fallen. As he did every morning, Hermiston was asking HYDROSIM to calculate the precise amount of spill from each reservoir needed to keep them from overfilling while avoiding a flood in the sensitive lower Columbia.

If the computer was going to balk, Hermiston had a backup, his slide rule. He pulled it from his desk drawer and began to run through the numbers, jotting subtotals and interim results on a notepad. He worked the slide rule like a concert violinist, positioning the middle gauge, then with his thumb, setting the crosshair where he read his result. He was an engineer from the old school. A slide rule didn't argue, and it made no error messages because it made no errors. When a computer wasn't calculating, it was just a TV with a blank screen taking up space.

Calculating spill was a fantastically complex job, a three-hundred-billion-dollar puzzle. It was the full-time job of the power master at Bonneville Power Administration headquarters. The BPA ruled the river, and Hermiston was the hand of God, having risen to the agency's top job twenty years ago after an equal period of toiling as a lowly engineer and planner. With a push of a button Hermiston could submerge a town, stop all shipping on the river, or cause hundreds of irrigated farms to fail.

On Hermiston's desk were little concrete souvenirs from each of the dams he controlled from his office. The faded lettering on one old paperweight said *The Big Man with the Big Picture*. It referred to the wall behind his desk, which was festooned with surveillance satellite photos of the Columbia River. From three hundred miles above the earth, the river still looked impressive, but you had to look hard to spot the dams.

Next to Hermiston's phone, pencils and pens overflowed from a coffee mug. There was an old plastic toy replica of what looked like Noah's ark lying on its side on a piece of varnished wood. Apparently it had once been glued to the piece of wood, as though Hermiston had received it as a joke award. The plaque on the base was too corroded, its punch line long forgotten. On a wall facing the satellite pictures was a gallery of photos from the old days. Hermiston had one for every dam on the river, black-and-white shots of the dedication day for each dam. Men in gray hats stood at podiums while derricks and heavy equipment towered overhead. In the oldest picture, tens of thousands of people crowded the dedication for the Grand Coulee Dam, their faces blurred into the common prayer of the Industrial Age, dreaming along with the engineers of the land of plenty that would be created for hundreds of miles around. In each picture, presiding over the ceremonies, was the round face of the man who had preceded Hermiston as power master and had conceived that a river as big as the Columbia could even have a master. The face of Frank Hale in the fuzzy black-and-whites still looked as hard as the granite bedrock that held his dams to the earth.

They were all Frank Hale's dams: each one an argument against nature and the natural skepticism of people whose struggle to survive on this hard land had caused them to shrink into the Pacific Northwest's vast landscapes. Frank Hale had grown up on a wild river and imagined a clockwork miracle machine of man and nature on a scale never seen before. Pumping out electricity and irrigation water, Frank Hale's dams would finally make good on the brutal unkept promise the American frontier had made to the common man. Hale's dream vindicated every one of their failures. The dams placed man in the foreground of the west. They turned a desert into a quarter of a million square miles of wealth for the taking.

Hale succeeded so well that his shrines eventually ceased to amaze the vast public they served. The dams melded with the natural order until they were as indistinct as pebbles in the sand, nothing more than the invisible stagecraft of prosperity in a region that up until then had bequeathed only poverty to its squalid settlers. The pictures on the wall told the story of how the crowds dwindled at the groundbreakings and ribbon cuttings over time. In the last picture on Hermiston's wall, only a tiny group of people was on hand to witness the dedication of the Dalles Dam in 1967. The crowd was small enough to make out the face of Bud Hermiston, engineering-school graduate, and a young evangelist for Hale's machine-river of progress.

"Are the numbers in from Canada yet?" Hermiston called out to an assistant in the outer office. Before he could run his calculations each day, Hermiston needed the Canadian numbers from the Canadian dams upstream. The illusion that Bud Hermiston controlled anything on the Columbia faded a bit at the Canadian border. The Canadian and U.S. systems were linked by treaty, which meant that while computers monitored everything on each side of the border, data was not shared between nations except by phone. The dams in British Columbia were the newest hydro projects on the river, and since the 1980s they had forced Hermiston to share his role as regional Poseidon with a pantheon of river overseers.

Hermiston had never met his counterpart in Canada, Jeff Markel. All he knew about him was that he was paid less than half of Hermiston's salary and had to share an office. The lack of such perks did not diminish Markel's power to affect things south of the border. If Markel released too much from his dams, it could wreak havoc downstream in Hermiston's world. Mica Dam was the first in the Canadian chain. It was every bit as impressive as any of the U.S. dams. If Mica ever failed it would wash out everything downstream until Grand Coulee. Hermiston knew if Mica failed with the waters this high, Grand Coulee might just be washed out as well.

It was the principle of the thing that irked Hermiston. The dams had been an American idea. The accident of being upstream gave Canada a power Hermiston thought it hadn't earned. The grand old Roosevelt-era BPA had become a slave to U.S.–Canadian relations, a concept so stultifying to Hermiston, it justified an invasion by the U.S. Army to acquire the Columbia headwaters and be done with this Canadian nonsense. "We're not going to be friends with the Canadians forever," Bud would say to anyone who listened, until his federal masters sternly advised him that such talk was "not helpful."

Canada wasn't the only problem. It had been much simpler in the good old days when the engineers ruled the river like the pharaohs. Even high water like this was much simpler back when there were fewer dams and fewer people demanding water. In the twenty years that Hermiston had been power master, he had watched the erosion of his authority. Now every decision he made was watched over and second-guessed by two-bit city councils and Indian tribal committees, not to mention environmentalists and fish biologists. Unheard-of water levels such as he was seeing now made everything more difficult and the effect of a mistake that much more costly. Anything he did today would make someone mad; make enough people mad, and Congress would convene weeks of hearings. Hermiston would have to trudge out to Washington and answer questions from politicians who couldn't clear a stopped-up sink by themselves without a room full of special prosecutors.

Today most of Hermiston's employees were lawyers not engineers. Most of the work of the BPA was to make sense of the billions of federal regulations that determined whether or not it was okay to flush a toilet. In Hermiston's office the bookshelves had long ago been appropriated to hold binders full of federal documents, certification procedures for water and soil quality, nuclear evacuation plans, complicated rate schedules for power customers, and the secret list of which areas along the river were to be flooded first in case the dams had to be drawn down in an emergency. Hermiston felt the whole impenetrable mess could be summed up in a few words. Rates would always go up, nuclear evacuation plans would never work, and in a real flood Indian lands would be submerged first. The federal documents contained complicated formulas for carrying out what everyone already understood, fates to which people were long ago fully resigned.

One corner of his office was appropriated to maintain a seismometer, which churned out reams of paper covered with wiggly lines. The seismic monitoring was required by a humiliating act of Congress called the Geology and Public Safety Act of 1992. This was a piece of Washington silliness that had stunned even a seasoned D.C. hater such as Hermiston. What in hell could a law do about geology? In a dam builder's world, fate rested with the earth and its continent-sized stones. There was no greater security. Real engineers understood that with the continental plates you took your chances, period.

"If an earthquake is big enough to take out one of my dams, you won't need some graph paper to tell you. If it's not, who cares about a few knocked-over lamps? Earthquakes are acts of God," Hermiston would say, as though he were referring to another engineer. "Honest work."

To Hermiston, a seismometer was no guarantee of anything; it was simply an irritating, pointless little trinket. Hermiston loved to deliberately knock into it or drop heavy objects such as books on top of its glass cover to see if anyone noticed the paper disasters he delighted in making. No one ever did. Two people at the BPA did nothing but catalog the data and send it off to Washington, where, Hermiston was convinced, no one ever even looked at it.

"Get that bastard Markel on the phone," Hermiston yelled to the outer office. "He's late again."

"Mr. Markel, line four." It was the cheerless voice of a federal lifer working the phones.

"Jeff, what the fuck are you doing up there in the Arctic, ice fishing?"

"You're not going to like it, Bud." The best strategy for a Canadian dealing with anyone south of the border was to get right to business. "Our levels are still rising," Markel said with distinct alarm in his voice. "I've got to release another four million acre feet this morning."

"Don't tell me you can't hold more back than that," Hermiston shouted down the phone line. "Four million is flat wide open. I've got eleven million people in this watershed compared to the few hundred Ted Kaczynskis who live up your way. I need a little cooperation upstream from you today, Jeff."

"You know I can't hold anything right now with this bloody snowpack hanging over my head."

Hermiston grunted. The Canadians used snowpack as an excuse for everything. It was true enough that a sudden melt at the higher elevations would send twice the water from a week of rain straight into the Revelstoke and Kinbasket Reservoirs in a matter of hours. But Hermiston was looking at his weather data. It said the rain was due to end in western Canada within twenty-four hours and that the temperature would remain cold and steady in the mountains.

"If you could just shut it off for a day, we could get ahead of the game down here. We're running full tilt. We've got so much power on the Intertie you could blow-dry Lake Tahoe without so much as a brownout."

"I'd like to help you, Bud, but until my levels stabilize I can't close anything down up here. Maybe tomorrow."

"Okay, maybe tomorrow. How's your erosion?" Hermiston picked up a chart that indicated the latest shipping channel levels. High water always meant more silt, which meant more dredging, and this was the peak season for shipping traffic.

"It's still rising, Bud." Markel scanned silt data from a half dozen locations. "I'm afraid there's a lot of Canada on its way down to you. This latest surge has pulled a lot of tonnage." Markel said he would fax the latest detailed report on Mica's runoff and hung up. Hermiston sat looking at his own numbers. He took a pen out of the old mug on his desk to take some notes that became doodles while he waited for the fax. His eyes were drawn back to the mug.

Vanport 1948, Aluminum City U.S.A. was the place where he was born. The city had vanished in the last disastrous flood on the Columbia, a flood that took everything Hermiston's mom and dad had in the world. Until 1948 Bud Hermiston's dad had already spent his life starting over. The flood made it one too many. He never recovered. His parents died two decades later, long since broken and waterlogged, like an old dock that gives way silently in the night.

As Bud grew up, so did the population, until it had increased tenfold along the river, his river. "Flooding isn't up to nature anymore," he said, looking at the little toy Noah's ark on his desk. When it was time to build another one of those around here, Hermiston thought to him-

self, the voice calling on Noah would not belong to God. It would belong to Bud Hermiston and the BPA. Hermiston picked up the heavy
printout of the daily water levels and slammed it down disgustedly on
the top of the seismometer table. The needle on the graph lurched across
the paper. "That was a good one, Richter nine." He laughed and waited
for the needle to settle down. He wished it were as easy to move the water in his river.

7

"We come in peace to the people of the Celilo nation."

Dressed in camouflage, Roy McCurdy handed a piece of paper through the cash window and demanded thirty thousand dollars.

"Small bills, please." Roy's voice was deadly serious. Duke couldn't help rolling his eyes. Joe Moses, the CEO and supreme host at Shoulder Moon Casino and Cultural Center located on Route 14 in Celilo, Washington, knew this was no robbery. Moses paused on the way to the roulette tables. Even if the gamblers waiting in line behind these two survivalist-dressed frontiersmen were losing patience, Joe was used to this kind of thing.

"May we help you, gentlemen?"

Moses was tall, wrinkled, and leathery. The men at the window were pale-skinned, the older one's face covered by at least a day's worth of beard. He was wearing camouflage gear and a woolen cap with big ungainly flaps that hung off his head like elephant ears. He was comical everywhere but in his piercing blue eyes. The younger man was neatly dressed and athletic-looking. He wore a baseball cap and stood silently shaking his head.

"No speeches. If they won't take the paper, let's just go," Duke whispered.

"We're here as bona fide representatives of the Sovereign Nation of the New Israelites." Roy stressed the syllables "bone-uh feed-ay" as though they would bestow some credibility he didn't naturally project on his own.

"We sure don't want to start off on the wrong foot with the New Israelites." Joe calmly examined the piece of paper the older man was holding. He'd met men like these two before, though this was the first he'd heard of the New Israelites.

"What exactly happened to the old Israelites?" Joe asked half seriously.

"ZOG?" Roy was happy to help. "ZOG is the enemy. The Zionist Occupation Government is at the United Nations directing the systematic dismantling of the U.S. Constitution. This is my son, Duke. We have come here out of friendship to unite with a free people."

"Uh-huh." Joe wondered how many weapons the man was carrying. Under the thick coat he couldn't really tell. He continued to stare at what looked like a homemade banknote. Printed on an antique dot-matrix printer, across the top it said *Tax Lien Reserve Note Backed by United States Treasury Obligations. Pay Holder Thirty Thousand U.S. Dollars.* On the back was a crude picture of an eagle and the words, *New Israelite Nation.* "Pleased to meet you." Joe sighed. He couldn't imagine what would motivate a person to ask for thirty thousand in return for something that looked like it was torn out of a coloring book.

Duke spoke up. "Excuse us, but my father has always had a little trouble with the U.S. government." He pointed at the gaudy Indian decor. "I'm sure you can understand that around here." On his cap was the bright red, single-feathered, big-toothed logo of the Cleveland Indians baseball team.

"Why would you gentlemen think I have any problems with the U.S. government?" Joe asked, trying to hide his revulsion at the image on the cap. At Shoulder Moon, Indians had no problems with the Feds, and they worked hard to keep it that way. Every tax-paying business in a five-hundred-mile radius from Celilo was painfully jealous of the money that sloshed through the casino like a dam blown wide open; there was unimaginable wealth at this place dressed up like a lost Stone Age civilization. The waitresses wore costumes of the squaws from old western movies. The slots that were mobbed day and night had names such as

"Sasquatch" and "Squanto's Last Meal" and "Big Wampum." The poker tables were in the fake "Longhouse" at one corner of the casino, where there was actually a small Indian museum adjoining "The Potlatch," one of the many restaurants where gamblers could eat fajitas and dried-up, overcooked lumps of salmon. As a final insult to the Columbia River right outside the front door, the salmon were flown in from Alaska. It was all about as Indian as the logo on this young man's cap. To Joe, the most Indian thing about this place was that he never talked openly about any troubles he might have ever had with the U.S. government.

"Unfortunately, gentlemen, we can't accept this kind of money here. But if there is anything else I can help you with, Mr. . . . ?"

Roy did not give his name. "You accept this green U.S. government money backed by your people's graves?" The statement was both absurd and perfectly true. For an instant Joe thought these two might be some kind of setup.

"I'm sorry," Joe said. "People just seem to like greenbacks in America. Bad habit, I guess."

"We're in a war with the U.S. government. It's a cover for ZOG."

"My people have waged a few wars with the U.S. government. We've discovered that war is not the best way to communicate with Washington." Joe smiled at the people waiting in line behind these two.

"Dad, no one's interested in hearing about ZOG. I think we need to move along."

"Look," Joe addressed the son. "If your daddy has something in his wallet we could actually use to get some cash, we would be happy to help."

"That's an insult. You would rather take some plastic card owned by Jewish bankers?" The old man was nearly shouting.

At the mention of Jewish bankers the people in line groaned out loud. "Hey, Adolf, go home to your gas chambers," someone called out. Roy turned.

"How did you like your U.S. government in Oklahoma City?" The crowd's last bit of patience and sympathy boiled away.

"Dad, we're going to have to leave now." Duke said it sadly as he reached into his father's coat pocket and removed his wallet while the old man stared at the people around him. Joe Moses motioned for his bodyguards.

"I'm afraid this is more about gas and expense money for the old man than ZOG," the son said quietly to Joe as he motioned for his father to step out of the cash-window line. "I think you can get a thousand from this card. I'll make sure that Daddy cools off." He handed a Visa card to Joe who walked up to the window and gave it to the cashier. "See if you can take a grand off of this."

"I will not let you take advantage of our friend." Roy raised himself up proudly and handed his wrinkled banknote to Joe. "I want you and your people to have something of value." He was most comfortable giving speeches. "I know you can't fight Jewish bankers on your own, but I promise this will be worth a lot to you someday."

"Thank you, sir," Joe said. As he put the piece of paper in his coat pocket he looked straight into the old man's face: Knotted and hardened with lifelong anger, it did not match the comical outfit he was wearing. Joe recognized it as a killer's face. He'd seen such faces before. His brother Charley Shen-oh-way had such a face, unsettling, brutal, without pity. Joe thought for a moment he would bounce these two when, to his surprise, the Visa card was approved for a cash withdrawal. He waved off his bouncers and handed the old man an envelope of cash. "Mr. Whillers, is it?" Joe looked at the name on the card. "Why don't you and your boy try to have a little fun?"

"Thank you." The son seemed to wince at the mention of the name. He ushered his father into the crowded, noisy casino. Joe noticed that the son did not carry the hardened face of the father. The young man's voice was familiar, though he couldn't place it. The formerly angry line of gamblers who had watched the scene huffed contemptuously and went off to drink. *Money is money,* Joe thought, but he remained uneasy. The whole scene felt like a setup, but these two seemed too dim to be anything but harmless. A casino was a magnet for assholes, and Joe had seen every kind of scam. "Why don't you run a complete check on that Visa card, just in case it's stolen," Joe told the cashier.

Once every few months Joe would have to charm and occasionally eject somebody for trying to cash homemade, white-separatist, neo-Nazi money. Hand-lettered or worse, printed with words like *White American Bastion* or *Anti-Federalist Treasury Note,* it was always the same. A couple of men would tramp in with heavy camouflage jackets, go straight to a cash window, and present their militia money. They liked the casino because it was on reservation land and, as they liked to say, was "free unoccupied territory." Indians had, by virtue of their defeat at the hands of the federal government, the very territorial autonomy these militia armies coveted as their right as "real Americans."

The militia play money generally came in one-thousand- or ten-thousand-dollar denominations. Its redeemers expected the Indians at Shoulder Moon to be sympathetic and simply cash the notes, no questions asked. Once refused, they would stand around at the window making speeches about ZOG and how it was sending United Nations troops to kill all the white babies. Gamblers on their way to the tables and slots hurriedly elbowed the men aside, as though they were eluding Krishnas at Sea Tac Airport. Eventually Joe would dispatch his bouncers, who listened as the men continued to howl about Ruby Ridge, fluoridation, or some other federal conspiracy, and were then gently escorted out the front door. For all their bluster, no incident had ever required coercion or an actual arrest.

These survivalists only reinforced Moses's suspicion that the white man was a gigantic millennial joke on his people. Coyote was hard at work producing the spirit world's particular brand of comedy starring self-proclaimed prophets peddling play money, seeking solace among the Indians, while threatening to bomb and kill their own. Such characters had always been part of the Pacific Northwest. Their voices hissed quietly in the constant drizzle of the backwoods. Timed with the end of the century, they had emerged from the frontier until they were an anomalous quirk of the foreground, comical and deadly.

Joe thought that in his lifetime Americans had grown, if anything, more obsessed with the frontier, slavery, pointless fears about Jews, immigrants, and nonwhites, suspicions and hatreds imported intact from Europe as though they were part of some nostalgia for the worst of the old countries. Joe saw that all the old arguments over freedom and tyranny settled by a half dozen wars still glowed like colored pins on an ancient map. Wandering befuddled and lost through new lands while carrying their old maps was the story of the white people: Coyote's unmistakable fingerprint. What else could explain all the lost faces night after night in his casino?

Joe was convinced that if there had been no white man, the Indians would have had to invent him. It took a meteor to extinguish the dinosaurs. Joe and his remnant civilization were the somnolent turtles, skittish iguanas, and invisible geckos from a proud planet of giants long gone. Without blinking, Indians watched their erratic, quick-to-anger, mammalian carnivore heirs fight over the scraps of the history they, themselves, had made.

They came in droves to the casino to plug the leaks in their American dreams. Shoulder Moon had a slogan crowded onto its festively colored matchbooks. *Good Luck Is Sacred Ground: Play hard, play fair, play again.* Shoulder Moon Casino had taught Joe that Americans were never more dangerous, entertaining, or easier pickings for cash than when they sensed a winning streak. They got drunk on the idea of winning just like Indians got drunk on corn whiskey. From Christopher Columbus to the present moment, with only a few bloody blips in between, the white man's streak had been going on for five hundred years. After generations of nonstop losing, Indians could finally catch a glimpse of the effect they were having. The grand lesson of history? On the ashes of Joe's ancestors, a civilization had been born that seemed dedicated to nothing more than going out with a bang. Coyote again.

Joe stood at a roulette table underneath an enormous fake wall-mounted fish. He was dressed in a red satin tuxedo trimmed with simulated rawhide fringe, which passed for a uniform. All the Indian employees except for the really serious bouncers in black suits wore a similar outfit. Joe had envisioned Shoulder Moon as "the most spectacular ambush since Little Bighorn." Bankers had told him that the Indian motif would clash with the casino. His own people had said that gambling would degrade tribal identity. Joe listened patiently while university-trained anthropologists and Smithsonian shrunken-head collectors who had spent their careers filling federal warehouses with his people's discarded artifacts, not to mention their remains, told him how he was plotting the destruction of his own heritage. He was quiet during all the hearings. He waited while all of the court cases were argued. He didn't protest when all of the legislation to stop Indian gambling was considered. He didn't cheer when every bill was defeated. Through it all Joe Moses waited. But when the proper permits were in his hand, he did it his own way.

Three years after opening its doors, Shoulder Moon was grossing in a year what it had cost to erect more than one of the dams upriver. The slots alone pulled in more business than some big casinos in Vegas. The parking lot had been extended and regraded four times since it opened. The square footage devoted to gaming had doubled, and there were plans for a new building with five new restaurants, a full theater, and a wilderness ride where people could shoot the rapids in mechanical boats that simulated the Columbia River long before the dams.

The casino was to have been the great equalizer. Joe's younger brother, Charley, had predicted that the luck of the Columbia Indians was fated to change. He had believed that good life would return. Charley had never imagined it would come in the form of a casino—that was Joe's contribution. Joe and Charley were a great team: Joe Moses the anglicized showman, Charley Shen-oh-way the visionary. They had played together and faced the elements together from the time they were young boys. From the rocks above Celilo, Joe and Charley would make pacts and pray to the salmon, vowing to show their bravery above all others who fished the falls. Beneath the carved stone face of Tsagaglalal, Charley and Joe would speak and dream for hours about the future.

Charley was in love with the old stories, grizzly bears descending from heaven or Great Spirit eagles flying out of the sun to settle the score. *"Tamala,"* he would say, which meant "tomorrow and eternal life" in Chinook. The only grizzly bears Joe had ever seen were stuffed and for sale in hotel lobbies. He dreamed of the riches in the white man's world. Charley had preferred to throw his lot in with the old world, and he'd been swept away, along with Celilo Falls, many years ago.

"Come on, red man. Dial up the Great Spirit." At one of the roulette tables a youngish, slightly chunky man named Doug Pollack was still up by a few hundred. Pollack was a successful trader who seemed to have redeemed his baby fat for a satisfied what-could-possibly-go-wrong gut, chin, and demeanor. He prayed to Joe: "Gimme red, gimme twelve, three on the quad, and a double street in the middle, gimme a goddamned cash-money winner."

Joe smiled at the faces around the table, stepped up, and spun the wheel. The ball's smooth rolling sound searched for a place to land with a smart and fateful click.

"Twenty-four," Joe called out in a gravelly voice. "Black wins." Around the table the regulars responded with sighs and nods. Like all hard-core gamblers, they believed each outcome was knowable. "Damn close," one muttered. One hundred and twenty-five bucks vanished into the pit.

"Next time, a winner," Joe said, knowing only the house had a sure thing.

When he wasn't busy managing Shoulder Moon from his office, Joe liked to work the roulette tables, presiding over the ball and wheel. Roulette was Joe's favorite game, and the more he played it, the more he was sure it was a game of skill. Certainty about roulette and every other game at Shoulder Moon was etched deeply into his seventy-one-year-old face. It was a face that promised good luck; at least that was the way the gamblers saw it. High rollers starved for a talisman had found Moses and his temple.

There were no higher rollers than the strange assortment of big shots who came to Shoulder Moon. Joe could see a greasy-looking white kid in his twenties, a regular from Seattle, CEO of some Internet overnight wonder worth a few hundred million. Betting against him was a tall man in his sixties from the town of Moses Lake; he was one of the many wheat millionaires who cashed his five- and six-figure federal agricultural-subsidy checks at Shoulder Moon. Joe felt the survivalist note in his pocket. It occurred to him that there was a lot of play money in circulation in his part of the world.

At Joe's roulette table were some regulars, including the Grassleys, an elderly couple from the little desert town of Ephrata, Washington, who owned a potato empire that shipped French fries to fast-food joints all over the Western Hemisphere. The Grassleys had a system, which they followed like a catechism, of betting on nearly every number on the wheel. Mrs. Grassley guarded the proceeds like a spider. Every once in a while she scraped a couple of stacks of chips into her big leather purse and sent her frail, nervous husband over to the window to cash them in.

Next to Pollack and the Grassleys was a woman named Rebecca who always came to Celilo alone. She drank strong gin and tonics, gripping her glass as though it were her only anchor in a howling wind. Her cheeks were red, and she always left the casino less than steady on her feet. At the roulette table she was quiet, placing her bets in a whisper. Winning and losing were interchangeable to her, not because she was rich, but because she so enjoyed being in a room full of people who all believed that their lousy luck was about to change. When she wasn't playing roulette, she was at the slots staring dreamily into the lights of the noisy bandits.

To Rebecca's left, sat the hard-betting security chief out at Hanford, Duane Madison. He often showed up in his Department of Energy uniform, but tonight he was very much off duty, in a loose-fitting Tommy Hilfiger sweatshirt that did a poor job of hiding his gut. At the end of the table sat a first-timer from Portland named Park Sun Yee, a Korean who insisted that everyone call him Burt. "Burt" had just won back-to-back five-hundred-dollar bets.

"What did I tell ya, Burt? Joe here's a fucking Yoda." Doug had bet five hundred, predicting that his luck would change when Joe arrived at the table. It had. He was up two thousand.

The Grassleys had hit a double street bet at six to one. But with smaller losses on a half dozen other numbers, they netted only about $150. Still, Mr. Grassley hooted, sorted the chips, and waited for further instructions from his wife. Joe loved the Grassleys. They had one of the best setups going.

"Damned if you folks don't lose almost as many chips as you rake in," Duane Madison said. He didn't think much of the Grassleys' system. "You're smart, that I'll give you. But where's the fun?" Though Duane had dropped another three hundred, he was still up a few grand for the night. "I'd rather stay home and watch the ants in my driveway."

"People on a fixed income can't afford to bet all or nothing like you do, Duane. We both win. It's just that we're going to take it home," Mrs. Grassley declared while Mr. Grassley nodded in agreement. He and his wife had never stopped believing that, despite their millions, they were just simple, penny-counting dust-bowl farmers.

"We could all probably buy the state of Wyoming with the Grassleys' fixed income," Pollack snorted. He had no system at the table. "Too much work. I need to feel it to bet."

"You can't win by feel here, Doug." Mrs. Grassley shook her head and looked at Joe. "He'll tell you, the Columbia is a haunted river. The white man can never win big here. There are too many spirits floating in off the water working against us." Mrs. Grassley winked at Joe. "My husband and I stick to small winnings, so the river ghosts don't notice."

"Lotta river ghosts out there these days," Doug Pollack said. "Killers."

"You mean the salmon murders, Douglas?" Mrs. Grassley perked up for a true crime story.

"They found another body last night." Doug liked to be at the center of a hot rumor. "Hard to figure, though. The Feds ain't saying much about it, and the local cops are having a cow over being shut out. The Seattle papers are full of it."

"They say it's some kind of Indian thing. Could that be true, Joe?" Mrs. Grassley spoke with the feigned incredulity of a seasoned poker player concealing four kings.

"People say all ghosts are Indian ghosts," said Joe, shaking his head. "Haven't heard a thing."

Duane Madison eyed Joe carefully and wondered.

"What exactly have you heard, Mrs. Grassley?" Madison asked.

"We've heard that there's a whole lot the Feds are keeping under wraps about the condition of those bodies."

"Closed caskets, all three of them. That's what I've heard." The potato queen laid a few fifty-dollar chips on the table. "I wouldn't get in one of those fish trucks if you paid me a million in cash."

"Million in cash just might change my luck." Madison laughed and stayed with red, adding a thirty-to-one off wager on the zero. "Do black people count as white in your haunted river rule, Mrs. Grassley? I ain't white but I'm winning squat."

"The same chance for everyone at Shoulder Moon," Joe said as he spun the wheel once more. "It's the law."

The ball bounced and clicked, and all eyes around the table followed it into the red, gold, and black blur of the wheel. In the pause Joe made a point not to think about the river murders. Indians got blamed for everything that didn't have an explanation. Joe thought about the river's ghosts, the people and places he had known as a boy. Watching the roulette wheel was like watching the river in the old days. Full of salmon and watched over by Coyote, Joe's wild childhood river was the source of all prosperity and security, the stage upon which life and death were played out.

The biggest ghost was Celilo Falls itself, long ago silenced but never quiet. On the spot where Joe stood, villages and tribes from hundreds of miles would gather each spring and fall for the salmon runs. The men would wager village to village over who would spear or net the largest fish, or the greatest number. It was easy to lose count. There had always been fish without end at Celilo. Fighting their way up solid walls of rock facing the river's torrent head on, the salmon would seek a path upstream, summoning an unearthly strength to breed.

Had he himself not stood in the raging waters with his lance and felt the life force draining from a thirty-five-pound chinook he had speared while hundreds of fish of equal size jumped around him, Joe would not have believed it. Celilo was the one place in the world where Joe, his brother Charley, and his friends could escape the bleak realities of growing up Indian in America in the twentieth century. By 1967 everything he had known along the river had been swept away by the white man's progress. Primal and terrifying, Celilo Falls was all that re-mained. Then one day it, too, was gone.

Joe blinked. He wished that the roulette ball would never land and that everyone around the table could stay forever wrapped in the antici-pation of their own dreams, that the present would merge with the past, that no success would be counted out in the currency of another's failure. Everything was possible. Joe Moses could even hear the roar of Celilo until the silver ball dropped. Red twenty-three.

"Indians like the rigged games best, don't they, Chief?" Joe returned from his reverie to see the face of the old man in camouflage from ear-lier in the evening parked in front of him. He had wandered over to the roulette table and was carrying several thousand dollars' worth of chips. His son was not with him.

"It looks as though you've had a good run over at the slots—Mr. Whillers, is it?" Joe tried to assess if he had been drinking. "I'm sorry I've forgotten your name."

"The name's McCurdy, Roy McCurdy. Glad to know you all." He smiled warmly at everyone except Duane Madison, who looked up sharply at the mention of the names Whillers and McCurdy.

"You weren't kidding about those river ghosts, were you, Joe?"

Duane Madison pulled in his modest winnings. He had seen the man earlier at the cash window and had been trying to place his face ever since.

"Five hundred on the black." The man said the word *black* with a sneer. He leaned over to Joe. "Do you always let people gamble their welfare checks like this? I thought you didn't take play money around here, Chief."

Joe moved his foot over to a switch under the table that alerted security to possible trouble. "Now I gave you another chance, a little while ago. I hope you're not going to get ugly now after we went out of our way to help you."

"One hundred on the red and two on the double street." Duane laid his chips down.

"The black is betting against black." The old man was clearly enjoying himself. "There's a sure bet."

"Did you just come here from a Klan meeting?" Mrs. Grassley looked up from her columns of numbers. "We're all friends at this table. Nobody's interested in your insults." Mr. Grassley looked alarmed.

"You think this is a fair game, lady?" The old man beamed his bitterness full onto Mrs. Grassley. "The chief holds all the cards in this room. White people like us step out of line, and all he has to do is squeal for the Feds and we're out on our asses." Mrs. Grassley said nothing and looked down at her pile of chips.

The woman named Rebecca stared at the man as though she placed him somewhere. "If you play long enough, you win. That's fair," she said as she placed two twenty-dollar chips on the low-end double street at five to one, then drained her glass.

Moses called the next round. "Place your bets. Hundred on the red for Duane. The Grassleys stay with the system. Burt doubles on the black. First bet from Mr. McCurdy, the unknown soldier with the big smile on his face over here, is five hundred on the black. Mr. Pollack stays on the sidelines, and we spin."

"Black six."

"Say it loud, boy, I'm black and a proud winner of one thousand cash-money dollars." McCurdy snatched his thousand dollars from the table. "Need a little self-esteem right about now?"

Duane was seething. The aggravation of losing another three hundred dollars had shortened his temper. "You make a lot of noise for an old racist fart."

"Destiny, Mr. Negro, destiny." He pronounced the word as "nee-gruh" and prepared to make another bet. "You're a long way from Africa out here in the desert. I'm trying to help you save your paycheck so all those crack babies back home don't go hungry."

Duane could feel his own primitive and righteous impulse to tear the man to pieces, but it was not the time or place for a showdown. There never was for a black man from Seattle. Contentment in the Pacific Northwest had given him an education, middle-class prosperity, friends of all backgrounds, and the belief that people like McCurdy were pathetic and absurd. Like Hendrix, Duane had simply found an escape from blackness by adopting a near-religious confidence. Duane needed none of the swagger of the ghetto culture to believe that people like McCurdy were animals whom he would not dignify with his own personal emotions. Duane thought of what Hendrix had said of such people.

Hey machine gun. I ain't afraid of your mess no more, babe
I ain't afraid no more
After a while, your, your cheap talk don't even cause me pain,
So let your bullets fly like rain

Duane's family had been in the Pacific Northwest for three generations. This guy had the look of a drifter just ahead of the law and a station-wagonful of ex-wives. No one else at the table quite knew what to say. Rebecca had won two hundred dollars from her wager with the old man, but the tension at the table made it feel like she had lost instead. Joe pressed the foot switch under the table. Frail, thin Mr. Grassley broke the silence. "What's your problem?" He coughed and continued. "You just won a thousand dollars."

The Grassleys had also won big. With forty dollars on the quad, one hundred on the black, and twenty on the double street, all of which contained the six, they pulled in $620 with a loss of only twenty on the side bets. "Your destiny is just dumb luck," Mr. Grassley said to McCurdy, anxious to avenge any rudeness to his wife. "Maybe you should move along."

A pair of the casino's bodyguards stood nearby. Joe quietly told them to stay. *"Mitlite,"* he said, using the words of his own language. *"Mitlite."*

The old man watched this exchange and turned to Joe. "Are you going to spoil all the fun now, Chief? America can't be very much fun for you. Tell us all how much fun it is to be an American Indian. How many of your relatives were murdered by Uncle Sam's jackboots so you could have your little Disneyland on the Columbia here?"

"If you're having no fun in America, Mr. . . . what's the name again?"—Joe could feel this strange man's rage touch his own—"maybe you should call your congressman. How about we give you a couple of free dinners? Would that postpone the race war for tonight?"

"Spin the wheel, Joe." Doug Pollack put down his cellular phone. "Uncle Skinhead here just needs his own talk show. One asshole, one talk show. That's America."

"Already have a talk show, and I'm afraid there's no postponing the war."

"Five hundred on the black." Duane placed his chips. "And is the name Whillers, or is it McCurdy?"

"Who wants to know? Two thousand on the red," Roy McCurdy called out, and laid down his chips, making two additional side bets, one thousand on the double street thirty-one through thirty-six at five-to-one odds, and five hundred on the single number thirty-two. He leaned in to Duane, pointing at the lettering on his sweatshirt. "So, homeboy, how much do you get paid to be a big round billboard for that Tommy Hilfiger faggot?"

"And your camouflage getup?" Duane asked. "Is that for trick or treat?" McCurdy chuckled at Duane with a seasoned hatred. Duane shrugged him off with a look of disgust. He knew Roy McCurdy. More federal agents knew that name than the president's, along with the name Maccabee Pond. Roy McCurdy had been screaming end-of-the-world proclamations over the airwaves ever since federal agents had surrounded Roy's house a decade ago. He shot his way out, his wife took a bullet in the head in front of her little boy, and the entire fiasco was televised live. The shoot-out at Maccabee Pond had ended the lives of a few agents and dozens of FBI careers. But none of McCurdy's bullets was ever traced to an FBI agent's body, and because the bullet that killed his wife had come from an FBI rifle, McCurdy had eluded all charges and was freed to pursue his defiance in other ways.

"I'm afraid it's for real, boy." McCurdy continued to point at Duane's sweatshirt. "What we have here is a colored boy doing free advertising for the white man." He drained his drink and spoke to the table. "We fought a goddamn war to free the black man, and they sign up to be slaves all by themselves."

"I'd still like to know about the name Whillers you used before," said Duane. He thought of McCurdy as dangerous only when cornered but more like a childhood bully in public. Still, McCurdy had succeeded in making everyone else at the table more tense. "Was he a friend of yours?"

"I know you." Rebecca had suddenly spoken. Her voice was loud and had the hint of a slur, but she so rarely made a sound that the whole table stopped for a moment. "McCurdy is the man from the Bible radio station. I hear your show all the time." Rebecca blushed a deep pink. She extended her hand as though she was in the presence of a celebrity, which made the other people at the table even more uneasy. "Tommy Liberty, he's on that station, too, right?"

"Tommy's my son, ma'am. It is always nice to meet a listener." He pulled a card from his pocket and gave it to her. "We'd both be happy to give you a VIP tour of the station anytime. But tonight I'm out here sinning along with you in this temple of Satan. Call me Roy, won't you?"

Duane looked at Joe. "If this here is Mr. McCurdy, why did you call him Whillers?" Duane was happy to pay attention to anything other than the money he was losing.

"You allow nigger cops to sit down and interrogate your customers, Chief?"

Joe ignored them both, called the bets, and spun the wheel.

The ball landed on thirty-three.

Another payday for the old man. Red paid, and so did the double street: thirty-one through thirty-six. He won six thousand dollars against a loss of only five hundred. Joe was powerless. To intervene in the middle of someone's streak would only cause a riot and ruin business for weeks if word got around. He scanned the room for the old man's son and didn't find him. Joe would have to wait until the old man began losing to bounce him.

"What's the problem? Too much luck for the Indian nation?" McCurdy was calling for a beer, a bourbon shot chaser, and a second beer to chase that. Rebecca ordered another round. A crowd was beginning to gather.

"Destiny. It is all in the voice of the earth: *wawa illihee*." As McCurdy spoke, Joe visibly flinched, and all of the Indians working nearby, including bodyguards, looked up.

"Chinook language," he said. "You are full of surprises tonight."

"*Wawa illihee*, voice of the earth. It doesn't only speak to you. One hundred and fifty years ago all of the missionaries and settlers in this part of the country could speak Chinook jargon. It was our second language, Chief." He emphasized the word *our*.

"*Mesachie tillikum*," replied Joe. "I don't need a lesson in Chinook from you, *mesachie tillikum*." The words meant "bad person."

"I'm afraid you're wrong about that. I'm no enemy of yours, Chief.

You and I are part of this land. Our daddies and granddaddies came right out of this dirt. We're not like these yuppies, your federal-farm Jew squatters over here, and the nigger."

The old man pushed all of his winnings, about seventy-five hundred dollars, onto the number fifteen.

"I did you a favor by cashing your card, sir." Joe spoke quietly to McCurdy. "Now I'm a little concerned that it wasn't yours. I'll have to call the police if you don't settle down."

The crowd had separated into blacks and whites, the opposite poles of an electrical current. Rebecca sat transfixed in the middle. She was dazzled as Roy took control of the whole room. It was like being in the presence of a star or a preacher.

Duane Madison stayed calm in the face of a streak of bad luck that appeared to have acquired a personal dimension. He smiled and put his remaining two thousand on red, drew five hundred off his Visa card, and put it on the fourteen for a side bet.

"Are you experienced at this, Mr. Aryan Brother, or can I watch you hand it all back and get thrown out on your white ass?" he said. "At least I wouldn't ever let a woman take a bullet meant for me."

The blood seemed to drain from McCurdy's face. Joe's bodyguards tensed visibly for a fight, but McCurdy, after a pause, took a long breath, looked over at Madison, and smiled.

Pollack had three thousand on the table. "This is fun," he said into the awkward silence. "I'd love to see you go down." Pollack placed it all on the red.

Burt, the Korean, was next. "This is about money only." Burt was a gambler betting the streak. It just happened to belong to the man across the table. "He is playing a game with you." Burt pointed at Joe. "They both are. I play black."

"The Korean is a smart man." McCurdy's voice rang out clear and strong. "There's no way I lose here, no matter how you rig your game. Indians can run casinos where white people can't. Indians can fish wherever and whenever they like because of the courts. You're just another rich guy with a lot of paid federal thugs to beat the shit out of me if I step out of line. But whatever happens tonight, I still walk out of here a white man. My people created this world. We play for keeps."

From across the room Duke McCurdy stepped through the crowd and found his father. He shook his head, alarmed. "You promised no trouble, no speeches."

"There's no trouble here, boy," he hissed at his son.

"We can leave now with plenty of money in our pockets and head home," the son was begging. "We don't need to do this. You said we came in peace."

"Stand away from the nigger and the Jews and come here, boy!" It was a command. The way he spoke to his son was more intimidating to the people at the table than anything Roy had said up to that point. The son, who was hardly a boy, obeyed.

"So this is how your daddy cools off?" Joe said. Even the body-guards took a step back. Rebecca sat next to Roy and his son, who she now understood was the same Tommy Liberty she listened to on the radio. She felt buoyed up by the excitement, pulled out of her own life and into another one. She pushed her pile of chips over to the black. She placed a few on the number fifteen next to McCurdy's.

The old man ignored the crowd and focused on Joe. "*Wawa illihee,* now spin the wheel. Destiny, destiny."

Joe spun the wheel. Roulette was not a game of luck. It was not even a game. It was like America's history—people with a common purpose, incited to suspicion and ill-willed anticipation waiting for balls to drop, condemned to live out the consequences. Joe looked up at old man McCurdy. On his face was a look of delirious peace. He didn't have to look at the ball to know where it had landed.

"Black fifteen."

He had won it all, $262,000 from a single number. Burt screamed and grabbed his three grand. The Grassleys had quietly played the streak along with the Korean and with a trio of side bets won fourteen thousand. Mrs. Grassley collected up the chips and motioned to her husband that they were leaving. She didn't thank the holder of this streak. Rebecca pulled five thousand dollars of winnings over to her purse. She had never been so lucky. She had occasionally been this drunk. The combination warmed her. But the money wasn't important. The magical evening was over; there was nowhere to go but home now. She grabbed her coat and dispersed with the crowd. Joe watched her, hoping that she didn't have far to drive.

Everyone else had lost. For Duane it was six thousand dollars gone for nothing. He walked silently from the table and went directly to his car. A total of fifteen thousand went into the center of the table. The old man and his son, who finally looked relieved, were still sitting at the table stacking up their winnings.

"I'm helping you out, Chief," the man said, his voice dripping with contempt. "You did almost as good as me tonight. We make a great team. Indians can't stand a fair fight. It always has to be a rigged game. I just evened the score." He leaned in close to Joe. "The money's for a good cause, you can be sure of that. And remember, Chief, not every murderous ghost thirsty for revenge on your river is an Indian ghost."

The casino bouncers stepped forward and gripped the old man's arms. He shook them free and walked out with his son and his winnings. Joe watched them go. He noticed how sickly and pathetic the father looked, an emissary from an unseen world. For an instant the son's humiliation struck him as the key to a perfect setup.

"Destiny, Chief. *Wawa illihee.*"

For the first time in many years, Joe Moses strongly sensed the haunted Columbia. But it was not his brother's spirit he felt. It was something else: Coyote had made the ball drop. A few minutes after the two survivalists left the casino, a clerk told Joe the Visa card had turned up stolen. "Whillers . . ." Joe remembered the name on the card. "First name, Dave." Joe felt the old man's play money still in his pocket.

"Do we call the Feds?" the clerk asked, knowing the loss would be made up by the end of the evening.

"No Feds," Joe said, still uneasy. "They probably already know anyway. Let the word get around about how well he did. It'll bring us a big weekend."

It had been a robbery after all. If Joe had simply cashed the note from these New Israelites, he would have only been out thirty grand.

Confirmation

The warrior heard sounds in the tall concrete shelter he called his long-house, and after an instant he made out the footsteps. He could see, up beyond the high walls of the tower, the circle of sky far above him. The clouds were thick and gray, but he could tell the light was waning; it was early evening. Silently he reached out and slipped his fingers around the handle of his long blade. With his other hand he grabbed the small harpoon that was his preferred weapon in combat. Though the abandoned cooling tower was open to the sky, darkness was thick below. He sought the scent of the intruder, but the air was heavy with the musty chill of a cave and the pungent signature of the bats that lived within. After a moment's concentration he found it: The intruder was no animal. Sound told the warrior that whoever it was, was not on a hunt. Even a poor hunter would have been more careful. The intruder was unaware of his trespass.

The dim pale sky dropped a single beam of light into the center of the tower and found a shiny bald head blowing with wisps of gray. The man stepped carefully around the debris on the floor of the tower. He carried a flashlight in one hand. His footsteps were sure. They took him close to where the warrior was crouched and ready to spring. The man wore an old torn trench coat and carried a briefcase as though he were on his way to an important appointment. He moved with little grace and carried no weapon, but the warrior lifted his blade as the beam of the flashlight danced nearby. Should this man see him, it would be his last vision on earth. Smohalla's task could not be accomplished if he was discovered. The warrior raised his harpoon, but the man hobbled past his hiding place without a pause toward a pile of debris the

warrior had not noticed before. The beam of the flashlight settled on a sheet of
soiled plastic that appeared to cover a pile of objects like a tent.

■

Jack Charnock looked around. Everything was exactly as he remembered. In the years since his last visit, nothing had changed. On the
day his son died, they had pointed to this portion of the wall, and he had
stared through his own tears at the pattern of stripes in concrete, gray on
gray. He could only imagine the body's position deep within the wall,
knowing that the heavy pressure of the reinforced concrete would have
obliterated it altogether: his son's life reduced to a smudge or a barely
perceptible striation of color without form. Teeth alone would have survived intact. It was this thought that possessed him as he had pored over
the government safety X rays of every inch of the concrete structure to
find the images of his son's teeth, gray on gray. The government required
the X rays to certify the structural integrity of this plant that was never
built. The X rays had been stored away, secure and retrievable in a government archive. Jack noticed as he had scanned each sheet of microfilm
that he was the only one to have ever examined these pictures. They were
part of the hollow rituals of the nuclear priesthood certifying that this
empty ruin was the safest, most expensive headstone ever built, engi-
neered to withstand even a nuclear attack.

After searching for weeks with a magnifying glass by hand, it was
frame 12778–61, grid coordinate 39-N through O, where he had finally
found them. The teeth appeared as whitish dots arranged in two neat
semicircles, one on top of the other. It was as though the pressure of the
concrete had first forced his son's mouth open and then as it solidified,
flattened his jawbones apart like the yawning mouth of a snake. He had
kept the picture with all the others he had of his family in a metal box
here. He had never shown it to his wife.

It was fitting, Jack thought, that this cooling tower was the grave
for a Charnock. He often wished that his father's still-radioactive re-

mains be brought here. But just as the government had told him when his son was killed that a Christian burial was probably not worth dismantling a billion-dollar construction project, the government was not interested in turning one of its lesser fiascoes into a monument to the nuclear misfortunes of one unlucky family. When WPPSS Number Three was abandoned, Jack Charnock thought it the best memorial of all to his son. He deeply cherished the solitude here. He took a deep breath and spoke quietly to himself in Latin. He had often wanted to bring his wife, Rebecca, to this place but had felt she wouldn't understand it the way he did. She didn't really accept the sacrifices that were a part of his world. She saw them as humiliations and insults to be avenged and redressed.

He pulled back the plastic to reveal an old broom leaning up against a green rusting patio chair from the 1960s, made out of steel tubing. A cushion gave the chair some padding and appeared to have given up some of its stuffing to mice. On the cushion was the metal box. In front of the chair and placed lovingly to face the concrete wall was a plastic-and-wooden toy rocking horse, painted in bright colors for a young child. Charnock carefully folded the plastic and set it to the side. With the broom he dusted off the toy horse until he was satisfied. Then he pulled out an envelope of old photographs, including the ghostly X rays and a shiny Bible, and sat down in the chair. He opened the book, switched off the flashlight, and allowed his eyes to adjust to the low light.

The warrior lifted his harpoon and moved toward the place where the man sat. His eyes knew no darkness. To the warrior the man was clearly visible inside the shadow. The chair he sat in creaked. The warrior knew he could kill this man with his eyes closed. He chose the place on his body that would be his target. The back of his chair was too high, shielding the soft places on his back. He circled around toward the front where he had a clear shot into the man's abdomen. Less than three lengths of a man separated the warrior from his prey, and still he was invisible. The warrior raised his weapon and set his strong legs for the throw.

As he saw the man's tears, the warrior felt his weapon grow heavier in his hand until his arm could no longer hold it. The warrior tried to move but was frozen to his spot, as though the man had commanded his body. The warrior looked into the man's face. He was oblivious to his surroundings, deep in the ache of his own mourning. The warrior was drawn into the man's pain until his own heart ached, heavy with loss. The eyes of the toy horse before him found the warrior's face and commanded him to be silent. In his mind he heard a voice. The first words were in a strange language.

"Transmutemini de lapidibus mortuis in vivos lapides philosophicos. And I saw heaven opened, and behold a white horse; and he that sat upon him was called Faithful and True, and in righteousness he doth judge and make war."

At once the warrior understood that this longhouse belonged also to the man. The warrior was the intruder here. The voice spoke once more.

"And I saw another sign in heaven, great and marvelous, seven angels having the seven last plagues; for in them is filled up the wrath of God. And I saw as it were a sea of glass mingled with fire: and them that had gotten the victory over the beast, and over his image, and over his mark, and over the number of his name, stand on the sea of glass, having the harps of God."

When the warrior took a step, he felt a familiar pain in his muscles and bones. In the painted horse he could feel the presence of Smohalla as never before. He could not resist reaching for it. With the tips of his fingers he gently touched the head of the horse.

"Sam?" Charnock closed his Bible and called out. He wiped tears from his face and looked around. "Sam? Are you here?" There was only silence. He switched on his flashlight and scanned the area. He felt the chill before he saw the hobby horse rocking slightly. "Sammy," Jack called out. It was not a question this time.

"Sammy, I have come to tell you that it is finished. The hard work is complete. All that is left is to see it through to the end."

That morning, Jack Charnock had gone into the office of the person to whom he reported—another kid, there had been so many to oversee him for so long—and asked to schedule a demonstration of his device, which was now finally assembled. Hobby Horse was complete at last. Perhaps that would show these young people that there was still important work to be done. A demonstration, just like in the old days, would improve everyone's spirits.

The young man had known nothing of the project and nothing of Jack. He seemed happy to see Charnock. He handed him a plaque and said there would be no time for a more formal presentation. He shook his hand and handed him the folder that said he was terminated. Jack had taken a minute to realize what was happening. "But what about the demonstration?" he had asked. "No need for it," the man had said. The pause was uncomfortable. "You know I studied your father's case in college. He was a brave man. You must be very proud," he said. "Did your dad's face really set off a Geiger counter?" Charnock nodded. The phone rang, and the kid took the call and turned away, waving as he did. Jack had said to himself that he would not move, that he would wait right there. He wasn't about to let an entire career at Hanford be dismissed in this way. But he turned and left the office when he realized that he would not be able to keep from crying. As he walked through the door the kid called out, "You've got a whole week to clean out your office if you want. You're paid up to the end of the year. Congratulations. I got you a full federal pension. Not bad, eh?" Then he had gone back to the phone.

"We're going to be together now, Sammy."

Charnock spoke out loud directly to the toy horse in front of him, still rocking slightly. He was convinced his son could hear him. "A regeneration is nearly upon us, my son." From his briefcase Jack pulled a baseball and golf ball. "The alchemist's stone. Kisty touched it, and he didn't even know. Now we will, my son."

His whispered his son's name once more and packed up his things.

He rearranged the plastic over the horse and chair and made his way back out of the empty tower where a van was parked. As he climbed into the cab it began to rain. As he pulled out onto the main Hanford road, it began to pour down in a torrent. He could barely see the green dome of the FFTF reactor off in the distance. He thought about what the young man had told him about being paid for the year and having time to collect his things. He smiled as he drove. It would not take him long to clean out his office. When he was done, Charnock thought to himself, it would be very clean indeed.

■

As the warrior watched the man leave, he thought of the woven baskets that he had seen as a young boy each spring in the wondrous markets of Celilo, each tribe with a distinctive pattern of decoration and weave. Some of the baskets were large enough for him to climb inside, where he could hide in the darkness. As he did here inside this tower, he would look up and see the disk sky above him until the faces of adults would appear there, too; whoever found him would reach in and pull him out again.

No one would find him here. He felt his heart with the sad man with the toy horse and photographs. Smohalla had guided them both to this place, where they were now agents of prophecy. It made him grateful for even the fleeting feeling that for the first time in thirty years, he was not alone.

8

Francine opened her eyes to find herself on the bottom of a pile of the dead and dying. *More bodies,* she thought. She peered out, wondering how long she had been asleep. She recalled the food being prepared before she closed her eyes. She could smell corn and potatoes on the fire and juicy bits of smoked salmon cut up on the warm stone next to the flames; yet the smell of death burned in her nostrils.

Smallpox. The faces around her were weak with agony and carried the blisters of death. Francine glanced at her hands and found them thankfully clear. She still had the strength to try to claw her way free. Faces on disembodied heads regarded her with accusation and agony. She plunged her hand through a pair of stiff arms. They came apart; bones separated. Wrists fell limply from forearms, and hands fell to the dirt floor. Fingers detached and lay coiling and uncoiling by themselves like fat larvae. The Indians were dying while she was not.

"*Chalk-uh-lope.*" She heard the voice of her mother. "*Chalk-uh-lope.*" An Indian word? There were so many she didn't know. Francine racked her brain, but she couldn't recall what this word meant. She saw her mother's white skin in front of her. She was walking ahead, holding out her hand, trying to lead her daughter out of the longhouse.

Francine wanted desperately to eat. She reached down and grabbed a piece of salmon, but bodies convulsed in anger everywhere she looked. She closed her eyes and placed it into her mouth. She chewed greedily, saliva ran down her neck, and all around her were the loud wails and moans of *"sitkum siwash."* These words she knew well. "Half-breed," they called her.

She looked up. Her mother was urging her to move faster, to put down the food. A tall man who scattered the crowd of sick people took her up in one arm. His hair was dark and long. In one hand he carried a long harpoon. She held tightly to his wide shoulder as they walked. Francine shouted for her mother to turn, but she kept walking. "Father," Francine said to the man carrying her, "walk faster." But as he got closer to her mother, he seemed to shrink and tremble. Sores broke out on his skin. When he stumbled and raised his harpoon, Francine screamed and fell from her father's grasp. He glanced once at his daughter, and with all his strength he plunged the harpoon deep into the body of Francine's mother, still walking ahead. Then he turned and ran back into the darkness.

When Francine ran to her mother, she saw that her face was gone, replaced by a mask of bare teeth and wide eyes. Francine backed away. "I'll fly," she shouted. She jumped and began to flap a pair of wings on her back, but she fell back into the path of the crowd of dying bodies creeping toward her. What had been wings were only crumpled and withered stumps of bone on her shoulder blades. *"Tepeh!"* she shouted, the Chinook word for "wings," as the dying Indians began to drag her toward a hole in the floor of the longhouse.

"Chalk-uh-lope," her mother spoke faintly from behind the mask. "Mother," she cried out. When there was no answer, Francine started to slip down the hole in the floor. She looked at the face of her mother and recognized it. "Tsagaglalal," she said. The floor of the longhouse disintegrated. As she fell into the darkness, she saw the outstretched hands of her dying Indian family.

Francine awoke and shook off her blankets. She was drenched with sweat. The claustrophobic memory of drowning in a crowd of people who resented her very existence was fresh like the smell of cooked salmon that seemed to hang in her empty room. But when she licked her lips, there was only the sour taste of morning in her mouth. She looked at the skin on her hands. Clear. She felt the bones in her back. What had been wings were her shoulder blades digging into the hard mattress— another longhouse dream. She could never separate the terror of claustrophobia with the complicated tangle of pain and unresolved feelings regarding her father and mother. She lay in her bed waiting for the trembling to subside.

Francine stared up at the painted ceiling and followed the worn and flaking gilded beams over to the wall where they met faded floral wallpaper. At the window, heavy dull-green velvet curtains cascaded down. The first light of sunrise found Francine's blankets on the bed—geometric, woolen, Indian—unlike the house, an Italian castle lost on a desert bluff overlooking the Columbia. She was not dreaming. This was real. This was Maryhill, her home. As she always did, Francine awoke a few minutes before her clock radio.

"Tommy Liberty on a Friday morning in white America."

"Give it a rest." KGOG was the only station that came in clearly at Maryhill. Francine reached for the snooze switch until she realized that she knew the person behind this voice.

"The idea that the United Nations is here because this country wanted it is one of those great Zionist myths. The blue hats that show up in other countries will come here one day. Listen to what Tommy is telling you. They are the police force of the occupation government. Mark my words."

It was her strange, alluring boatman from the other day. Recalling him brought back the mutilated body he had found in the river and the murders she was trying to forget. She thought instead of the boatman's face, and as she listened, she could barely imagine the gentle, awkward red-haired man with the smiling Indian on his hat from this shrill voice on the radio. It made her sad to hear him sound so convincing, as though he truly believed what he was saying. She scanned the dial for something else, but there was only more ranting, or Irish fiddle music. Every square mile of Indian country had a Bible-thumping radio station and a public radio station. Besides insipid spiritual advice and warnings of global conspiracies, the radio offered nothing to her people. She switched it off.

When Francine stood up, her black hair fell across her shoulders, and the morning light picked up the shine off the olive skin on her abdomen not covered by the T-shirt that hung off her breasts. Francine was tall, with wide squat feet. Her body was full of contradictions. Athletic, but with a soft face from which deep blue eyes beamed, conveying mixed blood as an unmistakable first impression. Her eyes had given her away since before she knew what it was they told the people who nodded smugly, sighed, or even recoiled when they looked into her face. Her eyes had betrayed her even to the boatman.

She grabbed a sweater, a pair of jeans, and a silk robe from a tattered Victorian drawing room partition. She draped the robe over her shoulders and walked into the long upstairs hallway. At the other end, hanging on a hook, was an old cloth coat signifying that her mother's nurse had arrived. For all of Francine's life, her mother had lain between life and death in a room Francine rarely entered anymore. Even glancing at the door returned the chill of her lingering dream. The garbled *chalk-uh-lope* was the only sound Francine had ever heard her say. No one knew what it meant. Francine had always taken it as a secret code, a command from a mother who, as far as she knew, had never even uttered her daughter's name. Perhaps, she wondered, it was the one clue that could tell her where to find her father, Charley Shen-oh-way. Charley was the man who appeared in her dreams—always in the distance, holding a fisherman's lance—whom she imagined would one day step from the darkness to make sense of her life. He was long dead, Indian people said. If there was more to the story, no one had ever shared the details with Francine.

Halfway down the hall, light poured through the door of the front bedroom. The master bedroom for her father and mother, it had been empty for many years. Windowed doors led out onto a small, spectacular balcony. Francine stepped through the doors into the cold morning air. The rains had paused for nearly three days. It was Friday. Since the two bodies had been discovered, the skies had cleared momentarily. The rain had stopped. On Tuesday the sun had shone for a whole afternoon.

On the bluff overlooking the river, a flock of peacocks wandered improbably, scratching at the desert granite, looking for the imported bird seed that kept them alive. The peacocks were an artifact, literally the last remaining descendants of the original aviary brought here by Francine's great-grandfather, Sheldon Hale. He had built Maryhill at the end of the nineteenth century with the staggering railroad riches he had brought west from St. Louis. The slow-stepping birds looked cast away, like the heart of the woman who had watched them since she was a little girl left alone to dream of long-departed princes. They were as lonely as the framed black-and-white photos of long-dead Indians that lined the halls of Maryhill. They were as lonely as this pink marble mansion built in the middle of a desert wilderness.

Besides being as out of place as an apparition, the mansion stood above the deepest well that had ever been dug west of the Mississippi up to that time. Old man Hale had also built himself a one-third-scale exact replica of Stonehenge and had himself buried underneath its giant stones. The grave site of Hale's son and Francine's grandfather, Frank, rested in a fake Druid religious site built on top of real Indian graves and overlooking what was then the biggest and wildest river of the American West. From his little-boy bedroom window, the Northwest's greatest dam builder had grown up looking down on the Columbia's whirlpools and cataracts every day of his life.

Maryhill was technically Francine's inheritance, but her uncle owned it now. The casino had bought Maryhill when, as a museum and tourist attraction, it had fallen into debt and disrepair. Joe Moses had an idea it could become a luxury hotel. But the Indians were sure it contained bad spirits. No one would work there. Maryhill remained what it always had been, pointless and beautiful.

Far below her, railroad tracks lined the riverbank on both sides. Just downstream from where she stood, the tracks branched inland, stretching toward the horizon and into the valleys. East and north of Maryhill, vegetation stopped and the high desert began. Off in the distance under a mottled gray sky, pink dust devils draped in morning sun gossiped rumors of rain upstream. From where she was standing, Francine could tell it was still raining in western Idaho and northward into Canada.

Francine could smell how the dry dust of the plateau met the sharp watery river breeze. She breathed in deeply and could unmistakably sense the long journey of the wind, its descent from the pine-rimmed mountains draped in snow, down across her desert home to the river and points west. Her father's people had taught her that everything she needed to know about the land could be found in a single lungful of air. Their ancestors had followed and watched a wind for millions of years that had roared off the plateau and found its way to the gorge of Nch'i-Wana, "the Big River," dropping the desert's stinging volcanic dust and carrying off the river's churning white foam to become coastal fog far downstream, where the river met the ocean.

Charley was Francine's blood connection to that world. She presumed it was he who named her Smohalla, after the legendary nineteenth-century religious prophet who had bedeviled the U.S. Army with calls for holy war against western settlers. Charley's people had taught her about Salmon Brother and how he was the *naami pyap*, or "guardian of life," for the peoples of the river.

This morning the river was high. To the Indians, high water traditionally meant good times; it was good for the crops, a friend to the salmon. A flood made the salmon stronger, got him to the ocean sooner, to return in abundance two years later. It would be a good year, they would say; but everyone who wasn't an Indian said high water was bad news.

Francine's mother's relatives, the Hales, were of course dam people, and dam people hated high water or any water that wasn't contained behind walls of earth and concrete. The name Hale appeared on the dedication plaque of every dam in the Pacific Northwest. The Hales and other engineers and industrialists had come to this land, looked around and saw a river to be harnessed for power, irrigation, and "the future," a phrase they all intoned as though they were selling a magic potion.

In her room, Francine had a photograph of Celilo Falls, the most magnificent untamed stretch of water the West had ever seen until the dams came. Her grandfather had taken the picture when he was scouting the location for what became the Dalles Dam. In it a half dozen Chinook and Wasco Indian men stood on wooden scaffolds holding wooden lances for spearing salmon jumping up the falls. The men were not facing the camera. They were watching the river and a giant salmon caught in midair. Francine had always dreamed that the very young man, third from the right in the photo, was her father. He would have been about that age. Francine's mother might have been with her father on that scouting trip. The picture could have been of the moment they fell in love. There was no one to ask. Her father was gone. Her mother had been in a coma for years. Her uncle, Joe Moses, had known them both, but he never spoke of those times to Francine.

Though evidence of her grandfather was everywhere she looked, Francine possessed only one artifact of his world, Frank Hale's old pearl-handled .44 caliber Magnum long-barrel revolver that she kept in her desk at the hatchery. He had carried it with him up and down the river for protection and to intimidate any doubter into believing that Frank Hale would do what he said he would do. The closest living connection with her grandfather was now the power master for the Bonneville Power Administration, responsible for all the dams on the U.S. side of the Columbia. His name was Bud Hermiston, and in addition to being a dubious family friend, he was Francine's boss at the hatchery. He was overseer of the vanquished world of Francine's Indian father, the concrete-and-steel world of her mother's family, and he ruled over the salmon's domain. Hermiston didn't much like salmon or Indians or biologists, but because the Feds required a salmon program and Francine was the grandchild of his best friend, he tolerated the hatchery and its half-breed custodian.

Charley Shen-oh-way's disappearance around the time Francine was born made her the sole survivor of a living legend. Her father and mother had been a scandal of two peoples. Her mother's near-death in childbirth, followed by Charley's disappearance and death, signified a clear verdict to everyone on the consequences of reckless love, a verdict favorable or not, depending on whom you talked to. Francine was either evidence of a curse or the blood legacy of an epic romantic tragedy. She grew up never knowing exactly which.

Francine stood on the balcony and pulled on the sweater and the jeans. In a roomy thigh pocket of her pants were the two metal-and-bone harpoon points she had found with the bodies she had seen, and a third one from the dresser in her room, one of the few trinkets Charley had left behind years ago. This older point was made entirely of bone and rawhide. Nasty murder weapons all three, and masterfully made. In a world of manufactured bullets, mass-produced fishhooks and blades, it was easy to forget how much ingenuity it required to craft something so deadly from materials that were once part of living beings. These were for fishing, but others like these were made to bring down elk. No Indian hunter ever forgot that his weapon was part of the closed and sacred circle of life and death, where an object that ended life could also represent the immortality of the lives that had bequeathed it to the hunter. She wrapped the three in a piece of white cloth and put them back in her pocket.

Francine found it hard to imagine that any Indians she knew would have killed one of the hatchery drivers and left the body to be found. She knew the mid-Columbia tribes had no leftover love for the dams, but killings like this seemed out of character. To federal investigators, though, the harpoon point likely implicated one hundred thousand Indians in three states and would cause months of trouble if the police tightened the noose around reservation land. Already investigators were lurking. The extent of the killings seemed to go beyond what Francine, herself, had seen.

Down below the balcony, marble tiles of Maryhill's facade caught the morning sun and shone pink against the sky. Francine loved her castle under the desert sun. Most Indian people thought Maryhill was haunted. To Francine it had always been her secret fairyland. She had grown up among its ornate velvet and fringed furniture, painted ceilings, and gilded carved walls and doors. Its long dark halls were hung with black-and-white pictures of Indians posed in traditional costumes doing things that were more or less obsolete by the time the pictures were taken. Both the faded European splendor and the faces staring out of the frames foretold the end of civilization, and made Maryhill feel like an uprooted outpost floating on an endless sea.

Looking out on the river below, Francine could see a man standing in a boat, fishing. She stepped off the balcony, went downstairs and walked onto the marble entranceway with its checkerboard pattern where she always expected to see Alice and the Mad Hatter. At the edge of the neat green lawn she found the narrow brushy trail that went from the house down to the railroad tracks and ended at the riverbank. When she got there she could see there were two men in the water.

"Is that a bear crashing through the brush, Otis, or just a white woman sneaking up on us?"

"Too noisy for a bear. Maybe two white women."

"Worse, I'm afraid." Francine was used to their teasing. "Half a white woman."

She made her way out onto the old Maryhill dock that jutted out into the water. The boat was anchored just about twenty feet offshore. Daniel Three Knives and Otis Stepping Cloud were working the channel near the riverbank. Otis sat in the boat while Daniel stood holding what appeared to be a dip net. In the boat were some medium-sized fish.

Otis and Daniel were full-blooded, old-fashioned Indian ugly from the Chinook and Clatsop tribes, respectively. Lumbering, quarreling, Daniel and Otis were her elders, playmates, and advisers. These two had passed for family for as long as she could remember.

"Jesus Christ, that hurts." Otis was shaking a bleeding hand.

"Jesus is not listening. It's just me, and Coyote." Francine laughed. "What did my Otis do?"

"He just cut his hand opening a beer bottle." Daniel was disgusted. "Bleed over the side of the boat. You can at least attract fish."

"Little early for beer, Otis?" Francine asked.

"Warm beer," he said, taking a long draw from a bottle of home brew. "Perfect for breakfast."

"See any kings today?" Francine always wondered what was running in the river.

"Always looking for kings." Daniel rotated the pole that held his dip net and planted his feet in the bottom of the boat. Bending his knees slightly, he pulled the dip net from the water and retrieved a single fish that looked about two feet long. "Always these dog salmon." He tossed it into the middle of the boat where Otis was ready with a heavy mallet. As Otis cleaned the fish with a swift, practiced hand, dumping the gutted remains overboard, Daniel maneuvered the boat a few yards closer to the dock using the long dip net pole. In the morning light he looked ancient. Francine could imagine that it was a thousand years ago, and she was the first European explorer come upon two Flatheads fishing the lower Columbia.

"But he's a real fish, anyway, and not one of your public-school salmon from the dam." Dog salmon were natural river fish. The hatchery produced only chinooks and sockeyes.

"Hatchery fish are as real as this river," Francine said. "You should be glad there are any at all."

"I'm glad of nothing, Two-Blood Daughter." Otis had many names for Francine other than her own. "I want no salmon from the white-man fish tanks." Daniel worked his dip net low in the river. He looked annoyed. "The channel is deep. You should tell the dam fathers to drain their river. It's too full. They don't listen to Indian people."

"Dam people don't exactly take orders from biologists. They made their own river and do with it what they will." She was annoyed that Daniel always associated her hatchery work with the dam. "Do you think the Indian people are special for being ignored?"

To Francine, Otis and Daniel were special. Their foreheads sloped back from the eyes, giving them the somber peaceful look of the coastal tribes two centuries ago who had no reason to believe the world was anything other than bountiful and in balance. As babies Otis's and Daniel's skulls had been molded in the traditional way. The practice of compressing the soft heads of infants between two pieces of wood bound with rawhide was a mark of distinction. It literally flattened the skull from the forehead back to the crown of the skull to no apparent ill effect. It was a traditional mark of beauty, and hundreds of years ago this was how Chinooks and Clatsops were distinguished from their many slaves.

From the moment the whites arrived, Chinook and Clatsop Indians were called Flatheads. To Europeans, flattening gave the tribes the strange look of apelike savages, which is how the original white explorers labeled them for all time when they began mapping the coast of Washington and Oregon back in the late 1700s. These days, Chinook mothers caught with their babies in the traditional wooden cradle clamps for head flattening were convicted of felony child abuse. The badge of caste superiority for a whole people had become a crime.

Otis loved to brag that it was actually a Flathead woman who provided the account of the first recorded landing of white people from a Spanish ship on the north Pacific coast. Her story had long ago become part of the Indian legend, which attempted to explain in hindsight how the world had completely gone to hell three centuries ago. According to the story handed down over ten generations, she had said, "They came on whales that grew tall trees from their backs. They wanted water from us. They looked like bears with human faces." The Chinooks promptly captured the strongest of these befuddled Spaniards and made slaves out of them. The rest they killed.

"They had to kill them," Francine had been taught. By the time the Spaniards arrived, the terror of the New World had long preceded them. The plagues of European smallpox traveled well ahead of the explorers and settlers, wiping out whole tribes in an advance softening-up campaign for the later Indian wars, best described as mere mop-up operations. The stories Otis told her as a little girl were terrifying and thrilling.

He explained to her the legend of Tsagaglalal, She Who Watches, who sent the sickened people to their deaths, mocking their faces of misery from the rocks above the river.

Francine tried to imagine an ancient world of plenty in which without warning, death arrived, a death so indiscriminate it left little to speak of, even in myths. The arrival of the whites offered the only tangible explanation of why the world had changed. The Spaniards were innocent. The Indians assumed they were murderers. Both propositions were true. The stories of the old ways were garbled and decimated, like the tribes themselves. Francine felt them living on in her smallpox nightmares.

"Flatheads and biologists make no difference in this world," Francine said to Otis. "Only Coyote can free the fishes." She evoked the oldest of Indian legends about the earliest days of the Columbia, when it was choked with glacial ice and blocked by walls of solid volcanic granite. Coyote's mighty floods, so the legends told, freed the waters to carve the face of the world unfettered by any obstruction.

"There's no steady work around here, even for Coyote," Daniel sneered while looking at the salmon meat that would be his supper for the next few days. "Coyote's no different from every other Indian taking a monthly government check."

All of the absurdities of Indian history were credited to Coyote, the spirit demon who handed out mayhem and misfortune and the very occasional bit of wisdom. It was a dubious bequest from the Creator. Indians could make better use of real miracles or something more messianic than a celestial comedian dressed up like a stray dog. But Francine liked Coyote just fine. She talked to him all the time.

It was Otis who taught Francine about Coyote. He was the man to whom all her little-girl questions were directed. Otis had watched as Francine took up the broken myths of the Indian and fashioned them into an explanation for the world as she saw it. He saw how the little girl puzzled over her mother's coma, how she longed for a sign, some flicker of recognition from the woman in the yellowed sheets. When she was a little girl, Otis would take Francine from the reservation to visit Mary-hill several times a week. A trust from the Hale estate had always paid for nursing care for Francine's mother.

Otis knew Francine would discover the limits in her Indian world abruptly as she grew up. He watched with love as Francine learned what she was and what she wasn't. Unlike some of the others around Celilo, he had never pitied her or held her in the contempt that a white woman typically provoked among his people, let alone one whose veins carried the blood of a Hale. He saw her watching things from the time she was a baby.

Otis once told Francine to look at the night sky while he told her a story of Coyote tricking some wolves, a dog, and two bears into climbing with him up a ladder of arrows. They sat together, far above the earth, admiring the view. But Coyote ran away back to Earth, stranding the animals forever as bright stars. He laughed, and the cold wind froze his breath into ice crystals that he blew into the sky, making all the dim, twinkling stars that filled the space between the animals. Coyote pulled down the ladder they had used and bragged to everyone on Earth about the beauty of the night sky. "Listen to Coyote howling at night," Otis had said to little Francine, her head tucked away under his big shoulder. "He's been bragging about those stars ever since."

Francine saw in the confusion of the stars Coyote's mischief staring down from space, not the more literal Big and Little Dippers of the white men. She especially loved the glittering swath of stars the white people called the Milky Way. Francine could see Coyote's breath flinging the leftover stars across the sky when he finally got bored with making patterns. The chaos of the sky matched her own lazy way of doing things. To Francine, Coyote was as real as Otis and Daniel. Other kids had parents. She had the three of them. They were the precious sanctuary of a little girl who was alone most of the time.

Long ago, Otis explained to Francine, Coyote had given her little seagull wings. Coyote had sneaked inside her mother while she was sleeping to attach them to her back before she was born. But his mother had discovered Coyote, who ran away, leaving the wings unfinished. In his rush to escape, Coyote had stranded Francine's mother like the animal stars. She was locked in a deep sleep near death, where she had stayed since Francine was born.

Under the sun and stars, Francine would remove her shirt and lie on her back and feel the two flat bones under her shoulders pressed into the dust. When she stood up she could see her wings clearly marked in the dirt. Francine called her imaginary shoulder-blade wings *tepeh*, using the Chinook word Otis had given her. Coyote had promised that *tepeh* would grow to full size some day when she really needed to fly. In a dusty corduroy pullover dress with little skunks on the front, saddle shoes creased and soiled from the Goodwill in Spokane, and a ribbon that heroically clung to her black hair, Francine would spend long hours by herself, tracing circles in the dust, inviting Coyote to come and see her little *tepeh*.

"Skookum chuck talapus," Daniel spoke as he maneuvered the boat up next to the dock, and the two men stepped off into it. Otis carried a cooler of fish. Daniel Three Knives was silent and fierce. Otis and Daniel had been partners forever, yet they seemed to have very little in common. Otis complained out loud in English. Daniel muttered under his breath in his native languages, Chinook and Shahaptian. Otis had been marooned in English by the instructors at the reservation school he was forced to attend long ago. Daniel preferred being marooned in his own culture. *"Skookum chuck talapus,"* Daniel muttered as he watched the bow of the boat. *"Talapus halo elitee Skookum chuck."*

"Cut the medicine show, and let's get these fish into the smoker," Otis replied, shaking his still-sore hand. It made him nervous to hear the words because he had no good reason not to understand them all.

Francine translated Daniel's words for Otis. "He's praying for Coyote to free the slow, deep water to help the salmon get downstream, Otis. Lighten up."

"Good luck, he's hung over." Daniel rolled his eyes with disgust.

As they tied up the boat and stepped onto the dock, a shiny Jeep

Cherokee with a stuffed cat attached to the rear window pulled up along the side of the road. A man in khaki pants and hiking boots was standing on the trail leading down to the water. A family of four peered out of the windows of the Jeep like they were driving through a park full of dinosaurs. "Do you folks work for the people in that house up there? *Por favor?*"

"What is it about white people and SUV rigs?" Francine said to Otis loud enough for the man to realize that they all understood English perfectly well. "We fish and cook for them in return for English lessons and a place to sleep, if that's what you mean," Francine spoke testily to the man. "What can we do for you?"

The man stuck out his hand as though he were feeding the llamas at a petting zoo. The same damn experience for the last five hundred years, Francine thought, people from the outer reaches of the solar system arriving without warning, acting like they owned the world. Americans could stake a claim in a place that they had never visited as easily as they might pick up a ballpoint pen.

"We were just driving by and wondered if that big house up there in the middle of the desert is a museum or if some famous person lives there."

"Well, nobody is supposed to know." Francine glanced at Otis. Otis glanced, head down, at Daniel. "But this house belongs to an actor who made that movie a few years back."

"That movie about wolves," said Otis, looking up. "We were all in it."

"What was his name?" Francine shook her head.

"You mean, Kevin Costner? Kevin Costner lives here?" The man lit up.

"That's the name, right, Otis?"

"Costner, yes," Otis said seriously. "Man Who Dances with Wolves is what we call him."

"That was the name of the movie, too."

"Is that right?" Francine replied.

"I loved that movie." The man turned back to his Jeep. "Honey, it's Kevin Costner's house."

"I've heard that he's a hero among Indians," the man said.

"We wait patiently for him to return," Francine said, betraying her bitter tone to the man who finally understood that he was not wanted, and quickly climbed back up the embankment and drove off while Francine and Daniel doubled over with laughter. Otis pointed at the lettering on the back of the Jeep as it sped away.

"They own the name Cherokee, you know," he said bitterly. "Just like they own Pontiac and Mohawk and Seminole, Dakota, Cheyenne, Navajo, and Apache."

"Who'd they buy 'em all from, Otis?" Francine asked.

"I would have made a better deal for those names," Otis muttered as he lifted his beer bottle to his mouth and drained it dry. Though he'd once had the idea that he could make money selling the name of his own tribe, Chinook, Otis discovered that the Pentagon had already given it to an ugly green helicopter.

"I think Otis was a snake in a previous life," Daniel said. "He acts like somebody's agent."

"Kevin fucking Costner," Otis continued. "Indian people had the right idea when the photographers came west a hundred years ago. We wanted to charge money to take our pictures. Indian people belong to their pictures. Taking a picture is stealing. We understood about pictures. We weren't backward, we were ahead of our time. The white men just laughed. Land you can own, they said, pictures no. We said, land you can never own, but your image is a part of you always. Now white people own everything. They have lawyers to keep and steal pictures now."

"One more thing we invented," Francine added, "copyrights." Otis loved to brag. It was one of the things Francine loved most about him. It was as though he kept in his mind a master tally of everything that rightfully belonged to the Indian people, which he could recite at a moment's notice. The plans and schemes that filled his head were thrilling and fantastic, but their absurdity always left Otis bitter, as hungover from his nonstop dreams as he was from his constant drinking.

"We should own the whole tobacco industry in this country!" Otis was shouting.

"And all the corn." Daniel reached for his cigarettes.

"And the salmon," Francine said sadly as she looked down at the surface of the river. She could see the sky above clouding up. "More rain."

A truck coming up the road and heading west was carrying the little painted castle logo for the U.S. Army Corps of Engineers on its side. It was a regular one-ton pickup with a large container mounted on its bed—one of the smaller salmon tankers that transported smolts from the upstream hatcheries to a designated release point past Bonneville dam. Francine knew it well. She waved at the driver as he passed.

"He's a little behind schedule," Francine said, looking at her watch. It was nearly nine; the salmon trucks were supposed to move in the dark to prevent overheating in the desert sunlight.

"How can you be late delivering a load of cat food?" Daniel looked up at the truck. He watched it disappear down the road.

"The trucks are good for the fish," Francine said. "It gets them safely past the dams. But these killings are making the drivers nervous. They won't drive at night."

"How many baby fish make it downstream alive?" Daniel said. "It's a bad business."

"Daniel, Francine is the Salmon Brother's best friend. We don't understand these things."

"What's to understand?" Daniel asked with sudden contempt. "I've seen the Salmon Brother fly up in the air to get past Celilo. Why does he need to hitch a ride downstream in a government truck? It's a bad business."

"What do you know about bad business?"

Daniel was silent. Otis walked away nervously.

"Don't ignore me," Francine continued. "The murders are all the talk up at Wishram. The Nez Percé say the drivers are stealing the salmon from the river and taking them to California."

"Do they also say who is killing the drivers?" asked Daniel, keeping his eyes on his work.

"Nobody cares," Otis said finally. "It's bad luck, these trucks. The salmon is a hostage."

"Otis, the Columbia salmon has been a hostage since they built Grand Coulee," Francine replied. Such sentiments split her like a stone. She believed in the hatchery program, yet she also understood Otis's bitterness. "I was talking to Daniel, anyway." She pulled the three harpoon points out of her pocket and tossed them casually in her hands. Both Otis and Daniel looked at them, then looked away.

"I fish with a net," Daniel said.

"So, who do we know who isn't using a net these days?" Francine handed a point to Otis who examined it closely.

"Looks like some Yakima trinket," Otis said, handing it back to her. "Don't recognize it."

"It's not Yakima," Francine shot back. "You know damn well it's a real Wishram or Tenino harpoon point. It's just like this one, which I happen to know was made right around here." Francine talked directly to Daniel. "If I can tell you where I found this, maybe you can tell me where somebody might have lost it."

"Why are you asking me?" Daniel looked up.

"Look, the fact that I have this little souvenir could get me into a lot of trouble." Francine was appealing to his sense of practicality. "Two drivers dead, one barge pilot dead, others missing—the Feds aren't exactly going to let this continue. If the killer is leaving clues behind, maybe he wants to get caught."

"Did you check the crime scene for whiskey bottles and eagle feathers, too? Everybody knows that Indians leave them wherever they go." Daniel walked toward Francine and held out his hand. He took the harpoon points and began to examine them.

"One of them is at least thirty years old," Francine said. "These that did the killing, I can't say." Daniel examined the harpoon points calmly and methodically. At one point he looked up at Otis, who quickly turned his back and paid no further attention.

"These were all made by the same person." Daniel handed them back to Francine.

"That's impossible."

"These were made by your father. There's his mark."

Francine held two of the points up to her face. The mark raised the hair on her neck and thrilled her at the same time.

"But they can't be the same," she said. "This one came from a drawer in my bedroom. This one came from the back of the man I found floating in the hatchery."

"Then maybe the killer has an even cleverer disguise. Maybe he really doesn't expect to be caught, as you say. Maybe the souvenir you found is for you alone." Daniel lowered his voice. "Or maybe you are the killer, like your father, killing to protect *nusuh*, the salmon."

Otis turned around and faced Francine. "What people do you belong to? If anyone asks, I'll tell them I'm happy salmon killers are dying. Will you say that?"

Francine felt a pit in her stomach. Blood was speaking. Hale blood. Indian blood. Being of two worlds meant that it was easy for anyone to assume the worst about her. "I'll tell anyone the truth," Francine said, turning toward Daniel. "How about you?"

"Then tell the Feds the person who killed the drivers has been dead for thirty years. That's what your evidence says." Daniel started up the trail to the road. It seemed to Francine that he was serious.

"Stealing from a crime scene is stupid," he said over his shoulder. "It puts suspicion on all of our people."

"What do you two know about this?" Francine said to Otis. "Daniel acts like I'm accusing him, and then he's saying my father is the killer." She watched for some sympathy, but there was none. She pressed on.

"Is that what you believe? It's crazy."

"I believe that smart biologists should not just assume that her people are all stupid criminals."

"I'm not accusing anyone. I'm trying to protect them." Francine's
voice cracked with emotion and frustration. Otis looked down at his cut
hand, still bleeding and now filthy with fish guts.

"Your father always said that the salmon would have their revenge.
It's part of Smohalla's prophecy. It's why he gave you Smohalla's name.
Whether he is here or not, he is a part of what is happening," Otis said
tenderly. "Your father was capable of anything if it meant saving *nusuh*."

"You know something. Why won't you tell me?"

"I know nothing. I only remember," Otis replied.

"It's hard for a drunk to believe what he remembers," Daniel said,
standing some distance away. He waved his hand for Francine to let the
discussion rest for now.

"Go home and bandage your hand, my Otis," said Francine, wiping
tears from her eyes and handing Otis the clean cloth from her pocket.

"I will. Spread your wings, little Smohalla. Forget the troubles."
Otis pinched Francine's shoulder blade between his stubby thumb and
forefinger. "*Tepeh!*"

"*Tepeh,*" Francine said. Otis never failed to warm her soul. She
turned to walk back up to Maryhill. She looked at the harpoon points
again. There unmistakably was the mark of her father on all three pieces.
Her father had made hundreds of such tools in a lifetime of fishing.
There were thousands of similar pieces all around the region in private
collections, museums, and junk-filled shoe boxes. There were plenty of
people who knew how to make such things who were alive today. If the
message was for her alone, what might it say? What might it mean?

Sometimes Francine imagined what it would be like if her father
walked through her front door. Bitterness made her blink tears. Legend
had it that he had vanished to save the same fish she took care of now.
Francine could only imagine saying one thing to him if he ever came
back.

"I knew you would come."

Francine felt the effort, walking back up the steep trail. *Tepeh*, she thought. The little girl in her wanted to use her wings to fly up the hill as she had done long ago, running home to breakfast and dinner. Francine, the biologist, couldn't help feeling that she had outgrown her wings.

The sun was hitting the marble of Maryhill, and the surface of the river and the whole earth glowed pink and deep blue in a dazzling morning mosaic, all for her. Perhaps it was something about getting older that made her uneasy, like staring at her own naked image in the mirror. She merely saw the flaws now, mismatched blue eyes and jet-black hair. Beauty wasn't enough. Underneath all the sunny mornings, truth swirled like the lost stone shrines of her father's ancestors that were buried under the rising waters behind the dams. She looked back at Maryhill again. The sun was hitting the window of her mother's room. The nurse was cranking it open and pulling the yellowed curtain back inside. Francine wondered if her mother even knew that it was morning.

9

Roy McCurdy was counting out piles of money while he listened to his son finish talking to a caller on the radio, lining up five-thousand-dollar stacks of hundreds as though he were piling ammo clips for an assault. He looked up at the picture he kept on the wall of his wife, Ida. "God's destiny for white America is right here on your kitchen table, honey. You and me can start something that nobody's going to be able to stop." His voice was full of an unaccustomed pride. He had waited so long for something like this to happen. Now that the options were laid out before him, he could think. The desperation of poverty and hand-to-mouth fund-raising—all that had seemed for so long to erode his patience and make him doubt his cause was gone. He carefully considered what to do next. Ida, the unhesitating zealot, had always found him wanting. If she could see him now, he thought.

"How much money is there?" Duke asked as he came through the door, his show over. Off the air Duke resumed being Roy McCurdy's son. They had not yet spoken of the money or anything else that had happened at the casino.

"Two hundred grand. This here is to pay off sixty grand in debt, so the New Israelites are clear now." Roy looked right at his son with one of his demonic smiles. "The rest goes to charity."

"Have you picked one yet?" Duke asked. As usual, Roy only wanted to talk about how his son had done on the radio.

"You were pretty good tonight, boy. You had them callers really going about taking over the United Nations." Roy preferred Tommy Liberty to Duke. Duke had made sure of it. After tolerating years of his father's disappointment, Duke had created Tommy Liberty out of his imagination to be an older brother he had never had, his father's favorite, the pride of the McCurdy family. It was a role Duke could only model, never equal. It was better than nothing.

"I never understand why some of these people call us." Duke's voice was soft now. He looked at the money on the table. "Why don't we leave here? We could hire people to work the station and go somewhere else for a while. I'll get one of my boats fitted out for a long trip. We can go down to California." Duke was anxious to get out on the water for a good long time. The desert always made him feel anxious. Being stuck in the trailer with his father was sometimes like being buried alive.

"Your mother would come back from the grave and slice off my balls for turning her boy into a faggot tourist."

"Mom liked to travel."

"For a good cause, maybe, to do something important, maybe. Your mother never pitched a tent except after a battle. Remember that, boy." Duke had one picture of his mother. She was holding his hand while they stood in front of the biggest bonfire he had ever seen. Duke was wearing a brand new suit of military camouflage. He was five years old, and he held his mother's hand tight and stared at the fire that seemed to be trying to suck them both in. The heat of those flames and the warmth and security of his mother's hand were unforgettable. The robe and hood she wore were magical to him.

Even knowing his mother was a leader of the local Ku Klux Klan didn't alter the purity and innocence the white robe brought back to the son who had lost her. When he thought of his mother he saw only this picture, her head and hair shrouded in the hood, her face framed as though embroidered, somehow, into the cloth.

"I'm taking a few days off." Duke said it as though he expected an argument. "I want to spend some time on the river. You can cover for me on the air."

"You want a vacation? That's your big plan, to go off to a beach and hand your money over to a bunch of hotel niggers and Mexicans who will keep you drunk so they can rob you blind? You'll miss the end of the world, son."

"There are lots of places to go." Duke looked at the table. The piles of cash his father was neatly arranging looked like soldiers in formation, ready to back every messianic plan his father had ever brought home to the dinner table: hostage-takings, bombings, kidnappings, murders, lynchings, and of course the radio station itself.

"And wherever I go, the end of the world will find me."

"How do you feel about history, son? That's where Roy McCurdy is going. Your daddy will be as well known as Ben Franklin when he gets through. With what we got here, we can take out the White House if we want. We don't have to settle for homemade 4H-Club explosives. We can get our hands on some TATB or SEMTEX, the big-time boom-boom. The world is going to know that Roy McCurdy isn't some misunderstood mental patient who kills babies in day-care centers, mail carriers, and people getting their passport photos taken in a federal building nobody ever heard of."

"People have heard of the White House." Duke chuckled. "You're safe there. Why don't you blow up the Lincoln Memorial?"

"Pearl Harbor. Think how many people remember Pearl Harbor, December seventh, 1941? How many times have I told you that all around the world people are going to remember the day when Roy Mc-Curdy finally stuffs it in the face of the U.S.A."

Duke had heard all of this many times. He hoped that his father would get distracted as usual, blow his money on some crazy business scheme, and move on. Duke preferred to concentrate on his boats. He could use a new engine for one of them, a hull job for the other. With the casino jackpot, Duke was counting on getting back on the river at the very least.

"It's destiny that we won this money, boy. It is our responsibility now to make our mark." Duke said nothing. He was going through a box of audiotapes that had come in the mail. "Did you have a look around that casino?" Roy continued. "Did you see who was in there?"

"Besides the Indians?"

"Open your eyes, boy. It was a giant roomful of big shots and new-rich niggers all holding fistfuls of cash. Do you have any idea how much attention we would get by taking over that nest of uppity Indians?"

"Did you happen to notice that the place is full of weapons and security guards and electronic surveillance cameras?" Duke didn't even look up from his box. "You'd get about a foot in the door before you were dropped with a thirty-eight slug like some sick elk. Indians don't need to call the police. It's their nation, and police don't investigate Indian shootings."

"Who says I'd even need to go in the door? I'm not talking about some Ruby Ridge shoot-out, boy. For this kind of money, we ought to be able to do something big, something your mother would rise up from the grave to see. We could watch the whole thing on TV from that couch over there, sipping Jack Daniel's."

"Whatever you say," Duke placated. "Just leave me some money. I want to be well offshore if you announce that you're in the market for TATB and get the attention of every federal agent in this hemisphere. You can't even buy a pickup-load of fertilizer or a drum of fuel oil anymore without drawing a SWAT team."

"Here's some boat money." Roy handed Duke a neat stack of hundred-dollar bills. "Got any friends up at Hanford?"

Duke ignored him.

"Come on, boy. They've got to have a few garage-sale leftover Jap bombs hanging around. I bet I've got enough cash here to shake one loose."

"Why don't you simply buy a few hand grenades, break into a federal prison, and demand to stay there for the rest of your life? It would be cheaper than trying to shop for nukes up at Hanford. If you even got close to something like a bomb, they'd throw you in a hole so deep, I'd never see you again."

"You're so serious, boy." Roy laughed until he was out of breath. "Tommy Liberty would find a way." The possibilities were stacked in neat piles in front of him. "I'm talking about destiny. A yellow bastard like you wouldn't understand that. If you believe in the power to end the world, then destiny cannot be stopped. There's no uniformed Fed that can change destiny. If we are the warhead, the means to achieve victory will come to us. Set Tommy to work on the air. He'll find someone to help us."

"What destiny are you talking about? Who declared this war? We're the only casualties. We have nothing. We have never had anything. I used to have a mother, now she's gone." Duke wanted to grab him and hold him and tell him that he, too, missed his mother, that he, too, wanted her back. He wanted his father to believe as he did, that wherever she was, she would be happier if they left the battlefield and went on with their lives.

The mention of Ida always produced a glint in his father's red and weary eyes. "I knew your mother, boy. She understood destiny better than I ever will. If we are the bomb that will bring down the enemies of the white Christian people, she is the lit fuse. What your mother would have wanted us to do every waking moment of our lives is fight. Maybe she's just a black-and-white snapshot to you, but she's talking to me right now. Don't try to tell me what she would have wanted."

"I don't see the enemies, and I certainly don't see the army, but I'm supposed to believe that this trailer on blocks is the command center for the beachhead of the righteous?" Duke wondered if there was any way to switch his father off, any limit to his fanaticism. "Outside of this trailer, people think we are lunatics. I open my mouth and people back away. Do you understand how different the real world is from what you think it is?"

"Real world? I know everything I need to know about the real world." Disgust and sarcasm tinged his voice. "Leave me here to do the work that needs to be done. Take your boats and float away. Destiny is bigger than any little boy's adventure. It will write your name for eternity, or erase you from this earth forever."

"Destiny doesn't care about people. You can slaughter all the people you want, and nobody will care. After the piles of flowers are taken away and the TV funerals are over, people forget. Killing people just rearranges carbon and water. You think my children will know who Timothy McVeigh is?"

"What are you talking about, boy?"

"Blood can be erased; even Hitler has a dubious claim on immortality. The Jews are right: People will forget Auschwitz someday. Destiny is for the big things. Like what made some rocks round and some jagged, and carved out the land we're standing on."

Roy laughed. "You're a smart fucker, boy—yellow and smart."

"I'll see you in a few days, Daddy. Try not to end the world until I get back."

Duke put the money in his pocket, grabbed his bag, and walked outside to let his father conjure alone. The lights far away twinkled in the desert air. They looked like the bobbing buoys on the water that comforted him when he was alone on his boat. Duke looked at the horizon. He had always tried to protect his parents from the contempt and ridicule he saw for their kind everywhere in the outside world. They had given him a strange life full of fantastic adventures, chases, secret hideouts, explosives, and guns. Raised to be a fugitive, but with no real talent for crime, Duke had grown up believing his parents may have been wrong, but what he saw around him, outside of their world, was wrong, too. The wrong people, it seemed, had walked off with everything in America. There was little left to dream about except lottery jackpots and other long shots. Duke's mistake was that unlike his parents, he didn't blame anyone. He concluded bitterly that he had been born at the wrong time.

He looked back to the trailer. Its lights were yellow in the darkness.

He could see Roy's face through the glass. He was still counting money. Duke looked up to the trailer roof and thought he could see the antennae moving slightly. This was strange, as there was no wind that night. Then Duke could see the trailer moving back and forth as though the finger of some unseen giant was gently jostling it. He could hear the pings and pops of fragile tinny objects being moved about. A car alarm howled in the distance. Duke felt the mild vertigo of ground motion and beneath his feet he could feel the earth itself moving. As he became certain of what he was experiencing, the ground resumed its stillness, and the air became silent again, save for the distant car alarm.

"Did you feel that, boy?" Roy called out the door.

"I guess it was a quake or something."

"It was an omen, boy. Things are about to change."

"Are you feeling all right tonight, Daddy?" Duke asked, but Roy had already gone back inside. Duke looked back out at the river. Far in the distance he thought he could see the flashers of an emergency vehicle, but he couldn't be sure. As he often did, he wished the water would sweep him away from where he was standing. Perhaps it would take him to one of the lights on the horizon, where behind a door someone would welcome him in as if he had only been away for a short time. "Welcome home," someone would say, and Duke would not need to speak at all. He would just know. The thought gave him a chill. He looked back at the trailer behind him. One of the consequences of being a McCurdy was the inability to distinguish between feeling trapped and feeling secure.

1 O

"Dead men are lucky," Otis said, making sure the office door was closed and that all of the casino's suited bodyguards had been waved away before he spoke. "The Salmon Brother speaks."

Joe Moses sighed and stopped humming an old song to himself.

The two men in his office were not bankers, nor were they wormy city managers or hat-handed chamber-of-commerce types from the little towns near Celilo, who flocked into Moses's office each day to pitch their latest plan for a potato museum or a new downtown garage for parking a few of the casino's spare millions. Daniel Three Knives and Otis were Joe Moses's Indian brothers who could call in debts without the use of a lawyer or other intermediary. If they wanted Joe's ear, Joe had to give it to them.

"This killing is good," Otis continued. Joe couldn't tell if the peppermint ambience meant he was using or just drinking mouthwash. "The white fisherman thinks that the spirit of the salmon is out for revenge."

"Over at Hood River they're having trouble getting drivers," Daniel added. He was neatly dressed and seemed, as always, to be burning with a quiet anger. "It's a sign."

"Nonsense," Joe replied impatiently. "The government will give them a raise, and this will be over." He reached over to pick up two ornately carved pieces of bone sitting on a piece of soft leather on his desk, game pieces for the ancient game of *tlukuma*. He began to absently roll them around in his hands as he listened.

"We can take the jitters of the white fisherman and make an event for Indian people." Otis waited to see if Joe looked at all curious. "We can hold a festival. Salmon Blood Dance: the forbidden ancient ritual that our people have held only once in a thousand years, where we will ask Coyote to free the fishes again."

"That's a good one." Joe rubbed his eyes. "I imagine you'll be needing the casino for this sacred festival. You realize that you missed the millennium?"

"It's the ideal location. You've got the interstates and built-in microwave and satellite hookup that will bring the national media. We'll get great coverage. You'll get great business." Otis stepped forward. Joe could see that his shoes were shiny, his pants clean of stains. Joe suspected he had borrowed everything he had on, including the dark flannel jacket that seemed just a bit large for him, and the salesman's leather folder he opened to show Joe a leaflet he had designed announcing the festival. "I say we print up about fifty thousand of these and put them up from Vancouver to Los Angeles, Seattle to Idaho. We'll also need a few hundred thousand dollars to make the traditional costumes."

"And do I need a choreographer from Vegas and a costume designer, Otis?" Joe chuckled and closed his eyes. The man's enthusiasm was credible, but to look at his yellowed eyes, his scarred face, and missing teeth brought back the human wreck he had become. Joe opened his eyes. Otis stood there smiling, unable to conceal that he was weaving slightly, either from morning drink or lack of recent experience with sobriety. Mixed with breath mints and cologne, the odor of bar urine, blood, and bus exhaust was still detectable. Joe had learned to ignore the people he couldn't help, yet Otis was nearly family. "Otis, what are we to do about the fact that there is no such thing as the Salmon Blood Dance?"

"We don't know that. Someone was dancing three thousand years ago when the mountain fell into the river and lowered the falls at Celilo so that the salmon could get upstream. Coyote freed the fishes. It's a fact. Even the scientists say this."

"The white man is believing in Coyote now?" Joe laughed. "There's your millennium. Daniel, are you in on this festival of Otis's?"

"Smohalla dreamed that the salmon will be free. Whatever we do now is a part of that dream." Daniel's voice was dark and serious.

"Smohalla dreamed many things," Joe said, disgusted that the name of the prophet might be used to stir people up. "My father knew Smohalla's dreams very well. My brother died trying to make them come true."

"Are you quite sure of that?" Otis asked.

"Sure of what?"

"That your brother is dead."

"What are you saying?" Joe couldn't tell if Otis was serious or just ranting.

"What if the harpoons that killed the salmon drivers were made by Charley Shen-oh-way?"

"How would you know that, even if it were true?"

"It's on the wind. I can hear the anger of Charley Shen-oh-way walking the earth. Sometimes he speaks. All of the warriors from the old times have come home to pray for the salmon, to fight for the salmon. We must make a celebration for them. Your brother will return."

"Forget the mumbo jumbo, Otis. What did you mean about harpoons?"

"Drunks know little for sure in this world. You know that Charley marked every one of the carvings he made while he was alive. They can kill even if not by his hands. But how do you really know Charley is dead? Could you prove it? What if Francine asked you about the fate of her father?"

The deliberate, accusing words of Otis in control caught Joe off guard. "Are you trying to make me angry? What I say to Francine is my business. Are you the police? This is none of your business or their business. I know all I need to know about the fate of my brother. Above all, this is none of Smohalla's business."

"Smohalla had no interest in business," Daniel broke in. "Like your brother, he had no business. Smohalla created festivals when it suited him. He started wars when it suited him. He was not afraid to use his power to make prophecy come true. Smohalla was not one of your Indian capitalists." Daniel was skeptical of business or work of any kind that wasn't fishing, building, or planting. "Smohalla taught that men who work cannot dream, and wisdom comes to us in dreams."

"With sixty percent unemployment around here, we must be some of the wisest people who ever walked the earth, then." Joe had long ago concluded that if Smohalla's wisdom ever made it into the dreams of the unemployed, it was lost by the morning in the haze of their hangovers. The casino was the only escape Joe had ever found from the endless struggles of his people; he wanted to keep it that way.

"You think that your bright casino and all of its money makes you clever and wise?" Daniel had fought the casino from the beginning but had never been a match for Joe's ability to charm dollars into the hands of anyone who opposed him. Daniel remained one of Joe's closest friends, but he would never admit he had been wrong about the casino.

"Indian people have been gambling at Celilo for ten thousand years, and selling baskets, knives, and slaves for all that time, as well. I'm afraid what I'm doing predates Smohalla by a few years."

"Shoulder Moon is just another way of taking away our dreams and replacing them with jobs. Men are not jobs. Charley Shen-oh-way said this. Have you forgotten?"

"Indians have been living in dreams for a century, starving and dying and talking nonsense, waiting for things that will never come," Joe said wearily. "A little work and a lot of money is not going to hurt anyone."

"Then why is your brother not with us?"

"My brother made his own choices a long time ago. His fight was not with casinos. My brother bet against the dams." Joe's face drifted off into a sadness that made both Otis and Daniel uneasy. "It was a bad bet."

"This is no dream, Joe." Otis broke the silence and pointed to his brightly colored leaflets. "We can make this work for us, no matter. It's a lucky break."

"Who exactly is this lucky for, Otis? Not for me. Shoulder Moon is under surveillance." Joe had noticed federal officers poking around the casino, asking questions every night since the killings began. "It's not lucky for the drivers, not for the fish, and not for Indians who talk too much and get blamed."

"Everyone is talking," said Daniel, raising his voice. "The dead men carry the face of She Who Watches." He turned to Otis. "Show him."

Otis pulled from his folder a photo of a face painted in stone. Its eyes were ringed with concentric lines and its mouth was wide smiling with a black square in the middle. "I have friends who take crime scene pictures on the reservations. These are from over near Richland."

"Tsagaglalal." Joe used the ancient name. "Everybody born on the river knows Tsagaglalal. What's your point?"

"The dead men's faces have been removed and replaced by hers. The face of Tsagaglalal is carved into their skulls. Some people believe that the victims are still alive when they do it." Otis pulled a picture of one of the dead men from his folder and handed it to Joe. The face of She Who Watches was about the only thing that could transform a tawdry set of murders into an apocalyptic shout from the spirit world. Tsagaglalal's face was a death sign, said to be the agonized, contorted smiling face that people took just before dying horribly in the plagues of ancient times. She was said to watch the place where millions of Indians passed into the spirit world in the decades before the white man came. Joe's eyes were drawn back to the image of the mutilated corpse; the work was grisly, methodical, expert.

"Someone knows what they are doing," Joe said.

"The police want it quiet, but Indians are talking," said Otis.

"Can Indians ever shut up? That's the trouble. If the cops have kept it out of the papers and only Indians are talking about it, who's going to get blamed?" Joe handed the folder back to Otis. "Probably the stupid bastard walking around with a folder full of leaflets and a picture of one of the damn bodies."

"What does it matter that Indians get blamed?" Daniel said angrily.

"Smohalla said death first, then life. What matters is the white man's fear."

"You actually think the white man is afraid?" Joe opened his hand and looked at the *tlukuma* pieces. The bones were warm in his hand, but not yet warm enough for playing. The smooth carved game pieces soaked up the heat as Joe rubbed them rapidly in his palms. When ready, Joe would be able to feel them breathing in his closed hands and would not have to look to know which bone was which.

"The white man doesn't care one little bit about your Indian spooks," Joe said with the certainty of years. "Unless you know who is doing the killing, you are only two old women, scaring yourselves with nonsense."

"This is Smohalla's work," Daniel insisted. "The police can investigate forever. They will never know what happened."

"The old warriors are coming home for the Salmon Brother," Otis said, stepping forward with his leaflets. "Coyote is calling them home. Coyote is calling your brother, Charley. We must welcome them all."

"You might have a point about that face. Last time Tsagaglalal showed up, she brought the plagues." Joe handed the pictures back to Otis. "This time I guess it will be a plague of Feds. They're all over this case."

"It is interesting that you are concerned with the Feds when your brother's daughter is one of them," Daniel said bitterly. "She accused me of murder two days ago."

"My very angry Flathead brother." Joe motioned for Daniel to sit down. "I'm sure Francine did not accuse you of anything you weren't guilty of."

Daniel resumed his seat while Otis approached the desk again. "I say while they all are investigating, we move in. This has big event written all over it. Serial murderer, Indian spooks—it may not scare people, but it will sell a lot of tickets." Otis leaned over. "I'm surprised at you. This is right up your alley."

"And Otis knows alleys, right?" Joe let out a big laugh and dispelled the tension. "You speak the truth. People would rather believe in spooks. The alternative is some drifter psycho. Drifters, psychos, and day traders with guns are what tourists really fear these days. Indian spooks are entertainment." Joe opened his hands and showed the *tlukuma* bones. From his drawer he took ten sticks, called *wowuk,* for counting the score. "With your salmon dance, we might even bring the real people back to Celilo, like the old times."

He began to hum a very old song as his hands moved rapidly with a rising-and-falling rhythm. With a mesmerizing dexterity, the two bones were passed from one hand to the other until in a moment it was impossible to know which bone was in which hand. Joe's stone-gray eyes presided over it all. Daniel divided the *wowuk* sticks into two piles, one for him and the other for Otis. When Joe ended the song, his hands stopped, and he asked a question.

"What shall we play for?"

"Only dollars," Daniel said. The game moved rapidly. In succession, Otis and Daniel chose a hand which Joe opened to reveal either the smooth *cola,* the "male" bone, or the *skaguilak,* the "woman" bone. Finding the male was the only way to win, but a player could also bet on another player's guess. In addition to the money that changed hands, each win was tallied with one of the counter sticks. If a player guessed correctly, the bones would pass to the winning player along with a counting stick. If you lost your sticks, you were out of the game. Holding sticks allowed you to keep playing even if your losses were beyond what you could pay. In this way fanatical *tlukuma* players would lose their houses, wives, or even children.

For eight hands only the woman bone was guessed. The maddening thing about *tlukuma* was how, over time, it seemed as though the man holding the bones could read minds. Players on a losing streak were reduced to second guesses and dreadful self-doubts, even though the odds of the game were never less or more than fifty-fifty. Within a few minutes Joe had taken nearly three hundred dollars, and Otis and Daniel were down to only two counter sticks.

"What the hell else can we play for?" Otis reached in his pocket for his last twenty-dollar bill. "I'm almost broke."

"What else would you like to give old Joe?"

"I play for the Salmon Blood Dance, that we make shitloads of dollars at the biggest Indian festival the white man has ever seen." Otis was probing to see if Joe had approved of his plans. He pulled twenty dollars from his pocket and let it flutter down onto the desktop. He paused for a moment, then chose Joe's left hand.

Joe opened his hand to reveal the intricately carved bone wrapped with a piece of rawhide in the center.

"Damn, the woman always finds me." Otis grabbed one of his *wowuk* counter sticks and placed it next to Joe. He was down to his last one. Joe hauled in the crisp twenty and resumed his song and hand movements. Daniel placed a fifty on the table.

"Coyote will free the fishes," he said. "I play for this."

"It is bad luck to wager about what is foretold by prophets." Joe shook his head and hummed louder.

"My bad luck is my own damn business." Daniel followed Joe's hands, intently matching the song's rhythm with movements of his own head.

Otis took another twenty from his pocket and bet it on Daniel. There in Joe's modern casino office plush with carpet, the trio was lost in a game that had consumed this part of the world for ten thousand years. *Tlukuma* was based on the greatest illusion, that the human mind and its next moves could ever be predicted. People believed they were matching wits with the holder of the bones, or hearing the smooth bone itself calling out from within the hand. No one would ever confuse this game for flipping a coin. The song made everyone's spirits and passions rise. A good game was more like a dance with everyone, winners and losers, moving and singing together.

"Left!" Daniel shouted the moment Joe's humming stopped.

In the open hand was the smooth bone.

"*Talapus* wins." Otis grabbed his two twenties and one of the *wowuk*.

"You tempt the spirits, Mr. Three Knives. I would stay away from this one." Joe handed Daniel fifty-dollars he'd won and suggested that Otis's companion might be run over by a truck in the casino parking lot.

It was Daniel's turn to handle the bones. "What is your bet, old man?" The song Daniel hummed was Chinook in origin, complicated, seductive, with erratic, unpredictable rhythms.

Joe placed a one-hundred-dollar bill on the table. "I bet that we know a killer."

Daniel stopped humming. "Are you going to accuse me just like your brother's daughter?"

Joe said nothing. The wager spoke for him.

Otis looked pale. "I know many killers."

"Memory speaks on your face, Otis," said Joe finally. "I think this is a good bet."

"The voice of my memory is drink. It knows nothing." Otis cautiously placed two twenties back on the table and whispered to Joe, "I woke up with a bleeding head and a strange dream."

"Otis needs a drink. Play the game," Daniel said, and began to sing.

"Left again," Joe said quietly.

"The old man knows a lot." Daniel handed Joe the smooth bone and his last stick. The game was over.

"But Otis knows more, I think." Joe smiled gently at his old friend.

"I have dreams. That is all," Otis said quietly. His head hurt from the bruises of drunkenness and unending humiliations of feeling that people looked right through him.

Joe looked down at the surface of his desk and saw the *tlukuma* dice rolling toward the edge by themselves. The movement startled all three of them and made it look as though an unseen hand was in the room. Otis backed away. Daniel stood silently, visibly nervous. Joe looked around for an explanation and found none until he noticed the hanging ceiling lamp. It was swinging.

"It's an earthquake." It was over by the time he had said it. The three of them were unsure if the motion of the earth had something to do with what they had been discussing. Otis was completely pale now. "It's only a small tremor," Joe said. "You look like a trapped badger."

"I'm fine."

"It is Smohalla," Daniel said. He needed no explanation. "He speaks for the Salmon Brother. He kills for the Salmon Brother. He wants us to help him."

The people along the river were anxious enough these days. Joe needed them to remain calm. The casino was already the focus of a lot of bitterness. He didn't need any angry gods lining up against him. Joe looked down at the printed leaflet Otis had left on his desk. "How soon can we begin plans for the Salmon Blood Dance?" Joe said, and Otis smiled broadly, showing the many gaps in his teeth. He ran to Joe and embraced him.

"I have good dreams. You will see. This will be a good dream."

Joe smiled and returned the embrace. Otis's bones seemed loose and fragile. His smell was powerful. Joe wanted to protect him. Otis's look of pure wretchedness, the face of life out of reach, the face of waiting, punctuated with hopeless schemes and harrowing brushes with death, was as familiar to Joe as Coyote, as terrifying and more real than the face of Tsagaglalal. It was the face of the one incurable plague of all their lifetimes.

Penance . . .

On the smooth stone where Smohalla had died, the tall warrior sat looking out over the valley to the south. He was not looking at the place where the Columbia and Yakima Rivers joined. He did not seek the mountain peaks in the distance, although he knew where they were, along with each contour of the valley below. He gazed only at a single twinkling light at the edge of the horizon, just below the sloping ridge of an ancient volcano he had always known as nuksay, "the otter." White men had named the place Maryhill. He blinked. The light blinked back. The warrior had killed and would kill again, but his resolve was weakening. He needed reassurance. The faces of the dead were watching him. The river bled with his crimes. He did not have long, and he knew there was much work yet to be done.

From his bag he pulled a wooden idol, a bird called Wawsuk-la, and began to sing a prayer over it, matching his tone and rhythm to the constant musical wind of Rattlesnake, or waxpus, Mountain as he had been taught to do by the disciples of Smohalla himself. It was a holy spot. He prayed for guidance and for the skill to elude those who would capture and kill him; there were many of those now. It would be much harder to elude these new predators as easily as he had eluded his friends and family, the people who had loved him above all else long ago, people for whom his only prayer was that they forget him altogether.

He had given up everything to do Smohalla's bidding, knowing and believing in him despite the ridicule that greeted the prophet's words everywhere. Smohalla had said the salmon would be free. Instead there were dams. The sacred places were walled in behind barbed wire and checkpoints. The warrior *had tried to argue to his people that this was a sign of the power of the sacred places. That they had been taken by the white man for building his doomsday weapons and his dams was an unmistakable sign of Coyote. It meant that the spirit of Smohalla was alive after all. But people had laughed at him and had gone off to their good jobs building monuments to the stranger's gods.*

Smohalla had said there would be many tests of faith before the end came. The warrior had argued that in time Smohalla would reveal all. But even the warrior, Smohalla's most devoted disciple, had not imagined that Celilo itself could vanish. How could such a place be taken when it had been as real as the sun for all of recorded time, from back before the first ancestors? But when Celilo was gone and the heart of his people was finally broken, no one but the warrior believed in Smohalla anymore. He was alone, and there was only one person who believed in Smohalla's last believer.

Because she was not one of his people, it meant nothing outside of his heart. But it made him ache to think of her. He often did, even now. She had come from another world. Smohalla would have said that she was a white devil, a test of his faith that he was failing. In this alone he had disputed the truth of the prophet. He knew she was like him, an outcast from her own peo-ple. A person far from the atiim, *he would say, "the sound of the falls." He longed for her embrace and to feel the warmth of her body. Though he was a strong and powerful warrior, his devotion to Smohalla and his rejection of drink and work made his people suspicious of him. They considered him a poor candidate for a husband. He was, among them, a loner. But she had not needed his paychecks. She wanted only for him to love her, and in return she gave him a tenderness he had never imagined, and knowledge of the people whose rav-enous hunger and duplicity to obtain all that was his had seemed, for most of his life, beyond understanding. He drifted back to when people called him Charley, drifting in memory until he could actually see her.*

■

From the first time she saw him, standing on one of the wooden platforms that clung to the roaring rock faces of Celilo, Charley Shen-oh-way was something that made sense in Mary Hale's world. She was in her late twenties, back home and hung over from college and other well-financed failures back east. At high noon Mary had stepped out of her shiny car and walked to the bank of the river. There Celilo was reeling from the peak momentum of the spring chinook run. The white of the falls at ground level smudged the sky into a creamy fog of sound and movement, and each footfall of land was a precarious raft surrounded by surging water. Everywhere men were standing with nets and spears, waiting for the silvery jumpers that seemed to fly out of the spray as if pitched by an unseen hand directly into the falls.

Mary walked into this roar of river and human laughter that braced the lungs with equal parts snowmelt chill, desert sun, and the smell of fish. Mary glanced at the man in the center, standing on the tallest platform at the farthest point from the riverbank, jutting almost into Celilo Falls. He was motionless against the vertical of the white falls, the horizontal flow of the river, and the featureless desert sky, which worked on the mind, erasing the illusions of balance that convince bipeds they can walk upright. Many an Indian had simply stepped to his death, overcome by vertigo and disorientation. Standing was a disadvantage in this world, and the salmon pressed for supremacy every way they could, eluding both fishermen and pounding current on their way upstream. *Nusuh,* the salmon, had been jumping like this for only a short while longer than the humans had inhabited Celilo. Celilo was the site of one of the few remaining fair contests between man and beast still waged on earth. The salmon belonged here. They jumped for love, fighting their way upstream to spawn and then die in the same streams in which they had been born.

As the salmon jumped over the falls, Charley would snatch them magically out of the air and pitch them onto the shore where boys too young to climb the platforms would catch and kill them. The women would butcher the salmon and stretch the pink meat onto wooden drying racks to become pemmican, the salty smoked staple of the plateau, as precious as gold.

Mary knew this yearly ritual simply as a blur of folklore on the road between home and Portland. She stopped only that one time to watch. The tall man with the long black braid, in the center of it all, had looked back at her. Standing against the white of the river enfolded in its tapestry of icy chaos, Charley's eyes locked with those of the white woman in the orange cotton dress. His head and shoulders were collared in a necklace of sweaty fog. Charley belonged here. On his face was an expression of surprise and amusement at being snared by a glance in the act of fishing.

There were other Indians fishing on the platforms, but to Mary, Charley looked as proud as creation. It was said by the tribes along the Columbia that eventually Celilo left its mark on all who encountered it. The Indians at the Celilo camp watched Mary and Charley and shook their heads: No good could come from the rich lady with the Buick convertible from the pink castle on the hill. She nodded at the tall, nearly naked man; Charley turned back to the falls.

Charley showed up at Maryhill a few days later. He brought an eight-pound chinook salmon, and they ate together under the stars. Mary showed Charley how the house pumped water up from underground wells near the river to the arid cliffs. Charley told Mary about the ancient burial grounds out near the long-unused stables. They talked until morning. From that night on, Charley would visit Maryhill two or three nights a week, coming and going silently on foot.

They knew little about each other at first. Theirs was a love that solved each other's persistent riddles in a world that was being quickly swept away. Later Mary learned that Charley Shen-oh-way was a notorious radical who openly practiced the Waa'sat religion of the southern plateau. The Waa'sat claimed white people were prophets, agents of Sah-ha-le-tice—literally, the Spirit Above—who carried with them death and riches. To Charley the dams were the embodiment of both death and riches. He preached the message of the prophet Smohalla, who declared that Coyote would free the fishes.

Charley learned that Mary was descended from the mythical captains of industry who had come overland from the east or by sea from the west to stake their claims along the Columbia. Charley had grown up hearing stories about Maryhill, the dam builder's house on the hill, the strange wondrous birds that lived there, and the white spirit people who stood at its windows talking to the sky. Mary had been one of those faces at Maryhill's windows, though Charley had never been close enough to recognize her.

To each other they were original, apart from history, not predicted in any prophecy, a motionless spot in the chaos of world's end and Celilo's torrent. To each other they represented all that was forbidden and over the horizon. Mary loved Charley even if she could not eat much of what he brought her. Charley loved Mary even if he had no use for Maryhill's faucets and much of its furniture. He loved her because she had found him. She was everything to him, until everything changed.

■

The memories left an emptiness. They made him doubt, made him long for her. He could see the tall ceilings in her castle, smell the incense from the dark cedar beams that crisscrossed the long hallways there. He had disappeared from the life of his lady in the castle when Celilo vanished. He hoped she had forgotten him, but because he had not forgotten, he knew she had not. What he could not know was anything of the child. He blinked again. Of this, he could only imagine the possibility. The light on the horizon was still there.

Since those early days, when he slipped back into the wilderness, he had fished and waited, living the old ways, remaining out of sight—a living ghost. The killings would eventually signal to the people he had left behind that he was alive. There were those who would know how to find him. The over-whelming force of the whites, aroused and focused, could kill him as easily as a bulldozer crushes a butterfly. But it was not necessary to escape. His mission was to set in motion events that would play themselves out after he was long gone. He was prepared for this. He looked forward to it. The memory of what he had left behind had wearied him over the years. He was ready for death.

He understood Smohalla's instructions, but much as he relished liberat-ing nusuh, *the Salmon Brother, trapped and humiliated in the barges and* tankers, he didn't understand how the sacrifice of these men would help to bring back Smohalla's river. Killing was easy for him. Uncertainty was hard. The pain of it brought tears to his eyes. He could not know if Smohalla's mission would succeed. He closed his eyes and pressed his head against his fist. As he did, he felt the earth moving, the flat rock on top of Rattlesnake Mountain cracked along its seam. Then there was stillness.

The warrior lifted his head. Smohalla had spoken. In his heart was joy, but there was also shame from needing to be reassured. The earth and time were moving at the behest of Smohalla. The rain told him this, as did the high water in the river. There was no longer any way of turning back. It brought him back to his own life, to the moment when he might have stepped away from everything he believed, when a woman begged him to be what he could not be. He had instead abandoned the one person who had believed in him. He thought of her now. She understood betrayal far better than he—it was like the shadow long ago that fell over Smohalla's heart when his people abandoned him.

Out on the horizon the blinking light had gone out. The stars exploded with brightness, as if they were admiring themselves in the smooth river mirror below. In the air he could smell that rain would come again tomorrow. The moon was getting ready to set. He would sleep now. He looked down at the bird in his hand and asked forgiveness. In the musical wind on top of the mountain of the rattlesnakes a father prayed not to his prophet, but for a soul that spoke from deep in his imaginings, from deep in the memory of the woman he still loved like no other. He could not know it was the soul of his only child.

11

When the alarms sounded throughout the Dittmer facility, everyone was there to hear it. High water had people working around the clock. Bud Hermiston was on his way out the door of his office when he saw that the floor lamp was rocking back and forth. His computer screen flashed the message *Terminal off-line. Initiating emergency file protection.* When Hermiston looked down he could see the floor move three full inches under the castor wheels of his office chair.

"It's a real quake, Bud. I'd say a four." One of the people outside his office shouted. From the readings on the seismometer Hermiston could still see jagged activity, steady but not severe.

Two assistants came running in clutching manila folders like security blankets. To Hermiston they all looked like Cub Scouts at a sleepover party. "Genesis is in reruns on this damn river," he muttered to himself and turned his wrath on the machine.

"Don't make me laugh with some piss-ass little tremor, goddamn you." Hermiston stared at it, willing the needle to go flat. "Now settle the fuck down." Hermiston's voice rose to a growl, then a shout. His staff crowded around the door to his office. They were used to the way their boss addressed Mother Nature and weren't the least surprised when the seismometer needle responded as if he had commanded it.

When the needle finally went flat, Hermiston quietly took a long gulp from his mug of cold coffee. "That was no quake," he said as the alarm stopped and the office was quiet again. "I guarantee you the only creatures feeling that were us and maybe some ducks." He grabbed the intercom and called for the Dittmer senior staff to reconvene in the conference room down the hall.

The phone rang. "That'll be Golden." Hermiston put the USGS officer in Golden, Colorado, on the speakerphone. "What's up, Glenda?"

"Hi, Bud. You boys a little rattled down there?"

"Didn't feel a thing, love. You sure a truck didn't just backfire in your parking lot? We're busy dealing with high water right now; your little quivering rocks don't interest us, Glenda." Bud was the engineer bureaucrat, mover of worlds. Glenda was the government scientist, mover of paper. She chuckled over the speakerphone.

"Sorry, but you know the drill, Bud. In the beginning God created the heavens and the earth, as in earthquake. Floods came much later in the story. I'm afraid I outrank you."

"Glenda, we're not studying for the ministry down here. What do you have for us?"

"The good news is we got you hitting in the low fours and close to the surface."

"Epicenter?"

"That's the bad news—I think. It's too early to say for sure, but we think this was centered at Elmer city, and it looks like an RIE."

"That's not bad news. It means there wasn't a real quake, and you shouldn't be wasting my time."

"Bud, a reservoir-induced earthquake is real. RIEs, volcanic eruptions, anything above Richter four is real. Have you heard from Grand Coulee yet? We've already got indications that rail traffic has been interrupted along the river."

"It's my next call, Glenda. Now all of us need to get back to building our ark. Do something useful. Organize the animals into pairs, load them on the boat, or stop this fucking rain. When you get a final report send it along, won't you?"

"Always a pleasure, Bud."

Hermiston scratched his head. "A little RIE. Goddamn." The alarms had brought all of the engineers, scientists, and lawyers over into his area. It was a small crowd, and among them was Francine Smohalla, who had heard the bells over in the hatchery. As the crowd moved to the conference room down the hall, Francine paused in the doorway until Hermiston was alone in his office. He poured another mug of coffee and collected his papers. He looked up at her. Startled, he spilled some of the coffee.

"Damn, Miss Smohalla, what are you trying to do?" Hermiston yelled and searched for a napkin. All he could find was seismograph paper. "I'm jittery enough as it is."

"Cup's too full, sir." Francine pulled a white hatchery rag from the pocket of her work pants and began to mop up the puddle. "Like a lot of things around here."

She looked directly at Hermiston. He shuffled some papers and broke gaze before she did. If he looked at her for too long, he could see the eyes of Frank Hale buried in an Indian woman's face: It always spooked him. "I'll thank you to let me take care of what's too full in this office."

Francine said nothing. "Stick to spilled coffee," he said to her. "Anything bigger, you'd better let me handle."

In the conference room the BPA senior staff, the stage crew that ran the river, waited for Hermiston to enter. As he did the room went silent.

"The official word is a Richter level–four quake. Reservoir-induced—some of you may know that as what's called an RIE. It is not serious, and there are no reports of damage, but we haven't had one of those in a while around here."

Hermiston looked down the long table. No one in the room had ever experienced any kind of earthquake or a serious flood before. Only the eruption of Mount Saint Helens in 1980 was within this group's memory, and that hadn't even involved the Columbia system. The RIE was real; he knew that. A reservoir-induced earthquake was something every engineer understood, but they were still rare. One of the biggest on record happened at Hoover Dam down on the Colorado back in the fifties. The weight of a reservoir applied to stressed rock naturally produced little nudges and squirms. Bud liked to say dams and rivers were like monks sharing a room in a monastery; it took a few years for them to get comfortable. But the water had never been this high behind Grand Coulee. The pressure had never been so great.

"Shouldn't we drain the reservoirs just as a precaution?" Francine spoke up. She hated the way everything was centered around Hermiston as if he were a high-school wrestling coach. It reminded her of the gym classes she had always endured as a young girl, where a dictatorial adult ordered around a bunch of half-naked children. Everyone totally deferred to the man at the end of the table. Francine had come to this meeting expressly to call for a drawdown, although she barely believed she had uttered the words in front of everyone.

"We've got the water to spare right now, that's for sure," she added.

Everyone at the table looked at Francine, then back at Hermiston. The Bonneville hatchery program did not have much credibility among the engineers; nevertheless, Francine had a point. The faces at the table waited for a response from Hermiston. He was silent.

One of the hydrologists on the Dittmer team timidly began to explain how many million acre-feet they could spare out of Lake Roosevelt behind Grand Coulee. Once the ice had been broken and the subject was on the table, everyone began shouting and arguing at once. Bud shook his head and looked down at his weather photographs. He was getting a headache.

"We can't do a drawdown in the middle of these water levels without rerunning 1948." Hermiston took a long swig from his Styrofoam coffee cup. "The water's just too damn high. We all know that. Earthquakes, on the other hand, never kill anything but a few sheep up here. Let's focus on the problem at hand."

"The problem at hand may be a much bigger flood if we don't take this seriously now." One of the other engineers picked up where Francine had left off.

"Did we all see a disaster movie or something over the weekend?"

A fish biologist starting an argument about geology, even if she was the granddaughter of Frank Hale, was about as welcome to Bud Hermiston as a scorpion in his pillowcase. Ever since the early eighties when the federal government had appointed a committee of engineers, farmers, biologists, and Indians to advise the BPA about the so-called "multi-use demands" of the river, Hermiston had had to listen to the opinions of people he would just as soon scrape off the blade of an earthmover.

"What I'm saying here is that holding water in Roosevelt may be a dangerous gamble right now." Francine kept pushing, delivering a lecture on hydrodynamics to the big man at the other end of the table. "We've got some slack for a while, but if this rain keeps up, we may lose our chance to draw Grand Coulee down later." Francine looked down the table. Hermiston was the only person listening to her. The others were watching Hermiston's face to see his reaction.

He could see in Francine's eyes a hint of the tenacity and javelin sharpness of her grandfather, Frank Hale. It made him nervous. As long as he thought of Francine as a half-breed Indian aquarium tender he could ignore her. As Frank Hale's granddaughter she was infuriating. "Excuse me, Miss Smohalla, but our job is to prevent flooding not to create it." Hermiston was icy with sarcasm. "If this is about your hatchery minnows, can't you give them a ride in one of our fish taxis or barge them downstream?"

"I'm not concerned so much about the fish this time," Francine continued, "it's the whole system. Maybe the quake is an argument we could use to get the Canadians to shut things down at their end."

Nervously Hermiston jabbed the end of a bent paper clip into the cuticle of one of his fingers until it bled. He squeezed the finger into his fist. Francine had another point about Canada, but he wasn't about to admit it. "There's no way to tell what caused this tremor. An RIE can happen just as easily when you take pressure off a reservoir as when you fill it up." Hermiston held up a satellite photo taken eight hours before. "We have one very simple problem." He pointed to the slender but unmistakable bulges behind each of the dams along the river. "Keeping this water here from going down here"—he pointed at the area around the city of Portland and then aimed his thumb at the ceiling—"while this water keeps falling out of the sky. Get it?"

"Exactly my point." Francine stood. She wasn't going to let this rest. The Dittmer team had forgotten all about the earthquake. The direct provocation of Bud Hermiston was a more urgent force of nature. "You can't shut off a river with a dam," she continued. "Whatever the river wants to happen, will happen. My grandfather knew that. He would never have attempted to use the dams to do what you are doing. The river doesn't need the Columbia gorge to get downstream. If you tempt it to go around the dams, it will. If you tempt it to go through the dams, it will. The river doesn't care. It's been finding different ways to the sea for the past three hundred thousand years."

"I don't need you to tell me this river's history, Miss Smohalla. The capacity of the dams is something your grandfather understood very well. The granite walls of the Columbia gorge can hold much more river than we have ever seen on earth. The dams are simply a way of restoring the Columbia system to what it was a long time ago, before human settlements, before time and nature eroded it into what we see now. The Columbia used to be a series of lakes connected by a sequence of waterfalls. If you think the river has no memory of these water levels, just go look for the stone-age pictures on the rocks near where you were born. Measure the petroglyphs at Celilo. The water in some years would have covered all the present dams to a depth of eighty yards."

"That was flowing water, Mr. Hermiston, not your Army Corps of Engineers' dam-stoppered river. Flowing water is living water. What you do with the dams by holding everything back is to tighten a deadly spring and kill the salmon, all so you can say you saved a few trailer parks and some Wal-Marts in Portland."

"If we drawdown the reservoirs it will just flood Indian lands. That was another of your grandfather's decisions. The Indian lands are all in runoff areas. You want me to give your uncle's casino a cold shower? Is that what you're asking for?"

"You are making this emergency into an excuse for slaughter. I've got salmon stuck upstream who won't make it to the ocean in time. When you finally do open the dams, most of them will die from shock in the turbines, or be killed by the nitrogen levels caused by the dam turbulence. High water traditionally helps the salmon, but not on this river anymore."

"So this is all about fish." Bud Hermiston was more comfortable. It was not a hydrological discussion anymore. Biology he could ignore for now. "We have a system for transporting fish. It's the most ridiculous waste of money I have ever seen, but it'll get your salmon around the dams. Maybe if you Indians would stop murdering your truck drivers, you wouldn't lose so many fish and I could go back to my job and we could get on with some important business."

"How do you know Indians are killing them?" Francine was more surprised than insulted to hear that he seemed so sure about this.

"I don't know, Francine," Hermiston said, looking at her as though she were a child who had made a stupid spelling error. "Because no one else would give a rat's ass about them, maybe?"

She stood up to leave. All of the eyes followed her to the door of the conference room. She turned back for a moment. "You can decide to draw the river down now or wait and the river will decide for you."

"Thank you, Francine. By the way, until these killings have been solved, I have orders to cancel the transport program—effective now. Your fish will just have to find there own way to the ocean."

Francine looked back, her face flushed and angry. "Why wasn't I told? I've got three million smolts that need to go out in the next ten days."

"We can't get drivers. Period." Hermiston said it with a smile on his face. "You want to drive them? Be my guest." There was an awkward pause. "Now can we go back to our jobs here?"

Francine locked eyes with him once more before she left. To her surprise she could see that behind his efforts to humiliate her in front of a roomful of engineers, he was clearly as worried about the water as she was. "Big dams," she muttered to herself as she walked back through the long corridor to the hatchery. "Little men."

1 2

"It works."

Silence.

"I'm telling you, Becca, Hobby Horse works."

More silence. Jack Charnock held the two balls stationary on the slanted, precarious-looking kitchen table so that they wouldn't roll off. They were about the same size. One was charred and stained, the other was a brand-new golf ball.

"I've solved the trigger problem."

"I hope you're not bringing chunks of radiation into this house." Rebecca Charnock crossed out a word and looked up from a list she was making. "And no mess on my tablecloth, please."

"There's nothing radioactive here. It was a perfect test. See?" Jack set the two balls against the chipped sugar bowl and saw that his wife was paying little attention to what he was saying.

"Did you get bananas?" Rebecca pointed to the fruit bowl nearly in front of her husband. He made an embarrassed face visible only to himself in his spoon, picked up an overripe banana from the bowl, peeled it, and not finding a knife, began using the spoon to slice it into crude mushy chunks for his bowl of cereal.

"You're making a mess." Rebecca stopped making her list, rose from the table, grabbed a paring knife out of one of the kitchen drawers, and set it before him with a crisp thud.

"You don't really need a knife to slice a banana," Jack said with the authority of an engineer. "It's more efficient this way." He didn't touch the knife.

As far as anyone knew, Jack Charnock had always been a middle-aged guy about whom the most interesting thing you could say was that his father was radioactive and his two best friends had blown their brains out years ago. People who discovered these facts about him were invariably shocked to learn he had anything so interesting in his past. On the long drives between the Hanford Reservation and his home in Richland, Washington, near the Columbia, Charnock himself often puzzled over his past. He could never sort out whether his father was a hero or a pathetic victim. Of his two best friends, he could never decide which was the greater mystery, that they had killed themselves or that they had ever been his friends at all.

Jack was a mystery to his wife, though she had cataloged each particular of his unmovable routines. She always knew what he would do down to the smallest detail—why was another matter. All she could do each day was watch as her sixty-seven-year-old husband walked out of her life. She ticked off the little preparations from an imaginary preflight checklist: how he would grab the brown paper-bag lunch she had made from the kitchen counter and set it down on the living-room chair, where he would forget it; how he would pick up his overstuffed, single-zip leather folder marked *HANFORD Pu-239 SpecDef Group* so that his massive ring of keys would fall out and crash to the floor; how he would pat his chest and load his empty white shirt pocket with three pens and a mechanical pencil; how he would fumble with the flimsy aluminum porch doorknob caked with four decades of white corrosion; how with a shriek from its hinges the door would open, and Jack Charnock would step through it without once looking back.

She knew he would have actually said, "Good-bye, Becca," but the sound would be lost in the dry crash of the spring-loaded door slamming behind him. Like all of the other punctuation marks in their lives, Rebecca knew the exact interval between the opening and closing of this door. The slam always made her wince. It said that she was alone in the house. Later in the day the same sound told her that her husband was home for dinner, which was not so terribly different from being alone.

Jack Charnock had walked out of and then back into Rebecca's life exactly this way every day of their forty-five years together. He had said good-bye to her as a young woman and as a mother with a little boy hanging on her skirts at the door. He had sat with her at the dinner table long after dark and after the child was in bed, talking about the details of his work, fabricating and refining plutonium for nuclear warheads. He spoke mostly of all of the bosses and politicians and ultimately presidents, whom he angrily regarded as stupid, greedy people whose advancement was undeserved and had come at his expense. He was condemned to toil under the supervision of uncreative minds with no understanding of the importance of his work.

Rebecca had married him back in the fifties because he seemed steady, had a good job and a burning sense of mission that she found attractive. Jack Charnock was a sufficient breadwinner but after four decades, his paltry wages were thin cover for a smaller truth. In Jack Charnock's mind there had never been anything but work. It made Rebecca chuckle to think of the salary that the government paid him. She wondered how much money she might have saved the U.S. government if she'd ever performed the perverse civic duty of telling them that he would have gladly done all the work for nothing. During her visits to the casino, she wondered how their lives might be different if she had been given up front all the money her husband squandered to support his plutonium gadgets, to wager at the roulette table. Certainly her luck could not be worse than his was. She was sometimes desperate to know this. Her husband had never once altered his routine or cadences through their son's milestones. He missed all of Sam's piano recitals, school plays, the Little League games, and bake sales.

There were to be more children than just Sammy. A daughter, Delia, had lived for a few days before dying of complications of severe birth defects. Another boy, Timothy, was stillborn. Rebecca was wounded and deeply suspicious of these failed pregnancies. They made her feel as though she was an instrument for detecting nuclear events, as though the plutonium in their lives had invaded her womb. She thought her husband had barely noticed her pregnancies or how badly they had ended. Jack considered Rebecca's worries about radiation to be nonsense. His father had survived a poisonous dose, and there was nothing wrong with their son, Jack would say.

Sam had survived. He was a healthy kid until his nineteenth year, 1974. In the summer of his senior year in high school, Jack had gotten him a summer job out at Hanford to make money for Stanford's tuition, a bill Jack had no intention of paying, even though he could not have been more proud that his son was accepted. They rode together to and from work every day that summer. The day of the accident Jack came home alone. He knew nothing of what happened, but realized as he drove in that he had once again absentmindedly forgotten to pick Sam up on his way home. He turned around to drive back to the shuttle bus stop where he'd dropped him that morning. "Don't worry," he told Rebecca, "I'll go and get him. Keep dinner warm for us." She had to shout to get Jack to stop. When she told him that Sam would not be there, that he wouldn't ever be coming home, he still didn't get it.

Seven hundred tons of liquid concrete fell on the boy at the WPPSS Number Three plant construction site. He was buried in a cooling-tower wall next to the reactor where his rock-and-limestone mummified bones still lie. No one discovered he was missing until the shift ended. Even with the same last name, no one at Hanford had put it together that father and son were even related. Rebecca's was the name on the application to call in an emergency. It had always been that way. Rebecca had thought working out at Hanford would bring Jack and Sam closer. Instead, her son was claimed by the nuclear winter that had given her husband warmth and a purpose all his life, and given her nothing. The WPPSS Number Three reactor was ultimately never built. Sam's death was a line item in an overrun budget of mistakes and design flaws. There had been no body to bury.

"Who is going to want this thing now?"

"The Hobby Horse just may be the most useful idea to come out of the cold war."

"Is that why they canceled it, Jack, because it was too useful?" Rebecca had heard her husband talking about Hobby Horse for more than half of his long years of Hanford. Hobby Horse was the Pentagon's first and last attempt to produce a completely portable and concealable nuclear device with a power of fifteen kilotons or less.

"Not canceled, not canceled, just mothballed," Jack corrected her. "Hobby Horse made too much sense to cancel. We've always been allowed to continue working on it as long as we didn't charge it to a budget."

"Do you think anyone from the army committee that dreamed up this idea is still alive to attend your demonstration?"

"No," he said defiantly. "Just me."

"Then why would there even be a demonstration, Jack?" Rebecca had always been her husband's chief adviser on office politics at Hanford, where Jack Charnock was continually running afoul of some manager or another. He did things his own way in the most pigheaded, solitary manner, and assumed that if what he produced met their specifications, the voices of the critics would be silenced. Rebecca often had the cruel task of reminding him how the world really worked. Jack's two best friends had been just as stubborn, but unlike Jack, they could be humiliated. They were incapable of ignoring how badly they had failed, how little anyone had cared about their work, how completely the world had moved on, leaving them behind. Jack saw none of it. He just plodded ahead. Rebecca marveled at and was always a little terrified of this strength.

"As usual you don't know what you are talking about." Jack was dismissive. "Why wouldn't there be a demonstration? A demonstration is required now that we have met the Pentagon spec. So there will be a demonstration, period."

"Don't they think you are assigned to some fuel-cleanup project, and won't they be upset to learn you are out testing homemade weapons?"

"I do my work. This is extra. They'll be happy someone had the guts to do it finally." It was inconceivable to Jack Charnock that his work might not have value, that his contributions might be overlooked, that he might ever walk out of his house in the morning with no place to go. As all three were perfectly true on this particular morning, Jack sounded less convincing than usual. Rebecca detected the doubt in his voice, and much as she longed to comfort him, she said only, "I see."

In all his years of working for the PUREX division of the Hanford Nuclear Reservation's plutonium-production division, Jack Charnock had missed work exactly six times; once for each of his children's funerals, once for each of the funerals of his two best friends, and once for the funeral of his famous father, Harold, the Radioactive Man of Hanford. Rebecca never doubted that all these tragedies hurt her husband; this she believed with the unwavering certainty of a pilgrim at Lourdes. But as he never spoke of anything other than his work, she never saw the miracle that would have proven he lived in the same world that she did.

Unlike Jack's unfortunate dead friends, whose wives had run off with other engineers from other divisions at Hanford and spiraled from riches into financial ruin, Rebecca and Jack had always had a kind of squalid stability just short of bankruptcy. Their own finances permitted them to meet their needs but would not permit an interruption in work. Jack never took a vacation.

Being passed over for promotions hadn't stopped him from putting every spare penny into one scheme or another. The Charnocks' garage and the shed out back were filled with Jack's discarded projects. There were models and prototypes of warheads and detonators, a plutonium space heater, machines that were going to use plutonium to blast tunnels through rock and make superfast, coast-to-coast, underground bullet trains that Jack dreamed would make America the futuristic utopia he thought everyone dreamed of.

Jack Charnock's cosmology was shaped by some imaginary mid-twentieth-century World's Fair. "Atoms for Peace" was his credo, but war would do. Plutonium had no more loyal friend than Jack Charnock. In the house of Hanford's Radioactive Man there was always a Geiger counter around. Jack's father would put it up to his face for fun to show the neighbor kids, doctors, and other gawkers how the needle went off the scale and the detector roared with clicks. The accident was the towering event in the life of his family. Jack had never stopped living in its aftermath. Like a cat mesmerized by a bobbing sock dangling above its head, he was a captive of the radioactive trance that had cast its spell over his father. The accident measured him, baselined him, was the starting point, the literal background radiation in his life. He could not even form the question to escape it. So fixed and certain was it that Jack had never once asked his father about the accident.

The accident had severely burned Harold's hand, and he had to wear black sunglasses all the time to protect his eyes. But to Jack, radioactivity was nothing to be feared. It was a magical force. Working close to neutrons and alpha and beta particles, Jack thought, was what he was meant to do. He never worried about his own health, and he never connected his work with the deaths of his two children. Rebecca never thought of anything else.

To Jack, element 94 was the culmination of all matter. In plutonium, God and chemistry merged. Its agent on earth was Jack Charnock. He knew its every property and nuance. To plutonium he had sacrificed nearly everything until all he and his wife possessed was the forties-era F-style house at 94 Argon Lane, built by the government back when Richland was the frontier home for the scientists and engineers who made the original Nagasaki bomb. Jack couldn't have been more proud of an address, but the F-model homes had long ago relinquished the status they once had as the prized residences of the most senior nuclear scientists. They had given up their value as well. Rebecca and Jack Charnock now inhabited an old relic on a side of town most people in Richland didn't realize had a history anymore, the living, haunting museum no one ever visited.

The nuclear industry had become as archaic as stonecutting, but there was no giving up on the elemental power of the atom for the people who understood it. It was tantalizing, like the philosopher's stone of the ancient alchemists Jack also revered. A power so staggering would have a use; finding that use was Jack Charnock's mission now that the cold war was over. The Richland house was a junkyard of special presidential proclamations about plutonium and the global fight against the forces of evil, all worded with cold-war urgency. Yet each new "project" or "operation" handed to him had rekindled the old inventor's passion and kept Jack Charnock ageless and childlike.

It would always end the same way; the project was quietly mothballed, or canceled. Jack's work was not quite right, the nation "had decided to go in a different direction." He was always informed by some unknown colonel from Washington, one of the floating, uniformed Pentagon scum that unerringly rose to the top and made the call to Jack, who always argued back to them that there must be some mistake. Rebecca bore the brunt of these periodic tragedies. She would look into the empty eyes of the little-boy husband she had fallen in love with and see an old man, the question "Why?" hanging from his lips. She was cursed to watch as he was abused by the same uniformed technocrats whose call he always awaited like a firehouse dog curled up by the door.

Jack and Rebecca's life together was the single constant in this world that had promised much but delivered little. Rebecca never could have left Jack. She had hung in there long beyond the point of leaving. He was all she had now. She needed to see how the story turned out.

"What if no one wants Hobby Horse, Jack? What if showing them how it works doesn't make them want it, but only makes them want you out of Hanford?"

"Nonsense, I'm a Charnock. They can't get rid of me."

"Does anyone around Hanford even remember what that means anymore?"

"I do. But don't think about that." Jack grabbed a baseball cap from the top of the refrigerator and swatted the dust off it. The cap was embroidered in red letters. *DOE Project Hobby Horse: Director.* It was old, from the days before Hobby Horse's budget was eliminated. Jack put the cap on Rebecca's head. "You forget. Hobby Horse is something they are going to love. It's small and practical. It's cheaper now than when we started. It's going to be useful for excavation, mining. It can be secretly transported on the back of a truck and used to explode a block of official buildings. A single-kiloton Hobby Horse hidden on the backseat of a car could take out a whole government in a single detonation without killing too many civilians. We made it through the cold war. We won because of plutonium. It can still help us. Hobby Horse works. I know it works. It's time to assemble it."

Rebecca was always surprised to find that she could still love the man who believed in such things. It was the most maddening part. She cared nothing for the cold war and the rest of it; she loved the belief itself. How could he have stayed so steadfast even as they had lost everything as a family? Rebecca could never tell if he was a genius or lost in a deep, inescapable rut. She envied his certainty, whatever it was based on.

Jack stood up, grabbed his overstuffed folder, and headed for the door. His large ring of keys crashed to the floor, and he stopped to pick them up. "Do you have your lunch?" Rebecca asked, even though she knew the answer. Jack patted his shirt pocket and looked around. "Have you seen my mechanical pencils?"

"In the drawer." She pointed and handed him his lunch bag. He started toward the door. Rebecca said "Good-bye, Jack" as the hinges on the aluminum door creaked. It crashed shut right on cue, and he was gone. As always, she didn't hear him call, "Bye, Becca." He didn't hear her whisper, "I love you," as he drove out of the driveway.

She caught herself smiling. She wanted his triumph and was secretly thrilled that this gadget worked. If her husband could make his demonstration and just one person told him that his work was brilliant, that it was exactly what they were looking for, that it was the answer to a nation's prayers, Rebecca knew Jack Charnock would gladly close the book on every slight and act of disrespect he had ever endured. Every bit of pain she had endured with him would have been worth it. But without such a triumph, she was just as certain that he would slowly work himself to death.

Rebecca turned away from the door and sighed. There by the drawer, where his mechanical pencils had been, was his lunch bag; he had forgotten to pick it back up. Rebecca shook her head and placed the bag in the refrigerator. She took the Hobby Horse cap off her head and hung it on a hook in the kitchen.

They had spent their lives together and yet knew little or nothing of what happened out of each other's sight. Rebecca had never once caught a hint of her husband's grief over the loss of their son. She had no idea now of the collapse of Jack Charnock's world and his determination, despite it, to see his proudest achievement through, his gift to her for all the bad times. Jack had no idea how much Rebecca feared for his life, that she prayed for his success, and would do nearly anything to keep her dogged nuclear soldier from sinking into the dark place where so much of her life had already vanished without a trace. Isolated and inseparable, blinking in the dark, listening to each other's breathing, Rebecca and Jack were like two lost angels dreaming of miracles, neither understanding how close they really were.

13

The moment he had agreed to hold a festival on the grounds of the casino, Joe regretted it. He had forgotten how much everyone wanted to be involved in events like this, from anthropologists at the colleges around the region, who had their own notion of what a festival like this should be, to tribes who wanted their own festivals. In short order, Joe had managed to draw out of the woodwork every parasite who had ever tried to hook itself to Shoulder Moon's success. Joe hated politics, but Indians seemed to have some natural taste for it when it involved their own people. Joe considered this another of Coyote's jokes, how the Indians signed away all their land without a fight for two hundred years, and now would spend days arguing over which tribe would get the table closest to the gaming floor for selling T-shirts.

Dealing with Otis had been difficult. With Daniel's help, he had cleaned up, but not drinking made Otis so unruly and out of sorts that much of the time Joe simply wanted to throw him into a tank of whiskey to shut him up. Otis was working on the order of the musical acts that had agreed to perform on the outdoor stage. Daniel sat silently.

"There are too many Irish bands," Joe declared. Anything involving Indians brought out all of the musicians from the public radio stations. These were the same drumming collectives and New Age fiddlers who always found Indian reservations to be an irresistible draw. "Aren't there any Indian bands?"

"Only a couple of really loud thrash-rock groups who need to come at the end."

"So it's going to be dulcimers and lesbian drummers all afternoon and then kaboom?"

When the direct line on Joe's desk phone buzzed, he picked up the receiver. "Send him in," he said. Joe motioned for Otis to put his leaflets and pictures away. The door opened and a casino bodyguard ushered in a large black man in a gray uniform: Duane Madison. Joe recognized him immediately.

"Mr. Madison, good afternoon. I'm sorry about your bad luck the other night. I hope you've forgiven us."

"Forgotten and forgiven, I'm just waiting for a day off to come to your table again and win it all back. I'm due for a streak." Madison was in fact obsessed with his losses. Back in the casino his fingers literally trembled with anticipation over winning back his six grand, to the point where it made it hard to focus on the real reason he had come to Shoulder Moon.

"So what can we help you with?"

"This is a courtesy call, Joe. You might say I'm here on a professional matter. As head of security at Hanford, the murders on the river have fallen into my basket, so to speak. I hope you'll forgive me, but there are a few questions I need to ask."

"I've noticed that these murders have made a lot of federal agents curious about Shoulder Moon. I'd be happy to know why and answer any questions you have."

"I'm afraid I have no control over the federal agents in this part of the country. They could be anyone from the FBI to the Department of Agriculture. The federal government has a piece of all the action in the Pacific Northwest."

"Except for us, of course."

"Well, of course." Madison was doing his best to keep things cordial. "And I can't say I mind that the government hasn't put its fingers in Indian gambling."

"There's still plenty of time for that." Daniel spoke suddenly, nearly spitting out his words. "Why are you here?"

Joe raised his hand to Daniel. "Forgive Daniel Three Knives, Mr. Madison, but I would like to know the answer to his question."

"I am here to ask about the man and his son who took home the big roulette jackpot the other night. You used a name when you spoke to them. I'd like to know how you got that name. The two men called themselves McCurdy, not the name you used."

"I called them Whillers," Joe said.

"Exactly."

"I was mistaken."

"You were. Roy McCurdy and his son, Duke, are a couple of notorious white-supremacist types from up near Idaho."

"I don't know about the boy," Joe replied, "but the old man is clearly behind enemy lines."

"That's a good one. One of the victims of the river murders was named Whillers. In fact, as far as we know, he was the first victim."

"Then I was quite mistaken."

"It's not as simple as that, Joe. If you'll forgive me, I have to ask. We can prove that a cash advance off of Mr. Whillers's Visa card was made at Shoulder Moon the night I last saw you. Now, we know Mr. Whillers was already dead, so somebody was using his card."

"The murderer."

"Not necessarily."

"You were at the table that night. The raving white devil from the stockades called himself Whillers. He used Whillers's card. He won about two hundred fifty thousand dollars, and I had to pay it all to him. What else do you need to know?"

"You didn't have to pay it. A stolen card is no good, so his winnings were invalid. You could have bounced him right there."

"Mr. Madison, I don't follow you. For one thing the card didn't come up stolen until he'd already won. You were there—you, yourself the object of most of his vile language. You saw the faces in that crowd. If I had turned Mr. McCurdy away after such winnings, for whatever reason, every table on the casino floor, this quiet office where you are now standing, this entire building would be a smoldering ruin, and you and I would have died in much worse agony than Mr. Whillers did."

"We know all about Mr. McCurdy. We know he's capable of murder, but for now we think he ended up with the stolen card by accident."

Otis had said nothing up till this point. Joe noticed that he was increasingly uneasy.

"It's why I'm here. We think he might have gotten it from the man we believe was the last person to see Mr. Whillers alive." Madison looked directly at Otis. "Mr. Peter Stepping-Cloud Jones is the name I have for you, sir, but I understand from everyone we've talked to that you go by the name of Otis."

Otis winced visibly to hear his reservation name, given to him as a little boy at the English school, a name he never heard except when he was in court. "Otis is my name, sir."

He adopted the servile demeanor around authority that both Daniel and Joe recognized and hated. "I didn't see anything. I just woke up with a headache and an empty bottle next to me."

"Hold on a minute, Otis," Joe interrupted. "Now, Mr. Madison, should I call a lawyer for my friend here? I think you've got some explaining to do."

"Otis here was seen in the parking lot of the Celilo liquor store on the night Mr. Whillers was murdered. As best as we can tell, Mr. Whillers made a purchase at the store. Shortly after that, he was dead, and some of the credit cards in his wallet ended up at a gun show near Walla Walla."

"I didn't see anything."

"But you did find a wallet, right?"

Otis looked over at Joe. He looked utterly helpless and afraid. Joe could see that Otis had perhaps seen more than his usual nothing this time.

"I thought it was just a dream," Otis practically whispered.

"Have you told the police about your dreams?" Madison was attempting to be sympathetic but was immediately rebuffed by Daniel.

"Since when do dreams belong to the police?" Daniel turned to Otis. "Can't you ever just keep your mouth shut?" Otis said nothing.

"As you like it." Madison could feel the chill. "We think we can prove Otis sold items from the wallet of Mr. Whillers to a document forger at a gun show, who sold the credit cards to a white-supremacist group, the New Israelites, over near Walla Walla, which is how we think it ended up in the hands of Mr. McCurdy. These New Israelites have a number of stolen—credit card scams going to finance their own funny money. You may have even seen some of their printed money, Joe. All we want to know is if Mr. Whillers encountered anyone in the liquor-store parking lot. It was the last place he was seen alive." He reached into his pocket and removed an envelope containing a single snapshot. "We're pretty sure Otis was there." He set the snapshot on the table as though he was laying down a full house. Joe picked it up. Otis had attempted to put his hand in front of his face to block the flash, but there he was, pants half down, standing in a rainy puddle. Joe looked at Otis, who had an embarrassed smile and was faintly quivering with alcoholic tremens.

"The picture was developed from a camera found in Mr. Whillers's truck," Madison added.

"That's very attractive, Mr. Madison. Is it only Indian people you are interested in, or do you plan on talking to Mr. McCurdy?" Joe was polite but left the impression that he wanted this conversation to end.

"We are interested in anyone who might help solve these murders. Talking to Mr. McCurdy is a little more difficult. But we'll catch up with him. In the meantime, I imagine you're aware that these aren't your run-of-the-mill killings. It seems that someone is trying to scare a whole lot of people. Don't you agree?" Madison looked from face to face. No one spoke. "Good afternoon," Madison said. Joe stood. When he could see that Madison was leaving, he finally spoke up.

"The people along the river are very concerned about this. We are organizing a festival to pray for the Salmon Brother. Otis here was just helping us to plan. I hope you understand just how disturbing this all is to our people, Mr. Madison."

"Of course." Madison smiled. "I hope you'll still let me come back and try to win back what I lost the other night."

"Shoulder Moon is always open."

Madison noticed that Otis was weakly smiling in reaction to the comment about the festival. "I hope you're going to keep me in mind if you remember something that might be important, Otis." The door to the office opened, and a bodyguard escorted Madison away.

"Dead men are lucky," Otis mumbled to break an awkward silence when the three of them were alone once more.

"Anyone would be lucky compared to you." Joe was angry and disgusted.

"Don't worry about him." Otis was suddenly restocked with nerve, now that Madison was gone. "Just think of the festival and all the money we're going to make. It will be the best commercial for Shoulder Moon. You'll see."

"I'm not worried about him. It's you, Otis, who worries me. I don't know what you saw, I don't know if you even know what you saw, but I don't much like being surprised in my own office in front of a federal cop."

"It was just a dream."

"It was apparently more than just a dream."

"Your brother, Charley, was in the dream," Otis said in a confessional voice. "His face does not leave my mind without drink. Could he be among us?"

"It is what I have been saying." Daniel stepped up to Joe's desk. "The warriors came home. Smohalla's words are true. If what Otis says is true, then your brother, Charley, is carrying the future of our people."

Joe sat down slowly. It appeared as though a great weight had been placed on his shoulders. For a moment he seemed far away. In his eyes he was thinking of the days long ago when his father had stood in line as a young man to be part of the ocean of laborers who descended on the land around the town of Grand Coulee in the thirties. Grand Coulee Dam made a boomtown of bars and whores, and Joe and Charley's dad made good money, gambled good money, and drank it away. When the dam was done the town vanished, and so did every salmon run that depended on the waters upstream for a thousand miles. It was Joe's first lesson in what the white man could do. His family moved on. Joe's first work was as a dam laborer, while his younger brother refused to work on the white man's river. He would not believe that men alone could defeat a river.

They were both equally angry about how things had turned out even if their lives were very different. While Joe worked construction, amassing wealth for his escape from the white man's time clocks, his brother, Charley—gentle, naïve Charley—had stayed close to the salmon, dreaming of how it all might be swept away.

"When he disappeared I thought there was no turning back. Celilo's disappearance killed him, I thought. It was the one thing he could never believe would vanish at the hand of man. He was wrong. Being wrong like that killed him. I was sure of it." Joe's face was full of fear.

"Smohalla dreamed that the salmon will be free," Daniel said. "Whatever has happened, we are all a part of that dream."

"Even if the dream is real?" Otis asked. He had never seen Joe like this. It was as though he had lost his confidence in the casino he had worked so hard to build.

"Charley told me the last time I saw him that I would be right about everything only until he returned. I didn't understand." Joe's face was full of the loss of his brother so many years ago. "Did he say anything to you when you saw him?"

"He said the word *tamala*. He shouted, *'Tamala! Tamala!'*"

"It's him, then." Joe's face was colorless now. "Has he been waiting all of these years merely to kill some truck drivers?"

"Maybe it is not your brother's actions that are important," Daniel said. "Smohalla alone sees the whole picture."

Joe looked around at the fixtures in his office. They were expensive, but he was aware of how little it would take to sweep away all that he had created under this roof. He looked down. On his desk was the black-and-white picture of She Who Watches, Tsagaglalal. At that moment she seemed to be watching only him.

14

Bud Hermiston was having difficulty shaking his uneasiness. Knowledge was a dangerous thing where dams were concerned, and no one had more of it than he did. When what he knew about concrete, steel, and rock couldn't quiet his nerves, he would take his helmet, goggles, and slide rule and go have a look around. Hermiston felt his own anxiety put an added load on the dams. He would go see for himself that the place where Grand Coulee Dam joined the earth was as secure as if it had been made that way from the beginning. "It's all a part of creation now," he said to himself. "She could withstand another ice age if she needed to."

Hermiston loved going down inside his dams. Far below where there was only uncounted tons of masonry holding back uncountable tons of water, he was content. But he understood that others would take his poking around as evidence of impending disaster, or at the very least, bad luck. Inspections were common at all the dams, but personal inspections by the commanding officer of the Columbia system were rare. Since the dam complex had become the favored target of environmentalists, there was little Hermiston could do without raising eyebrows and making news. He arrived at Grand Coulee before dawn and would leave well before the shift change. No one whose mouth wasn't shut would know he had come and gone. He was looking forward to getting a little breakfast in Wenatchee before the long drive back to Bonneville.

An elevator took him down to the bottom of the powerhouse where the air was close and sweet with ozone. The generators roared. Because the dam was trying to contain the heavy drainage from the rains, only five of them were operating. The big spillways were closed. Gas switches slammed open and shut like hammers, channeling power out to the northwest grid where it would be divided and stepped up in voltage for the long trip west, east, and south. As he walked the long high corridor past the rows of transformers, the electric hum made the fillings in his teeth quiver.

At the end of the corridor was a bolted steel door that opened onto a narrow staircase. Hermiston went inside, and as he descended, the electric sounds were replaced by the deep voice of water and rock. There were no elevators from this point down. Beyond here, the only electricity was the occasional illumination from incandescent bulbs, whose energy had been falling water moments before. At the bottom of the staircase was a much longer corridor, stretching the full width of the dam and barely the height of a man. On the floor of this corridor, nine large steel hatches were laid out in a line from one end of the dam to the other. Hermiston walked stooped until he reached the hatch at the far end. He opened it, switched on his hard hat's high-intensity lamp, and climbed down the stainless-steel ladder that led all the way to the base of the dam.

Here the noise was a tight blanket of sound, echo woven back on echo until the hum in the air was indistinguishable from the hum in his bones. To Hermiston it was a joyful sound. The dam spoke to him down here. He sat still for a moment. Grand Coulee was holding as much river behind her as she ever had. She had never done it for this long, more than three weeks, and for all that time the river had continued to inch upward while Hermiston resisted a drawdown. He looked around. He was far below ground, below the reservoir itself, which pressed down on every molecule of rock with a force of hundreds of thousands of pounds per square inch. Water this deep, under this much pressure, supported no river life save bits of decaying matter that had fallen from the surface. No freshwater creature could survive down here, just one way that the dams changed the character of the river. Hermiston took a deep breath. This was where the dam anchored itself to the earth. On every side of him was the ancient rock of the Columbia plateau carved by volcanoes, ice, and floods; above him, there was only concrete.

Hermiston reached out and touched the wall. It was wet. He rubbed his fingers together and saw that the water was not clear. The moisture was a mixture of water and silt. It was not the result of condensation. The fine, fully dissolved silt could only have come from the reservoir above. Hermiston listened. This time he noticed a slight, high-pitched whistling there among the roaring voice of the dam. He tried to place it. It seemed to be coming from the center. If there were a fault in the dam, it would be better to have it nearer the edges of the span with their three angles of support. Hermiston gathered a sample of silt and placed it in one of the many empty film canisters he kept in his raincoat pocket for collecting samples. He labeled it with the time and location.

He climbed out of the shaft and moved all the way to the center. Carefully placing his head down on the shaft hatches, he localized the sound in shaft number six. He could also feel a vibration. "Fuck it," he said to himself, and opened the hatch. Peering down inside, he could see nothing but the ladder disappearing into darkness. As he descended, the vibration he felt on the surface was more evident in the rungs of the ladder he gripped on the way down, and it was getting stronger. He kept descending until he was less than one hundred feet from the bottom. His boots were waterproof and thick with steel reinforcement, so he didn't feel the water until it was almost above his knee.

It was bitterly cold. He looked down. Because the water was thick with silt, the light didn't penetrate the opaque surface. By the count on the wall, he was more than three-quarters of the way to the bottom. There was more than fifty feet of water in the shaft. The silt made it hard to see any movement. He slowly descended until he was submerged chest deep. A silvery object was slowly circling in the center of the shaft, tracing out a distinct whirlpool. Hermiston reached out and grabbed a small fish, a salmon, dead. The dam had mutilated its flesh, but it had probably died from the effects of nitrogen poisoning. Concentrated nitrogen was a by-product of turbulence through spillways and turbines.

The fish was ghostly, but it told Hermiston what was going on below the surface. This was not standing water. It was circulating from some point A to a point B. Not good. Hermiston took a deep breath, fastened his helmet and goggles, and climbed underwater, holding tight to the ladder. Maybe he could avoid bringing down a team of divers and attracting attention if he could just see for himself what was going on. Almost immediately he felt the water's downward pull. He gripped the rungs of the ladder, but they were coated with slippery silt. He continued his descent, counting the rungs he passed, trying to peer over his shoulder in the direction of the water flow.

He had descended six rungs when he saw the crack—a black slit in the concrete that appeared to be about two feet wide at its widest point. The moment he saw it the current pulled him from the ladder. Water was pouring through the crack and sucking him toward the opening where a number of dead salmon were already swirling amidst chunks of their own flesh. Hermiston felt pain in his lungs as he slammed against the wall of the shaft. His hard-hat light went out. Darkness swallowed him, bringing on panic. In a matter of seconds he would be swirling like the salmon. Carefully he calculated his bearings and reached up to where he thought the ladder would be. Nothing. He shifted to the right, and with his legs he tried to push off from the wall, where he was pinned by flowing water. If he broke free, he knew floating would rob him of his bearings, and vertigo would make it impossible to do anything but flail around until his lungs burst and he drowned.

His only chance was to push off with his legs as hard as he could and hope the force would propel him to the other side of the shaft where he might grab a rung. He struggled to keep from exhaling. Cold and lack of oxygen were making him dizzy. He pushed. The water was strong. It meant the breach extended far below. But Hermiston's legs were stronger, and when his head bumped against the metal rung, he grabbed it and desperately clawed his way upward. He counted as he climbed. His head broke the surface at eleven rungs. He knew he hadn't sunk that far when the light went out, but he couldn't be sure. If the water was rising this fast, something would have to be done.

He climbed out of the shaft and sat in the dim corridor light to catch his breath. The cold hurt his skin. The balls of his fingers throbbed with pain from his climb. Slowly he stood up. His beloved dam had almost killed him; or was it the river he had spent his life trying to control seeking its own revenge? Hermiston made his way back to the surface. The security staff and other BPA employees waved at him, but they knew enough not to ask why he was soaking wet. "Little moist down there today, Freddie. Woke me right up," he said to the man at the top-side checkpoint who was about his own age and had been working at the BPA and the Army Corps ever since Hermiston was an engineer just out of college.

"Dam's got a lot of river to hold these days."

"She'll hold it."

"Of course she will, Bud. She's as scared to get on your bad side as the rest of us."

"Just keep that in mind, Freddie."

"I will. Is everything okay down there?"

"She's fine. How come you aren't out collecting your pension?"

"I will when you do, Bud."

"Never happen, Freddie," Hermiston chuckled. It was their running joke about being the two most senior employees at the BPA. "They'll have to drag us out of here someday."

"Never happen, Bud."

Hermiston winked a good-bye, stepped outside, and paused at the railing to let the wind dry him out. He looked down for any sign of anomalies, eddies, or telltale spots of soaked ground at the bottom of the dam. There was nothing. He looked downriver. In the morning light the water was beautiful. It appeared that the rain would come much later in the day, if at all. The sky was clear. The high walls of the Columbia

Gorge stretched off into the distance. Water was high, but still the river was dwarfed by the dam. Everywhere Hermiston looked he could see evidence that the river of the present moment was merely an inconsequential trickle compared to what it had once been. Twenty thousand years earlier the Ice Age had ended with such violence that creation itself could barely match. The modern Columbia was born in a torrent no human could comprehend. A dam of rocks and silt glued together by ice and gravity had burst in what was now Montana, emptying ancient Lake Missoula, a body of water triple the size of Lake Superior.

Hermiston shrugged off his near-drowning and reminded himself of the far greater forces that had made his world long ago. A flaw in the bottom of a dam could be fixed. He would see to that. As he stood in the chill wind he pulled out his trusty slide rule and calculated the high-pressure concrete patch that would seal up the tiny breach. It might take a week or so. If it was the only consequence of this one-hundred-year high water, then Grand Coulee was still the engineering miracle it had always been.

In the grand scheme of things, a little whirlpool like the one he had just witnessed was nothing. It could not compare to the ancient floods and cataclysms. Hermiston always had in his mind a picture of the first flood that heralded the end of the Ice Age. He wished he'd been around to see it. In the scenario he imagined it had been in the morning on a rare clear day when energy from the rising sun had finally melted through ten thousand years of frozen debris.

It began perhaps as a sluice of mud opening around a jumble of massive Mesozoic tree trunks that were warmed first, due to their dark coloring. Free from the ice, they became buoyant and loose. As they moved they tore channels in the frozen debris. Lake water sucked into the spaces left by the tree trunks, spiraled with the force of a drill bit, pitting and caving great holes into the ice at the base of the dam.

From the air at the right moment, he might have seen a single tsunami wave, possibly two hundred feet high, radiating across the surface of the entire lake. The final cataclysm must have come seconds later as the momentum of the draining water caused the floating remains of the ice dam to literally flip like a swamped canoe, spinning it as easily as a child blows a pinwheel. Propelled by centrifugal force, the misshapen mountains of ice erupted across the plateau like milkweed. Hermiston imagined that the sound of this ice dam breaking loose and the roar of the lake water suddenly exploding out from under it must have been among the loudest sounds ever produced on earth.

In geologic time this catastrophe had happened just an instant before Bud Hermiston showed up on the planet. There were few places where one could inspect the recent aftermath of a major geologic event, and Hermiston liked living along the Columbia River precisely because it felt a little like being an eyewitness to the book of Genesis, where the elemental forces of good and evil were ever present.

Every tossed boulder, gouged blind canyon, virtually every geographic feature of the land west of Montana and north of Crater Lake owed something to these cataclysms that heralded the beginning of the modern epoch. Every plant growing along the river was descended from a seed deposited by its silt. Every splash of white water on the Columbia, every one of its awesome waterfalls, was now a tiny echo of that long-subsided flood. There was a single word for it: the *jokulhlaup*. It was an Icelandic word referring to the devastating flood caused when volcanic activity melted and boiled pack ice, causing it to break up in a fast-moving sludge that surged overland, carving and crushing everything in its path. But no one word could ever be precise about a cataclysm that only the luckiest human being could have witnessed without obliteration.

In modern times each of his dams had altered something of the river's flow patterns. The last big change came in 1967 when the Dalles Dam silenced one of the last remaining echoes from the ancient *jokulhlaup*. For the first time since the Ice Age, Celilo Falls, one of the most spectacular features on the river, and the site of the oldest continuously inhabited human settlement in the hemisphere, was submerged. The energy that for thousands of years had produced the spray and churn of the largest falls after Niagara in North America was swept away.

Hermiston had not been sorry to see Celilo go. As a little boy he had stared in awe at the noise and chaos of the falls, but he had always been afraid of and a little disgusted by the Indians who gathered there to fish. Stinking of salmon and poverty, they swarmed over their rickety scaffolds and wooden platforms to spear or net the jumping chinooks on their upstream spring and fall runs. To Hermiston the Indians seemed like pests, ants with funny hats whose only advantages were in numbers. Even the Indians' trucks and modern tools looked rusted and backward to him.

By his reckoning the Indians had just found an unlucky obstruction for the salmon and were impaling and clubbing the giant fish at their most heroic and vulnerable moment. At least the salmon had the courage to jump Celilo Falls. The few times he had seen the peak chinook runs at Celilo, Bud had always rooted for the fish. Everything about the Indians blended into the unsavory sense of the primitive that had repelled him like some unsightly stain he might come across in a public rest room.

"We should have left them alone." Hermiston chuckled to himself. "Because of the dams they stopped fishing and went off to become millionaires. The bastards should thank me." The cold was getting to him. He would finish drying off in his heated car. He walked off toward the parking lot and thought of the string of unsolved murders that had shut down the salmon transport fleet. In his mind he saw the white lifeless eyes of the fish that had been slowly swirling in the whirlpool down below. There was plenty besides high water making him uneasy.

15

Rebecca Charnock was alone in her kitchen with the radio on. She listened as she cleaned up from a dinner of half a grilled cheese sandwich and a cup of tomato soup. Skillet, saucepan, plate, cup. One of each. A glass was half full of gin and tonic, her first and therefore not quite ready for the sink.

"This is Roy McCurdy sitting in for Tommy Liberty here on KGOG radio. We're talking about this federal conspiracy called Social Security. With me is a Miss Lateesha Robinson. Am I saying that right, Miss Robinson?"

"That's correct."

"And I understand that you are out of the Social Security office up there in Spokane, is that right?"

"That's right, but I don't know what you mean about a federal conspiracy. You'll have to explain that to me."

"In a moment. We're just looking for some basic information about the Social Security system."

"All right. I'm happy to help."

If Jack had made it home that evening, the radio would have been shut off for dinner, and Jack would have eaten Rebecca's leftover half sandwich in addition to one of his own. At his place there would have been drops of pickle juice from a jar and fork he always brought to the table, many crumbs, and smears of mustard. He loved to spread mustard on the top of his grilled cheese. Usually his glass of beer would have foamed over from a bad pour, and there would be a beer-soaked napkin to throw away. For dessert he would have had a bowl of ice cream.

Tonight she cleaned her very few dishes slowly, stalling what would be a long, lonely evening. She didn't feel like listening to music whenever she was alone like this, and when the wind was howling off the desert, music made every noise outdoors seem like an army of prowlers. Voices comforted her. The ugliness and hatred that went out over the radio was somehow secondary to the fact that these were live human voices. There were other people in the world. As she drank, it was easy to ignore the ugliness and listen only to the sounds of the voices.

"You see, Miss Lateesha Robinson, our listeners don't know a lot about Social Security. They get their paycheck each week and see what the government takes out and they have a lot of questions."

"Well, I can certainly understand that. I sometimes have the same questions about my paycheck."

"Now you have been working there at Social Security for a few years now, right?"

"Twelve years."

"Twelve years of collecting a paycheck from the U.S. government, and I guess, Miss Lateesha Robinson, you are a quote-unquote 'person of color,' is that right?"

"I'm regional manager of the Social Security Administration here in Spokane, and yes, I am an African American. Now, do you have any questions about Social Security?"

Rebecca was surprised how different it was listening to Roy McCurdy now that she had actually seen him in person the other night at the casino. She found him just as offensive on the air as she had in person, but there was something about knowing him that made her feel more involved somehow. It was as though she had been let in on a secret game. McCurdy was baiting his guest just as he had provoked the people around the roulette table. The guest thought McCurdy was seriously interested in the Social Security system. Rebecca and the rest of

McCurdy's audience knew different, and knew that the guest would be the last to understand what was really going on.

"I would like to know, Miss Lateesha Robinson, why you have to assign a number to all the white babies in this country?"

"Everyone needs a number in order to get their Social Security. You have to have a number to get your Social Security, I have to have a number. That is how the system works whether you are white or black."

Miss Robinson was beginning to express exasperation with her interviewer. Rebecca smiled and refloated the ice cubes in her glass with gin. She knew what was coming. It was always a question of how long to stay tuned before the level of outrage made listening repellent and she changed the station. The more she drank, the longer she could go. She secretly hoped the woman would just hang up before she was humiliated on the air. Rebecca wondered how Roy McCurdy had convinced Miss Robinson to come on his show in the first place. Rebecca looked out through the window at the driveway. It was dark. No sign of Jack. She could see herself in the glass. She was wearing a new dress she had bought with her winnings the other night at the casino. She had bet with McCurdy. She smiled as it occurred to her that it was like the man on the radio had given it to her. It made her feel a trifle guilty and excited sitting there listening. Like many voices on the radio, especially when she was alone, especially when she was past her second gin and tonic, Roy McCurdy seemed to be talking to her.

"But it's the white babies you're after. Isn't that the truth, ma'am? Let's just think about it here. The money from Social Security comes from the white people. It mostly goes to black people. Can you admit that at least to our listeners?"

"I will admit no such thing. Who are you? I was told that this was going to be a program about saving Social Security."

"Of course you want to save Social Security. You take money from the white race and give it to blacks and Jews. Which is why all the white babies in America are given a number by the government. It's so they can always get their hands on our money."

Rebecca winced and nodded when she heard the click of the phone. The guest had hung up. Rebecca was relieved that she would not have to hear what was to come. What fascinated Rebecca most about McCurdy was how he conveyed a total sense of control over his own fate. That messianic certainty was reassuring to Rebecca, even if she found the details of what McCurdy called for disgusting. It made her feel important, like the old days when her husband was working on top-secret bomb designs and they both seemed to be at the center of the cold war. There seemed to be so much possibility: Once the world had to listen to what they had to say. Now she waited for Jack to come home, knowing that his credibility would have eroded a bit more, their lives a shade more dim.

"Miss Lateesha Robinson wants to save Social Security." Now that his guest was gone, Roy laid on the sarcasm, practically spitting out her name. "The niggers all want to save Social Security. But it's the Jews who want you to have a number so they can find you when it's time. The Jews have already given your Social Security number to the United Nations and the World Bank."

Rebecca stopped washing dishes at the sink. This kind of talk couldn't have been further from what Rebecca had been raised to believe, but oddly, she found that in the safety of her own kitchen, letting herself go along with what was being said as a kind of joke—an innocent game, really—drew her into the voices on the radio. It was just like when she watched the psychics on cable TV; believing, even though as the wife of a scientist she knew it was ridiculous, made it all the more exciting. So she believed Roy McCurdy for a moment, and suddenly she was one of his powerless Americans fighting against the global conspiracy.

"Folks, I'm here today to say it's mostly too late to do anything about this. The numbers have already been handed out and put on computers, and the white people in this country have all signed up voluntarily. Most of the babies with numbers are white because white people are people with real addresses. But folks, how can we have hope when those same white people with the mailboxes and telephone numbers are stupid enough to follow the government's instructions like sheep? So I ask you all: Why are we numbering all the white babies if the government of the United States of Israel in Washington, D.C., doesn't have a plan to exterminate the white Christian race in America?

"You didn't ask any questions when you got your Social Security card in the mail, did you . . . did you?" Roy paused filling the air with silence, an old radio trick. Rebecca leaned in to the speaker, shaking her head slowly as she did.

"I didn't think so," he said suddenly and louder than before. "You know, people, it's really hard to have any kind of hope sometimes."

Rebecca blushed and then laughed out loud, cutting the silence with her voice. "You're a bad one, Mr. Roy McCurdy."

"Take down our phone number. I'll be right back after a message to tell you how you can get involved in the most important battle since the Revolutionary War. This is KGOG radio, the voice of the free people of the high desert."

Rebecca went back to her dishes during the commercial. She didn't need to take the number. It was committed to memory in the same way soap jingles used to take over her mind when she was a busy housewife stocking the larder for a growing family. The reminders of those days were many, especially when Jack left her alone. She listened to the radio as a distraction from her own memory. Like her trips to the casino, the radio was a staged reality, and she could make her part as big or as small as she wished simply by changing the size of her bet. She could dial the phone number and risk it all or just stay in her kitchen listening. Rebecca thought she might, one day, call. But so far she never had.

"Citizens, free people of the real America. You all know who you are. It is time to do something big." Roy was back. Rebecca turned away from the sink, and leaning on the scarred avocado-green Formica counter, she looked over at the radio as though it were a neighbor gossiping at her kitchen table.

"The problem in America is that people think they are powerless when they're not. You may think that the waves of dark-skinned savages are unstoppable and that you have to just roll over to the communist godless conspiracy to pollute the white race. You may think there is nothing to be done. You may think that if the government wanted you and your family and your property that there would be nothing you could do but toss some harmless firecrackers their way before ending up crispy and dead like David Koresh, or full of federal lead like the people at Ruby Ridge. You may think that just because federal agents shot and killed my own wife—my beloved Ida—you may think that just because the government jackboots kill an innocent woman—the mother of my own child—kill that woman dead, that I would lose hope. But you see, I don't lose hope. Tears I lose every time I look at a picture of my beloved and think about the happiness that we stupidly thought we were free to have in this land. Tears I may lose, citizens, but I do not lose hope."

Rebecca had put down her dishcloth. McCurdy's voice was full of emotion. Rebecca had heard him talk about the death of his wife before, but it seemed different tonight. Maybe it was that she was alone. Maybe it was that she knew his face now with its deep-set wrinkles, the eyes of sadness behind glimmers of anger, and the humiliation on the face of his boy standing there next to his raving father at the casino, the face of a motherless boy. Maybe it was just the gin. Rebecca put a hand to her cheek and felt tears. Her own losses in life had made her feel powerless. She certainly had never thought about her grief in quite this way before. She sat down shivering at her kitchen table of forty years, a table that she had expected would never be empty like this, that she had expected would always be surrounded by the faces and voices of her children and their children. She had to admit to herself that she had lost hope.

"You may think that our enemies have all the money and that there's no way for you to ever catch up. You see them dangling prosperity in front of your face and telling you to work harder, or buy shares from the stock exchange. You watch their entertainers singing and dancing on their television networks. They're good, don't get me wrong. But what they're doing is lulling you into thinking that everything is fine if you just sit there and do nothing." Roy paused again. "You aren't really so stupid that you would believe that, are you?"

McCurdy's voice was almost a whisper. He took a deep breath, aiming his lips at the microphone. Rebecca waited for his big finish.

"You may believe that you are powerless, but just come out of your sleep and think about what you could do if you absolutely had to, if your life depended on it. Maybe you're not so powerless. Maybe, in fact, each one of you quiet souls is actually a fight-to-the-death soldier. I'm willing to bet that some of the things you have around the house are damn good weapons. Look around. You can cook up some serious bang with common household chemicals. I'm not suggesting that anyone actually do anything, of course. Uncle Sam wouldn't like me to do that. So for Uncle Sam who's out there listening, nobody should do anything illegal or dangerous. This is just one of our mental exercises." Roy chuckled. He knew the line that could get the radio station shut down, so he didn't cross it, but because his listeners knew that line just as well, Roy's program was like an elaborately coded language where all the messages were really only about one thing—crossing the line.

"I just want you to think about what you have around the house that might actually help a white people's army. I'm as sure as I sit here that in your house there is something you haven't considered before, something that you may have looked at every day of your life until now without a thought. That object, that idea, the old collection of stamps that may be valuable, something, anything, if you think about it, could be decisive when the battle begins for the liberation of the United States of America. It is time for something big, citizens. If you can think of something like this in your household, you know whom to call. We are not powerless, and the thing is, people, they know it. They know that we can crush them in a moment if white America can only wake up in time. You know whom to call."

Rebecca was surveying her kitchen to find something to help the desperate-sounding man on the radio. It was as though she were back at the roulette table, feeling the thrill of a streak and nervously calculating her largest possible wager. She looked at the hooks for winter hats next to the screen door. She looked at the electric can opener, the refrigerator magnets mostly in the shapes of fruits and vegetables, but there were a few large, round, and metallic magnets that her husband used to bring home from Hanford. These magnets were strong. When he was alive, her son Sam had loved to play with them.

Rebecca looked over at the phone and realized her heart was pounding in her chest. The object in her house that matched McCurdy's description, her largest possible wager, the thing she could least afford to lose yet might be exactly what McCurdy was looking for, was her husband, and his device, Hobby Horse. A life's work, ignored by the government, might now find its true value.

McCurdy was taking a flood of calls now from people who were offering up their Civil War–era pistols they stored down in the basement, metal drums for storing gasoline, old computers, and scrap metal for recycling. A man offered up a pair of diesel-powered generators. One woman had a collection of Elvis photos that she wanted to donate. She didn't know what it was worth, but she said she wanted to make sure it didn't fall into the hands of the people at the Smithsonian. Roy was happy to oblige and repeated the phone number.

"I know you are out there, someone who wants to change the course of history in America. Nobody is more American than a person who believes they can make history. Within your grasp is that power." Roy paused again. "You can change the course of history by simply picking up your telephone."

Rebecca looked at her hand. She was holding the telephone receiver. Her heart was pounding. How could this man be so sure of himself to speak his piece and let the world decide the value of his ideas? It was all her husband had ever wanted—the chance once in his life to show the world what he could do. Unless she picked up the phone, it occurred to Rebecca that Jack might die without ever getting the chance. It didn't matter that this man on the radio was crazy. He might be lucky in a way she had never been. All she would be doing really was placing a bet. She drained her glass. Rebecca's head was dizzy from standing up and walking over to the phone. She knew the number. Her hand dialed it. Rebecca Charnock watched, waiting for another ball to land.

16

Duke McCurdy nudged the throttle forward and eased his way past a flotilla of cement barges headed downstream. The rim of the northern cliffs was pink with the dawn that would not reach the surface of the river for at least fifteen minutes. The air in the shadow of the gorge was cool. The line of cliffs was leveling off, signaling that he was entering high desert country. Stunted and clumped, the trees looked suffocated by the arid basalt rock they somehow clung to. All along this part of the gorge, life argued with stone in somber recitatives that ranged from the dubious to the astonishing. A Douglas fir seedling grew horizontally out of a rock face seemingly devoid of light and runoff, while a lush carpet of wildflowers lived off mossy sediments trapped by an ancient crater far above the riverbank. Duke's eye watched the northward lip of the gorge for the most astonishing of these living outposts, Maryhill Mansion.

Like anyone who ever wondered what the pink castle was doing on the granite lip of the Columbia Gorge, Duke had heard the story of Maryhill. He had heard how it was built by railroad industrialist Sheldon Hale as a gift to the Romanian princess he fell in love with in the late 1800s. According to legend, it was home to her only long enough to give birth to a son, Frank, who grew up and built the dams that changed the lands along the river forever. The princess grew to hate her castle in the desert, and she died lonely and heartbroken, her husband gone on to other conquests, his son soon to follow. Since he had first heard the stories, Duke had thought of Maryhill as one of his stones. It was another erratic, a geologic anomaly like the flood-rounded rocks in his collection, like all of the anomalies clustered around the Columbia River that suggested ancient apocalypse and false paradise. Dropped here by a flood of eastern riches, Maryhill Mansion was the most godforsaken waste of money Duke had ever seen.

Duke steered closer to the bank and saw a rickety dock with a dented aluminum rowboat tied up next to it. A makeshift affair, the dock was held together with wires and smelled of creosote, with none of the elegance of the older carved steps that led from it all the way up the gorge to the house. It occurred to Duke that before the dam flooded this part of the Columbia, there must have been another dock a few hundred yards toward the middle of the river. It was probably still there underwater, Duke thought, mossy and haunted with river creatures, like a piece of Atlantis.

The *Queequeg* idled and inched up to the dock. Duke expertly cut the engine at just the moment to avoid a collision. Duke was worried that he might tear the dock completely away from the shore. He dropped anchor and fixed lines from bow and stern. Just before stepping off onto the dock he saw himself in the mirror in the cockpit and removed his Cleveland Indians baseball cap and hung it on a hook. He made an attempt at adjusting his shaggy red hair. His heart was pounding. He couldn't explain why he was here. Since he had spoken to the woman at Bonneville, she had stayed in his mind. He felt sorry and angry for saying the things he had said. It was a strange physical imperative that summoned him to redeem himself, but each morning since he'd last seen her he had lost his nerve. He clung to what nerve he had left as he pushed this last distance upstream to Francine's door.

Maryhill was almost straight above him, perched on the edge of the cliff as though floating in the low clouds itself. His father would have scouted this place for a kidnapping or a bombing. Duke wondered if he would have even noticed the beauty of the place. Up on the rocks with his back to the river, he felt as though Roy were watching him through crosshairs. Roy would pull the trigger, disgusted that his son was sneaking up to the house of a "brown-skin." He imagined himself falling, wounded and bleeding, back to the water to die on the deck of his boat.

A peacock greeted Duke at the top of the cliff stairs and waddled along with him up the marble steps to the front door. He rang the bell and then looked around at a view so utterly breathtaking that he forgot what he was doing here and why he had come at all. His soul told him he belonged here. Such an expansive view of the world was as far from the suffocating clutter of his father's Airstream as he had ever been.

Duke could see that Maryhill was built at the edge of the rain shadow that separated the lush coastal forests from the high desert. To the left, pink stone from ancient lava stretched to the horizon broken by wind-rounded buttes and mesas that seemed unearthly. In front of him were the volcanic peaks of Mount Adams, Mount Hood, and far to the south, Mount Jefferson. Down below, the Columbia spread out to the left and right, its deep blue framed in pink and green. Streaks of white signified boats. Standing here Duke felt the full force of the river. Everywhere was evidence of the even more powerful forces that tore out the river's channels long ago.

"Pretty nice front yard, and I don't ever have to mow it." Francine's voice startled Duke, and as he turned around he nearly stepped on the peacock. A loud, ugly squawk assaulted the morning tranquility. Francine was dressed in a black linen shirt and gray corduroy trousers that fit tightly on her hips and legs. On her feet she wore delicate soft boots made of light colored leather, expertly stitched with beads and pieces of bone. They rode handsomely up to her mid-calf. "It's Mr. Tommy Liberty," Francine said with a big smile. "Are you collecting for the Four Horsemen of the Apocalypse?" Duke just looked at her jet-black hair, her blue, oriental-shaped eyes, and her dark skin. She was no white woman. It made his heart race.

"I've been listening to you on the radio. I can't tell if you are a great actor or a serious mental case."

"Please call me Duke. The other name is just for the radio."

"I see, you're a half-breed. I'm relieved to know you're a great actor, Mr. Duke McCurdy." Francine looked around. "How did you get here?"

"That's my boat down there." Pointing at it settled his nerves. "It's a beautiful morning to be on the river."

"It's rare these days to have sun. They say it's going to start raining again by the afternoon." Francine looked out at the river again instinctively, noting its level. "High water."

"You can see everything from up here," Duke said, looking back at the view. "I can see how someone would grow up to build dams if they saw this sight every morning."

"They say that in the old days you could hear the roar of the falls up here and smell its spray. Back then there was a spring river, a summer river, a fall river, and a winter river, all different like each day's sky. The dams made it all blue and flat, day in and day out. I don't much care for dams."

"Do you see that outcropping there?" Duke pointed at the ridge of rock on the southwest shore. Francine nodded. "Now look far to your left on this side of the river." Francine leaned out over the stone and marble railing above the black-and-white chessboard tiles on the front veranda. "If you look carefully, you can see an outcropping almost exactly like it, nearly a mirror image there on the opposite bank."

"I see it."

"It's where a twenty-thousand-year-old flood punched through the rock and dug the gorge."

"Very good, Mr. McCurdy. It's also why Maryhill is on this spot. This bend in the river is where the Columbia meets the Cascade Range. The river had to go somewhere, so it made the gorge. My people made this house."

"So the home of the greatest dam builder in this part of the country is on the site of one of the most spectacular natural dam breaks the world has ever known."

"Geology, I understand, Duke McCurdy. The psychology that put this house here is more of a puzzle." Francine motioned for Duke to come inside. "But I've got plenty more mysteries in here if you'll have a cup of tea."

"I hope I'm not disturbing you." Duke stepped through the thick, ornately carved door. "I really wanted to apologize for the things I said the other day."

Francine said nothing and led the way down a wide hall past a room full of black bronze sculpture. "They're Rodins," Francine said matter-of-factly as they walked on. Duke gaped at a brilliantly appointed parlor, a library with bookshelves from ceiling to floor, a room full of old weapons including a coat of arms. "My great-grandmother's," she said, pointing with her thumb as though she had given this tour many times before. Duke noticed that the carpets were faded and in some places worn through; that the carved wooden pieces seemed dulled by soot; and that dust floated through sunbeams, which spiked the darkness from behind red-and-green velvet drapes. But the interior of Maryhill was still impressive. Footsteps echoed in the silences.

Francine led him to a large formal dining room with a massive wooden table and intricately carved beams running the length and width of the ceiling. At one end was a set of swinging double doors. Here Francine turned around. With her hand on the doors she beckoned backward. "I call that the spirit world. In here dwell the living." Through the doors was a big metal-and-tile kitchen that was in serious disrepair and looked straight out of the 1940s. There was a tiny refrigerator and next to it a wall-hung rotary phone. A toaster oven crusted with use sat on the counter next to a set of well-chipped porcelain canisters shaped like smiling pig heads. The ancient-looking range-top stove had a coiled electric hot plate on top of it and a cast-iron teapot steaming away.

"The stove hasn't worked in years. But we don't really need more than this. Fixing things in this house isn't cheap." On the table a large woven basket in the Chinook style contained Francine's personal provisions. She never used the kitchen cupboards. Inside it were bags of rice, a Tupperware container filled with cornmeal, boxes of raisins, and some bread. In plastic bags wrapped with rubber bands were pinkish slabs of dried salmon pemmican. She ate the Indian-style dried salmon meat constantly because it was easy to keep edible, of no interest to mice and insects, and of the Indian foods she grew up with, it was the only one Francine knew how to make herself.

"I can make you a sandwich if you'd like. It's a little early for lunch." Duke said no and thanked her. Francine found as she pulled articles for making tea from her basket, that it comforted her to bring this man into her world behind the velvet, wood, and bronzes. "I'm afraid this kitchen was mainly a place where servants worked. Family didn't generally come in here."

"Have you lived here all your life?" Duke asked. "I figured this house was owned by the BPA."

"Not anymore," Francine said. "It's Indian land now. The BPA handed it over twenty-five years ago when Frank Hale died."

"I was always told this place was haunted." Duke breathed in deeply. The air was scented with the cool breath of Maryhill's porous stone. It was the aroma of old varnish on nineteenth-century beams and the stale smell of abandonment.

"Do you believe such stories?"

"Maybe. If you hear something enough times it's the same as believing it, that's what I know. Ever since I was little we called this the haunted house. Little boys don't need much coaxing to believe in something like that."

"Do I look like a ghost to you?"

"No. The story I heard was that because the place was built on Indian graves when the lady of the house died here a long time ago, Indian spirits made her come back to life every night to walk the upstairs halls searching for her family. They say you can hear her calling for them in an Indian language."

For a moment Francine glanced upstairs to where her mother lay and wondered if she would be proud to be considered so notorious with the local boys. She went back to filling teacups.

"Do you think the people you talk to on the radio really want to start a war against blacks and Jews?"

It made Duke uneasy to have the subject of the conversation shift so abruptly. He was just starting to feel good about being here.

"If they believe it, it's not because of me. Lots of people were raised to believe that kind of thing. It's what they talk about because it's what they know best. I'm not changing anybody's mind."

"So you think talking about Jewish conspiracies and how blacks are subhuman is the same as other people talking about fishing or football?"

"There are radio stations that do those things all day long. It's the way it goes nowadays. Everyone has his own drivel to believe in. Prophets and sports DJs scrawl prophecy and conspiracies all over, and there are more than enough people in the world to give every last one of them a congregation. You can bet there's somebody out there to believe in anything."

"Do you believe all the things you say on the radio about the world?" Francine handed Duke his tea.

He thought for a few seconds. "I believe that there's nothing I can't say on the radio. My daddy always said what was on his mind on the radio. He's got scores to settle with the world. My mother didn't much like this world, and then it killed her. I don't think much about what I say as long as it sounds right. I don't know that much about the world, only about its end."

"It just seems silly to me, all the things you say about conspiracies and racial wars. It makes me laugh sometimes when I listen to what comes over your station."

"It's not so ridiculous, you know, what Tommy Liberty says," Duke said slowly. "For instance, blacks and Jews fighting a war against the white race could happen. Blacks are mad at us. Jews are mad at everyone. If we're going to survive we have to stay madder than them."

"I thought only Indians worried about their survival in America."

"Everyone worries about survival in America." Duke chuckled as he sipped his tea. Francine noticed that as he spoke about these things his jaw locked and he gritted his teeth. "You're taught from the time you're born to believe in the American dream. By the time you die with your fingers bleeding and sore from just holding on, you understand it was never about anything but survival. The American dream is the biggest con in all of world history." Francine thought about that for a moment.

"But you are a Nazi. Why would I have anything to do with you?"

"Because you don't believe that I'm a Nazi." Duke smiled at her. He had not yet said anything to end the conversation.

"You either are or you aren't." Francine got the feeling that he was playing a game with her. "Which is it?"

"It's not so simple. Let's just say that I'm a disappointment to my parents. They wanted me to be just like them. Isn't that what all parents want? What did your parents want you to be?"

"I don't really know." Francine wondered if she would have been a disappointment to her mother or her father. She often wondered what her father would make of her work at the hatchery. Was she saving the salmon there or overseeing their humiliation in some watery reservation, a concentration camp for fish? The thought had crossed her mind. "Maybe trying and failing to be a Nazi is worse than being one."

"Maybe trying is exactly the same as being one."

"So you tried to be like your parents but you failed."

"I'm a disappointment."

"No, just a half-breed." Francine drained her cup and took a long breath, slowly shaking her head as she did. She was drawn to this man. Understanding why made her feel it all the more. "I have to say, for a disappointment, you sound pretty convincing on the radio."

"My mother never heard me on the radio. She died a long time ago." Duke sat quietly, thinking about his mother and sipping his tea.

"Do you believe that this house is haunted?" Francine asked suddenly, shaking free of the memory of her absent father.

"Why do you want to know?"

"Just answer the question."

"No."

"But you're wrong. It is. This is the house I was born in. I am its ghost. Upstairs, my mother is that woman you heard about as a young boy, only she's still alive. The graves on this land are my family's graves. Indian and not."

"So you are one of the Hales?" Duke let Francine explain. He realized he'd made enough mistakes already.

"Frank Hale is my grandfather. His daughter, Mary, is my mother. You have something in common with her."

"What's that?"

"She was a disappointment to her parents, except she didn't try not to be."

Francine motioned for Duke to follow her. They walked back through the long dining room to the wide staircase in the front hall. He ascended into brilliant light streaking through stained-glass windows that caught the desert sun to the east each morning. He looked back toward the front of the house. Through the clear windows above the big carved door was the river again. The contrast of brightly colored sunlight and dark blue water made Maryhill seem like the heaven his mother always spoke of from the Bible. He wished he could see her in such a place now.

At the top of the stairs Mary Hale's nurse had emerged from the sickroom with a tray of bandages and cloths from her patient's morning routine. Francine and the nurse paused in the hallway.

"I'm going to visit with Mother for a while. Please don't disturb us."

"Very good, ma'am." The nurse smiled. It was an occasion when Francine went into her mother's room. "She's doing very well today." Which is what the nurse always said. Francine stood at the door and beckoned for Duke to enter the room.

"This is my mother. As you can see she's quite alive."

Francine touched her mother's frail tiny hand that stopped shaking as her fingers made contact. Save for darting eyes and trembling hands, Mary Hale lay motionless in the center of a metal-frame hospital bed. A bedside table was piled with medicines and lotions and a little makeup kit. On her face were streaks of rouge, her lips were outlined in red, color that her heart no longer provided to yellowing skin. Her expression was frozen but still relaxed, as though she was not exactly miserable in this state. Duke could not tell if this impression was a consequence of the nurse's makeup job or a glimpse within her.

"What do you think she sees?" Duke asked.

"We think she can see and hear everything, but she can't tell us. So we don't quite know." Francine's resemblance to her mother was strongest in her deep blue eyes. The old woman's darted back and forth, alternating between the ceiling and a point across the room on the large carved mantle above an enormous fireplace that hadn't been used in decades.

"Hello, Mother. How are you this morning? Did you sleep well?" Francine peered into her mother's face, seeking eye contact or recognition of any kind. There was none, although Duke could see Francine had long ago stopped expecting it.

"She knows you're here, right?" Duke asked as Francine fluffed up the pillows behind her head.

"She knows that people around her love her; she knows that she's home. Beyond that it's just a guess. For thirty-three years we've all been making guesses about her."

Francine went over to the window pulled back the heavy drapes and flooded the room with sun. It made Mary Hale look smaller and more frail. Her eyes widened in response to the light, and Duke thought he could see her trying to lift and turn toward the window. She had been stunningly beautiful once. Gray highlights shone from long hair that spiraled off her head in an impressive braid and lay coiled by her side, giving her the appearance of royalty. Her hands, pink and crisscrossed with blue veins, were rolled up into fists nearly at right angles to her wrists, obviously atrophied and useless. On the floor next to the bed, a green bedpan indicated both her body's health and her helplessness.

Duke felt sad and was tempted to ask the real story of why

Francine's mother was caught this way between life and death. He had always thought terrifying ghosts roamed the dusty halls of Maryhill when this real woman had been here the whole time. The shame of her helplessness was a more ghostly terror than the stories little boys might conjure in their Halloween imaginations. Francine quietly stroked her mother's hair and adjusted the blanket. Of all the dams on the river her father had built, dams Duke had traversed so many times by boat, it occurred to him that Mary Hale was one more. Behind her eyes a life force seemed to press up against its barrier like the water behind the concrete of the Grand Coulee, arresting the natural path of her life in midstream. The ravages of a life torn from its channel were visible on her wasted body, ravages that a dammed river tastefully concealed beneath its surface. In Francine's blue eyes was the loneliness of a child waiting for answers that never came.

"She nearly died a long time ago. It was when my father disappeared. I don't even know the whole story. Her body was found pretty much like this in the river. No trace of my father was ever found. You can say it was a miracle or a curse that she was revived, but she has not recognized anyone or spoken an understandable word for more than thirty years. She has been like this since the falls vanished."

"Which falls?"

"Celilo. They could once be seen from this window before the Dalles Dam flooded everything up this far. My father fished the falls. There is a picture of him here."

Francine pointed to a black-and-white photo on the dresser of a man standing on a platform holding a wooden pole over rushing white water. The man possessed thick black hair that hung below his shoulders, Francine's other distinctive feature.

"Your mother married an Indian? That's why you're not white." The words left his mouth before he knew what he was saying.

"They didn't exactly get married," Francine responded curtly. "I was hoping that I had more than enough white blood for you, Mr. McCurdy. You seemed to think I did the other day."

"I'm sorry, Miss Smohalla." Duke's face blushed a deep red. "I didn't mean to insult you."

Francine smiled. His reaction to her mixed blood was at least honest. She had never heard an apology from any of the others that concealed their disgust or interest behind silence. "You must be some disappointment to your parents," she said with sympathy. The man's mouth seemed to betray him as often as her eyes did. "Call me Francine." She placed her hand on the old woman's forehead again and gently brushed back a lock of her hair. "I think Mother likes you."

"What is she looking at?" A relieved Duke followed the old woman's eyes from the ceiling to the opposite wall.

"It's hardly visible now, but there is a mural of the old river painted on the ceiling. And over on the mantel she has always looked at Smohalla's bird there. My father left it behind. It's very old."

The carved wooden bird looked like a child's toy as it hung on a wooden rod. Francine twirled it with her wrist and the bird seemed to dance around the rod. Mary Hale's eyes followed the bird's movements. When it came to rest Francine made sure its eyes faced forward toward the bed.

"It's an oriole. The bird came to the prophet Smohalla in a dream on Rattlesnake Mountain long ago and told him the story of how Coyote would free the fishes. Just before he died, Smohalla told the story to the Chinook people. But Coyote did not free the fishes; instead, the dams came. Then Rattlesnake Mountain was fenced off by the Pentagon and became part of the Hanford Nuclear Reservation. Smohalla's prophecy was a bad joke, so the people became angry with him, with my father who was his messenger, and most of all with Coyote. I'm told that my father always believed the prophecy even after the dams came."

"Your mother, too, it seems," Duke said while looking at her face still intent on watching the little wooden oriole.

"*Chalk-uh-lope.*" In a soft voice, slightly hoarse, Mary Hale spoke.

Francine moved back toward the bed.

"*Chalk-uh-lope,*" she said again.

"It's the only thing Mother has ever said since her accident."

"That's interesting that she uses that word," Duke said.

"We think it may be some Indian word my father taught her."

"No, it's Icelandic." Duke walked over to the bed. "*Jokulhlaup,* is that what you are saying, Miss Hale? *Jokulhlaup?*" He said it more slowly the second time.

"Your grandfather must have known the word. It's the Icelandic word for an ice flood. It's the ancient word for what happens after the breakup of an ice dam that frees the water in a frozen lake.

"*Jokulhlaup.*" Francine repeated the word and touched her mother's hand. "So that's the name for what carved out the Columbia River twenty thousand years ago."

"That's what I was trying to tell you about the view from your front door. The evidence of the *jokulhlaup* is everywhere you look."

Duke had gone over to the window. Francine joined him.

"This house is right on the edge of an ancient flood."

"You're saying that this was lakefront property at the end of the Ice Age?"

"Here's something even better." Duke put his hands gingerly on her shoulders. They felt smooth and solid with muscle under her shirt. "The *jokulhlaup* was only the second biggest flood you can see from this window. All that desert rock out there is an ocean of lava four thousand feet deep all the way to Idaho. Your great-granddad built his house next to and on top of two of the biggest floods the earth has ever known."

"They say he was looking for high ground." Francine laughed and leaned back into Duke's chest. She could hear her mother's breathing behind them, calm and rhythmic.

"She's sleeping." Francine's eyes filled with tears. Duke placed his arms stiffly around her. She held them to her and let her head fall back into his shoulder. "I try to imagine not being able to make yourself understood, and just when I think I get it, I remember that she's been like this for more than thirty years. That I have never been able to understand."

"I wonder if there's more."

"What do you mean?"

"More that she wants to say about the *jokulhlaup*."

"I suppose it has to do with how much my father loved the old river, before the dams. It's why she fell in love with him. My mother hated her father. Frank Hale wanted to own the river, to make it his slave. I was always told that's why she took up with a full-blooded Chinook."

"It must have been hard for them to believe that she was really in love with an Indian."

"Why is that?"

"Because Indians are at war with white people."

"Maybe that's why my mother fell in love. She was trying to end a war. While your folks were trying to start one." Francine was speaking to herself now as much as to Duke. After a moment she looked up over her shoulder. "Don't you get sick of talking about wars and the end of the world all the time?" Duke took his arms away and nervously looked over at the clock next to Mary Hale's bed.

"I should go," he said after a moment.

"Do you ever tell your river stories on the radio?"

"No."

"Why not?"

"I think I should go." Duke wanted to return to his boat. It was familiar. This place and this woman were not.

"You sure scare easily," Francine taunted, but only because she couldn't bring herself to ask him to stay. "Maybe that's why you're a disappointment to your father."

Duke stood his ground. "You don't know anything about my daddy."

"Why don't you tell me something? You know about my family, all of a sudden."

Duke went over to a chair near the fireplace and sat down. Francine sat in the chair near her mother's bed.

"When I was growing up, I learned to be scared to see any black face because of how it would just set Daddy right off. It's one of the first things I can remember in my whole life. When I was little and we were living in Seattle, we pulled up to a red light in our old beat-up Dodge cop car. Daddy drove a cop car that had black doors and a white body, where you could still see the sanded-off star on the hood under the rust. On the middle of the backseat where I always had to be, there was a metal speaker for when the cops needed to talk to the criminals they were hauling in to jail, I guess. That old Dodge burned oil and every time we stopped, blue smoke poured in through the windows and made us all sick, which is why Daddy hated to stop at any red lights or stop signs.

"At an intersection one time there was a well-dressed black man in the car next to us. I could see that he was also a father. He was driving a new blue Chrysler New Yorker. I recognized it because it was the kind of big car Daddy always talked about getting. In the back was this little boy in one of those fancy car seats, all strapped in. I was standing on the seat with my arms on the back of Daddy's dirty torn-up headrest.

"I smiled at the kid, and he started to wave just as the smoke from our car begin to blow into his window. He made an awful face. His father looked over at us, and the windows on both sides of his car began to go up. They were electric, the first time I had ever seen electric windows. Little kids are suckers for electric windows. When they were all the way up the boy turned away from me and looked over at his daddy. I noticed right then that my daddy was giving the man the finger. He started screaming about the "real America" and how he had put his life on the line for it. He was swearing and cussing, using all those words he only hauled out for niggers and Jews and my mother sometimes.

"The light turned green, so Daddy stepped on the gas to pull ahead, and as he did he deliberately swerved into the side of the car, putting a nasty gash on the Chrysler's right front fender as we roared away. I don't remember much else. I was thrown back and hit my head hard on the speaker. The last thing I saw was that little boy looking at me as I flew through the air. He was my enemy now, the first enemy my daddy ever made for me. Then my head cracked against that metal thing and I was knocked out. Daddy didn't stop swearing and yelling at that man in the Chrysler until we were almost home. When I came to, I realized that he'd started yelling at me for getting blood all over the backseat. I couldn't move. I can only remember staring at the ceiling of the car, feeling the warm blood from my head drip around my ears, dreaming of how safe that little boy must have felt there in his car seat.

"My daddy taught me to look for enemies. I always found them. I never hated the niggers and Jews the way Daddy did. He just made them my enemies. I scare easily for a reason."

"And your mother?" Francine nearly whispered.

"She taught me about the rocks, the desert, and most of all, the river. She called it a river that went out of Eden, like in the Bible. She loved this land. She used to tell me that out here you can see the end of the world and its beginning wherever you look." Duke put his head in his hands. "She's been gone a long time now."

They sat in silence. The only sound was Mary Hale's breathing and an airplane engine off in the distance. Finally Francine stood up and went over to where Duke was sitting. She placed her hand on the scar, which she could see clearly now on the back of his head, and pulled him gently to his feet. Duke placed his hands on her shoulders. What was forbidden and dangerous was not impossible, he thought. Trees could grow from wind-scoured rock like the walls of the gorge. As Duke closed his eyes and searched clumsily for her lips, he could feel his body surrendering. Her hand coasted down the curve of his lower back. Her lips were wide and smooth, and they swam over his, giving him the sensation of breathless headlong motion without end.

As he walked, carrying her down the hall, her legs locked around his hips, her arms on his neck, he watched only her eyes. Under the loose shirt he could feel her breasts roll with the rhythm of his footsteps. Now he stood alone in her room as she closed the door. He reached her bed and looked down below to a boiling ocean of woolen counterpane and sheets that wrapped him in the smell of what was about to happen: the power of wanting her, the sensation of her touch as she freed his body from his clothes, the sureness of her hand guiding him, their motions parallel in the way a deep current finds its pathway downward, commanded by momentum and gravity.

Francine thrilled to his surrender. Her hands brought him inside her and guided his face to her neck and breasts. The weight and solid urgency of his bones and muscle relaxed her. She pressed her face into his chest, felt him find her center and push beyond; this man had made her feel safe. She had made him, if only for a moment, brave. They were pieces of a flood tossed up on dry land. They belonged together, Francine thought, because they were torn apart. Duke looked deep into her eyes and buried his hands in her thick black hair.

"They have always betrayed me, my mother's eyes," she whispered.

"Hate betrays me," Duke whispered back. "Who can escape his tribe?"

"We have escaped already." Francine wiped his shiny forehead with her cheek. "There are no tribes anymore, only names. Coyote says names are at war with the world over all that has been lost since the beginning of time. That's why they betray us."

"I don't really hate the world, you know." He looked away from her as he said it. Francine saw shame on his face.

She whispered, "I know. I don't really hate my mother's family. They did what they had to do. They created a new world out of one that was dying. Now I feel that world is nearing some end. I'm afraid of what comes next."

Duke looked back at her. "You don't have to be afraid of what comes next," he said, "of this I am sure."

Spent and drifting into sleep, they lay in Maryhill's velvet daylight until night fell. The moon through the window awakened Francine for a moment. She looked over at Duke sleeping peacefully next to her and wondered if her father had been as nervous about being in this house, and then as comfortable. She mouthed the word *jokulhlaup*. On her face were joyful tears to know anything of what her mother was dreaming after a lifetime of missing the faint signal. She looked over at the tranquil face of Duke. She kissed him silently. Perhaps *jokulhlaup* was an Indian word after all, she thought—it's how Coyote freed the fishes.

17

Near Route 11A Duane Madison was well away from the river. The rain was making him nervous, as was the fact that he hadn't seen the sun for more than a week. Everything had been making him nervous since badly mutilated bodies wearing federal uniforms had started showing up along the river. In the shadows he saw strange intruders. He hadn't been able to shake the feeling of being watched since the first body had been found, but the rain was his worst problem now. The sensors around his high-level waste pens indicated that there was more than enough groundwater to support migration of some of the nastiest substances known in the universe. In the 200 area the cold war was still warm. There was more high-level nuclear waste here than any other piece of real estate outside of Chernobyl. When it rained, the waste liked to move, splashing into the air, vaporizing in the chilly humid atmosphere like warm breath or soaking into the saturated soil, moving, like everything, toward the Columbia.

Duane Madison knew his sludge was on the move because he could hear the sirens from the groundwater alarms. They sounded like idiotic car alarms after a Saturday night of vandalism in Seattle, but here the sound actually meant something. There were three levels of sensors in the 200 area. Sirens signified level one, along with white strobe lights, warning of the presence of surface water. Level two actually activated pumps when the water level around the concrete basins exceeded their maximum. The pumps skimmed surface water off the top of the basins and pumped it into another tank where it would be tested for toxins and radioactivity and then finally pumped into a waiting basin. The basin was built for storing such contaminated rainwater and all the dead animals and birds regularly found wandering confused and sick all over the 200 area. Level three warned of an imminent explosion. There had never been a level-three incident at Hanford.

Duane checked his instruments. All eight pumps had been tripped overnight. He stepped outside for a moment to assure himself that the pump motors were whining along with the alarms. Yesterday it had been only three pumps. Federal regulations required that there be a noisy alarm system to warn of the obvious. With the weary disgust unique to federal workers of the modern era, Duane wiped the cold rain that the sirens were shrieking about off his face. Duane wondered why he wasn't just another form of nuclear waste after all his years at Hanford.

'Cause I work cheap, he thought. I'm too valuable. Duane glanced for a moment at the dosimeter on his vest. The "safe" stripe was green as always. He looked out toward the cluster of buildings nearest to him. Everything was quiet except for the alarms. Far beyond in the 400 area, a pair of headlights was moving. It was the only activity he could see, and even it was unsettling. Before Hanford was a nuclear reservation, Madison knew it had been a home to river Indians. Since the murders began, it seemed as though their spirits were returning to be among the nasty chemicals that Madison worked to contain. Every light seemed sinister. In the distance, light reflected off the eerie, greenish, spectral dome of the FFTF, the only operational research reactor that had so far managed to avoid landing in the vast techno–garbage dump Hanford had long ago become.

He wondered what the Indians from long ago would think to come back and find their world looking this way. Maybe they were looking at it even now. A Hendrix tune came to mind about aliens returning to Earth only to find the stars in the wrong places and everything burnt. It seemed to describe perfectly Hanford and the Indians he was certain haunted the place.

Duane sang to himself as he watched the headlights around the green dome of the FFTF reactor. At least it was up and running. It could produce electricity and had its own little node on the northwest power grid. It also contained real enriched plutonium, the hot stuff: Pu-239. FFTF was an authentic breeder reactor, the only one in the United States and the pilot project for a multibillion-dollar reactor program called Clinch River that had been canceled back in the eighties. The plan for FFTF was to recycle all the spent fuel at Hanford into weapons. During the cold war you needed to be one of the warhead-delivery boys with a level six, the highest DOE security clearance, to even step on the FFTF parking lot. But there was no use for FFTF anymore. It was a radioactive keepsake from the cold war's trillion-dollar science fair.

Every once in a while they used the reactor to test space-shuttle parts and materials for satellites or occasionally some unfortunate creature was loaded into the center of the reactor and bombarded with radiation to see what happened. Duane had once been inside FFTF to interview for a job. They asked him polite questions about fission containment, implosion yield, and if he'd ever seen a thermonuclear detonation, then never called him back. Duane was a former police detective, a nuclear chemist, an expert in hazardous-material security, but he had never seen a bomb. At FFTF Hanford's old pecking order still ruled. Chunky, buzz-clipped nuke boys in white shirts who smoked too much, drove Oldsmobiles, and still dreamed of building bombs were the lost aristocracy at Hanford. You could find them here and there, parking their immaculately maintained cars in the few reserved spaces left over from the seventies. They were like old generals—proud, irrelevant, and nearly extinct. The tables had turned. It was the nuclear garbage men such as Duane who got paid the most and infested Hanford like high-tech rats.

He walked back inside and opened the equipment closets near his office. There were boxes of clean tools and sealed hazardous materials suits enough to equip a team of ten. "We all work too damn cheap," Duane said aloud to one of the empty helmets hanging on the rack. The price of one of the HAZMAT suits nearly equaled his salary. "Use once and throw away, except for us reusable parts." There was going to be a lot of overtime if this rain ever stopped. Records indicated that the last time it had rained this bad at Hanford was back in 1948, when the number of sheep around here outnumbered the tons of nuclear waste and when all the rain-related headaches were far downstream near Portland. Back then, Vanport, Oregon, was lost, torn from the ancient riverbed and scattered downstream like pillow feathers from a shotgun blast.

When the rain finally stopped, and the extent of the seepage was known, the real work would begin. The pumps would be designated low-level waste and scrapped the moment the sun came out, regardless of how well they worked. According to the stacks of regulations, they were to be pulled up, sealed in concrete, and disposed of at only a slightly lower urgency than the evil sludge in the high-level basins they were formerly protecting. It meant that Duane and one of his crews would put on their sealed HAZMAT suits and, with a pair of forklift trucks and a crane, reinstall and test eight brand-new half-million-dollar pumps. The sensors had to be reset, every bit of data recorded hourly, each teaspoon of liquid accounted for, and each activity exhaustively cataloged in an EPA incident report that could easily run to five hundred pages if the rain kept up.

All this took most of a week, and when it was done, the crane, the forklifts, and a week's worth of toxic suits were all trucked out to the 200 east pit to be dumped with the barely used pumps and every tool, bolt, sock, handkerchief, coffee stirrer, and Styrofoam cup Madison and his crew had generated. Each piece of debris got a federal number and became part of the EPA report. Copies were made and hurriedly sent off to Washington where they were filed away in a less toxic but only slightly more orderly dump: the National Archives.

The regulations authorized replacement purchase of sixteen more pumps. Each big rainstorm at Hanford meant another $10 million to the defense contractor who made the devices, the same contractor whose name was on the desk calendar in Madison's office, the pens he wrote with, the contractor who sent computerized Christmas cards to his family each year. Duane got lots of Christmas cards from companies inside the beltway that he presumed prayed for rain or even more lucrative disasters out at Hanford.

He thought the buzzer was another alarm at first, until he heard the voice on the intercom. Duane walked toward the door. Sheets of raindrops swarmed through the porch lights as he snapped them on and opened the inner door. A man who appeared to be in his sixties wearing a felt hat straight out of an old movie stood squinting into the thick glass of the outer window.

"I'm afraid I've taken a bad turn here in the dark. Is this the two hundred area?" he said over the intercom.

Duane looked out at the headlights of a vehicle parked a few hundred feet away. They were angled upward, which suggested that his vehicle was already in a ditch. "You look like you might need a tow."

"Well, yes . . . I tried a bit to rock her out, but it's very muddy. If I could just make a phone call, perhaps."

"I don't know who you would call. I'm it around here until the morning crew comes on. Now, could I see some authorization, Mr. . . . ?"

"Yes, Charnock, Jack." He fumbled around in an old plastic litterbag stuffed with papers. "Here we go." He handed Duane a clear-plastic Hanford clip-on badge holder, thick with ID's and parking-authorization slips, and struck the cheerless pose Hanford's relentless checkpoints made a habit for all employees. Duane scanned the old badges. This guy had been around here a long time. On top was a current photo tag identifying him as Jack L. Charnock, scientist. The badge was purple, level six. Duane whistled.

"About the only thing you can't use this for is getting out of the mud," he said as he pulled his raincoat off the hook and stepped outside. "Come with me. I'll pull my truck around. It's a big one. We'll get you taken care of."

Inside the DOE truck, equipped with winches and sampling equipment for dealing with all of the special circumstances of Hanford, such as getting a flat tire in a hazardous waste dump, Duane could see that with his soggy hat off, Jack L. Charnock, scientist, was almost completely bald. He was a large pink-faced fellow with a big mole on the left side of his forehead. There were two sets of glasses on his head. A large pair sat on the top of his forehead and what appeared to be a pair of narrow reading glasses rested on his nose. His shoes were caked in mud. Duane gunned the engine and pulled out of the parking lot. "You work down at FFTF?" Jack Charnock nodded.

"I thought all they did over there anymore was zap gerbils with neutrons."

"Not exactly." Charnock's voice betrayed the sting of knowing that the old bomb-building days were over at Hanford and that his line of work was more footnote than topic sentence. "There are certainly cheaper ways to kill small animals. You could feed them grass from out back of your building." Charmock had only contempt for the 200 area and its garbage pits. He represented the original wartime mentality, the old nuke hustle where all that mattered were bombs and fighting Communism, and the other details were trivial. To Duane, Charnock was a Manhattan Project adrenaline addict looking for another war, another fix, oblivious to the trail of destruction he and his kin had left behind.

"My work is fuel design. The only honest job left out here," Charnock said proudly. Duane tried not to laugh.

"You one of the pellet men, then?" Duane had seen hundreds of reactor fuel rods with their pellets of spent uranium that sat in the eerie blue water of the high-level waste pools. "Pellets, sure. I've done some U two-thirty-eight design." Charnock sounded as though working with uranium interested him about as much as cleaning latrines. "But my specialty is the larger shapes, the rings, hemispheres, and cylinders, all the stuff you can make with Pu two-thirty-nine."

"Plutonium?" No wonder he had the level-six clearance, Duane thought. "Then I'm surprised you're working at all." Since the eighties Hanford and Savannah River's weapons plant in Georgia had shut down all plutonium production. With the cold war over, no one needed plutonium for weapons, and because it made such a good weapon, Pu-239 cost more to protect from theft than it was worth producing electricity.

"I don't do it for the money. Plutonium-fuel design is the chance to work with a genuine miracle."

Duane looked at him doubtfully. Plutonium had produced more environmental cliff-hangers than miracles at Hanford. All of Duane's Gomorrah-sized waste pits involved plutonium. "It's going to be some miracle if they ever clean it up out here. That's for damn sure."

Charnock began shaking his head and cupped his hands as though he was cradling a small bird. "Son, with all due respect, you're a garbage-man. All you've ever seen are rusted reactor cores and scorched, crumbling uranium pellets that look like dog food. Pu two-thirty-nine is like no other substance on earth. It's a real metal, but it can be hard like quartz, soft like pewter, or sticky like wax. It has five distinct states between its solid form and its ultimate melting point. Plutonium burns like paper at room temperature but when heated, unlike any other metal, it contracts rather than expands. It can be molded into perfectly detailed impressions finer than bronze without machining. In flat sheets it is stronger than stone, but formed into a sphere as an alloy with the rare metal gallium, it begins to throw off neutrons, becomes hot to the touch, goes critical, and left alone replays the first few moments of the universe right before your eyes."

Duane liked this guy. He was a true Hanford original—brilliant, raving, obsolete. "It's also poisonous and radioactive with a half-life of about twenty-four thousand years. Are you by any chance working on a line of designer jewelry?"

"Great question." There was a gleam in Charnock's eye. His voice rose to recite a speech Duane felt sure he'd given before but which still moved him. "All metals are poisonous. Plutonium is no different. All so-called precious metals are useless. Plutonium two-three-nine is unique in human history. It is the first substance we have created on this planet that wasn't here when we arrived. Everything else is something we mixed up or burned up. Plutonium is what I call the philosopher's stone."

"Then I call it the most toxic headache and mess any philosopher ever produced in human history."

Duane chuckled and backed his sleek, muscular Department of Energy four-wheel rig up to Charnock's van, which was so covered with mud, it was impossible to tell what color it had been before sliding down in the ditch. Charnock pointed to the rear wheels. "The right one is pretty well dug in." Duane wasn't worried. "I've got a bunch of chains in the bed," he said. "We'll tie down to the rear axle."

Charnock opened his door, and abruptly the sirens made him stop and listen. He looked nervous. "Did those alarms just begin?"

"They've been going for two days now. It's the rain," Duane reassured the befuddled-looking scientist. "Don't worry, it's not an air raid. This is just a low-level incident. You're in the two hundred area, Mr. Charnock. We got nothing like all that hot-and-steamy, weapons-grade material you folks work with."

Charnock grabbed a chain and began to wrap it around the rear frame. Duane joined him after a moment and secured a second chain around the axle. "Watch where you step," he told Charnock. "Stuff's on the move around here. It's what tripped the alarms." Charnock was standing with his head uncovered. The rain was pouring unimpeded over his face. He shouted, "I love rain! It kills the dust!"

"You're one crazy fucker," Duane said, but Charnock was right about the dust. It was everywhere at Hanford, much of it radioactive and all of it virtually undetectable. Rainwater was something the Feds could at least watch. Duane opened the back of Charnock's van, stepped up onto the bumper, and peered under it. He could see that it was carrying a heavy load of some kind. The wheels were deep in the mud. He looked around and saw four strange-looking padded boxes. Inside each one was a shaped and padded lining like an exotic egg crate made to hold something besides eggs. One was full of baseballs; another, of golf balls. The others were closed and, it appeared, locked.

"Looking at my homework?" Charnock's voice startled Duane.

When he turned around, Charnock's steaming breath was in his face. It smelled of coffee and the cherry lozenge he was sucking on. "You coach Little League or something?" Duane asked as he climbed down. "No," Charnock said. "Just like baseballs, that's all."

Duane reached down to touch one of them and then thought better of it. Charnock was still standing near him. The red of the taillights made his mouth and eyes look black and empty, like a doll's.

"The golf balls I like because of their physics. I don't play," Charnock said.

This load of odds and ends alone could hardly be responsible for sinking the rear axle of the van into the mud, but Duane didn't want to hang around in the rain to figure it out. Duane secured the chain and climbed down.

"Now get up front and steer us out while I pull," Duane said. He walked up onto the roadway, feeling the chain for loops or knots, when his foot caught a smooth chunk of granite and slipped out from under him. Down on his knees in the water, Duane slid like a fish down into the ditch where he was swallowed up to his elbows by the muck under Charnock's van. The alarm sirens and the engines of the two vehicles drowned out his voice, and all he could do was wait while the cold water soaked through his pants and boots.

"Charnock!" Madison screamed, but there was no answer. The sirens gave him the creeps and reminded him just what the rain-filled ditch might be carrying out of the 200 area tonight. The door to the truck opened. Duane hoped Charnock was looking for him. But the voice that came out of the cab was from the radio turned up loud.

"This friends, is the opening battle in the final subjugation of the white race."

Charnock was stumbling around. He could hear nothing but the radio. He had turned it up and leaned over on the passenger side to see where Madison had gone, and stopped moving when he heard the voice of a woman.

"Am I on?"

"Hello, ma'am. You are on the air. How are you going to help the good Christian people of this nation tonight?"

"I'm sorry. I've never called a radio program before. I guess I'm a little bit nervous."

"That's all right. Everyone gets nervous at first. Just tell us what's on your mind."

The woman laughed, but only out of politeness. "I have something, or my husband does, something that I think you will be very happy to have."

"Can you tell me about it?"

"It's not really something I should talk about on the radio. I'm sure my husband would be upset if he heard me talking to you. Maybe if you give me your address I could send you some information. This is something my husband has worked so hard on, and the government doesn't realize what a wonderful man he is, how much he has done for this nation."

"He's a government worker, is he?"

"Yes, for more than forty years. It just breaks my heart how much he has given to this country, and you know, they never have taken him seriously."

"Well, ma'am, I don't have a lot of time left in the program to talk about unhappy government workers. Does he work down at the Social Security office, too?"

"No, he's from Hanford." The way she said it brought tears to Jack Charnock's eyes. He was listening to the voice of a woman he had once courted, who had once looked into his eyes as he explained the things he would do in his life, the woman who would hold his hands and say she wanted to ride along wherever he would go. He had not heard his wife speak in that voice for decades, since long before his children died. It was the voice he was listening to now.

In the silence after she said *Hanford*, Jack just stared at the radio, his hands on his face soaked with tears. Duane Madison shouted up at

Charnock, who looked down to see clods of mud Duane was heaving out from under the van to get his attention. He got down on one knee and spotted Duane just behind one of the wheels.

"What are you doing down there?" he asked.

Duane screamed for Charnock to get a rope off the truck.

Charnock seemed to be in a trance. He was half oblivious to Duane, helpless under the truck and wallowing around in a pool of potentially radioactive mud. Charnock turned back to the radio to listen.

"Still here, ma'am, and we're going to take a break now, and I want you to stay on the line so I can get some information. But I thank you so much for calling, and I'm sure your husband out there will be very happy you did. It's twenty-three minutes past the hour here on KGOG: all the real news without all the Jews."

Slowly, Charnock reached over and switched the radio off. He wiped his eyes and once again stared down at Duane Madison, realizing for the first time that Duane had been helplessly stuck for several minutes.

"I'm so sorry. I didn't see you slip." Charnock reached Duane a length of rope.

"I thought I had lost you," Madison said as Charnock lifted him out of the mud. He was as strong as he was clumsy. As he brushed the mud off himself as best he could, Madison eyed this strange bull of a man wearing two pairs of glasses. "What in the fuck were you listening to?"

"It's some religious program. I usually pay it no mind, but I thought I recognized a voice. I'm sorry."

"I thought you were going to have a Nazi prayer meeting right there in front of your radio." Duane was more incredulous than he was irritated. "I'm screaming for help, lying in this nuclear slime, and a nuclear physicist has got the Aryan Nation's greatest hits blasting all over Hanford."

"I'm sorry, I've got nothing against your race. I wasn't thinking." Charnock seemed to have no idea what he was listening to and looked as though he'd seen a ghost. "It's about the only station that comes in out here. They talk about the UN mostly. I don't really pay much attention."

"Excuse me?" Madison shook his head. "Don't you know who those lunatics are?" Charnock's face was blank. "I'm afraid I don't." Charnock looked slightly embarrassed.

Duane walked back toward his truck and shouted back at Charnock. "They're just about the stupidest people you're ever going to find out here. And who are you, some kind of plutonium salesman or a sensitive environmentalist who wants to save all the plutonium on the planet?"

"Really, I'm sorry."

"It's all right. Let's just get out of here." Duane started his engine and with his head out the window, he guided the van out of the ditch. The chain creaked with the strain of the van's weight, but after a moment Charnock's van was squarely on the road, caked with mud but drivable. The scientist ran over to Duane's window.

"Thanks again. I was really stuck there without you."

"Don't mention it." Duane was wet and cold now.

"And you were right about me."

"How's that?"

"That is what I am, an environmentalist for plutonium. Not many people know that about me. We could be friends."

Duane chuckled though he wasn't sure if the man was joking. "We love visits from environmentalists over here in the two hundred area. Nice meeting you, Mr. Charnock. See ya around."

Back inside his office Duane stripped down and put on a new pair of coveralls. He was soaked to the bone. As he stepped into the shower, he tossed his clothes into a laundry pile and noticed that the dosimeter still pinned to his shirt was no longer green. He reached down for a closer look. It was bright red. He had taken a full dose of something. Duane went over to the cabinet and grabbed the Geiger counter and waved it over the wet clothes. There was nothing. Duane was confused. The counter registered no radiation on any of the mud, his hands, face, even his boots were clean. It was a relief that he hadn't been wallowing around in a waste pit but still the dosimeter was bright red. He'd never seen it like that.

"Bloody rain," Duane muttered to himself as he stepped into the shower. He scrubbed himself thoroughly and painfully. The alarms were sounding in the background. The dosimeter thing was peculiar. Charnock was peculiar. Madison stepped from the shower and dried himself off. As he did, he walked over to his computer and scanned the staff list at Hanford for the name. It wasn't there. He searched again, wider this time, and found it three times. The first and largest entry, was about a Harold Charnock: one of the routine underlings on the original Manhattan Project. Special Isotope Team. Injured in 1952, he became his own special research project. The Radioactive Man. The next largest entry was for Samuel Charnock, killed in 1974 during the pouring of concrete for WPPSS Number Three plant. He was nineteen. An investigation had been inconclusive.

Jack's entry was smallest and last. He had worked at the same division at Hanford for more than forty years, but all that was noted in his record were two promotions, the last for perfect attendance. Madison realized why he hadn't found Jack's file on the first pass. He had been recently moved to the retired list. The decision had been made the week before, to take effect in a few days when his many badges would also expire. Madison thought it odd that he hadn't mentioned it. He looked over other details in Charnock's file. He was technically a waste-disposal engineer, but he had worked the longest on an obscure weapons program called Hobby Horse. The small plutonium-bomb project had been suspended quite a while ago, according to the records. Madison noted with some surprise that Mr. Charnock had responsibility over a small quantity of weapons-grade Pu-239. There was almost no weapons-grade plutonium left at Hanford. The old production reactors were shut down, and all the fabrication plants had been mothballed after the Soviet Union collapsed.

Madison looked out the window to his office. The gray obscured the riverbank and shrouded the old reactors clustered along the Columbia. The 100 area where the original Hanford reactors were was one of the few places it was safe to walk around without a suit on. Madison often took his lunches out there. His favorite place was a picnic table at the old B reactor, built in 1945, where the original plutonium for the Nagasaki bomb was made. The reactor had been stripped and sealed. But there was a plaque on the locked front door declaring that the B reactor was on the National Register of Historic Places. There were no plaques on Madison's high-level waste tanks. There was no need. Pu-239, the most famous toxic element at Hanford, had a half-life of twenty-four thousand years. It would easily outlast the recorded history of any nation on earth. The Hanford 200 area would be a historic place as long as humans had the good sense to avoid it. In his mind Madison tried to imagine the volume and weight of the stockpile of Pu-239 the records said had been allocated to the Hobby Horse project. It was supposed to be housed at the FFTF reactor, but it occurred to Madison that such a quantity would not be terribly difficult to move.

There was one non-nuclear building in the 200 area. It was a ruin, a ghostly old white barn from one of the farms that was bought out when the Pentagon bomb makers came. It was still standing, defying the desert wind. *Only a real historic landmark could survive this hell,* Madison thought. He couldn't see the little shed as he looked out his dim windows, but he knew it was there. There had been prairie grass, fruit trees, and struggling wheat fields here once. Those long-dead farmers would have wept with joy to see this rain. He peered into the fog. Every shadow looked like a figure running into the darkness. Madison blinked and turned away from the window to watch his instruments. He listened to the honking of the alarms, twiddled the crimson dosimeter nervously between his fingers, and prayed for the rain to end.

18

For a week Duke's presence at Maryhill had transformed it for her into a real place. It was as though time itself had sat up, stirring the ancient dust. On the morning of their seventh day together, Francine could feel something was wrong. She awoke to the sound of rain against the window. Duke was standing next to the bed. His foot was on a chair, tying one of his boots. He wore no shirt. When Francine looked up, he stopped what he was doing and sat down on the mattress.

"Where will I find you?" she asked.

"I'm taking the *Queequeg* up to Richland. My father will be wondering where I am."

Francine pulled herself up to a sitting position and let the blankets fall away from her body. In the overcast light of thick rain clouds, her skin looked almost black against the white sheets.

"The river is rising. I need to beat the barge traffic." Duke stood up and walked to the other side of the room where his shirt was. "I'll call you."

"Why do you look like I'll never see you again?"

"I'll be coming downriver in a day or so. I dock at Astoria, a place called Goose Point Marina."

Duke was all business.

Francine pulled the blankets up over her shoulders. "You are afraid of something—what?"

"Not at all. I said my father will be worried."

"Worried, why? That you'll go soft if you spend too much time with a half-breed?"

"It's not like that." Duke pulled on his shirt.

"It was just a joke," Francine said. "Would you like some breakfast before you go?"

"No, thank you. I'll get something on the road."

"Your father is against quiet breakfasts?"

"He's against quiet. Breakfast is okay."

"And you?"

"My father is different. He's like someone off the boat from the old country, except my father dreamed up the country he's from, and we're its only two citizens, and we have no intention of coming to America. Ordinary things like quiet breakfasts make no sense to him."

"Is that what your coming here was—ordinary?"

"No." Duke blushed deeply. He looked up at the ceiling. "It's not ordinary. We're not ordinary. But we're not part of his plan. Outside of that world nothing exists for my father. My father doesn't even know what I do. I grew up thinking everybody like me lived in trailers and made plans for war. I learned about the river from my mother's stories about the end of the world. I learned about boats only because when I was a kid I went to the boat races alone. Roy's never seen the *Queequeg*. He hates that I spend any time on the river."

"Maybe he needs to manage without you for a while."

"He can't. He's not like other people. He'll just get himself killed, and I can't be responsible for that."

"Then I'll go home with you now, and he'll see that you have your own plans."

The idea of walking through the doors of the trailer and introducing a woman, this woman, to Roy had never occurred to Duke. It made him sad and more anxious to leave.

"Francine, my father is not someone you want to tangle with. He's the real thing. He doesn't need to look at the calendar to decide what to do. When the world didn't end on January first, 2000, my father wasn't disappointed; he took it as more evidence that the job was his."

"Then turn him into the police if you think he's that dangerous."

"But I can't even do that. In America what my father does is legal. Give him a gun, put him in an office, he's just another slightly eccentric coworker. Until he does something to end the world, Roy McCurdy is a free man."

"Legal or not, you would never turn him in." Francine could see that Duke had no choice in the matter. He would have to honor his father.

"I would never turn him in. He's all I've got."

Francine put her arms around him and buried her head in his chest. "So there is no freedom for Duke McCurdy?"

"I think freedom begins after my father ends the world. There hasn't been much freedom in this one."

"You still believe in him, even though you know he's wrong?"

Duke turned away, stung that the source of his misery and loneliness were so evident. "I forget that you just weed out and throw away all of the defective salmon you find in your fish tanks. You don't understand. I can't explain it. Fathers answer to strange forces from worlds far outside the home. By the time you understand them, you realize that they are the same forces that move you. I can be angry with my father, but I can't deliberately hurt him. I would be a freak of nature if there wasn't somewhere inside me where I believed in him totally."

Francine sat back on the bed. "I wish I could say that what moved my father moves me. The emptiness is what hurts. In a way, you're lucky."

"Maybe I am," Duke whispered, and grabbed her hand.

Francine wanted him to know that she understood things. "You know, you're wrong about the salmon. I don't throw away the defective ones. They're the most anxious to make it into the river. I think sometimes that it's the defective fish that lead all the rest to sea out of a pure force of desire. Each salmon is a freak of nature, capable of swimming up waterfalls and navigating thousands of miles by stars they can never see clearly. The salmon do what they don't understand, what they can't possibly understand. They do it without ever questioning their absurd fate to swim upstream and die."

"What do they think of your hatchery tanks?"

"I don't know. Sometimes I think the concrete walls confuse them. They know they should be in the river. Sometimes I think they blame me, that they hate me. But I believe they do something even more maddening—they forgive me." Francine was weary from this lifelong confusion. She really didn't know why she took care of the salmon. It certainly wasn't an interest in biology. She knew it hurt her to stay near the river, yet there was nowhere else to go.

Duke picked up his jacket and moved as if he were about to leave. "You live in a castle; I live in a trailer. Look at your mother for what happens when wrong people get together."

Francine flung down her blanket. "America is a nation of half-breeds and strange combinations. Look at me. Aren't I what happens when wrong people get together?" Duke started to embrace her, then shook himself free and stepped into the doorway. Francine could see that something in him did not want to leave.

"Look, I'll come back. It's not what you think." He pointed to the window. "I think there's trouble on the river. Let me go and settle some things. I would love to find a way for you to have your world back. That's a promise." He stepped through the doorway, and Francine listened to every step as he made his way down. She heard the creak of the large front door. She pulled on a robe and stepped to the window to watch his boat pull away from the dock. As she watched the river out her window, she could see that something was indeed different on the water. Francine observed the *Queequeg* nose out into a visible downstream current. She grabbed a pressed uniform from her closet and ran downstairs to the kitchen. Out on the river a pattern of waves had replaced the water's normally smooth surface: The waves branched like spokes off a steel beam that stretched out as far as she could see in both directions. Midriver, the dredged shipping channel was moving faster than the shallows, a river within a river.

Francine was certain Hermiston had opened the dams even before she arrived at Bonneville. Driving into the hatchery parking lot the air was heavy with spray from water falling through the spillways. This was serious runoff, and it was raining heavily.

"How long do you plan to continue this, Bud?" Francine got him on the line the moment she arrived at the hatchery. She was still wearing her coat as they began to argue.

"As long as I need to, Francine. A routine drawdown to meet seasonal targets is nothing to be concerned about."

"The other day you told me that opening the dams was impossible, now they're flat open."

"I didn't say anything was impossible. You said you were looking for fast water for your baby fish. Now you've got it. Why are you griping at me?"

"You know exactly why. Open like this, the dams are death to the salmon. I'm due to release the whole hatchery tomorrow. Without drivers to take them downstream I'll lose every fish."

"Then make more fish, or find a way to make yourself some more drivers. At least the dams aren't killing them."

"Did something happen upstream?"

"Let me worry about what's going on upstream. There is nothing about this that isn't completely routine, so get back to your fish and leave the river to the experts."

She hung up. She was angry with McCurdy for being such a coward. She was angry at whoever was doing the killings. She was angry at Hermiston's power over everything. She was angriest of all with the Indian people who seemed content with the murders. Everything had been thrown into confusion. With no drivers, Francine's only option was to release the fish directly into the river. If they weren't killed in the turbines and spillways, nitrogen churned into the river by the violent turbulence and spray would poison them. Any hatchlings that survived would be too weak to avoid the creatures that lay in wait for tasty, defenseless baby salmon.

She looked out the window of her office. There were two transport trucks parked. One, stained with blood, was still a crime scene covered with yellow police tape that fluttered in the wind. The other, larger truck was idle. She walked out to it through the rain.

Inside the cab she oriented herself to the controls. Driving the vehicle would be the main challenge. Pumping the fish in and out and keeping them alive for the trip—that part she knew well. She had helped design most of the equipment. The keys were on the seat. She started the engine and sat looking at the transmission. When she was reasonably sure she had found first gear, she moved the shift lever and let out the clutch. The cab lurched forward and then settled down. She was moving.

There was not enough room in the parking lot to practice putting the truck into second gear. She would just have to take her chances out on the road. Fortunately she could maneuver the tanker close to the hatchery transfer equipment without having to deal with reverse. She parked and walked back toward the hatchery tanks.

The fish were moving rapidly. Francine looked at the water temperature to see if it was elevated. It was not. Yet her fish seemed agitated, as though they understood what was about to happen. Francine took a deep breath. The river was strong in her nostrils. The open spillways all the way down the river produced clouds of drizzle that were pushed toward the sea by desert air that used the ancient river channel on its way west. She wondered if the salmon could smell the spray. Perhaps even the mist falling on the surface of the hatchery tanks contained messages the fish were bred to receive for thousands of years. Droplets of river water were calling these salmon to the ocean. As she watched the hatchlings, she sensed that they were eager, as she was, for life to start.

The salmon were transferred by means of a hoist that lifted tanks full of baby fish up into a holding area where, by opening a trapdoor, the water and fish swam down a short ramp and into the tank. It was as close to simulating a fast-running stream that they could manage with stainless-steel pipe and wire mesh. Francine wondered what the fish thought of swimming down a black hole, but she was grateful that unlike a lot of equipment, this setup didn't kill many of them.

It took all morning to load the tanker. By the time she hopped into the cab, it was early afternoon. She would have time for only one run today. She estimated that working alone, it would take a full three days to get all the hatchery smolts into the river. As she started to put the truck into gear, she looked into the mirror as if to ask why she hadn't thought to do the transporting herself long before this. As she pulled out onto the roadway, it occurred to her that she was now a target for murder like the other drivers. The realization made her angry at Hermiston once again for putting her in this position. She pulled on the brake, idled the truck, and ran inside her office.

In the bottom drawer of her desk was the revolver. She loaded it. It was heavy, but she knew how to use it. She placed the gun on the seat and immediately felt safe. A .44 Magnum would protect her from any harpoons or other ghostly Indian nonsense. She put the truck in gear, cursed loudly to herself, and headed out onto the highway with the same confident swagger her white ancestors had brought to the high desert. White beats red. Gun beats spear, especially this gun, the gun of her grandfather Frank Hale. Aim at the shadows and blast away until nothing moves. It had worked for him. It would work for her now.

She turned on the windshield wipers and pulled the revolver closer to her on the seat. Looking at the gun, she felt like a Hale. Headlights in the oncoming lane illuminated her face in the glass, an Indian face. She was hunter and hunted, an Indian shadow dodging bullets in the darkness. Like McCurdy, she, too, had been drafted into battles not of her own making. As she drove toward the release point with her hand on the pistol, she tried not to feel ashamed.

19

A Toyota pickup truck and a beat-up van were already parked next to the trailer, so Duane Madison pulled his much larger rig around to the other side and stopped next to an old Buick Wildcat. He looked at the van as he sidestepped the mud puddles and walked up to the trailer. In daylight Duane couldn't place the vehicle. He knocked sharply at the front door of the trailer. There was no answer. He could hear music inside. He reached down and picked up a number of pink-colored leaflets that had been left on the doorstep, advertising an Indian festival to be held in two days at the Shoulder Moon Casino. Thinking about the casino made Madison wince over his losses and the whole ugly matter that had brought him here to question Roy McCurdy in the first place.

Madison knew this trailer was the only place McCurdy called home, and that it was also a radio station, without looking at the two satellite dishes and broadcast antennae in the yard. He knew its sounds and tirades as he would some familiar late-night TV evangelist one might watch with the fascination of driving past a fresh car wreck. But McCurdy had always seemed more ridiculous than dangerous, his silent listening supporters more like a pool of suckers, eager to part with their cash, rather than an army. It was still amazing to Madison, looking around at the humble, squalid trailer site overflowing with rusting junk and stinking garbage, to see just how much could be made with so little. He knocked again.

Madison called out, "Hello."

He reached down to the doorknob to see if the door would open. The door was flimsy. The knob was loose. Madison twisted it easily and froze as he distinctly heard the click of a round being chambered into a gun. He let go and took a step back.

"Hello, I'm looking for a Mr. Roy McCurdy." Duane moved away from the door. He had left his own weapon in his truck, thinking it was more trouble than protection here: Now he had trouble and no protection. "I know someone is in there. I'm going to knock one more time."

On the second knock the door swung open rapidly, and Roy McCurdy was standing there, smiling.

"Are you leafleting my doorway, boy, or just littering?"

Duane could see no sign of the weapon he was certain he'd just heard. His police training took over when he suspected a hidden weapon. But he felt it put him at a disadvantage here, making him seem afraid of someone whom he considered to be nothing more than a crackpot. He looked down at the leaflets he was still holding.

"I believe these are yours, Mr. McCurdy."

Roy took the leaflets and scanned them. "I got plenty more of those inside. The drunken Indians over at the casino are planning a big hoopla. I plan to go. Are you?"

"I doubt it. I've come to ask you some questions, Mr. McCurdy. Do you have a few moments?"

Roy looked him over, paying particular attention to his uniform. When he noticed the words *Hanford Security*, he stepped outside onto the landing and closed the trailer door behind him. "It's my lucky nigger from the roulette table. I never thanked you for helping me win the biggest jackpot of my life. You looking for your cut or something? We're on the air now, and I don't have a lot of time."

McCurdy's tone and vocabulary made Madison want to slap him. People like Roy were the object of tantalizing myth. By the time they were teenagers, every black man in America had fully worked out a plan for what he might do when confronted by someone like Roy. Madison was just disgusted by this silly old man who appeared to be ready to kill the moment he said hello, a man for whom there need be no further provocation than showing up in black skin, a man who would give no warning.

"You are Roy McCurdy, right?"

"You know who I am." Roy was smiling. "Do you realize that this is sovereign territory you are standing on, boy? You left the United States of America the moment you got out of your truck over there."

Roy sounded so casual and confident, he might as well have been standing in front of the White House rather than this dented-up trailer in the middle of nowhere. Duane thought that there was no person more infuriating than someone with no shame. He reminded Duane of the clearheaded Muslim faithful who were convinced they had a guaranteed passage straight to heaven for killing designated infidels.

"I'm afraid I had nothing to do with your winnings the other day. You won the money on your own as far as I can tell. I'm here on another matter. This is a neighborly call, Mr. McCurdy. I don't want to take up much of your obviously valuable time. Someone made some charges on a credit card recently, and we'd like to ask you about them."

"I don't have any credit cards. Don't believe in them."

"This card was not in your name. It was in the name of a Dave Whillers. Does that ring a bell for you?"

"It's not my name now, is it, boy? Why would it ring a bell?" As defiant as he sounded, Roy actually seemed relieved by the question.

"I'm not here to play games with you, Roy. You used the name Whillers the other night at the casino. I heard you. A half dozen other people heard you. Now this Mr. Whillers's luck ran out about the time your luck began to change for the better. So naturally I have to wonder how you got your hands on a credit card that wasn't yours. Especially if, as you say, you don't believe in them."

Roy just stared at Madison for a moment. It seemed to Duane that he was looking for a weapon. "That's some uniform you have there, but I don't know if it gives you the authority to come out here and trespass on sovereign land. That's just a uniform for one of those fancy federal janitors over at Hanford, isn't that right?"

"This is a Hanford matter. Mr. Whillers's body was found inside Hanford. Where did you find his credit card?"

"Jesus, one dead trucker, you'd think it was the pope or something. Is he one of those fish drivers the Indians have been killing for the past month? Do you think you can pin one of those murders on me?"

"I'll pin anything I can on you. For instance, I think it's strange that you know the man was a trucker. I didn't tell you anything about him. And I'm not the police, exactly, so maybe it's better that you talk to me because I can certainly make sure the police come out here to search your radio station. They might not care about knocking you off the air while they search through every scrap of paper. We do need to figure out how you ended up with a dead man's credit card."

As he spoke, Madison could feel an urge for revenge that had nothing to do with the racial invective that was being directed at him; rather, it was all about the money he had lost to this man at the casino. He wondered what six thousand dollars' worth of payback from these people might look like. Meanwhile Roy seemed to grow calm, eyeing him with a gleeful, untroubled contempt.

"Mr. Madison, I don't think I would have pegged you for a sore loser coming out here to bother us peace-loving people. Do you need some food stanps?"

"It looks like you folks need to recycle some more beer cans to generate a little cash. Maybe you can work something out with the judge, beer cans for bail."

"You got a lot of guts just standing out here on my land, a jackboot nigger janitor in a uniform, telling me how he's going to send in the police. You've got a death wish threatening me at all." Roy's confidence hadn't wavered. "Do you have any idea who you're dealing with?"

"I think so. We think an Indian, this Indian, might have sold Dave Whillers's credit card to someone like you, someone who pays for false IDs, who writes bad checks, who prints his own fake money, someone who's the pretend president of his own country. Ever seen this man, Mr. President?" Madison held out a picture of Otis. It was an old mug shot, not the picture of him standing in the parking lot. McCurdy glanced at it and shook his head.

"I don't have nothing to do with any Indians, I'm afraid."

"All you need to do is tell me where you found the credit card. We know a lot more about this than you might think."

"Mr. Madison, I don't need to do anything at all right now. Even if that picture there showed me actually killing this unfortunate fellow who lost his credit card, the police wouldn't come near this place."

"So you think the U.S. government is afraid of your little trailer nation?"

Roy laughed, and said, "You are one brave nigger to be talking to me like that. But maybe you should ask your Fed bosses why nobody told you that the U.S. government has had enough trouble from Roy McCurdy. Everybody knows Roy McCurdy wouldn't have anything to do with some murders over fish. You better stick to chasing tree-hugging faggots over at Hanford, or find some fish-worshiping Indians. You've got nothing on me."

The headlights from a car driving up the hill flashed in one of the trailer's windows. It made the gray fog seem like night. The car crunched over the dirt-road gravel and lurched to a stop next to the Toyota truck. Duke was in the driver's seat and had his window rolled down.

"Can I help you?" he shouted. Duke was alarmed to see Madison standing in front of the trailer door. He shouted to his father as he got out of the car. "Daddy, the station is off the air. That tape you got on is off its track. All you can hear on the radio right now is a bunch of muffled noise. You need to go fix it." Duke turned to Madison. "Excuse me, sir, but this is a little emergency. It will only take a minute."

Roy stepped inside to adjust the equipment, which gave Duke time to assess the situation. "What can we do for you? Have we met before?"

"I was just asking your father a few questions. Duane Madison is the name."

Duke recognized him from the casino. Recalling the incident gave him a knot in his stomach. Duke could imagine no motive but revenge that might bring him here. Duke glanced over at Madison's truck, noticed the Hanford patch on his uniform, and imagined another motive.

"What's a nuclear guy like you doing all the way out here talking to my daddy after what he did to you the other night in front of a whole casino full of people?"

"The credit card your father used the other night belonged to one of the murdered drivers for the Bonneville salmon program."

"It was bought at the gun show in Walla Walla, where they sell stolen credit cards all the time. I'm sure you knew that before you came out here. Did the credit-card company send you out here to collect?"

Duke was as wary as his father about uniformed visitors. He glanced over at the Toyota truck parked next to the trailer. He wondered if there was another visitor inside the trailer. Hearing Madison speak about the murders made him think of Francine, which he had been doing pretty much nonstop all the way back from Maryhill.

"You're Duke, right?" The younger man made Duane more wary. He looked carefully, but at first glance he seemed to be unarmed.

"Why should I give you any information about anything? I don't know you. If I know anything about you, it's that you hate my father for what happened at the casino. You've got no business out here."

"All that may be true, but according to the BPA, you brought in a body a week ago from out in the river. Why don't you tell me some more about that?" Duane felt in full control of the situation now. People like this took up too much time and space in the world: He wasn't going to give them any satisfaction.

The skin on Duke's face tightened as it heated up. Madison's smile told Duke that he spotted his flush pink complexion. He wanted the man gone. Hatred welled up in him in ways he could never generate on his own. He felt like a McCurdy.

"The body was floating in the river. I rescued it. You should thank me."

"We've been trying, but you've been busy. We've tailed you ever since you brought it to an Indian woman at the Bonneville hatchery. Can you explain why you would do that rather than go to the Coast Guard?"

"I don't like uniforms."

"She was wearing one, I think."

"She wasn't a jackboot." Duke caught his breath.

"Jackboot nigger. Is that what you wanted to say?"

The door opened, and Roy came back onto the landing.

"That's enough, son." He stepped up until he was face-to-face with Madison. "I'm not afraid of your *n*-word, boy. But we're tired of playing games, Mr. Duane Madison. It's time for you to get out of here or the president of the New Israelite Nation will have you shot. Unlike in your country, I don't need to worry about a nigger-loving Supreme Court."

Roy was holding a pistol. Duke's head was down. He was praying.

"Son, we know you were with this woman this morning." Duane ignored Roy and continued speaking to Duke. "Can you tell me what she said to you about the condition of that body?" Duke blushed red.

"She had nothing to do with that dead man."

"Now that isn't even close to what I asked you, is it? Why would I think she did?"

"I'm through talking to you. You've got no business with me and no business with my father."

Duane couldn't resist a last remark.

"Tell me one thing then." Duane winked at Roy. "Does your daddy know you sleep with half-breeds?" Roy looked at his son. His smile was gone. Duane was beginning to feel as though he had managed to recoup some of his losses from the other day. He didn't see the punch until it landed solidly against his jaw. Duke had grabbed Duane around the neck and was trying to push him off the landing and onto the ground when Roy intervened. "That's enough, son. Let's just let the janitor boy go back to his atomic mops."

Duke was ready to kill; it was a feeling that he had long ago concluded he wasn't capable of. He didn't really know if it was the mention of Francine that made him seethe, or something about the memory of his mother and uniformed intruders that had turned the tables. Duke took a breath. He looked over at his father. Roy seemed amused. Duane had not fought back. He had taken the punch and ended up on the ground, but he quietly stood up and dusted himself off.

"I guess niggers aren't the only folks with buttons to push," Duane said. "I'll see you later. The next time it won't just be me."

"The United States government surrounded my home once before, nigger man. They won't do it again. They know no one will leave here alive next time." Roy unchambered the round in his pistol and put it in his pocket, holding up the round for Duane as he did. "If the world hasn't ended by the next time I see you, I'll make sure this still has your name on it."

Duane walked back to his truck. The two McCurdys stood there smiling at him as he roared out of the driveway. There were four vehicles in the parking lot, the Buick, the car Duke drove, the Toyota truck, and the van. Four vehicles, two people; Duane wondered if there were more people inside. He looked again at the van in his rearview mirror. The road curved, then he was gone. Only when he felt his tires sliding on the pavement did he let up on the gas. He was well down the road when he was able to crank up his stereo and collect his thoughts. *What a country,* he said to himself. The American Dream was a big mouth and a heart full of bitterness.

Duane knew that the old man was right about the police. Those who weren't secretly sympathetic with Roy wanted nothing whatsoever to do with any McCurdys ever since the shoot-out at Maccabee Pond. It was as though by leaving him alone, they granted McCurdy his hateful toy nation. As far as McCurdy was concerned, Madison understood he was on his own.

It had been a lark coming out here. Duane had presumed there was no real connection between McCurdy and the dead man with the credit card, but he had not expected such a reaction from the son. When Madison had gone over the report federal investigators were circulating, he'd seen the list of bodies and found the name McCurdy again. The same boat that brought body number two in had been seen docked at Maryhill where Francine Smohalla lived. There were questions about the woman at the hatchery, but Duane had no idea that mentioning her would produce such a response. He puzzled for a connection. He thought again about the van, but the old man's last remark about the end of the world was not just a taunt like the rest of his racist bile. Madison looked over on the seat next to him. The pink leaflet announcing the Indian salmon festival at the casino was in two days. Maybe he would show up.

He was relieved to see no headlights following him. His lips were dry. He licked them. They were still dry. He turned up the heat and the volume in his truck. It was stupid, but it made him feel safe.

2 0

Roy watched Madison's truck leave, then turned to his son. "Go inside, boy. I don't have time for this now."

Duke shuddered as he passed his father, as though he expected to take a blow. Roy followed him into the trailer where a visitor was seated at the kitchen table in front of a stack of money.

"This here is Jack." Duke was relieved that the visitor would stall whatever was coming. Without looking at Duke, Roy introduced him to the wispy gray fellow in the kitchen. "Jack Charnock, meet my good-for-nothing son who's intent on getting us all in a world of trouble."

"Pleased to meet you." Charnock's voice had a quiet intensity that came across as sadness to Duke. "Your father says that you love boats. I used to love to go fishing on the river years ago when I was a boy. I haven't done that in a while."

"Is that your truck out front?" Duke stepped up and shook Charnock's hand.

Roy smiled and pointed at the money on the table. "It's our truck now, but I don't think the word truck gives it proper respect, somehow."

"The truck is only the way she gets around," Charnock said. "The technical term we use back at Hanford is 'delivery vehicle.'"

"What does she deliver?" Duke looked carefully at the money in front of Charnock, trying to imagine what his father might have found for sale at Hanford.

"Destiny. You might say Mr. Charnock is the New Israelite Nation's secretary of defense."

Duke looked more closely at the truck through the window. It was not immediately apparent whether it was loaded up with weapons and explosives or was itself some kind of weapon. "I gather, for this kind of money, you aren't here to mow the lawn." Duke estimated there was about $180,000 stacked neatly in front of Charnock. They had shaken on a deal well before Duke arrived. Duane Madison had been an interruption.

"Mowing lawns"—Roy winked at Charnock—"there's another use for the Hobby Horse, mowing the South Lawn of the White House."

Charnock chuckled nervously. "That's not what I had in mind."

"It's just a joke, sir." Roy turned back to his son. "Duke, what Mr. Charnock makes possible is what your mother and I dreamed of long before you were born. What we are going to do is give him a stage on which the world can finally see his brilliant work."

"You work up at Hanford?" Duke asked Charnock. He could tell when his father was completely serious. "Is that why that other fellow was here, looking for you?"

"I think the nigger was looking for you, Duke," Roy said. "Thanks to your boats, and your new half-breed girlfriend, you almost got Mr. Charnock here spotted. We might have lost him." Duke flinched again. Roy softened his voice and continued, "But like I said, this is destiny."

Jack Charnock said nothing. Duke could see that he seemed not to know where he was and wasn't interested in finding out, so Duke asked once again. "Excuse my father, sir. Did you say you work up at Hanford?"

"I'm retired. The truck out there is carrying one of my longtime projects. It's something the government never had a use for. I made every part. It's no business of theirs anymore. But I'm finished with it now. Your father can have it. I have only two pickup trucks. I was thinking that the third device might fit on one of your boats."

"Be a hell of a lot more useful hauling plutonium than hunting women." Roy's taunting of his son made Charnock uncomfortable. "Be honest now, Mr. Charnock. You aren't retired. Tell my son how the federal government fired you after more than forty years without ever promoting you so you might live out your life on a decent pension. That money you're looking at is your security now. The New Israelite government takes care of its citizens."

"The money is for my wife."

Duke looked more carefully at Charnock. "You're selling my father plutonium from Hanford? Is that what's in the van out back?"

"Not just plutonium, son. Mr. Charnock is a very important man."

"Is that true?"

Charnock nodded nervously.

"Are you completely out of your mind? We all could go to prison for life." Duke realized how close Madison's arrival on the scene had come to blowing the whole scheme open. Nevertheless, Roy was as calm as Duke had ever seen him.

"Not here," Roy said triumphantly. "Plutonium's legal in my country. It's a matter of national defense. Now just let any of the U.S. armed forces try to arrest us."

Duke was more interested in the technical details. "What specifically have we got out here now? I'd like to here it from you, Mr. Charnock." Charnock was happy to oblige. He beamed at Duke, as though he were speaking to a Pentagon general.

"You've got eighty kilos of Pu two-thirty-nine machined into three bomb-grade interlocking spheres. Placed inside the center of the Hobby Horse implosion devices, they become three bombs that can be detonated by remote control, using the ignition unit I invented for the Hobby Horse program. The sequence of explosions to produce the necessary implosion is controlled by the electrical ignition system of a six-cylinder engine reaching a speed of five thousand rpm. At five thousand rpm the krytrons—big high-voltage spark plugs—fire and the precisely placed explosives surrounding the plutonium core begin a wave of compression. A baseball-sized piece of plutonium reaches the diameter of a golf ball one one-thousandth of a second later, and the chain reaction begins, somewhere between five and fifteen kilotons each."

"A fucking Toyota truck, boy." Roy was very excited. "That nigger security guard was looking right at a bomb and didn't see it because Jack here makes them look just like Toyota trucks. Isn't that right, Jack?"

"It doesn't have to be a Toyota. It just needs to be small." Charnock was gathering up his money and getting ready to leave. "The original Pentagon specifications called for a nuclear device that would avoid detection and fit in an ordinary family car. You could easily put it in a Ford or a Chevy or, as I said, your boat. It works off the ignition system of any six-cylinder engine."

"How far away do I have to be with this remote unit to make her work?"

"Within a mile, and it should be clear reception." Charnock pointed to the two pairs of buttons on the unit. "This starts the truck. This is your accelerator. When the light goes on, you're at five thousand rpm, and this button fires the igniters."

"And I go flying right into heaven?"

"The only way to be free of the explosion is to use a timer and be at least a mile away."

"How much devastation would something like this cause?"

"It's made for knocking out hardened concrete targets at close range. Its radiation dissipates quickly and the blast zone, while intense, is small. Like I said, if you're a mile away and behind a good rock, you'll be fine."

Roy picked up one of the pink leaflets from Shoulder Moon Casino and handed it to Duke. "We could park right outside the front door of that Indian casino during their fish festival and break some world records for trouble."

Charnock stood up. "You're wasting your time and money using this in a crowd. It's made for bringing down buildings. If you want my advice for something like that, I'll be happy to help. All I want is for the world to see how useful these devices can be."

"You're a true American, Jack Charnock, and a hero to the New Israelite Nation. Why don't you buy your wife some flowers on the way home?"

"Thank you. That's a good idea. I haven't done anything like that in quite a while." Jack seemed to be at peace as he walked out the door and toward his muddy van. Duke noticed that he had forgotten the bag of money on the table. Roy reached over to grab it, but Duke was quicker. "Not on your life, Daddy."

"Mr. Charnock, you forgot this."

"Oh, my. My wife says I forgot my head a long time ago. Thank you." Charnock climbed up into the van and turned the ignition. "Flowers, we never could afford them."

"You can now," Roy said, and waved.

After Charnock drove off, Duke turned to his father and met Roy's hard, rough hand. The pain burned in the bone around his eye, the skin of his cheeks, and caused tears to pour from his eyes. He could feel his eye begin to swell and tasted blood in his mouth, but it was the accumulated memory of all the blows from Roy that caused him the most agony.

"Who is the whore, boy?"

"She's none of your concern."

"She's half what then, if not the spawn of a whore?"

"She's Indian," Duke said, and was immediately sorry.

"As long as she's not black, it's okay? Is that what you're trying to tell me? I see right through you, boy."

"You don't know anything about me." Duke was terrified of his father, but he was more angry than afraid this time. His feelings for Francine gave him strength. "You're angry with anything I do that's not in your control. I have my own life."

"It's no decent life, with decent people. It's not worth remembering. Nothing about you is going to be worth remembering by anyone after you're gone. You think your life is yours to do with what you want, as though God's plan for the white race was to live peaceful, boring lives in the suburbs? Is that what you think, boy? Remember what the Lord said to Jeremiah: You shall have your life as a prize of war because you have put your faith in me. Your life is mine, boy. I would think you would want to live your life with some respect for the values your mother died for."

"I don't think it matters what woman I'm with," Duke said, resigned to defeat. "You can't forgive my mother for walking in front of a bullet thirty years ago. It's the only reason anyone pays attention to the McCurdys. Because she died, we're famous freedom fighters instead of just another family of bankrupt wackos living up in the hills."

"We're about to give them another reason to pay attention," Roy said, his voice losing the scolding tone and quickening with excitement. "Time is short, boy. We've got work to do. If I can't choose my life, you're not going to choose yours. This is why we're here. Don't you feel it?"

Duke looked into his father's eyes and saw the excitement of the old days. Another bonfire of burning crosses, and Roy was determined to light it. Duke could see the only thing that had changed was that he was alone now.

"You wish I died instead of her."

"Nonsense, boy." Roy rubbed his eyes as if to say that the thought had crossed his mind. They both were silent for a moment. Duke looked at the Toyota truck in the driveway. If it did what the man Charnock had claimed, and his father somehow managed to detonate it, any thought of a life of his own choosing would be over. If the target were the casino at Celilo, there would be no life with Francine. Choosing a life, Duke thought, was simply the act of deluding oneself into thinking such a thing was possible.

"We're going to change the world, boy, and we don't need any help from your Indian girlfriend."

"She's not my girlfriend. She's a biologist I met on the river who is trying to stop the murder of the fish drivers."

"Well, forget about her, or I promise you I'll do something to make her forget about you."

Duke ignored the remark, even though he understood that his father was capable of anything.

"Do you actually believe that Hanford old-timer has built a pluto-nium bomb?"

"Of course I do, and even if he hasn't, there's enough explosive in the detonator he's rigged up to reduce a city block to dust and human gravy. But it's going to work. I can feel it."

"How did you find him?"

"His wife called the radio station one night while you were gone. I thought she was a little off center. Then he showed up. He's a real nut, just like us. Thinks he was put on this earth to do plutonium's bidding. Been working quietly for the U.S. government his whole life. It's perfect. We're going to bring down ZOG with one of her own children."

Duke looked at the leaflet from the casino. His own anger at being trapped in the circumstances of his father's destiny made him think he could do nothing to stop Roy, but as usual, he might keep him from making a fool of himself.

"I think you've picked the wrong target."

"Why? It's absolutely perfect. Think of how many people will be there. Thousands of Americans from all walks of life. The media will be there along with tree huggers and whale protesters. The place will be crawling with federal workers gambling away their paychecks. Security will be nonexistent because it's Indian property. It will make Oklahoma City look like somebody's project for shop class. It's perfect."

Duke shook his head. His father always counted bodies. "It's just people. Killing people doesn't change anything. How many do you kill? Oklahoma is one-sixty-eight, Charley Whitman with a rifle in the Texas Tower, twenty-three. Plane crash, couple hundred at most. Cambodia, two million dead. Hitler, six million. Hiroshima and Nagasaki, quarter of a million. We broke all the records for death in the last century and dis-covered that human lives are cheap. They simply grow back."

"You going to war against some rocks and bushes, boy?"

"What if you could bomb a time rather than a place? What if you could place a charge that when detonated would bring down a civiliza-tion? What if there was a bomb that erased all of the roads in America?

Or what if people woke up one morning and there was no way to get from here to there? What if money all of a sudden had no meaning? What if there was no way to communicate, like after the Lord saw the Tower of Babel and scattered the people of the world, giving them different languages? You can't change the world by killing, only when you force the living to change."

Roy looked at Duke, and his face was tender in a way Duke had rarely seen it. He was listening to his son with rapt attention. "You know, boy? You remind me of your mother tonight."

"You said one time that my mother would know and be hurt if I ever forgot her."

"That was a long time ago."

"I did forget her, of course. Any five-year-old boy would. What I never forgot was the guilt that I helped to kill her. It took a long time to realize now that feeling came from you, not her."

Roy looked away from Duke. The years that had passed since he had lost Ida suddenly showed clearly on his face. "I didn't know how to be a father, let alone a mother, for all these years. You can't choose these things. They choose you. I just did what I could to keep her memory alive. It's what she would have wanted."

"I think she wouldn't have cared about that. I think she would say that the memories of people are like the wind, without weight, shifting with the weather. History is written in stone. If you want to be remembered, you must find a way, like the Indians did, to make the stones speak."

"Your mother used to admire the Indian bastards. She used to look up at the stone pictures the Indians made and say that they will outlive America." Roy took a deep breath and looked down at the hand that had moments ago struck Duke. "Please forgive me, son." Duke looked again at the truck parked next to the trailer. "I miss your mother. I guess I want people to die for that. She would say I'm weak for wanting that, but I can't help it. She would say that you are right about killing."

"Charnock said his bomb could be fitted onto a boat engine, right?"

"Yes, he did."

"Then we have three chances."

Duke felt somewhere inside that he had come to a decision.

"For what?" It pleased Roy to listen to his son.

"To make an old woman's dreams come true." Father and son embraced for the first time in thirty years. They both were thinking of a woman. Only Duke knew they were not thinking of the same one.

2 1

Francine tried to keep her speed up, but she was too concerned about the fish in the tank to go terribly fast. There was a line of traffic behind her, and the high-beam headlights from the angry drivers on Route 14 who were trying to get her to pull over so they could pass her made it impossible to look into her side mirrors without getting a headache. Light from oncoming cars made the already poor visibility from the pouring rain even worse.

She could feel the weight of the truck in each turn in the road—thirty tons of water and salmon sloshing around in the dark. She wondered if it would actually be worse for the fish to be simply dumped over the side of the dam. They had evolved over millions of years to migrate through water more efficiently than any other organism on earth. Instead they were riding around in the tank behind Francine's seat as she fumbled with the eighteen-wheeler's transmission.

The confined space concentrated her sense of the hatchlings as a single entity. They were no longer many, but one—just as *Oncorhynchus tshawytscha,* her beloved chinook, went from being millions of single unconnected creatures out at sea to a mad tribal plunge upstream to spawn and die in unison. She thought she could sense something like the power of their collective presence in the tanker behind her.

The power of creatures linked by a single mind as the salmon were was what she imagined her father had once understood. He had channeled the spirit of the salmon like an old-time prospector who could smell the presence of gold, or like a douser finding water with a stick. She whispered *"nusuh"* to herself, and thought it a much prettier name than *Oncorhynchus tshawytscha*.

Francine watched the mileposts to see when she was nearing the drop point. To protect the fish from the effects of nitrogen, she would have to put them back in the river at the farthest downstream point. Past Bonneville Dam the river was free. Francine wondered what the effect of Hermiston's drawdown would be on these lowlands. She knew that the Indian settlements that went right up to the bank would be in the greatest danger of flooding. She also knew that with this much rain and the dams wide open, any prediction was more of a guess. As she looked toward the riverbank, she thought she could see high water, but as the brush cleared and she looked out over to the Oregon side, everything seemed quiet and completely normal. The road here was very close to water level, but it was clear.

She turned right. The road took her down below the highway at milepost 93. Lumbering over the railroad tracks, she winced as she rocked back and forth. Francine had selected all the drop points for the transport program. This one was on the trailing edge of the river's wide bend to the north. It caught a swift, deep current, perfect for swimming and for hiding from predators. As she drove across the gravel lot that led down to the river she noticed that the water had crept up well above the usual release point. It was up around trees along the riverbank. Francine pulled alongside the water so the tanker was closest to the river drop point. The cab ended up almost in the trees. Branches overhung the windshield. She cursed under her breath. She had hoped to avoid backing the truck up, but she would have to use reverse to get out of this marshy riverbank. The water was about as high as the top of her wheels. She dared go no deeper. She idled the truck, secured the air brakes, and climbed down to operate the pump.

The water came up to her waist as she walked around to the rear of the trailer where she released the wide drain tube and aimed it toward the surface of the water. When she was sure that the angle of the truck would fully empty the tanker, she switched on the pump. The water was cold through her pants, but she focused on the silvery glints of hatchlings as they emerged from the tube and disappeared beneath the dark surface of the river. She heard a noise and looked up to see a pair of white seagulls perched on the top of the trailer, watching. To Francine they looked almost smug. All at once one of the predators fluttered down and in an instant plucked a struggling hatchling from the surface of the water.

It flew up into one of the trees, trailed by another bird. The demise of a single hatchling was the signal for a dozen birds to descend to the water to feed. Francine noted that it took a few seconds for the fish to orient to the river, but that was more than sufficient time for the birds to snatch them up and carry them off. The panel on the tanker indicated that it was about half empty. She looked up and saw a bird boldly eviscerating a hatchling with its sharp beak, eyeing her as it did, even taunting, it seemed to Francine. Predators were part of the natural order. She couldn't fault them, yet she also couldn't help feeling they were improperly taking advantage of the situation. Francine waded back to the cab of the truck to get her pistol. She would even the score.

She stepped back down into the water and peered into the mist, allowing her eyes to again adjust. As they did, a man seemed to step from the darkness. Just as in her dreams, he had long black hair and carried a long lance. He moved toward her holding the lance aloft, preparing to throw. Francine backed up.

"Who's there?" she cried out.

Her voice seemed to immobilize him. Francine took a step closer, and it seemed for an instant he was going to run away.

"Mary?" The man's face was incredulous, his voice unsteady. They both seemed to be dreaming. Francine could see a Herculean struggle, as though a force compelled him to strike against his will. He aimed his weapon. Francine raised her pistol to meet the threat and fired just as he hurled the harpoon with terrible force. But as she felt the hammer fall, she knew exactly who he was.

The force of the discharge knocked her off her feet into the slippery mud, saving her. The harpoon glanced harmlessly off the door of the truck and splashed into the river, but a single agonized shout indicated to Francine that her bullet had struck its target.

"Father, Father!" she screamed, and ran to the truck, where she pulled a powerful flashlight from the door pocket and dove into the trees, unafraid and desperate in the darkness. The sound of the gun had alerted vehicles on Route 14, including a police cruiser that swerved into the lot with its lights blazing. Observing that the truck was a BPA salmon tanker, the officers immediately called for backup.

Francine could hear nothing but the hiss of the rain and her own breathing. Every few seconds she cocked her head to listen. Police radios barked and crackled unheeded, and her flashlight's beam danced in the green darkness, finding only the trunks of trees. Recklessly Francine slogged ahead. The high water covered undergrowth, tangling and knotting around her ankles. Only by making high, slow steps could she make any progress. She stopped and scanned the surface of the water with her flashlight from the high side of the bank down to the river, looking for ripples: There were none.

She assumed that anyone trying to escape would head up the bank toward dry land. The snap of a branch pierced the air. She aimed her light at the source of the sound. There at the base of a tree trunk were drops, not rain, hitting the surface of the river. When she looked up, she understood in an instant that it was blood from her father's wound. He was already gone. As he jumped from tree to tree, Francine could just make out his form heading down the bank toward the river.

When she tried to move toward him, she tripped on the underbrush; her legs would not move forward. She strained with her back and shoulders and thought of her little-girl wings. She was so delirious, she imagined she could fly to him as she had always dreamed she would. She tried to fling herself toward him, partially freeing herself as she did, shouting, "Tepeh!"

He gave no answer. She shouted again, this time the word nusuh. Her flashlight caught his face and made him avert his eyes. She could see his face was trembling and absent of color. The bullet had struck him in his abdomen near his left side. It seemed to Francine that he was drinking the vision of her in. He could not have seen her before, yet he recognized her as his daughter. As Francine started to speak again, he put his hand out, pointing at the ghostly colors of the police lights on the edge of the trees. He gestured for her not to follow. Though he looked weak, he lifted himself into the center of a kayak that up until that moment had been invisible in darkness. With a single swift kick he propelled himself out of the trees and away into the swift current of the river.

"Father." Francine choked out an angry whisper as she heaved the flashlight into the river. It took many minutes before she had the energy to wade back to the tanker truck, which was still dutifully pumping out its cargo. A crowd had gathered out by the police cruiser, everyone fooled as she had been, looking for a fugitive to emerge onto dry land. She stayed in the shadows while she reached around on the ground to pick up the harpoon that her father had used to try to kill her. She stowed it on the truck in a rack below the tanker.

"Did you see anything?" someone called out.

"Not a thing," she said.

An officer approached. "Could you understand those shouts?"

"Indian words, beats me," she said, then added, "Got the damn fish into the river, anyway."

Francine looked out at the spout of the tanker, now empty, still in the water. The gulls and seabirds were gone, as were the baby salmon. Like her father, they had gone to take their places in some poorly understood natural order. As she had always done, Francine stayed back to clean up the mess it had all made.

Matrimony

Pain and exhaustion had put Charley in a state between waking and sleeping. He could feel his weakness in every breath. He couldn't shake the face of the girl from his mind. It was his beloved Mary. It was the face of Smohalla. For a moment he had wanted to run to her. For a moment the pain of the bullet vanished. For that moment he wanted only to bring her aboard his kayak and paddle back to the longhouse to sit and tell all of the old stories and chew on pemmican and laugh with the sound of the river in the background. None of it was possible, so he vanished into the river that made no sound and swallowed up Indians like history.

His wound was not fatal. It was not even that serious; that much he could tell. He was certain now of the prophecy that had moved him all of these years. He had lived it from the moment he had slipped into the river on the day Celilo had died. All of the sacrifice now made sense, even if he could not foretell how the story would end. It caused him great pain to realize that he had had his first and last glimpse of a child, a daughter, from the love and union with the white woman Mary Hale. Playing the events over in his mind, he searched for a clue she might have given him that there was life inside her. He knew now this daughter would be looking for him and that finding him would be her death sentence. It was important that the end come quickly, he thought. His part was mostly finished now.

He shifted in his kayak and paddled the small craft toward the bend in the river. This was old Chinook land, the sandy edge of a continent. This was where Nch'i-Wana took his broad last steps into the ocean, into forever. Astoria's bridge loomed above, and the lights of the smoky city of timber, pitch, and paper-plant stench were visible but gave out no stronger illumination. The tops of trees wore collars of low-hanging fog. He was gray as the water and therefore invisible, as he had always been.

Under a long-abandoned timber dock reeking of creosote and rust, he tied up his craft. There would be a bag of white-man clothing and a wallet with a very small amount of money tucked under the planks. He found it and tossed the bundle to the dock and slowly climbed up. He could feel the warm wetness from his wound. He wondered if his injury had also been a part of the prophecy. He had concluded after seeing this girl who could only be his child that the prophecy called for him to fling his lance at her, that killing her had been part of the prophecy's fulfillment. He now knew that the simple act of belief had been all that was required. It had, he noted as he winced with pain, saved both him and her. Like some modern-day Abraham, he felt no guilt from the offer of sacrifice, only the humility that comes from having had contact with forces greater than he could ever hope to understand.

He dressed slowly. The chill made buttons and snaps more than the usual challenge. The touch of the coarse fabric against his skin was welcome, and soon he felt warm. He found the stairs that led up to the street and made his way to the old waterfront streets of Astoria, a place that for generations had been hiding people who did not wish to be found, as all real seaports did. He found a warm, familiar place beneath red neon letters that flashed Bath. It was an old-style steam room with a short bar, which he knew well. A few people raised their glasses to him as he sat down. "Hello, Charley," they said. He was known here, and unknown. The bar was filled with men waiting for ships or just returned from the sea. Men like him, he thought, who had slipped through trapdoors to leave other lives behind. He ordered a glass of water and sat quietly, noting that one of the most unusual things about the white man's world was how easy it was to remain invisible. Even for thirty-three years.

The pain of seeing her face burned into him deeper than her bullet. He had lived two lives now and was beginning a third, as a father. He shook his head. He could not shake her. He had thought his path had been to follow the salmon, to find the people who were their murderers. He had found his daughter instead, and she was no murderer. Charley could see that the long path he *had followed ended here. The work for Smohalla was done. He was Charley Shen-oh-way again. Weariness combined with the smell of drink in the musty bar made him think about the last time he had seen Mary. In that moment when the two people he knew as family were there with him next to the river so long ago, they had lost him, but now they were discovering that just as certainly, he had lost them.*

■

Joe had been in baggy blue overalls and a white shirt. Charley's older brother held in his hand the tall, wide-brimmed hat that had identified him all his adult life. In his ears were wide gold-hoop earrings. Unlike Charley's, Joe's hair was crudely cut. Too short to be tied back, it wildly followed the contours of his head. In the blue morning light it looked black and thick like charcoal smudges. Moses's face was shiny and handsome in a more manly way than his brother's. It was frozen in the half-adult, half-child mask that had always made the Chinook tribe seem mysterious and unreadable to outsiders. His wide lips were striking above a powerful round chin, a face continually vigilant and poised for battle.

Charley spoke first. "The salmon must know we are with Coyote-Who-Frees-the-Fishes. The dams are not ours."

"The salmon stopped listening to Indians a long time ago." Joe was more of a realist. If the salmon heard any messages, they got them from the dam builders nowadays, not from Indian wizards. "You think the salmon care what we think every time one of them gets ground up in the turbines at Bonneville?"

"You would have to think that way to cash my father's paychecks." Mary glared at Joe.

"Why don't we just feed Devil Woman here to the salmon, Charley?" He didn't look at her. The white woman was trouble, had always been trouble, and was powerless to stop what was being done to the river. "Maybe if you say some magic words, we can get all the whites to just drop what they're doing and sail back across the Atlantic."

"Don't let her get to you." Charley stood motionless, feeling the balance point in his spear. "And she's right about your paycheck, Brother."

"Whatever you think of me, Charley, it's a lie to say Indians have nothing to do with the dams. Where do you think the money comes from? Trading beaver pelts to Frenchmen with beards and kayaks like in the old stories? The dams are the life here now. There is nothing else. Every Friday from here to Idaho, the bars are full of Indians busy drinking off their construction paychecks. The salmon know who builds the dams, and they know who's sleeping with the dam builder's daughter."

"The dams are made from Ice-Like-Stone. Ancient walls from the long winter come back. The salmon were born of the ice. They and we shall be born again," Charley intoned.

"Charley, have you ever seen Grand Coulee up close? Do you have any idea how much concrete is there? That's no ice dam up there, Brother. Behind it is a lake two hundred feet deep in places. This new dam will raise the river here, too. You swim out there now, and we'll never see you again. It's over. Celilo and everything that went with it will be gone the moment the river fills."

Charley was only half listening to his brother. Near the deep side of the rock the slenderest ripple creased the surface of the river. Slowly, he raised his spear.

The moment the ripple returned, he struck. The spear entered the water like a stiletto, and immediately the surface near the rock exploded in violence, as though the river itself were bleeding. It looked to Joe to be a twenty- or thirty-pounder. Mary saw the head of the fish come out of the water and crouched down to watch the struggle.

Charley read the vibrations in the shaft of the spear to tell him when to heave the fish out of the river. Unlike less-experienced fishermen, he did not jerk his spear, instead allowing the chinook's own motion to bind the barbs deeply into its flesh. Charley stood nearly motionless. The weight of the fish could be measured by his protruding thigh muscles, which danced like narrow stilts under his skin. As the salmon began to weaken, Charley bent his knees slightly, taking a deep breath and hoisting the spear up into the air. Both points could now be seen harpooning the side of the great fish. One had pierced the fish clean through and was dripping blood from the opposite side of the salmon's shiny dorsal fin.

Charley heaved the fish, and it landed neatly, spear upright, next to the rock by the bank. He had pulled his gutting knife from the leather pouch at his hip and pounced on the bleeding fish, its life quickly receding. With a single motion Charley opened the belly, and reaching in to sever the main vein at the base of the head, he inverted the chinook over the bowl he had placed on a mat in the soft cleared area next to the rock. Through the triangular hole near the heaving gills, blood first poured, then trickled into the bowl. As the level reached the brim, the fish stopped heaving and died, as though its life had been transferred intact like an egg yolk separated into a dish.

Joe stood by, filled with a familiar deep pride and admiration for his brother's prowess. He had been watching him and the most majestic of the river's creatures since Charley had taken his first steps as a young boy into the roaring center of Celilo. Joe never failed to be moved by his younger brother's skill and grace. Each motion echoed a generations-old ritual that was about to vanish forever. Joe's voice caught in his throat as he realized that in this chilly inlet next to the falls, the ten-thousand-year-old unbroken song of Celilo was ending.

Charley gutted the fish, then quartered it, leaving the head and tail as separate pieces, which he arranged carefully around him. The bowl of blood he emptied into the leather pouch and tied it tightly. He gathered up the pieces of fish and walked down to a place on the shoreline where the current had some speed.

"I am just a small voice in time, like you." Charley turned to Joe. "Just as the blood will vanish in the river, our voices are hidden in the wind of the canyons to be found by the listening ones."

Joe hated this talk as deeply as it moved him. He turned to Mary. "This will kill him, you know."

Joe didn't like outsiders seeing the sacrificial ceremony, especially this final one. It angered him as much as the danger his brother seemed bent on. "Charley, if you go through with this now, it will be as pointless as some circus stunt." He looked at Mary, who was shivering with cold. "She will merely have an adventure to tell her grandchildren."

"*Aut-ni* is no stunt." Charley used the more ancient Shahaptian word rather than the Chinook word for "blood." It was a word Joe hadn't heard since he was very young. "Brother, you are born of this blood. You know this as deeply as I do."

Every child knew how the blood of the first salmon would show the rest the way upstream from the ocean. The sacred salmon ceremony had always preceded the weeks of gambling and revelry that surrounded the spring chinook run and that turned Celilo twice a year into a Stone Age Las Vegas. But it was not something Joe had thought of or felt for quite some time. "No amount of blood and magic talk is going to get the chinookers over the dam, Charley. They've got the white man's fish ladders to lead them now. They don't need us anymore."

"The salmon must know that we will be waiting when they return. The river has given us many signs. We must answer now."

"*Tlukuma* will say, Charley, *tlukuma*." Joe produced a pair of carved dice and some *wowuk* sticks. Charley smiled and picked up his *tlukuma* bones. He motioned for the three of them to sit down. Mary watched as Joe sat cross-legged and using his knees as a drum, slapped out the old rhythms as Charley sang. To the haunting music he switched the differently marked bones from one hand to the other with lightning speed.

It was the most ancient of games; the drums and songs called to spirits who coaxed good fortune out of an uncooperative world. The winner had already been decided. The game was merely a way to learn his identity. There was no word for luck in the Chinook language, the tongue of a race of inveterate gamblers who didn't believe in playing the odds, only fate itself.

"You think that the old Indian brothers were wrong to never tell us about what is happening now. You think the dams prove that Smohalla was wrong, that Tsagaglalal is only lines painted on a rock. The white people's knowledge of Nch'i-Wana is only a few facts about water and rock. They work miracles with this knowledge and break the hearts of the Indian people. But Coyote knows all the miracles, and he knows the path from the mountains to the sea."

"That path is blocked now. Celilo will soon be silent. It is finished."

"The white men who built the door also made a key. Even if they do not know it is the key. Coyote will find it and free the fishes someday. That is my wager."

"For Celilo then, I guess." Joe had not listened carefully to his brother, and he was not going to say good-bye. Charley let his head fall back as if in a trance. He held his closed fists out to Joe, who hesitated, then chose left.

"You lose," Charley said as the bone with the intricate carved pattern of stripes and two thin pieces of leather thong tied at either end lay in his palm. Charley opened his right fist and revealed the other clean bone. He handed both of them to Joe and pointed up at the face of Tsagaglalal. "Call to her when the time comes, and I'll come back to your splendid temple."

Mary had observed all of this in silence. "There is no one else who can call you home?"

"Only Tsagaglalal."

"Then you lose, Charley Shen-oh-way." She turned away from him and faced the river with her bitterness.

The red of the first morning sun glanced off the pink basalt stone of the gorge. Tsagaglalal's face was on fire. Charley unbraided his hair. Walking back to the river's edge, he placed his hands in the water and one by one released the pieces of the fish, which sank immediately away. He looked back at Mary for the last time. Her hands were cradling her stomach. She did not cry, nor did she look up. She stared at the surface of the rising water. Wearing the leather pouch full of blood, Charley stepped into the river and began to swim toward Celilo.

Against the current, the cold water drawing his skin taut like a drum, Charley battled the onrushing cascades of the river he had only known as Nch'i-Wana, the "Big River." As he swam, the river rose, covering the familiar footfalls and rock landmarks that had always been his guides through the white water. The current buffeted him and forced him to find oblique pockets of calmer water, spaces between the current to make his way slowly forward. As he reached the middle of the circular falls he found a smooth rock shelf that was now well submerged by the rising river. Slowly he stood wedging one of his feet between two rocks for balance. He waved the bag of blood, marking the direction the fish should swim toward his people's platforms and nets he knew would be empty this year. Finally he untied the bag and with his eyes closed he poured it onto the water.

He uttered the words *Orinico, Orinico Noh Way Tah Tah Nch'i-Wana.* Calling to the salmon out in the ocean, believing as his people had always believed, that the blood of the first salmon caught by an Indian would show the way for *nusuh* to follow. The blood started downstream and then, snagged by an eddy, the red bubbles dissolved into a pool formed by the rising waters. He felt cold. The river was different. This last dam was making the water behave as it never had before. He jumped into the current to try to reach the far bank and swim to a small cave where he had always gone as a boy when the river had sapped his strength. He would try to find that place now in the rising unfamiliar waters. But out in the current he was lost in the depths of a river pooling over everything he had ever known. As his mind's map of Celilo was being erased, the water drew him downward.

■

Charley took a long pull from the glass of water in front of him and looked around at the few people sitting next to him in the bar. Alcohol was a disguise. It occurred to him that this was its chief attraction. Drink disgusted him, but he could not deny its power. The pain of his wound was receding. He looked down to see that he had stopped bleeding. "Medicine." He chuckled, drained his glass, and buttoned the cloth coat he was wearing.

"Got a ship, boss?" The bartender picked up the money Charley had placed next to the glass. At first Charley didn't realize the man was speaking to him. Then he looked around. The bar was almost empty.

"No ship, just a last voyage, almost finished, almost home now."

"It's always nice to come home." The bartender filled Charley's glass and leaned close to him. "Whiskey this time? For the end of a voyage? This one's on me. You know they say the river is coming home, too."

"Is that right?"

"There's talk that all this rain has weakened the dams."

"There's been a lot of rain."

"Hell of a lot. Never been this much. Barge boys are nervous. Nobody wants to be out on the river when it happens."

"When what happens?" Charley looked around again. Now the bar was empty. He had seen no one leave.

"I thought you knew, boss."

"I know only about the salmon. I know they will soon be free. More than this I do not know."

"Then you know everything."

Charley drained his glass again and looked around. The unfamiliar whiskey burned in his stomach. The bartender's back was to him. The bar was suddenly full again.

"What did you say, boss?" The bartender turned around as though greeting him for the first time. "You get a ship?"

"No ship, I said. Just a last voyage, almost finished, almost home." Charley smiled. He realized that Smohalla and Coyote had just spoken. They were gone now. Charley understood everything. There would be one more journey.

"Can you tell me how long it will take to get to the casino upriver?"

"The Indian place at Celilo?"

"Yeah, the Indian place." Charley smiled as he said it. "How long is the drive?"

"About two hours, maybe a little less. Is that home for you?"

"Yeah, I guess it is."

"That's good, boss. It's always nice to come home."

Charley was almost home. It occurred to him that this sensation was the perfect combination of joy and sadness. He thought to himself that this must be what it feels like to have lived a life after all. The thought warmed him. He pulled the whiskey on his breath into his lungs. The taste was sharp like smoke from an old forest.

"Medicine," he said to himself, and walked out of the bar into the misty Astoria night.

2 2

Joe Moses was waiting when the woman entrusted to his care marched up the front steps of Maryhill. All of her wrath was for him. He took the full force of her fist on his chest and stumbled backward as she buried her head in his shoulder. Francine had been carrying the lance her father had thrown at her and left behind. When she dropped it, it echoed off marble and mountain as it rolled down the stairs. Francine picked it up, brandished it at Joe like a weapon, and rushed by him into the house's tall atrium.

"How could you have not told me that he's alive!"

"I didn't know myself."

"And you expect me to believe that."

She paused long enough to look deep into his eyes before breaking his gaze and shouting with disgust. "There's no time to even talk now! They've organized a manhunt!" Francine bounded up the stairs three at a time. "They'll kill him now."

Joe walked slowly. He had been listening to this woman since she was a tiny baby. Holding the harpoon, she raged from one room to another. The house seemed to be pressing down on her from all sides, as if it were part of a conspiracy to hide the truth from her. As Francine ran by her mother's room, she felt a curious, unexpected affinity. Others had locked both of them away here: It astounded her that they had apparently been willing to pay any cost to keep them from knowing anything. Perhaps that was the reason she had been sent here to live.

Francine pulled a long fabric bag from her closet and began to pile into it every artifact associated with her father, especially the harpoon points—the two she had collected from the murders, and the one her father had left her. She jammed the harpoon into the bag. When it didn't fit and instead its sharp point tore through the fabric, she pulled it from the bag and with a shriek of exasperation broke it over her knee. The shaft of the lance did not break easily. Her leg ached as she stuffed the pieces into the bag and zipped it closed.

"This is a surprise for many people, not just you." Joe had been standing in the door watching Francine struggle with the harpoon. "Tell me what happened."

"That's a good laugh. You have the nerve to ask me to explain? Why should I tell you anything?"

"You've seen him."

"Of course I saw him. I was pumping out the salmon tanker at a drop point downstream from Longview. He stepped out of the trees, and thinking I was one of the salmon drivers, he tried to kill me. I didn't realize who he was until I had already shot him. I tried to find him, but he slipped into the river and paddled away in a kayak. He's wounded, and because I fired a shot, everybody knows about him now. I couldn't stop the police. They'll find him before we can ever get to him."

She ran into her mother's room. For a moment she looked at the wooden Smohalla bird on the mantel, her mother's companion. She left it there, stuffed some remaining artifacts into the sack, then raced down the stairs. She opened a door near the kitchen and walked briskly back behind the house to where her vehicle was parked. Joe followed, barely able to keep up.

"Did he know who you were?" Francine slowed in response to Joe's question. She had been asking it to herself ever since she fired the shot.

"I don't know. Maybe."

"Did Charley say anything to you?" Joe was nearly whispering. Francine looked around. The sound of her father's name was thrilling, as was her uncle's genuine tenderness for his brother. They were standing near the monument to Stonehenge built by her grandfather, slabs of dark stone in a circle with benches in the middle. Francine slowly walked over to one of them and sat down.

"I thought he was going to say something, but he didn't."

"What do you plan to do with those things?" Joe pointed to the bag stuffed with artifacts.

"Get rid of them. If the police find them, it's over for all of us."

"You mustn't try to interfere now. What is happening is prophecy and cannot be changed. If your father is to be found, he will be found. If he is to get away, there is no power to prevent it."

"I'm surprised to hear you, of all people, speak of prophecy. Aren't you the original self-made Indian?"

"Much has happened. There is much to doubt now."

"Let's just say I've got a backup plan in case you're wrong, or in case this is just another lie meant for me alone." She took a step toward her car and then turned to face Joe.

"Look, I am going to take these to a place where they will be safe. I don't know how I will feel when I return. If they catch and kill my father before you explain to me why my life has been a hell filled with lies for thirty-three years, I may never forgive you. So I'm going to give you a chance right now before I go."

"It would be difficult to tell this story in a week, let alone a few minutes."

"Try it."

"What do you most want to know?"

Francine sneered. "Start with the last time you saw him alive."

"It was the last happy time along the river, in the days before Celilo disappeared, when your mother and father turned their backs on their families. They were too much in their own minds to ever listen to anyone's advice. Charley loved your mother. The Hales hated Charley. He knew that there was no future, so he returned to the river, his first and only true love. You made it complicated. They weren't planning on you."

"Complicated for whom?" Francine practically spit out the words. "I planned for none of this." She wept and placed her head in her hands. Joe leaned toward her and touched her shoulder. The skin was warm and firm. He was not accustomed to comforting children, and he had rarely, if ever, shown affection for his brother's child, whom he had raised for good or ill.

"We wanted to protect you from the bitterness. The Hales blamed the Indian people for your mother's condition. Indians accused the Hales of having Charley killed. Your mother and father only cared about the river, the salmon, and their love."

He began to tell the story. Francine sat quietly on the stone bench, watching Joe's wrinkled hands carefully replacing her dreams with the real story of how she came into the world. The tall stones cast shadows that vanished when small white clouds, blown swiftly by the desert breeze, blotted out the sun for a few moments. As Francine watched and listened, it occurred to her that this was history, shadows swallowed by larger shadows, with each life a brilliant burst of sun that lasts until the next cloud.

Joe spoke calmly and steadily until he came to the end, the part where Charley was swimming out in the rising river and only his face could be seen. Here his voice recalled the pain of watching the two most important people in his life disappear along with the falls.

■

Mary saw him go under as she climbed up on the tallest rock. For the first time she could see how the dam had raised the river into a swirl of undercurrents. The spray was replaced by deep, powerful channels churning downward with many times the momentum of the natural falls. Joe knew the river as well as his brother, and he gripped the tlukuma *bones in his hands, waiting for his brother to reappear.*

"Charley!" Mary removed her shirt, and before Joe could get to her, she was in the river swimming toward the last place she had seen Charley. She didn't get far. The current that Charley fought was too much for Mary. Joe

watched as she was swept out into the channel and rapidly bobbed downstream.

Charley saw Mary go into the water and tried to swim toward her. He was now facing in full force the same water that the chinooks fought. But the thickened current slammed him instead back toward the rocky cave now filling up with water. It was too deep to stand. The churning water and silt buried him like desert sand. Charley Shen-oh-way's boyhood refuge had become a watery trap. In the dark and cold his body convulsed for a time. He clawed at the rock and mud and then floated free, dusted by river silt, sheltered by the rising river below and the pocket of air his face would find above.

"You lose, Charley," Joe whispered, and dove to find his brother, but when he came to the cave there was nothing. The opaque and unfamiliar waters had buried everything. He stood alone at the edge of the river looking downstream for any sign of escape. It had finally taken everything from him. Joe had to step back through new mud to reach the shore. He stood for a moment, watching his family's wooden fishing platforms slip below the water. The river would rise much farther before it would stop. Until the last moment he had wanted to believe that even in the face of all that was changing, the old ways made sense. Charley's strength and courage was actually something to believe in. It was what made Joe hate now.

Being Indian was the curse of belief. The more an Indian believed, the more he died, and everything around him decayed until there was nothing left now but the maggot generation Joe had been born into. They lived in the pungent garbage and vomit of history and called themselves natives. What had his people done to deserve such a curse? Charley had loved the woman named Mary because she was as close to the river as he was.

■

Joe looked over at Francine. She was crying.

"How can he be alive, then?"

"Because he never died. It is the only explanation. Perhaps it is like Celilo—unseen, but still there below the surface of the water. Charley was never found, and by the end of the week Celilo was gone. Celilo

Falls, where the bravery of men and the power of the salmon were tested by the gods every year without fail, the spray of which was believed to be the breath of the earth itself, had vanished without a whimper."

It had broken his heart. It had made him able to accomplish all that came after. In that moment Joe Moses walked away from all that he had known then, and he was certain again, as the memories swirled inside him, that somehow the salmon had been warned.

"I hiked downstream an hour later and found your mother at dusk barely alive, caught in some newly flooded trees. She had been in sight of the dam when she blacked out. The last word I heard her speak before she went into the water was Charley's name. After that she said only the word, *jokulhlaup*, which is the white man's word for Flood-That-Carves-Stone. I thought it more of Coyote's tricks. I pulled her from the mud and sand and brought her back, helpless and pregnant, to Maryhill. Half a year later you were born. I thought you were Charley's message from the place he and Coyote had gone. You squirmed in a blanket next to your mother, who never once awakened from her coma to nurse or comfort you. The doctors said it was you fighting inside her that had kept her alive."

"And my name?" Francine asked.

"If your parents had any plans for what to call you, they told no one. I gave you your name."

Francine clasped the hands of her uncle. Her eyes were moist. "Then he doesn't know my name, either."

"No."

"Why is he killing the salmon drivers?"

Joe paused and wrinkled his forehead. It was clear he had agonized over this question for some time.

"There is a prophecy that your father believed in, that Coyote would someday find that path for the Salmon Brother from the mountains to the sea. I think he disappeared to save Celilo, and he believes somehow that he can. I don't know exactly what he is doing; I don't know if he understands fully; but if I know anything about my brother, it is that he will give whatever life he has left to make the prophecy of Smohalla come true."

"He has already given his life."

"He and your mother have given their lives. Let's hope it is not for nothing."

"We have to find him before they do." To Joe, it looked as though her step was heavier now, as though she were carrying more than the evidence of crimes she was determined to hide. She stepped into her vehicle and drove away. To Joe, it suddenly seemed like only a moment had passed since he had last seen his brother. The Dalles Dam had ended Celilo Falls; it had broken the hearts of his people; it had taken his brother; and it had broken the most powerful family in the Pacific Northwest.

He stood up and walked from the Stonehenge garden, relieved to be free of the impotent relics of a civilization even more lost than his own. He set out for the edge of the lawn where he knew a narrow trail disappeared into the brush. He followed it for a long time up to the highest point on the cliff, where it ended. There before him was the face in the rock, Tsagaglalal. Her eyes looked down upon him, smirking, as if to say how wrong he had been. A feeling from the old times stirred in his blood, mixing with the aches in his joints from the climb. He was old. There was not much time. He searched around in the brush beneath the rock until he found the oil lamp. It was a large metal-and-glass signal lantern from the railroads. In the days when Joe and Charley were boys, they would climb up here and light the lantern and fashion hooks and nets for fishing Celilo. He shook the lantern until he ascertained that it was full of fuel. Its deep red glass was dusty but intact. Charley had stolen it long ago. Had he known its use even back then? Joe fumbled for a match. He waited for the wick to take the flame and then placed the cover over it. The lamp bathed the rock in red light. It was their old signal. Joe set the lamp beneath the face of Tsagaglalal, looked out at the river, and wondered if at that moment Charley was watching him.

23

Duke had the *Queequeg* out of the water and up on a trailer and was just beginning to negotiate it out of the parking lot of the Goose Point dock when he spotted Francine running toward him. She had left her truck running with the door open and was holding a bag that she tried to hide as she jumped up onto his running board.

"Take this, quickly." She pressed the bag up against his window. "There isn't much time." Duke couldn't hear what she had said so he mouthed the words *hold on,* and slowly pulled his rig out of the way of other boats.

"Are we running away together?" he said as he rolled down the window. He motioned for her to climb into the truck with him. Taking the *Queequeg* out of the water unexpectedly had provoked enough questions. Duke maneuvered his truck out onto the highway to elude anyone paying attention to them in the marina. Francine noticed his anxious movements.

"You're afraid to be seen with me."

"Not at all. The marina is not a good place to talk. I'll explain later. Tell me what happened."

"I need you. Everything is different."

"That's true enough," Duke said. "I've got a new job to do now, me and the *Queequeg.*"

Francine paid no attention. "I need you to take this bag of my father's *ik'ik*s. Some are murder weapons now. The police are hunting my father everywhere on the river. I last saw him down near Longview. I have to find him before they do."

"You don't have a father. What happened at Longview?"

"I drove the salmon to the release point. He found me. He tried to kill me with this *ik'ik* like he did with the other drivers. He recognized me, I think, but I shot him before I could tell who he was. He got away."

"You found your father after he went missing thirty-three years ago, and you shot him?"

Francine had not fixed the details quite in that way until that moment. She burst into tears. "He's been alive all of my life. Now I don't know if I will ever see him again."

"What do you want me to do with the bag?"

"Hide it, destroy it. It's really all that links my father to the murders. Maybe I can help him. You're the only one I can turn to. They'll search Maryhill when they understand exactly who they're looking for. They may know already."

A drizzle began to fall. Duke switched on his wipers and seemed to come out of a trance. He took his eyes off the road for a moment and looked at the river. "Your bag is safe with me."

"Thank you." Francine looked at his face and noticed that one of his eyes was seriously bruised. "What happened?"

"Roy and I kind of had it out. He knows about you."

"How could he know?"

"Apparently the Hanford cops have been tailing us as part of their investigation."

"They told Roy?"

"It's just some of the normal harassment we get. They love to keep tabs on us. They'd love to shut us down. They never will."

"Roy did that to your face?"

"I was defending your honor."

They were silent again. At first Francine thought that Duke was making a joke. She looked at him and could see that he was completely serious, proud of whatever had happened.

"What is this job you're going to do?"

"Job?"

"You said you had a job. Is that why your boat is on a trailer?"

"I'm taking the *Queequeg* upriver to Lake Roosevelt. There's no way to get around Grand Coulee except on a trailer."

"Why don't you rent a boat up there?"

"Because no boat can do what the *Queequeg* will be able to do when I get finished with her."

"The powerboat races?"

"It is something like a race, yes."

They drove for a while in silence. Duke spoke first.

"You know about this festival up at the casino, right?"

Francine had forgotten about the preparations her uncle had been making for weeks now. She wondered if it might be canceled because of the manhunt for her father.

"It's in two days."

"Are you planning to go?"

"I hadn't thought of it. If my father is still at large, I suspect I'll be busy."

"Don't go."

"Why do you say that?"

"I'm just saying don't go. I can't explain. You'll be safe at Maryhill. It's on high ground."

Francine noticed for the first time a calm that he had not had on any other occasion she could remember, certainly not the morning she had last seen him.

"Let me off here." Francine pointed to a parking lot off to the right. Abruptly, she recalled that she had left her truck running back at the marina. "I'll hitch back. I need my truck."

Duke slowed the vehicle and pulled off the road. As he did, it occurred to him that he would not see Francine again. He reached for her hand. It was cold. He pulled it to him. She resisted.

"If you or your father do anything to hurt my people, I'll hate you forever, Duke McCurdy. I need your help, not your spooky advice. Promise me that you'll take care of the bag."

"I can only promise that you will never hate me." Duke pulled her toward him.

She continued to resist, but in desperation she fell into his embrace. "Is that how Duke McCurdy tells a woman he's in love with her?"

"I'll keep your bag safe. But I wouldn't worry about your father. If he's stayed out of sight for thirty-three years, I can't imagine the police finding him in a day. He's probably trying right now to find you."

"Maybe so. I guess I understand what you were saying back at Maryhill."

"What did I say?"

"I should believe in my father because he's my father, even though it's wrong to murder, wrong to be full of hate, and wrong for him to have made me a freak of nature."

"That's something you said. I think you have always believed in your father, Francine Smohalla. That's why you take care of his salmon."

"Why can't we escape from these things?"

"Because we have to see how it all turns out. Good or bad, if we run away we only miss out on the ending."

"What are you really going to do upriver?"

"I'm going to take a little boat ride and look for white water."

"There's no white water above the Grand Coulee Dam."

"So I'll make some, a present for your mother, to win the heart of her daughter. One *jokulhlaup* coming right up." The moment he'd said this out loud, he realized that he understood something that had caused him pain all of his life.

"If you want to win my heart, just take care of this bag." Francine laughed at what seemed to her to be a little joke, kissed him, and then stepped from the truck to walk back to the marina. She got a ride almost immediately. Duke watched her in his rearview mirror. The tears rolled down his face. Now he understood another riddle that Roy had been shouting about all of his life, destiny. He could suddenly say he had one. It was not what his father would have wanted, but Duke was certain that when he was finished, Roy would be proud of him.

24

It was not the many bats or the creeping rodents he could hear flee-
ing nearly underfoot, or the musty smell of guano and death that unsettled Duane Madison as he moved deliberately toward the precise
coordinate twenty-three degrees off true north. He aimed his flashlight
at the wall of the cooling tower and gave a startled shout as the beam
found the face of a toy horse slowly rocking in the darkness. The movement was from desert rats, but the painted face of the horse, faded with
age, was macabre and outlandish. He looked down at the folder, which
had recorded the position of the body, time of day, and other details in
an incident report, which could have easily been recounting the discovery of a lost wrench, or some worker's lunch box surrendered to wet concrete. The death of Sam Charnock was simply another detail.

This was the place. Madison looked up again. The objects, a paltry
shrine to a dead boy, confirmed it. Madison peered around with his
flashlight and found the chair and a metal box with a heavy clasp on the
front. In it were pictures of the boy with a younger version of the man he
had met in the Hanford mud, and a woman whose face in the pictures
seemed to know what was coming. Madison paused to look at the X rays.
He couldn't tell what they were at first, then the semicircular pattern of
teeth gave it away. He looked up at the wall. On it in charcoal were some
words written in Latin.

Transmutemini de lapidibus mortuis in vivos lapides philosophicos.

He quickly copied down the words and looked back at the toy
horse. It nagged at him. The eyes seemed to follow him around the

room. He hated old antique toys like this, stylized painted clowns and eerie puppet faces, white people's toys. They were faces of nightmares and horror movies that made Madison wonder why white people seemed always to surround themselves with things that would scare anyone half to death. Even the words *hobby horse* seemed wrong, evoking some sequestered notion of play in rooms no one entered, like this one for a dead boy named Sam.

A thought crystallized. Hobby Horse had two meanings here. It was a little boy's toy; it was the life's work of a father. A plutonium bomb to memorialize a dead son. Son and father reunited in work and play, across time and death.

> *Fly on my sweet Angel,*
> *Fly on through the sky,*
> *Fly on my sweet Angel,*
> *Forever I will be by your side*

Madison looked at the horse again. Its eyes seemed to be watching something. He followed their gaze with his flashlight until he found a stack of two familiar boxes. Duane searched the dark, dusty floor as though an alarm had been triggered. The boxes were both open, their inner round compartments empty. A Department of Energy control number indicated that the boxes had contained weapons-grade nuclear materials, Pu-239.

The boxes had been tossed here as though discarded. They were not part of the shrine. The plutonium, which would have been machined into baseball-sized spheres, was gone. Each detail that fell into place quickened Duane's pulse. He could see the rows of baseballs in the back of Charnock's van. All around were other boxes of non-nuclear but just as restricted explosives, TATB, and chemical-bonding ingredients used in shaping and amplifying nuclear explosions. He tried to imagine the ratio of plutonium to the chemical explosives from the litter of boxes and get a sense of what he might be dealing with here.

He grabbed the boxes and the metal footlocker full of pictures and ran back to his own truck. In the employment file he had pulled up an address in Richland, 94 Argon Lane. He thought about going back to his office and initiating the complicated sequence of alerts to declare a nuclear emergency, but it would take hours of paperwork and broadcast the discovery to the entire planet. If there was a chance to catch Charnock before he could either sell the plutonium or configure it in some way where it could produce a nuclear explosion, he might end this thing here. Charnock would surely know the signs of an all-out federal nuclear theft investigation and would have probably made plans to ditch the Pu-239 in a hurry. Duane raced past the checkpoint and on toward the city of Richland.

The empty plutonium cases and boxes of explosives were in the back of his truck. The footlocker was on the seat next to him. As he drove, he tried to calculate what the most immediate threat was from this apparent theft. There could have been as many as six machined warhead-grade quantities of plutonium in each of the boxes. According to the project history in Charnock's files, the Department of Energy had given about that amount to the Hobby Horse project back in the seventies. There had never been test explosions at Hanford, so whatever plutonium had been granted to Charnock's team thirty years ago was still around and as fresh as if it had arrived yesterday. Madison figured four, perhaps five bomb devices were possible, based on what he had already seen.

The rain was heavy when he reached the driveway of Jack Charnock's Richland home. A woman answered the door.

"Good afternoon, ma'am. I'm from out at Hanford, and I wonder if it's possible to speak with your husband?"

Rebecca Charnock looked at Duane for a moment as though she recognized him. When he said *Hanford,* her face became set and hard.

"He's at work today."

"I'm afraid he's not."

Rebecca leaned against the door. "You Hanford people have brought a lot of bad news to this house."

"I understand, Mrs. Charnock. We know what happened to your son years ago. Right now we don't have any reason to believe that your husband is in danger. I have a few very important questions. May I please come in?"

The door opened, and Rebecca walked quickly back into the kitchen. She wet a paper towel and was wiping her face, trying to compose herself. She wordlessly motioned for him to sit down at a time-scarred Formica dinette table on which sat a vase of brilliant roses and irises. They seemed out of place here. Madison placed the metal foot-locker he had brought with him from the cooling tower on the table next to the vase. Rebecca Charnock glared at it. She flinched as Duane opened the metal clasp and placed an envelope of photographs on the end of the table nearest her.

"Do you know what these are?"

Rebecca stepped over to the table. She shuffled through the X rays. The family snapshots were familiar, old friends. She hadn't seen them in quite a while.

"Where did you get these?"

"Never mind that. Do you know what they are?"

"These are pictures of my family. They are none of your concern."

"The X rays are of the concrete wall where your son, Sam, is buried." He pointed to the neat rows of teeth in the blurry gray film. "The place is abandoned now."

"I want to know where you got these. And where is my husband?"

"Your husband apparently found these pictures out of literally millions in the Hanford safety records and took them for himself. I found them all collected in a little shrine inside the empty cooling tower where your son died. I think your husband has been going there for many years, Mrs. Charnock."

"Where is he?" she whispered.

"That's what we are trying to find out right now."

"How can that be? Check the records. My husband has never missed a day of work in his life; he's never called in sick; he's never been late. Why would he start now? You should march right back over to his office and ask him these questions yourself."

"Do you know that he's been terminated?"

"What?"

Duane pulled some papers from his pocket. The signed termination document from Charnock's employment record indicated that his last day on the job had been three days earlier.

"This is your husband's signature, isn't it?"

Rebecca stared at the documents with fascination and horror. Jack Charnock had never once done anything to surprise her in all their years together.

"How long has he known about this?"

Duane pointed to the date at the top of the page.

"He was formally terminated a little over a week ago."

Rebecca sat down. "So this is how it ends with you people." She turned the termination document over and over in her hands as though there was some additional meaning to the years Jack Charnock had spent at Hanford that might be coaxed from a single page of fine print.

"Not quite." Duane looked around to see if there was any indication that the house was being used to hide the plutonium he was now convinced had been removed from the Hanford site. "Some very dangerous nuclear materials that your husband was responsible for have gone missing. If I can't get an explanation or locate either your husband or the materials immediately, I'm going to have to call the governor and have him declare a nuclear emergency. That means anyone wearing a uniform in a thousand-mile radius from where we're standing will have the authority to hunt down your husband like a stray dog. So for his sake, I hope you can help me."

Rebecca looked long and hard at the X-ray pictures on the table. She arranged the colored snapshots of what had been her family around them. "You live with someone long enough that you know exactly the thoughts they are thinking. Twenty, thirty, forty years go by, and this person who has shared your bed, the man who has sat at your table every single day of those years no longer has anything new to add to what you know about him. He has nothing new to say. There's nothing he can do anymore to surprise you."

Duane watched as Rebecca talked. She kept staring at the pictures, her eyes filling with tears of sadness overlaid with a greater anger.

"That's the moment of greatest mystery. Because you no longer believe there's anything new, his capacity to surprise and shock you is infinite. It's as though one day he comes out of the hollow shell of his life like it was some flimsy costume to roam the world free of expectations. That's my Jack."

She looked up at Duane. "Do you know that he has never once mentioned the death of any of his children to me, not in twenty-nine years? We have never spoken of it. I thought he simply finished with all of it long ago. But I was wrong." She pointed to a photo of Jack and Sam Charnock standing together happily somewhere at Hanford in front of the unearthly green dome of the fast flux reactor. "Father and son were close, after all."

"Mrs. Charnock, have you ever seen these words before?" Duane unfurled the scrap of paper on which he had tried to copy legibly in Latin. "Your husband wrote them on the wall where your son is buried."

She repeated the words softly and then translated. "From death to life is the stone of the philosopher thus transmuted."

"Your husband told me the one time I met him about a philosopher's stone. He said it was his name for plutonium two-thirty-nine."

"Do you know how hard my husband worked for this country?" Rebecca was looking at the words and pictures before her on the table. Duane could see that her mind was racing. He didn't know how much longer she would be willing to help him.

"Mrs. Charnock, we don't have much time. If your husband is planning to do something with that plutonium it could end up killing tens of thousands of people. We have to stop him."

"He would never fight for himself, you know." Rebecca looked straight at Madison as though she had worked something out fully in her mind. "In all those years he let them ignore him, let others take credit for his inventions. He would just watch helplessly as his important projects got canceled. My husband, you see, is an idiot when it comes to politics. I'm not. It's why we've stayed together all these years."

"Mrs. Charnock, when was the last time you saw him?"

"Just a moment, Mr. Madison. You're the fellow who lost all of that money at the roulette table a couple weeks ago, aren't you?" Duane was feeling as though this was beginning to get away from him.

"Mrs. Charnock, I'd prefer it if we could just keep it to a discussion of your husband."

"I remember you very well. You sat right next to me, but I'm sure you don't remember. You were too busy paying attention to Mr. McCurdy. Come to think of it, you may be more involved in all this than you think."

"What do you mean, 'all this,' Mrs. Charnock?" He could see in her eyes now that she knew much more than she was saying.

"I thought I was the one with the secret life. I thought I was the only one with the surprises. It would never have occurred to him to call Mr. McCurdy. That's why we're together. God in heaven knows that I would have left years ago after everything that has happened. But I stayed." Rebecca Charnock touched her husband's young face on the snapshots. "Where are you, Jack? Was all the money just for me?" She looked back at the X rays. "I should have known. Jack Charnock is a ghost of Hanford, like his father, like his son. He would want to be there when it goes."

Rebecca Charnock put her head down. She knew at that moment that her husband wasn't coming home. She knew that the money in the box in the kitchen was to be for her, that she had set in motion a chain of events that she could now see was a beginning only for her. Her husband would have one more project to finish. Whether he was chased down by the Feds or was able to make his Hobby Horse do what on paper he knew it could do, he would not be coming home. Rebecca stood up and went over to the refrigerator. In it was a bag lunch. She took it out and clutched it like a doll.

"Mrs. Charnock, tell me what is about to happen." Duane could feel everything around him slipping, like he was driving into a fog. The mention of the casino and McCurdy had come out of nowhere. He was afraid. Somehow an investigation into a series of grisly murders had led to this unbalanced woman, who looked like she was capable of killing him with a single glance. "How is McCurdy involved in this?"

"What if you had worked all of your life to make this world a better place and not for one day did anyone take you seriously, not for one day. Think of it. What if you had seen every disappointment, if you had looked into his broken and beaten face every time he came home from another humiliation and could do nothing but try and patch him up and send him back to the same hateful place. For more than forty years you watch the man you had pledged your life to, sink away like this, and then suddenly you see a chance to help him. Would you do something to help this person who had given his whole life for nothing? Would you make it possible for him to leave a mark, to show the world that he was here?"

There was a long pause. Duane looked around to see if there was anything in the room that might help explain what this woman was talking about. If she had been waiting for an answer from Duane she appeared not to notice that he hadn't given one.

"Mr. McCurdy gave my husband something the government never gave him in over forty years. Mr. McCurdy wants to bring down the U.S. government, and after what we've been through, I can't say I much care anymore."

"Mrs. Charnock, did your husband give Roy McCurdy materials for a nuclear bomb?"

Rebecca got up from the table and went over to a box on the counter. She reached in and counted out a pile of money. She walked back to Duane and handed him the money.

"It's six thousand dollars. I believe that's about what you lost the other night. Mr. McCurdy wouldn't want you to have it, but I think my husband and I owe it to you."

Duane looked at the money and set it back on the table. "Keep your money, ma'am." He finally recognized Rebecca as the mousy, quiet woman he occasionally saw at the casino. The seriousness of this situation had fully dawned on him.

Rebecca continued with a smile. "You know, Mr. Madison, because of you, Roy McCurdy was able to pay good money for my husband's hard work. Of course I insisted that he pay. That's another reason why we've stayed together all these years. He would have just given it away."

Duane knew this was beyond him now. The bombs might have been at McCurdy's when he was there two days ago. He knew there was little likelihood they would be there now. "Mrs. Charnock, if you have made it possible for Roy McCurdy to use a nuclear weapon, we're all losers."

"Don't bet on it," she said as Duane nearly ran out to his truck. "My husband always said that his inventions would make the world a better place. I'd believe him."

"Don't go anywhere, Mrs. Charnock. We're going to want to talk some more with you, I'm sure. I hope for all our sakes, your husband decided to get drunk or have an affair and that he shows up on your doorstep tonight."

"You don't know my Jack very well," she said as Duane rolled down his window and turned on his engine.

"Sounds like you don't, either." Duane gunned his engine and grabbed his secure cell phone from the dashboard. "Just don't go anywhere, ma'am."

He pulled out onto the road to head back to Hanford. He knew Mrs. Charnock was right and that she wasn't going anywhere. He put in a call to the office, dialing a number used only for emergencies. Officer Westcott answered the phone.

"What's up?"

"We've got a very serious situation all of a sudden."

"Don't worry. I've already got the arrest warrant. We're on our way to pick her up now." Westcott's voice was breathless.

"What are you talking about?"

"I thought you knew. An old man stopped by this afternoon with a bag full of Indian stuff, spearheads and those same barbed hooks we found sticking out of that murdered driver we found. He said they belonged to a woman named Francine Smohalla and that his son was mixed up with her and that you would understand."

Madison's pulse quickened. He nearly shouted through the phone. "It's McCurdy. Is he still there?"

"He said you would know him. He left the bag and drove off about two hours ago."

"Jesus fucking Christ! Did you see what he was driving, Westcott?"

"Nothing special. I think it was a Toyota pickup or something like that. But I examined the bag. This is a bag full of murder weapons, Duane. This Smohalla is the one who claimed she was shot at while driving one of those fish tankers and started this manhunt. It was just a front, Duane, the hatchery—she's the killer."

"We've got bigger problems all of a sudden. Now listen carefully to me, Westcott. I want you to put out a full-scale nuclear-emergency call to FEMA. I'll be there in a few minutes. It seems that there's enough plutonium for a serious bomb on the loose from Hanford and I think your Mr. McCurdy might have been carrying some of it. We don't know yet if it's just one bomb or more than that but here's another name for you: Jack Charnock. He's a retired Hanford worker. We think he took the Pu two-thirty-nine, and with McCurdy, is planning to use it sometime soon. I'm betting Charnock is the only one who knows how to detonate. He's the key. We've got to find him."

There was silence for a moment. "I've got two cars on their way to the casino at Celilo to pick up Smohalla. Should I call them back?"

"No, she may know something about McCurdy. But we're going to need every available federal, state, and local authority to help locate these nukes before someone has a chance to use them."

"Roger. Duane, do you think this is related to the murders?"

"Do I believe someone would try to end the world over a fish?" Madison chuckled, but as he said the words they didn't sound so ridiculous. "I think there are people around here who would end the world just because there's nothing good on TV. Sit tight, Westcott. Make the call to FEMA. I'll be right there." Duane had another thought. "Come to think of it, there's no reason to go back to Hanford. Just make the call and meet me at the casino."

Madison thought about the anger loose in the world. It was hard to take seriously. It was, in fact, a lot like the millions of waste pools and leaking drums of nuclear sludge that it was his job to contain at Hanford, the by-products of the modern world. McCurdy reminded him of the easy part of his job. Big, nasty, easily traceable toxins that could be detected and bagged before they could do any harm. Then there was Charnock, a slow leak, anonymous, quiet, and detectable only after its damage had been done. There were millions of slow leaks at Hanford. They could be diluted and diverted and slowed down, but they could never be contained—like the anger in the world. Even with Duane Madison's best efforts, it would all someday find a way into the river.

And so castles made of sand fall into the sea, eventually.

Madison drove hard, Hendrix blaring in his mind, stereo silent so he could monitor the radio traffic. His truck slammed into the curves, scattering gravel and emptying puddles. He rode the rear end of every slow driver he came upon until they pulled off the road. At the top of the hill leading down to the casino he saw what he thought was the glow of red taillights, a car stopped in the road. He slammed on his brakes, coming to rest just beneath the Indian rock painting overlooking the town of Celilo. The road was empty. The rock painting, usually invisible at night, was on this night bright red. Its eyes and mouth seemed like black caves bored deep into the stone. The light gave the face a three-dimensional appearance that made it look almost alive. He couldn't see the source of the light, and he didn't wait around to discover it. He gunned his engine and continued on toward the casino. All Madison could place were the black eyes bathed in blood red and looking only at him.

·
·
·
·

25

"My son, Sam, would be about your age." Charnock uttered this without warning as he cleared four holes he had just drilled in the mid-deck of Duke McCurdy's boat and positioned a heavy metal plate containing the same number of bolts, each of which looked like it had come from a battleship.

"Where is he now?"

"Oh, he's a professor back east. My wife and I never see him. He's got all sorts of important work—you know, physics, computers, mathematics."

"Don't you know how old your own son is?"

Charnock paused. "You forget after a while. When you have kids you'll understand." He took a step back from the plate he had bolted into place. The cover of the engine was off and wires from the ignition system ran to the metal plates.

"Work the winch; I'll set her."

Duke had hooked a chain to the tubular frame containing a sphere constructed from individual tiles. Duke was fascinated by the craftsmanship. He cranked the pulley used for lifting and installing boat engines, which easily lifted the device up over the deck to where Charnock settled it in place and began driving the bolts. The machine-gun screech of the air driver filled the workshop.

Duke looked at the *Queequeg*. On blocks and out of the water, she was awkward and impotent-looking, but every bit of work he had ever put into her was visible. It was like poring over a trove of mementos.

Each scar and patch and daub of paint had been an episode of a young man's independence, a respite from the tirades and menace of his father. This last bit of customizing would end a long journey. This final act of independence would both free him from his father and honor his end-of-the-world madness. Duke could see exactly how he and his father were different. It made him calm. This was a present to Francine much preferable to himself. There was clarity here, where in his own jumbled soul of hatreds and fears, there was none.

She might not understand it immediately, yet the salmon would tell her. Duke would join the rocks and boulders that had always fascinated him. He was about to make his mark: This was the perfect plan. It was a gift for everyone he had disappointed in his life. His mother and Roy would eventually understand that, like Francine, he was a part of some natural order. He motioned for Charnock to step over to a table where he had tacked his map.

"Here is Mica." Duke pointed to a line above which a blue lake stretched east and south. "This is Kinbasket Reservoir. I'm certain that you'll be able to park somewhere on top of the dam. Nobody ever goes there. Nobody ever will after this. Mica's failure will wash out every dam downstream to Grand Coulee. That's where I'll be."

Charnock studied the map.

"How high is the structure?" Charnock was doing numbers in his head.

"About six hundred feet above the river on the downstream side."

"The explosion will crater the dam to about two hundred feet and the force of the water will do the rest."

"You should detonate before dawn. It will give people time to evacuate. I'm not an expert at this, but I estimate the flood wave will take most of the day to get to Grand Coulee, and then I'll give it another boost." There was silence. The two men stared at the map. Duke looked at the place where Shoulder Moon Casino was. He looked for Maryhill. It would certainly be above the flood. Just as certainly the casino would be washed away.

"Have you said good-bye to your wife?" Duke asked.

"No, but she'll understand."

"How about your son?"

"Yes, I did. He's happy about all this." Charnock took a deep breath as though something that had troubled him for a long time was finally settled. "Have you said good-bye to your wife?"

"Not married. But my folks will understand. And of course Roy is the inspiration for all this, anyway."

"You know, I would like to thank your father."

"For what?"

"For giving me this opportunity."

"As I understand it. Your wife had as much to do with it as Roy. She got you two together."

"Of course that's perfectly true, but my wife doesn't know all the ins and outs, you know. She's going to have a fine life now with all that money you paid me. Your dad says we have a lot in common. The Feds killed your mother and my spirit. To you and me, they've got a lot to answer for, I think."

Duke looked at Charnock. He seemed so harmless, so matter-of-fact. His world was the clever details that constituted his device. He gave his life as an anonymous trinket in a larger deed. He seemed to assign it no particular value compared to the inanimate forces he had spent his long undistinguished career serving. It occured to Duke that this was perhaps why the man was, in fact, so dangerous. The quiet angers and slights in this world, where only the few could ever hope to win, collected over time—dripping, spilling, channeling like the rain until they were a force nothing could hold back. Duke could see himself in this way, a rivulet of a cascade. What had made him feel alone was the thing that most bound him to the world.

"Wouldn't you have rather used these to bomb the Russians back during the cold war? Wasn't that what all of the nuclear weapons were for?" Duke considered this the riddle that described his own puzzlement with the modern world.

"Hobby Horse is the name of the project that developed these small portable bombs. They weren't for the Russians. They're like any invention. They're built to do something useful. There was nothing useful about the cold war." Charnock's face darkened. "Nobody even cares that we won. People always talk about preventing another world war. Look around you. World peace is what's destroying this planet.

"My father survived World War Two. He survived a nuclear accident that would have killed most of humanity. In those days you could talk about survival. People actually lived through the bombing of Nagasaki. Now it's all different. Everyone who experienced the cold war is going to die. The casualty rate is one hundred percent. You see, son, you can live through a war and they call you a survivor, maybe even a hero. But no one ever survives peace. We all die wondering what we might have done differently. My father never wondered about things; he just survived. I'll bet your father never wonders about things, does he?"

"No. My father's always been at war." Duke felt as though this funny little man had been put on the earth to speak to him at this moment.

"Young man, I spent my life wondering about things. I was trying to understand this substance called plutonium. They always said it was something to do with the future. Plutonium was going to be a big part of the 'World of Tomorrow.' There were going to be plutonium-powered trains and coffeemakers. I know now that plutonium has nothing to do with the future, only the past."

"It's getting late." Duke was conscious of the schedule. There would only be a day's head start. "You need to show me how to work this thing and then get on the road yourself."

"Yes, of course."

On the console of the boat, Charnock had installed an additional meter. Wires were strung from the console and out on deck where they disappeared under the engine cover. The sphere, bolted down, was covered with a blue plastic box, giving the whole unit the decidedly low-tech look of an outhouse. Duke could not have imagined a better camouflage.

The same almost laughable look had allowed his father to escape serious attention for most of his life. Duke thought this a good joke. America dreamed that its field of battle was reserved for nuclear titans in a war over righteousness, only to find itself defenseless against an Armageddon of rags and rusted jalopies leaking oil and tawdry revenge.

Charnock pointed to the tachometer. "You must reach five thousand rpm to sync the firing sequencer with the pulses of electricity coming off your engine. This is a diesel, so it won't like revving that fast for long. Also, your ignition system won't work as a detonator, so I've rigged up some spark plugs like those in a gasoline engine. Turn off any electricity on the boat when you get ready to detonate. There shouldn't be a problem, but just to make sure. When you reach five thousand rpm, just pull this lever. You'll know it worked when you see the blue light. It'll be the last thing you'll ever see."

"I'll try to steer myself close to the lip of the dam."

"You'll need to be right next to it; otherwise the reservoir will absorb the nuclear shock wave. You want the concrete arch to take as much of it as you can. And try not to detonate until you actually see the effects of the approaching flood wave. You don't want this explosion to cancel the force of the wave. It's not completely clear if fifteen or twenty kilotons will take out Grand Coulee. With the wave behind you, though, I'll bet you've as good a shot as a strike from some Soviet missile."

"How do you figure?"

"It's pretty much a guess, but up at Hanford we had to draw up contingencies in the event of an attack. Grand Coulee was one thing that we figured needed a direct strike, otherwise you couldn't shake her. But the dam people are the only ones who really know what she can take."

"I wouldn't call them this week, Mr. Charnock." Duke smiled at him.

"They sure won't be answering the phone next week." Charnock laughed awkwardly. Neither Duke nor Charnock wanted to think about human casualties as a result of what they were about to do. The whole thing seemed to Duke neater without them.

"Will it be like Hiroshima? Tens of thousands of dead people and more waiting to die?"

"No, Hobby Horse is a blast bomb, not a radiation bomb. Near ground zero, nothing survives. A few miles away, there will be lots of shattered windows and anyone sheltered behind a rock, out of sight of the bomb should survive. There aren't many people up there by Grand Coulee, anyway. The flood is going to be more of a problem than any blast, the way I've got it figured. All I care about is that the wave makes it to Hanford. There's a concrete tower there that I would love to see come crashing down."

Charnock stood thinking for a moment, then his face lit up and he began to chant quietly to himself.

"Put up the flood, or water, upon the black and soft matter or earth of the stone. Beat this black earth into powder, and mingle it with man's blood, and so let it stand three hours. Distill it on ashes with a good fire; and then it shall be water of the fire rectified, and so hast thou three of the elements exalted into the virtue of the quintessence, namely water, air, and fire."

"Is this some kind of religion for you?" Duke found himself uneasy around Charnock's mystical zealotry, as he was around that of his parents.

"It's what I meant about the past. Plutonium is not something for the future. It's the ancient philosopher's stone, the virtue of the quintessence. It is a spirit from the past come to haunt us here in this millennium and show us the way back. I'm just an insignificant gatekeeper, like you."

"Like Coyote." Duke suddenly thought of something Francine had told him.

"The animal?"

"The Indians say the salmon know the way back to the sea no matter how much time passes. They say that Coyote is the gatekeeper. He frees the fishes."

Charnock seemed proud of the comparison. "The more names a thing has the more important it is."

"You should get going. You won't get slowed down until you are al-most there. There's probably still some snow in the mountains around Mica."

"What about the border?"

"The Canadian border?"

"Yeah, do I need a passport?"

"Should be no problem. Do you have a valid driver's license?"

"Yep."

"Then they'll wave you across. I guarantee it. They'll probably be thrilled you're going to visit the upper Columbia. Nobody ever goes there. You're not going to be bothered."

"How can you be so sure?"

"It's the best part of this plan." Duke laughed. "The Feds think ter-rorists would never smuggle explosives into Canada. They only look for bombs coming the other way."

Charnock coughed nervously. They both understood it was time to get on with it.

"Good luck." Charnock grabbed his tool kit and climbed up into his truck while Duke cranked open the door to the shed. Dawn was breaking. The morning air was damp and heavy with rain, the clouds low and dark.

"Good luck, Jack Charnock," Duke said as his truck pulled for-ward. Duke could see that the boat trailer was riding low on his shocks. The load was heavy. Duke hoped the roads were clear near Mica. Charnock turned on his windshield wipers, and they threw raindrops into Duke's face. Charnock waved, and rumbled down the driveway. As he closed the door to the shed, Duke swore he heard Charnock call him by another name—Sammy.

26

"Twenty-nine," Joe called out to a chorus of groans as people around the roulette table watched the ball. Joe Moses looked for his brother in a sea of heads extending to the four walls of Shoulder Moon Casino. He had not stopped looking since he had left the lantern on the rock. Each night he had hiked back up to refill it with fuel and Tsagaglalal's smile taunted him once more. He did not see his brother in the crowd.

Joe's usual table had the best view from the floor level of the casino's traffic pattern. It had always been his intention that signs for elevators and exits pointed at nothing, and the thick carpeted walkways only led people cleverly back toward the gaming tables or the slot machines. Joe was regretting this design decision at the moment. There was gridlock wherever he looked, no way to walk a straight line and get anywhere, and even when not mobbed, there weren't that many people who could walk a straight line at Shoulder Moon after seven in the evening.

Word that Charley Shen-oh-way was alive and wanted for murder had spread among the tribes. People were on edge. They asked Joe what he knew. Knowing nothing only increased his own longing for his brother. People said Charley's return would be a sign from Smohalla himself. Those who had seen the red-lit face of Tsagaglalal assumed she had brought him back from the dead. People spoke openly of the return. Joe had not made up his mind about what his brother's return might mean exactly. He struggled with this as he cleared the house chips from the board. Fiddle music from an Irish-sounding band named Treetoad was giving him a headache.

"I wouldn't have thought there would be so many people interested in a festival for fish, Joe. Was this your idea?"

Mrs. Grassley, at her usual place, was interested in her winnings, as was her husband, who stared at the table through his plastic oxygen mask and carefully stacked chips. Between bets they looked up to observe a parade of meticulous outcasts slowly winding its way past the roulette table.

"So many people have causes nowadays," Mrs. Grassley remarked with the contempt of a self-made millionaire. "When I was a girl we never had time for such things."

A woman staggered by with a tattoo that began on her neck and continued up onto her shaved head, concluding with three eagle talons, one on her forehead and one on each cheek. Her arm was around another woman dressed in leather from head to toe and festooned with patches denoting various Indian affiliations. They scowled at Mrs. Grassley when they saw her looking their way.

"What tribe are they from, Joe?" she asked, as a bird-watcher might express interest in an unusual bug.

"Don't know. We call them Wish-ums," he said with a smile. "A Wish-um is a person who was told by someone that they had Indian blood. They don't know any more about it than that, so they sew on some patches, make up a story, and wish it to be true."

"I would think that a tattoo like that would make it hard to hold down any kind of a job."

"Not in this economy." Doug Pollack was in his usual place and also winning tonight. "If you can breathe, you can get a job. This year the people in our mailroom got signing bonuses and their tongues pierced." Pollack made a five-hundred-dollar bet on four numbers.

The festival had brought a different crowd to the casino. Mrs. Grassley looked out at angry people, some Indians, most not, everyone calling for an end to something. "What I don't understand is, why in this day and age people would want to go back to the past, where there were none of the things that make our good life and this bright future possible?"

"The festival wasn't my idea, to answer your first question," Joe said finally. "But in my life I have always found the past and the future to be a very volatile mixture."

A number of people carried signs or wore T-shirts bearing the face of Tsagaglalal. Her face was on the banner that hung over the casino's main stage: *She Who Watches says, "The Salmon Brother Is Our Indian Brother."* Ordinarily the stage would be headlining some distinctly non-Indian act such as Jose Feliciano or Paul Anka. Crowds had jammed the auditorium to hear speeches calling for war against white fishermen, calling for the government to declare the salmon an endangered species and a restoration of unrestricted treaty fishing rights for the Columbia tribes.

Otis had been right. People streamed into this "Salmon Blood Festival" as if they were going to Mass. To Joe it had brought back a vision of the old Celilo when traditional people would gather and gamble and sell and bitch about everything and anything. Here it was the same. The tribes were different, but on this night Shoulder Moon was once again the ritual marketplace of outrage and commerce that it had been in the old days. Joe thought even his brother would recognize it.

There were gamblers and Indian activists, and the ordinary curious types who got bored easily, looked for T-shirts, and drove home drunk. Small-time crusaders passed out business cards, spoke of their Web sites and the world's demise. Crystal readers, psychics, and diet gurus all offered a path to complete enlightenment. One group wearing hand-painted signs walked up and down the rows of flashing slot machines demanding a ban on electricity and the burning of fossil fuels. No one looked up from their buckets of coins. One man called for the destruction of clocks, which he claimed were the root of all evil in the modern world. Joe chuckled at this. There wasn't a clock to be found anywhere at Shoulder Moon. Clocks gave gamblers an excuse to go home when they were winning. You couldn't have that.

Outside the casino some white fishermen were shouting abuse at everyone arriving at the festival. "No more favors for Indian millionaires!" A sign said, *Save the Salmon, Kill an Indian.* Joe knew well the bitterness Shoulder Moon had produced all along the river. He had seen such signs before, just never so many in his own parking lot. He didn't like looking at them, but a half dozen television cameras tethered to a row of TV satellite trucks were apparently thrilled to be beaming pictures of the protesters all over the region, just as Otis had predicted. A contingent of state troopers watched it all with mild interest. So far it had gone smoothly. Every game was going. Every table was full. The slots were running nonstop. Joe was once more holding his net astride Celilo's torrent of plenty, gamblers and cash standing in for white water and salmon. He spun the wheel.

■

Francine stood backstage. Like her uncle, she stared out at the crowd looking for Charley. She had been warned not to come, and the casino was not a place she enjoyed visiting. Even as a young girl she detested her uncle's sparkling temple of money and Indian hokum. But tonight the festival made it seem like an enormous baited trap. She imagined it drawing her father into this cauldron of unsettled scores, angry faces shouting and grumbling to the music of Irish fiddles. All tribes, white, Indian, with nothing in common other than the chance to get drunk and shout about something and wager their paltry sums. She looked for her father's face and thought about Duke and his warning for her not to come here.

"It's a sign from Coyote. Shaking Head Woman has come. We must have done something right."

Otis had walked up behind her and placed his hands on her shoulders. As if on cue Francine shook her head and turned around, startled. He was holding a clipboard and wearing a headset, signifying that he was in control. "It's surely a sign from Coyote, if Otis is running the show," Francine said.

"You mean it's the end of the world." Daniel Three Knives stepped out of the backstage darkness. "What brings the biologist down here to see Indian show business?" The three embraced and looked back at the crowd, which was mostly on its feet jumping and swaying to the music. Otis was in his element. He was also tipsy, of that Francine was certain, although she couldn't tell if it was out of excitement or drink. She thought it best not to pay too much attention. Otis had a full flask of whiskey in his pocket but hadn't touched a drop. He hadn't given drink a thought since the hundreds of people began streaming through the doors of Shoulder Moon. There was no stopping the First Annual Salmon Blood Festival now, whatever his condition might be. Daniel would see to it that Otis didn't do anything completely stupid, no matter how happy or drunk he got.

"They are still hunting for my father. I want to find him first if he's alive." Francine had not stopped replaying the moment she had fired the bullet and heard her father's cry of pain.

"He's alive." Daniel sounded much more confident than her uncle had. They would have found his body by now. "Alive, they will never find him until he wants to be found."

"Do you think he would come here?"

"Indian people have heard that he is alive." Daniel pulled Francine back to where the sound of the music was not so deafening and they could talk. Otis followed but said nothing. "People are saying that he is a messenger from Smohalla. Your uncle has made the sign for him to come. Have you seen the face of Tsagaglalal?"

"She is covered in blood," Otis said. "It is her will that the white salmon thieves die."

"Your uncle has placed a light on the rock, the sign from when we were young boys. If your father sees it he will come here," Daniel explained.

"If he does, he'll be arrested," Francine said, skeptical and worried that the Indians' loose talk of omens and well-intentioned spirits would just hand the cops an ambush. "The place is surrounded."

"They are just security guards," said Otis. "When the Feds show up, I would start to worry."

"There are probably dozens of undercover Feds in the crowd right now."

"Not likely, we know everyone." Otis smiled. "Anyone we don't know is surrounded. Like that guy out there." Otis pointed at a face a few yards back from the stage on a security monitor. "He might be trouble but can't do anything because my people are all around him."

"Your people."

"I've got a hundred paid undercover security men who get two hundred dollars in chips at the end of the night. Stick around. It will be the best part of the festivities."

"One hundred of Otis's closest drinking buddies with money in their pockets sounds more like the casting call for a riot." Francine looked into the monitor. In the first few rows of the crowd she thought she saw Duke's face. A second look, and the face was too old.

"Do we know who this guy is?" she asked, pointing at the monitor.

Otis answered. "We know him. He's an antigovernment type. He won a big jackpot a few weeks ago and couldn't stop ranting about race wars and destiny."

"Why do you think he's here?"

"Not a clue. He did all right here the last time. Maybe he's looking for another payday. We've got three people on him. Is he a friend of yours?"

"I'll make it four." Francine studied the face of Roy McCurdy. Anger and bitterness had passed from father to son, but Duke still had in his face a tenderness long ago relinquished by his father's. She thought again of Duke's last words to her.

"A gift to your mother to win the heart of her daughter. One *jokulh-laup* coming right up."

Francine recalled his warning. It took her a minute to locate Roy. He was backing away from the stage, working his way out of the crowd, and gazing up at the ceiling of the theater. A look of rapture had enveloped his hard face. "A father, moved by mysterious forces" was how Duke had described his dad. The density of the crowd below her made Francine dizzy. Roy was making his way deliberately back toward the casino. All at once Francine realized why she had been warned. The thought sucked the breath right out of her as it formed in her mind.

"I know why he's here," she said suddenly and directly to Otis. "I've got to get to him." She stepped up to the edge of the stage.

"He's not someone you want to provoke, Francine," Otis said.

"I've already provoked him. Maybe I'm just the one to calm him down." Francine paused, teetering at the edge of the stage. The music was blaring. Francine's skin was drenched. Otis could see that she was terrified of the crowd.

"If you step down there"—Otis placed his hand on her trembling shoulder blades as he had done so many times when she was a little girl afraid—"think of your wings. Use your *tepeh* Coyote gave you to fly over the bad things. Coyote will protect you."

"If I really had wings, Otis, I would fly over the world and find my father. We're both stuck here on earth, I'm afraid." She took a breath, gathered her courage, and ran quickly out into the theater.

People were packed together around the stage. They did not move to make way as she walked by them. She looked ahead, trying to keep her eyes on Roy McCurdy and bumped into people in the crowd who answered her roughly with jabs of their elbows, shoving her sideways. The air was thick with drink and sour breath. Anger lay heavy over the room. "Don't push me, bitch." A man rose up offering his rage to Francine. She looked for a way around him and found only more people blocking her way. Francine felt the crowd swallowing her, answering her eye contact with threats of physical harm she could see on each face. As he moved well ahead of her, she could still see the gray head of Roy McCurdy, who was having as much difficulty making progress as she was.

A vertigo she knew only from her nightmares consumed her. Faces of Indian people locked on to Francine's blue eyes. Bodies moved to block her. "Excuse me," she shouted. "Please let me through!" As she moved forward, hands and arms pushed her to the side and back until she had completely lost her bearings. The stage music drowned out her voice and seemed to be coming from everywhere in the room. It was no longer a catchy Irish song but urgent drumming accompanied by wails and shouts. The farther she ventured from the stage, the more the light dimmed. The stationary bodies seemed to grow in the darkness until the crowd was towering over her.

Whispered from the lips of the Indian people who passed her from one pair of arms to another were the words *sitkum siwash*. Half-breed. She was exposed, naked. The faces around her were drunk and weaving, their eyes crazy. She could see bottles hidden in pockets and in wrinkled paper bags wet with saliva and grease. The floor below her was slippery. She felt a blow to her back, turned around, and saw a woman retching openly and laughing along with a crowd of men. Ropes of vomit and mucus hung from her face like strings of beads. She howled at Francine and opened her blackened mouth containing a single tooth. The woman could have been Francine's age.

She struggled to keep from falling. Terror and the disorientation of the music and stage lights made it hard for her to tell what she was seeing. Ahead of her any sign of Roy McCurdy was gone. He had made his way out of the crowd or had been trampled underfoot, which she thought was about to be her fate. She looked at the people around her. There were faces from many tribes. They all shouted at the stage, dulled and made desperate by drink. The plague had spared none of them: It seemed to Francine that these souls were like her salmon, whose lives consisted of circling in a featureless tank from which there was no escape, and at the end, no meaning. In the faces of the people, she saw the contempt she had always feared from the salmon. *"Sitkum siwash."* She heard the syllables again. They did blame her. They all blamed her.

Hands tightened around her arms, and she felt someone's breath against her bare neck, a woman trying to kiss her. The woman's eyes were rolled back in her head as she pressed her lips against Francine's face and plunged her hands into Francine's thick hair. Someone else's hands clawed at her breasts, forcing her down to the floor. She tried to resist, but the crowd seemed to be feeding on her, faces staring, arms reaching for a piece of her before she was torn to bits.

"You're killing me. I am not to blame." The crowd pressed down on her, squeezing her breath. The last words were lost in her empty lungs. She struggled to get back on her feet, but someone was holding her head down. All she could see was the glisten of the beer and vomit on the slippery floor and the unsteady knees all around her. She started to lose consciousness. Her last sensations were of being kicked in the stomach and chest as she descended to the floor.

Francine saw that a bed of flowers was softening her fall. She looked up at the sky. It was suddenly sunny and warm. She felt for her wings and tried to catch the breeze on the hill and fly up and over the river to safety. She flapped them and to her surprise she began to take flight. *Why do I forget my wings? I should use the* tepeh *Coyote gave me,* she thought. She felt herself rising toward the blue sky, and as she did, the sky darkened and the noise of the theater returned. She opened her eyes to see the faces that had been leering over her were below her and full of their own terror and amazement. She had shown them all, she thought, as she felt herself coughing violently. "I have wings," she said as her breath returned and she looked out at the crowd.

"Smohalla has come." The voices spoke, but not to her. She looked down and became aware that she was in the arms of a powerful man who had plucked her from the floor and was holding her safely aloft, keeping the crowd at bay. His long hair was black, streaked with gray. He wore a white shirt that made his skin seem as dark as the river at night. He was holding her as though presenting her to the world as an infant for the very first time. "What shall I call you, Daughter of Charley Shen-oh-way?" he asked. It was her father.

"Call me that," she said, holding her hands to his face. His flat nose and wide forehead were her own. He had been her *tepeh.* He was staring at her blue eyes; the eyes that told the world she had no roots had now brought him to her.

"Aren't you injured?" Francine said. "I know I hit you with at least one bullet down at the river."

"Let's go now." Charley began to walk forward, and the crowd parted before him. Francine settled her head on his shoulder. His smell was leathery, with the salty hint of salmon and the river on his skin. She sobbed quietly into his shirt and held him tightly. The stage had gone silent. Everyone in the theater was focused on the apparition in their midst.

"Smohalla has come. Coyote will free the fishes." Older Indians got down on their knees before Charley and wailed these words and others, signifying the fulfillment of prophecy. Young people watched and wept openly and reached out to touch him. "The old ones said you would come for *nusuh*."

"I have come only for my child. It is for Smohalla to care for *nusuh*," Charley said to the people nearest him. "That is all I know. My work for Smohalla is finished."

Few people heard him. All around Charley and Francine, voices swelled. "Smohalla has come."

The moment he had seen Francine go down, Otis had stepped from the stage and was making his way toward her and Charley. He ran in front of Charley, who stopped and put Francine down. "Charley," he said as he recognized him, then echoing the last words he had heard Charley speak in the rainy parking lot the night of the first killing: "*Tamala, tamala.*"

Charley looked at him. "No, I do not know you. The bottle writes its name on your face. Today has come." Charley motioned to the drunken crowd that had nearly trampled his daughter to death and looked back at Otis, his voice full of disgust. "The disease kills. You are the disease."

"Then your return is the cure." Otis embraced Charley, and a calm came over his face. He looked to Francine like one of the tribal elders he once had been. The fear and powerlessness she had always seen in his eyes, along with drink, were gone.

"I am no cure for you." Charley pulled away from his embrace and delivered a bitter whisper to Otis. "The disease is the cure for you." Francine was pulled by the obligation to defend Otis, the closest person to a father she had ever had. But she could not step away from the imaginary father she had dreamed of all her life, now become real in the form of this strange man. She turned away from Otis.

He stood alone in the crowd, his fingers on the flask in his pocket. As Francine and Charley made their way toward the casino surrounded by chanting people, Otis lifted it to his lips. A drop of whiskey that ran from his lips mixed with the tears already there on his face. He looked at Francine and saw for the first time that, as he had always told her, she had wings.

■

Joe had noticed the commotion off toward the entrance to the theater and could see that a number of his security men had headed in that direction. Joe halted the roulette game for a moment and tried to listen to the radio traffic to determine exactly what was happening. Distinct on the radio was the sound of the chanting—"Smohalla has come." He looked down at the table and saw that a large bet had been placed on the double zero, $31,000 at thirty-to-one odds.

"Look who's making the big bets again!" Mrs. Grassley said to the man who had quietly stepped over to the table. Joe had already recognized him.

"Mr. McCurdy, is your lucky streak still hot?" Roy was smiling. Joe thought he looked less angry and dangerous than the last time he saw him. He seemed to be genuinely enjoying himself, almost like one of the many lonely, retired men who showed up on the elderly singles bus tours that stopped at the casino. He had a thin wallet in his hand and in his front shirt pocket an object that looked like a small radio or a remote-control device for a television.

"Looking for a sign from God. I feel real good tonight, Chief. But I'm afraid you should have taken the night off."

"Why is that?"

"This fish festival or whatever you want to call it—seems to me it just gets in the way of your main business here at the casino."

"It's just for one night, Mr. McCurdy, and it's not keeping you from placing bets as far as I can tell."

"I just don't understand Indian people. You moan about your lost lands, but when some white judge says you can build anything you want on this worthless reservation land that the U.S. government put you on in the first place, you build a casino." He removed the device from his pocket and set it on the table next to his wallet. "Your contribution to this world is a place for Indians, niggers, and gooks to get drunk."

"What are you drinking tonight, old man?" Doug Pollack was looking at the size of the reckless bet McCurdy had just made. "Looks like Charles Manson is about to lose a bundle. That's some quality entertainment. Spin the wheel, Joe."

"One more time, Chief."

Joe was eyeing the object McCurdy had set on the table. It looked like nothing more than a toy with multicolored buttons arranged in a crude face, but like McCurdy himself, it seemed to smile back at Joe, bristling with menace. He gave the wheel a firm turn, excused himself for the moment with a smile, and put the radio up to his ear where he could hear his security people shouting about uniformed police inside the building. Police had no jurisdiction inside the casino. Joe wanted to leave the table but could do nothing until the ball landed.

"There's your sign, Mr. McCurdy," Mrs. Grassley noted with a sneer. The ball had landed on number eighteen. McCurdy said nothing as his $31,000 went into the pit. It was an awkward moment. Everyone looked at McCurdy. He opened his wallet and laughed. It was empty. He reached down to the device on the table and pressed a green button. A small light flashed and in a screen the number 890 appeared.

"There's my sign," he said.

"This table is closed," Joe announced, and walked off nervously toward where the police were now visibly facing off with the crowd. The

Grassleys, Doug Pollack, and the other regulars drifted off into the casino's well-lit chaos.

■

Duane Madison swerved into the parking lot and skidded to a stop in front of the main entrance to the casino. He pulled the service revolver from his days as a Seattle cop from the glove box and stepped down onto the muddy ground. In the parking lot there were media trucks on one side, a ragtag group of white fishermen with signs, trying to get their attention, on the other. The action was inside.

He headed for the door of the casino and walked by a crookedly parked Toyota pickup. He looked in the windshield, leaning on the fender as he did. The cab was empty, but the bright-red engine lights were casting a glow on the steering wheel. He took a step away from the car and without warning it started. For an instant Madison thought he had done something similar to sitting on a bumper and triggering a car alarm. As he watched, the engine raced, as though someone was pumping the accelerator.

Madison pulled at the doors. They were locked. The hood was latched and immovable. The bed of the truck was covered and locked. A large wire harness with a thick braid of cable snaked its way from the steering column to a hole in the cab where it disappeared into the back. Madison peered through the rear windows to see what was inside. Darkness. He looked down. Whatever it was carrying was a heavy load. The tires were sagging and the truck bed seemed to be sitting almost directly on its axle springs. As he stood there, the idle of the truck began to increase.

It came to him suddenly. "The engine is the fucking detonator. A nuke car bomb. He's here already!" Madison barked on his radio. "This is going down."

He ran through the front door of the casino and into the middle of a face-off between a line of police and a group of Indians. A woman and an older man were being taken into custody. The man was passively offering his hands to a pair of handcuffs while the woman was resisting and being restrained as she shouted.

"There's not much time! He's already here! Everyone is in danger!" Francine shouted, and struggled as she was cuffed.

Madison recognized the terror on Francine's face. "Have you seen him?"

Francine looked at Madison, relieved that someone was finally listening to her.

"He's out there in the casino."

"We didn't call in any federal reinforcements." One of the Washington State cops stepped between Madison and Francine. "Everything is under control here. This is a murder case. You can be on your way."

"Where is McCurdy?" Madison shouted past the officer at Francine.

"He's over there by the roulette table. They don't believe me."

"I believe you. Is he armed?"

"I don't know. They stopped me before I could get near him."

"We've got to get these people out of here!" Madison shouted to the officers, but they stood their ground. Mention of the name McCurdy had changed them. Madison motioned for three officers to accompany him out onto the gaming floor, but no one moved.

"You're on your own, federal boy." The officers stayed put. "We made our arrest. Roy McCurdy is none of our concern."

"You're crazy. He plans to vaporize this whole place with you in it."

"Then you can go in and stop him."

Madison looked around, the only black man in the crowd, alone under eyes that beamed contempt and needed no words. It had followed him here like an unpaid bill and cared nothing for how hard he'd studied in school, or any other aptitude or merit he had always tried to place between him and the color of his skin. From the time he was a boy with ocean in his nostrils, the Pacific Northwest had always felt like a place where everyone had come to start over. Here Duane knew only that he was the nigger; he felt for his gun.

"Don't do anything foolish, federal boy." The tallest of the officers smiled at Duane.

"There is a bomb in this building. McCurdy wants to kill us all."

"That's a good story. Federal government always has a good story when they show up, like down there in Waco; hell of a story. Like I said, federal boy, you're on your own."

"I see." His heart pounding furiously, Duane took a step back and looked from face to face. America's tribal war paint didn't wash off. They would die for no good reason, just so no one could say they saw them help out a nigger. The gamblers hadn't even looked up from their games.

"You have no authority here." Joe Moses and a dozen of his well-armed security personnel suddenly surrounded the police.

"That's good." Duane took a breath and nearly chuckled. "The Indians are the cavalry."

Duane stepped away and the crowd parted. It seemed to Joe that right there in front of him his brother had materialized out of the air. Joe walked straight up to Charley, scarcely believing it was him.

"I only believed you were dead," he said, ashamed and through tears.

He returned to the moment by the river when he had given his brother up for dead, holding in his arms the half-dead body of the woman his brother had loved, watching his entire world vanish with Celilo. It had been such a long way to come alone.

Charley's eyes lit up. He stepped toward his brother. The officers held him back. "You have done well."

"Let them go," Joe said to the cops. "My brother. I can believe now that Smohalla has come." Joe was overcome. He grabbed his brother's hands and stared into his eyes. Charley looked back with a playful smile as though it had been Coyote who put him up to a trick that had lasted both of their lifetimes.

"We win. Coyote showed me the key." It was as if they were picking up a conversation left off only the day before. "He hid it with the white man so it would be safe." Charley sighed calmly as though they understood how everything would turn out now.

"These people are under arrest for murder." The cop who had been speaking to Madison drew his gun and pointed it at Joe.

"Pull that trigger, and my people will make sure there won't be enough of your body left to fit into a can of cat food. You can do nothing here, Officer. Put your guns away." Daniel Three Knives stepped up to the cops, along with a few dozen Indians who seemed greedy for a fight.

"Then we'll arrest them the moment they step off this property."

"Joe, Daniel, forget about us. McCurdy is going to blow up the casino." Francine pointed at Madison. "It's why he's here."

"McCurdy just lost thirty grand," Joe said. "He's out of money. He's carrying no bomb." Joe pressed the Talk button of his radio and was about to say something when Madison spoke sternly.

"I know what I'm talking about, Joe. It could be a fifteen-kiloton bomb. It's in a truck in the parking lot, and we think he can detonate it from in here." Madison rushed by Joe and the Indians who had surrounded and were disarming the cops. He approached the roulette table where McCurdy was standing with the remote detonator in his hands. The table was between the theater and the front entrance. Unlike every other crowded gaming table on the floor, this one was empty but for McCurdy, who was watching the number rise on the controller and smiling. The gamblers all around him paid no attention to anything but their own games. McCurdy was surrounded by bright red light reflected off the carpeting and walls. It made his eyes into dark, deep-set, hollow caves like the head of a wooden puppet. The big stuffed salmon above the roulette table seemed to move with the flashing of the slot-machine lights.

"One thousand four hundred," Roy called out, looking at the rpm on the detonator. "You here for the fireworks, nigger, or do you want to place a bet?"

"Put that down, Roy, and I won't shoot you."

"Two thousand two hundred. I don't think you want me to let go of this. Go ahead and shoot, but it would be kind of a shame if I'm the only one here who misses seeing the light of creation."

Madison could not tell by sight how the detonator worked. McCurdy's thumb was poised over a red button in the center of the controller. His other thumb was pressing a black button. Madison could pull the trigger now and put a hole the size of a poker chip in his skull, but if McCurdy was right, this was going to be ground zero.

"Three thousand nine hundred. We're not far now. You think I'm the only one with a firecracker? Place your bet, janitor boy, red or black?"

■

Otis had climbed back onstage to drain the flask, letting the abrasive sting of the warm whiskey settle into numbness. The musicians had stopped playing. He looked at the crowd, which was growing agitated at the presence of police and pushing to get a glimpse of the apparition who had cut his heart out twice in one lifetime. The chanting for Charley and Smohalla had not subsided. He thought of the little girl Francine who used to run to him with her hands outstretched to show him a flower, calling him Daddy and asking to hear the old stories of Coyote again and again. Otis watched the lights on the audio console and thought about how much he thirsted to have had any control over the events that had swirled around his people, defining his life on the margins where whiskey turned impotence into rage. Otis picked up the radio and turned up the volume to eavesdrop on chatter he was no part of.

Madison's voice on the radio was clear. "It could be a fifteen-kiloton bomb." The words silenced the chatter. The only other thing he could make out was the name McCurdy. The man Francine had been chasing and trying to stop.

"A bomb," he said to himself. "That's a good one. Someone finally called the cavalry."

Otis looked back at the console and the main switch for the PA system that shut off the casino's constant canned music and opened his microphone to deliver an announcement all could hear. He gripped the microphone as though it was the last solid rung of a crumbling ladder and pressed the Talk button.

"Stop what you are doing and leave as fast as you can. There is a bomb in the building. When you are outside, keep going. Get as far away as you can. The bomb could go off at any time."

Otis relaxed his hand. It was white and his knuckles ached from the desperation of his grip. He sat back. There was silence until the wail of panic began to swell, slowly at first. He sat back and smiled. He thought of the river and those stepping-stones that made the water divert around them. He closed his eyes and felt the diverted course of history flowing around and over him.

■

Joe heard Otis and understood immediately. The crowd of gamblers torn from their own worlds had become a mob of a single thought: escape. Joe had no idea what to make of Madison and McCurdy's standoff. He would protect his brother and niece from the crowd and hope for the best.

"Come with me, quickly. We must make it to the office corridor before we're overrun."

"What of Otis?" Daniel shouted.

"He's back in the theater. If he's smart he'll stay put backstage. If he's as drunk as he sounded, he'll be torn to pieces. We can't help him."

"What of the bomb?"

"If it goes, none of this will matter."

Joe looked to see if he could still see Madison and McCurdy. They were either already overrun or had taken a different route away from the crowd. Charley, Francine, Joe, and Daniel cut straight through the poker tables and headed for the near wall. Joe fumbled for his keys. If the crowd saw an open door they would storm it. The noise was rising behind them. The confusing pattern of walkways in the casino and the lighting that obscured the walls and exits accelerated the crowd's panic. Joe could hear the sound of chairs and tables overturning as he stepped behind a gaudy column. Joe looked behind him.

The fake windows and doors in the longhouse area of the casino had fooled hundreds into stampeding down a dead end. He could hear screams as people were pressed against the flimsy wall and the sound of glass breaking as people tried to kick out the fake windows and doors. The pressure of the crowd forced people through jagged openings in the decorative wall that led only to a concrete outer wall. Then with a crash the entire structure of wood and aluminum collapsed, burying people pinned and impaled on broken Indian artifacts and plastic tribal masks that seemed indistinguishable from dying faces.

Joe watched it all, his work being dismantled by the same anger and primitive impulses that Shoulder Moon was built to draw from its customers and off which it lived. Everywhere Joe looked, the crowd was dense and desperate. The floor was rubble. Most people had lost their bearings. Two bodies lay bleeding and motionless as people stepped over them, hurled forward by the momentum of the crowd. Joe had his keys out as he reached the unmarked door. In a moment he opened it and pushed everyone through. As he slammed it behind him, he heard what he thought was the loud report of a gun until the sound of the slamming door covered it and everything else.

■

The people nearest Madison and McCurdy backed away when they heard the PA announcement. Initially, the panic flowed fearfully around them, the mob seeking a sign that they were running away from, and not toward, the bomb. But the people emerging from the dark auditorium didn't see Madison and McCurdy, and quickly the mob came between them.

As he struggled to keep his balance, Madison realized that they were all about to die unless he made a decision. He tried to remember what he had read in the documents explaining Charnock's Hobby Horse device. He knew it was made to work off an engine but the trigger involved something he was having difficulty remembering. McCurdy stood, oblivious to the crowd looking at him.

"You're going to be a part of history, nigger. Are you ready for the world's first atomic lynching?" McCurdy looked down at the detonator. "Four thousand five hundred."

Madison thought of the boxes in the back of Charnock's trunk, the baseballs and golf balls. He remembered implosion. The trigger was a precisely timed implosion. The engine had to reach a certain rpm to match the trigger sequence. A six-cylinder pickup truck redlined at about six thousand. The trigger point was somewhere between 4,500 and 6,000. There was no time; Madison knew what to do. "You're about to be killed by this nigger, you nasty little shit. And a seaful of angry brown people is going to stomp your body into pink gravy." Madison aimed at McCurdy's hand and fired.

The bullet grazed McCurdy's wrist and he dropped the detonator. It slid under the roulette table. McCurdy jumped down onto the floor to get the device, and as he did, Madison saw the surge of the mob from behind the collapsed wreckage of the longhouse structure. They ran hysterically out onto the floor, responding to the sound of the gun, and clearing the floor of tables and chairs. Madison got one more shot off before McCurdy disappeared. He had no idea whether McCurdy was dead or had recovered the detonator under the table and was about to end it all. Madison turned and ran for the edge of the room away from the doors as the mob reached the front entrance. They began breaking the glass and tearing through the half dozen retail shops with doors that opened onto the parking lot. On the floor as he ran, there were hundreds of dead and bleeding people. It occurred to Madison that a bomb was unnecessary here, that a nuclear explosion would erase the evidence of the carnage all around him.

He ducked into an entrance for the theater and saw an even more horrible scene. The corridors on both sides of the stage leading to the emergency exits were packed with screaming people. Madison couldn't see what people in the front of the crowd could see, that the doors were blocked with garbage and supplies for the casino's restaurants. He could tell by the sounds that there was no escape here. Madison vaulted up onto the stage and ran to the back looking for a loading dock door that opened outside. He ran by a man backstage.

"You don't see us. We have always been invisible."

Madison turned around to recognize Otis, obviously drunk, holding a long knife and sitting calmly on the floor.

"Otis, is there a way out through the loading dock?"

"Coyote forgets our faces, too. Coyote recognizes blood." Otis looked directly at Madison. The microphone was next to him. Madison realized he had announced the bomb and that he had been injured somehow, perhaps when people stormed the stage on their way to the blocked emergency exits. "Only blood flows into the river and speaks to *nusuh* and Smohalla. Only blood."

Otis raised the knife and tore through his pant leg, and while Madison watched in horror he plunged the blade deep into the inner side of his left thigh. With knowledgeable precision he severed his leg artery and looked up at Madison as the blood squirted forth.

"The door is open, for both of us now. I am the offering for the first salmon, showing the way." Otis looked up, sat back on his hands, and stared at the red backstage light on the ceiling watching its image dim until it, and the world, went dark. Otis didn't feel his head hit the floor. Only Madison heard it as he reached the door, opened it to the outside, and stepped off the loading dock into a muddy puddle.

■

The second bullet hit McCurdy in the lower back and almost immediately the floor around him was wet. He felt no pain. In front of him the detonator was just out of reach. Charnock had designed it so that letting go of the accelerator button did not slow the truck engine. He could see the number, still at 4,500 rpm. He tried to move forward and heard the roar of the mob sweeping around the table, sheltering him. He reached down for a moment to try and see where he was hit and felt warm moisture. His legs were numb. He brought his hand back to his face. The fluid was not blood. It was urine. He was pissing. The bullet had paralyzed him. He tried to slide using his arms when he heard the sound of people on top of the table. It was heavy but still rocked as people climbed, stumbled, or were pushed over it.

The table began to rock violently and McCurdy tried to get out from under it as he inched toward the detonator that had slid into a pile of chips. His fingers grabbed at it frantically, pulling it into his hand. As he got control of it, he reached his other arm out and tried to pull himself up to a sitting position to see the unit in the darkness under the table. The crush of people was too much, even for the thick wood, and it toppled onto its side, landing squarely on McCurdy's outstretched arm. The pain was overwhelming. The force of the table shattered his shoulder, knocking him back on his stomach and slamming his face into the carpet. The detonator slipped out of his hand and one of the last things McCurdy saw was a foot kicking it inadvertently across the floor still showing the number 4,500. As he looked up again, he saw the faces of the mob above him, none of them white. They swept over him like an avalanche. It was a boot slamming into his neck and crushing his windpipe that killed him. He thought about his son, destined to succeed where he had failed, and about his wife; he was soon to be by her side again. His last word was *destiny,* mouthed silently by bloody lips. It was spoken not in hate: To his own great surprise, Roy McCurdy died grateful.

27

Jack Charnock looked for the rest room in the rain. He had arrived at Mica Dam in the late afternoon. It looked like nightfall. The clouds hung low and heavy above the trees, and the reservoir stretched out flat and forever, like a gray desert. It was a tranquil place, the air equal parts hard-edged arctic and soft forest rot. The dam, for all its immensity, was an intrusion. Charnock was determined to have one last dignified piss before doing what he had come here to do. This feeling made him chuckle to himself as he stepped around puddles on his way to the visitors' center. He had been carrying a full bladder for the last two hours in the truck but the river had been pressing against Mica Dam since the 1980s.

Charnock tried the door. It was locked. He could see a sign for rest rooms on the wall in the darkness. He knocked. All he heard was the hum of transformers punctuated by the sound of ospreys in the tall trees. Above him the five-hundred-kilowatt power lines were draped like civilization over the timeless wilderness that lay beneath each human breath. He knocked again, a sound of his own making. It comforted him.

"May I help you? The visitors' center is closed."

The voice came from a rusty intercom speaker that he hadn't noticed. He looked up and saw the closed-circuit camera. He started to speak, and the voice interrupted him.

"Press the Talk button."

Charnock found the button and replied to the lens of the camera like it was an old friend from Hanford.

"Hello, just looking to use the rest room. I've been on the road for a while."

Jeff Markel saw the image of the visitor in his monitor and wondered why anyone would trudge all the way across the small lake of a parking lot in the rain when he had about six million acres of British Columbia on every side to do his business. Markel couldn't figure out how to suggest officially, as an employee of BC Hydro, that this soul should relieve himself right then and there. He admired anyone with the old-fashioned self-respect to look for a rest room this far out in the sticks. Markel pressed the intercom.

"All right, wait there. I'll be right down."

The lights came on in the visitor center and Markel appeared with a key to a heavy padlocked chain that barred the doors to entry like a painful regret. The visitors' center was immediately familiar to Charnock. It had the quality of righteousness that had surrounded the early days at Hanford where everything was grand and true—Genesis preceding Exodus. The walls were covered with ceiling-to-floor pictures of the construction of Mica Dam. Its mighty statistics proudly told of the forces man had marshaled for the betterment of the planet, as nothing but a dam could ever portray. A faded scale model under glass, complete with little trees and spidery powerlines, showed the dam's principle accomplishment: holding back the Columbia's headwaters, a reservoir capacity of "24.6 trillion cubic metres." Charnock noted the Canadian spelling of *meters* and wondered if anyone who wasn't an engineer could possibly fathom 24.6 trillion of anything.

"Men's room is to the left. I guess you could use either one, though. Nobody's been in here in years." Markel looked at the wonder on Charnock's face and felt a kindred spirit. "You a dam person, then?"

"Close, I'm from Hanford downriver. I guess we nuclear types are like your children. Falling water, spinning turbines, splitting atoms."

"What are you doing up here then?"

"I don't know. I've always wanted to come up here and see where the river begins. I love the power of stored energy waiting to be unlocked. It's my whole life. That's a whole lot of energy you've got there on the other side of this concrete, but nobody pays much attention to such things anymore."

"You're right about that. Cell phones and pagers get more respect than a dam. Wonders of the world unite, I guess." Markel smiled at this eccentric visitor but he had had the same thoughts nearly every day he came up here.

"I've been driving all day. Excuse me." Charnock stumbled into the men's room, hoping for once that the fellow who had let him in assumed, as everyone he had ever tried to intimidate had concluded, that he was simply a harmless old man.

Pissing calmed him down. It relieved him and settled him about what was to be done. The dam and reservoir were an invitation. Though little more than a gigantic pile of rocks and earth, Mica was every bit as impressive as the Grand Coulee of his youth. As he contemplated the forces that held back the river, the forces that built the dam, and the energy locked in the sphere of plutonium out in his truck, it was as though this dam had been built for the very purpose he was there to carry out. Everything up to this moment had been a test. Nagasaki had only been a test of Hanford's plutonium, its fearsome potential driving the years of the cold war, building like the rain filling the man-made lake behind the dam. Now the promise of these industrial monuments was about to be fulfilled. "Atoms for Peace," the mantra of Charnock's career, the philosopher's stone, was the key to the forces all around him.

He walked from the bathroom, rejuvenated, surprised to have no doubts about what he was doing. He had never felt as confident about his role in the world. He thought of his two best friends who had ended their lives long ago. They had lost hope, derailed by petty scandals. Only he had remained pure, above suspicion, true to the belief that the forces of mind and matter were one, that he was an agent of the irreversible. When he gave his life, it would be for something permanent. Hobby Horse could move mountains and free rivers. In an instant he would undo what it had taken three generations of laborers to build. They had thought they were improving the lot of those who lived by the river. For a time they had, but they had also wound the spring of a catapult, a spring that he would now release.

Charnock contemplated the forces pressing up against the earthen barrier of Mica Dam and estimated that his fifteen kilotons would set a force five thousand times greater in motion. The falling wall of water, ice, and mud would gather momentum as it overtopped each dam downstream. Eight hundred miles away, if Grand Coulee Dam was breached, it would grow five thousand times again to become by far the greatest man-made force applied at one time since the beginning of time itself.

"The Greatest Power Mankind Has Ever Known," the overstatement in big black letters hung over a glassed-in case display in the visitors' center that showed how many Canadian cities the dam could light. The exhibit was dark, but there were little buttons for people to press, showing how little of the dam's capacity it took to power their hometowns.

"You would like to have seen this stuff all lit up. We closed the visitors' center quite a while ago. Nobody ever comes up here except to fish and ski. Those that do would rather not know that one of the biggest dams on earth is just around the corner. People would rather play Adam and Eve in the woods." Markel liked this fellow. He thought about inviting him inside to show off all his turbines, the sodium hexafluoride insulators, and sophisticated switching equipment, but Charnock seemed ready to move on.

He smiled as he looked at Jeff Markel. "This is quite a place. Reminds me of Hanford, out to save the world except the world packed up and went somewhere when we weren't looking." Charnock jingled the keys in his pocket. "Is there a way to drive to the other side of the dam?"

"The road past the guardhouse goes out onto the dam but there's just a service road on the other side. It would be better to go back down and cross the bridge before Revelstoke and come up the highway." Markel didn't want this fellow to leave. "Where are you headed?"

"Actually, I really just wanted to see what it looked like from the top. On the one side a giant lake, and on the other a giant river six hundred feet below."

"It is quite a sight."

"My friends back at Hanford would love me to bring back a picture of the river from up here. We live in the desert, you know. This is heaven."

"Heaven, with a lot of free parking. We've been having a lot of trouble with this high water. If I let you drive out there you can only stay for a minute. The light is pretty bad these days. You better have a good flash."

"Don't worry, I do," Charnock said, without realizing what he was saying, and thanked the man. "I'm Jack Charnock and I want to tell you how grateful I am to you for making this fellow's journey that much easier. Who can I say is the master of Mica Dam?"

"Jeff Markel's the name. I'm chief engineer here. Thanks for stopping by. Bring some friends next time. We'll be here."

Charnock walked out into the rain. He felt determined and exuberant, if a little sad for his new friend Markel. There was nothing to do. Even if he warned him, Markel could not get far enough away in time to avoid the effects of the blast. The flood would make its own rules. There would be no calculating that until it started. Charnock started his engine and drove up toward the dim lights of the guardhouse visible in the distance.

He passed it and the gate was open, the guard waving at him as he passed. The road descended slightly before leveling out. Even under these clouds the sensation was of flying along a groove carved into the top of the world. The dam filled an ancient chasm, and out over the water the dome of rock seemed poised in tenuous equilibrium, holding back invisible forces like a kite in the wind. Charnock drove on until he was at the very center of the span. The water of Kinbasket Reservoir stretched into the distance. The water was high. It seemed to be seeking the top of the dam. Charnock imagined the force of gravity holding on to the mountain with white knuckles, holding, feeling the pressure rise with each raindrop, waiting to give way. On the spill side of the road there was only sky. Off near the horizon the thin line of the Columbia wound its way to the next concrete obstruction.

Charnock took a deep breath. In his pocket was a photo he removed and set on his dashboard, a picture taken just before his father died. Harold Charnock, son, Jack, and grandson Sammy were together on the front steps of Harold's house. Sam was sixteen in the picture. There was still plenty of boy in him. In himself Jack could see the hope from the old days when his work had seemed to matter and so much had seemed possible. His father was proud to have even made it long enough past his accident to have known his grandchild. Jack could see in his eyes that death was near.

For the picture, Harold had taken off the thick black glasses that the nuclear accident had forced him to wear for most of his life. The light from the camera's flash must have hurt him like a blow to the head, but he had not complained. His arm was around Sam, holding him close. Sam was laughing. Jack was looking straight at the camera, his face slightly preoccupied. Rebecca had taken the picture; she had wanted it, insisting that they pose. Perhaps she had suspected all of their fates.

Jack saw his father and his oldest son as martyrs of the nuclear age. He would now join them, a fact that explained his calm here at the top of the dam. He looked at the thickness of the earthen dam all around him. He could not be absolutely certain that Hobby Horse would bring down this structure. He counted on the high water to help him. It made him feel that this was predestined, that he was taking his place in geological history and leaving the petty history of humans behind. If Mica came down, there was every reason to believe that the force of the flood reaching Hanford would slam into the place where his son's body lay and tear it from the desert like a hose on wet clay. Hobby Horse would free his son, reversing his life's greatest regret.

Jack smiled and placed the truck in park and pulled on the emergency brake. With the engine idling, he turned a switch he had installed on the dashboard to the right. He looked through the window of the cab into the back to make sure a red light was now green. It was. He turned back around. He looked at the tachometer. The engine was at nine hundred rpm. He put his foot on the accelerator, pressed gently, and watched the needle rise.

■

Markel had returned to his office near the control room for the dam. He warmed up the cup of coffee he had with him throughout the day. His meeting with the visitor from Hanford had unsettled him. He liked the fellow, but his aimless attitude cut too close to Markel's own misgivings, which he would have been happy not to be reminded of on a cloudy day on the edge of nowhere, with the river still creeping upward. He had chosen the dam business over nukes because it was a good job for an engineer and not part of some creepy and forgotten priesthood. Charnock seemed like a missionary with no talent for converting the natives. Markel preferred dams because they required no convincing.

He often thought about the world ending and how he would learn of it in this remote outpost. Would they even notice it up here? Or would he simply continue to send power out to long-abandoned cities where it would just dissipate over power lines, always traveling, never finding a room to light, an armature to turn, or an appliance to bring to life.

The ring of a single small bell answered his thoughts. A teletype in Markel's office was spitting out paper. It rang a few times, announcing some downstream dam's plans for runoff, a warning for people living along the river. Markel looked at the paper. It was upside down but he could see it came from Hanford. He walked over and tore the paper from the machine and began to read.

It was a warning to U.S. law enforcement about a security lapse at Hanford. There was no mention of Canada. He saw the words, "estimated fifteen-kiloton plutonium bomb." The report described a vehicle, a small pickup truck with a camper. The report declared that secure facilities from Portland to Spokane needed to be on the alert. Markel read alerts like these with a Canadian's comfort that trouble never came north, it always traveled downstream. A casino near the Dalles had been targeted, but the bomb had been defused in time, according to the notice. At the bottom of the paper he saw two names, and recognized one. Markel was dizzy as he grabbed the phone and rang the guardhouse.

"Did you let that truck through the gate?"

"Affirmative, he's been out there about two minutes. Can you see him from where you are?"

Markel looked up at the closed-circuit monitors on the dam. There in the fog were the dim lights of a small truck parked directly at the center of the span.

■

"Nature first doth beget the imperfect, then proceeds she to the perfect . . . *lapidus philosophorum.*"

Charnock mumbled prayers he had said for many years, captions from his many strange dreams, alchemy and physics merging. As the needle moved closer to five thousand rpm, he rushed to repeat them all, to thank those upon whose shoulders he stood. "This is it, Kisty. You don't have to regret anymore what you have done." Charnock looked outside at the quiet misty rain hovering over the reservoir. On every side fir trees stood straight and tall.

He was left with silence. The engine was racing now. The needle had nearly found its place. He looked back at the picture. On the steps of his father's house was the Geiger counter he always carried with him, the one they used to play with at home. Behind where they were standing was a sagging carved pumpkin from that year's Halloween. Jack hated Halloween. His father always made such a spectacle of it, dressing up as Frankenstein. The children always demanded he show them how holding the Geiger counter up to his face sent the needle off the scale.

Jack had never said a word, never put on a costume, never gone for trick or treat. He had just quietly watched each year how the neighbors looked at his father like he was a freak, his father the greatest hero of the cold war performing like a circus clown. The son watched the needle in the truck rise like the old Geiger counter. It was one more game of "Hide the Radium." All at once he looked down at the seat where the large switch with a heavy braid of wires sat. He placed his hand on it. The tears rolled down his face. "I found it, Daddy," he called out. "I win."

Five thousand rpm. One breath. It wasn't the wisdom of the alchemists that caused Charnock to press the switch. He waited for the light. Through the windshield it was suddenly a cloudless day. Even the trees were blue, he thought. Then he disintegrated.

■

Markel saw a flash on the monitor, and then it went dead. There was only a second of silence. The control room was near the top of the dam on the northern edge of the chasm where the switching equipment was housed in thick concrete like a bunker. The shock wave instantly took out the lights and moved the walls of the room by sixteen feet until it was less than half the size. Pieces of the wall shot out like teeth from a broken jawbone as the concrete was bent and compressed by the blast. A half dozen shards of concrete penetrated Markel as easily as bullets. He had no time to bleed. The heat wave followed the shock wave, sucking the air from the room and shattering the control room's three-inch-thick, bulletproof glass. Markel was still alive when the motion stopped.

Outside, trees and rocks along the shore had been vaporized or lay around like fallen twigs and pebbles. The blast had carved a one-hundred-foot depression in the dam and had produced a crater that extended across the dam and out into the reservoir, depressing the water level until Kinbasket seemed empty; but the water was in fact an enormous wave of stored energy from the plutonium. The water that had not been turned to steam had reared up in a tsunami that toppled trees and pulverized everything in its path until the wave of sludge, now with a mass a thousand times greater than the water alone, halted, then turned back to swing like a pendulum toward the dam. It was this moment between swings that Markel observed as silence. Mica Dam had held until that point.

It was only a roar and a creaking sound that could be heard as the wave approached the crippled dam. Markel heard it and knew it was over. The wave hit squarely in the center, the dam's weakest point, split- ting it down the middle, plowing through the rock like it was loose sand. It crumbled and fell as trillions of cubic meters of water overtopped and then fell freely the six hundred feet to the riverbed. It took less than three seconds for the dam to be scoured down to raw bedrock and deposited at the bottom of the chasm. Markel and everyone else on-site were dead before they hit bottom.

The hills echoed with a sound not heard in two hundred thousand years. The ospreys knew the sound and left their treetop nests. From deepest shared memory, they knew to fly ahead of the wind to survive.

2 8

A guard at Revelstoke Dam, downstream from Mica, spotted the flood wave. There had been no warning from Mica. No one had survived. Five minutes elapsed from the time the wave was spotted until Revelstoke, too, was gone. Sixty-four hundred megawatts had simply vanished from the power grid. Bud Hermiston sat in an office at Grand Coulee. He had come here ever since the first alert about a missing nuclear weapon, had watched the lights disappear on the grid monitor, signifying that first Mica and then Revelstoke were off-line, obliterated by the flood. The wave was moving at thirty-seven miles per hour and from the first aerial sightings at dawn was estimated at nearly three hundred feet high.

"At this rate, the wave will slam into Lake Roosevelt and meet Grand Coulee in ten hours. What you need to tell me is how big was that pop up at Mica," Hermiston shouted at the man in his office. Duane Madison had issued the nuclear alert as a precaution. The death of Roy McCurdy and the disarming of the truck bomb at the casino had made him feel the worst was over. One hundred ten people had died in the chaos. The casino burned to the ground, but there had been no explosion. The first report from Canada had come a few hours later.

"The bomb at the casino was about ten kilotons. From what we can tell up in Canada it was bigger, about fifteen to twenty."

"You want to tell me about any more of your Hanford party favors waiting to go off, Mr. Madison?"

Duane paused. The plutonium found in the casino bomb represented about an eighth of what he estimated Charnock had gotten away with. If he was right about the Canadian bomb, maybe half the stolen Pu-239 was accounted for. That still left about twenty kilotons. "We can't be sure. We're doing everything we can to locate the rogue warhead. The better question is whether the dams can handle this flood."

"Well, son, I'm going to let you in on something. The next dam in its path is Keenleyside, just over the Canadian border. It has no fucking chance. You hear me? When it goes in about ten minutes, it's going to add more energy, speed, and water to the wave, and it's going to threaten more and more people living in the floodplain. There's only one thing standing in the way of that wave and every city along the river all the way to Portland."

"Grand Coulee."

"That's right, and Grand Coulee can stand just about anything that can be thrown against her. She was overbuilt. Frank Hale made sure of it back in the thirties, because no one had really believed until she was finished that it might be possible to halt the mighty Columbia with a concrete wall. But we did. She's as much a part of the earth now as the granite around her."

"Does that mean she can take this?"

"That's why I'm asking you about firecrackers."

Hermiston pulled his slide rule from the leather case on his desk and ran once more through the calculations he had been making all morning. He had done three sets. The first applied the full force of the flood to the dam. The second calculation took into account the structural weaknesses he had secretly observed down below the powerhouse from the earthquake and high water. The third calculation applied the force of the flood to the dam weakened further by some explosion similar to what had taken out Mica. Under the first scenario, Grand Coulee would hold. Even under the last, she would most likely stand, according to the numbers on Hermiston's ruler. If she didn't, the flood would march to the ocean, taking out everything in its path, including ten Columbia dams and at least one dam on the Snake River. Flood pressure would actually reverse the Snake's current and crush Ice Harbor Dam like brick through a picture window.

The second scenario was inconclusive and probably the most real. In her current weakened condition, with the water this high and no bomb, she might hold, but she would be so unsound that she would have to be drained, demolished, and rebuilt at a cost a thousand times greater than that when she was finished in 1941.

"I told you, we're doing everything we can to locate the last warhead. It's not easy to hide a nuclear bomb."

"How hard can it be?" Hermiston sneered at Madison. "These people hid one of them in a parking lot and the other in a vehicle that crossed an international checkpoint."

"We'll find it."

"Then Grand Coulee will hold."

"And if we don't?"

"There is no way that a fifteen- or even a twenty-kiloton explosive can hurt Grand Coulee Dam. But that's not all we're dealing with here. The flood contains more energy than a thousand of your bombs. The flood is all the energy it took to build all the dams, all the energy it took for all the water to find its way into all the reservoirs released all at once."

"It's big."

"It's most like the force that carved the Columbia gorge out of solid lava and granite a quarter of a million years ago, and if it finds a weakness in the concrete span from one of your little mushroom clouds, then Portland just might look like Atlantis by tomorrow night."

"So we evacuate."

"We evacuate and hope you find the last popper."

"Meanwhile we've got the roads to Grand Coulee completely blocked two miles all around. There's no way a vehicle we don't know about is getting anywhere near the dam."

Hermiston picked up his radio and called up to the last crew left at Keenleyside Dam. "Is the chopper there yet?"

"Landing now."

The voice on the radio spoke over the shouts and screams of an emergency evacuation.

"You'll have about five minutes to get out of there once you see the wave. Don't mess around."

"We're about to send you a picture, Bud, are you getting our signal?"

"Affirmative."

Hermiston switched on a video monitor and the words *Keenleyside Remote 1* appeared over a background of color bars. Hermiston turned to Madison.

"You're about to see the future, son."

Madison watched the monitor. The picture was of a tranquil morning scene on the edge of a lake.

Hermiston looked closely. "It's not far now. Those are homeless birds flying ahead of the wave. The flood took out their nests. The wave will be right behind them."

"Are you sure we can't weather this, Bud?" The voice on the radio spoke again. "We've got the spillways wide open and the powerhouse at full."

"Get in the fucking chopper. I'm telling you there's no chance Keenleyside will hold."

The camera jerked away from the person Bud had spoken to and pointed back out at the horizon. Suddenly, it looked closer. A sizable wave had appeared, raising the water level. It was visually disorienting, like tracking rolling surf in the ocean. The power of the approaching wave could be seen on both banks where large Douglas fir trees snapped in the distance as they were mowed down and torn from the ground.

"It's not that big, Bud, maybe seventy meters. I think we should sit this out."

"That's not the big wave you're looking at, it's just a ripple leading the way. Now get on the fucking chopper."

As he spoke, a giant black fist flecked with white spray seemed to plunge out of the mountains and into the reservoir.

"The wind is picking up. Can you feel that?" The pilot sounded nervous. The camera was aimed directly at a wave that might have been five times the height of the preceding ripple.

Hermiston shouted. "Pull back to a wide shot. I need scale to make the calculation." Hermiston jotted some numbers down, glanced at the topographical map on the table, and made a quick calculation with the slide rule that hadn't left his hands for hours.

"Jesus Christ!" someone shouted over the radio.

"It's four hundred meters tall. Get out of there now. We need to see the impact. Fly downriver, and get a shot of the dry side of the dam."

On the screen the wave actually seemed to disappear for a moment, absorbed by the wide flatness of the reservoir until its effect caused the surface to rise up in the foreground like a monstrous line of surf taking aim at a beach. Madison looked at the riverbanks where water and debris were carving a swath through trees and rock. As the flood channel widened in the middle of the reservoir, the wave got shorter, but as the channel narrowed again, the wave shot up taller than before, bearing down on the dam.

"Why isn't that chopper moving?" Hermiston was screaming at the television screen. "Go now, goddamnit."

As if commanded, the camera image drifted upward then jerked clumsily around as the shooter held on and looked for another shot. For a moment the camera was just pointed uselessly at the sky. On the radio, voices could be heard exclaiming and cursing. "That's a real wind, and it'll be worse down below," the pilot's voice could be heard saying.

"Get down there!" Hermiston shouted again.

The screen went dark, and Madison shouted, "Oh, Jesus!"

"They're fine. We just lost the signal for a moment." Hermiston didn't take his eyes off the screen. "It's back now."

The picture was jumpy as the pilot struggled to keep the chopper level. The camera was aimed back at the dam. All looked tranquil except for the scores of birds all over the sky that seemed to be flying out of the top of the dam itself. All at once, on either side of the span, two streams of water appeared. An instant later the wave rose until it towered above the lip of the dam and then crashed over it as though it weren't there. The chopper ascended until it was directly over the place where the dam had just been. The camera was aimed at a watery ledge, white and green as it thundered its way down to the valley floor. Every few seconds a tree trunk or a mangled elk or other large animal could be seen bobbing in the spray.

"It's holding," a voice on the radio said.

"Not for long," replied Hermiston, and as he said it, the ledge of green water fell away as though a drain had been opened below. The dam, at first hidden by the water cascading over its top, had collapsed, opening a chasm. The entire reservoir seemed to rush headlong into the gorge. Hermiston looked at his watch. Keenleyside Dam was gone. It had taken nineteen seconds.

The chopper hovered over the torrent that was raging downstream. No one spoke. Finally Hermiston looked up. "We got nine hours to move a hundred thousand people and then nine more to move two million more." The lights flickered in the office. Up on the grid, all three Canadian dams were off-line. "The city of Vancouver will be having blackouts right about now. Seattle is next," Hermiston said, and pointed directly at Madison. "If you have any trick for finding and disarming that bomb, you'd better fucking try it now."

Madison said nothing. Hermiston went back to his calculations. Madison walked over to the map and pointed at a place about two hours away downstream. "I'll be here," Madison said, "if you need to reach me." Then he walked quickly down to his truck, startling a half dozen gulls in the parking lot as he swerved, tires squealing, out onto the road. They flew ahead of him for nearly a mile along the road toward Maryhill.

Extreme unction

The room was as he had left it. The shapes, colors, and especially the smells were foreign. They rushed back into his nostrils, trailing with them his most perfect memories. She lay at the center of her fortress of rounded edges, ringed by softness beyond his imagination. It was the same impression he had had more than thirty years before, when he came here naked and weary of his own world's hard edges. As he looked around, it seemed as though this room was the doorway into the solitary place where he had spent the past three decades. Staring aimlessly upward there on the bed that had once been theirs, she looked as lonely as he did.

Slowly the warrior placed his large rough hand against her forehead. Her eyes found his, and she stared deeply into his face. He stood for a moment like this. Her lips quivered as though she were trying to say something. Nothing came. Her eyes darted to the wall opposite the bed. He looked over his shoulder. There was the bird he had received from Smohalla, the one he had left behind to watch over her in his absence. Its painted wood was faded, but the eyes were sharp and black, as her eyes were as sharp and blue as the day he had left.

He looked at her body, twisted and emaciated, a body he had once possessed. Her hair was still blond, but age had made it sickly with streaks of gray. He bent down and knew finally what had been his sacrifice for all of these years. He understood what Smohalla had asked of him and understood that he had given it without knowing what his life might have been had he refused. On the bedside table was a picture of Mary Hale as she had been then, along with the picture of Charley Shen-oh-way standing in the white spray of Celilo

Falls, strong and tall. He closed his eyes, slowly knelt down, and placed his head in Mary Hale's delicate bony hand.

"I still love you, Boston woman," he said.

■

Francine and Joe both heard him say it. They had brought Charley to Maryhill to escape from the carnage at Shoulder Moon, which lay burning and in ruins. What the panicked crowd had not destroyed was set ablaze by the white fishermen, while the police made no move to stop them. McCurdy's disarmed bomb was quickly carted away in a black truck from Hanford full of men in yellow bubble suits, who looked like creatures from another planet. The mere presence of the bomb had produced its own crater, inside which any score against Indians could be settled, where chaos radiated like deadly fallout, where streaming particles of hatred would haunt the place long after the fires were extinguished. Joe had watched the rioting in silence as they drove away.

It occurred to Francine as she opened the door to Maryhill that it was hardly an escape from chaos. Her father had left the place in ruins thirty-three years before, and left her with scores to settle. She wondered if settling scores with Indians was permitted in her mother's bedroom. Charley had broken the silence as he looked upon what remained of the woman who had called him down from Celilo.

"She's not from Boston," Francine said. Her two parents had appeared together many times in her dreams, but here, the real people who had given her life looked weak, frail, and spent with little life left in them now for her. Charley smiled back at his daughter, still grasping Mary's hand.

"That is what she would always tell me, that she had never been to Boston."

"In old Chinook language all Americans are from Boston," Joe explained, placing his hand on Francine's shoulder. She was torn with relief and anger over what she had seen. Joe had not given the total loss of the casino a thought since arriving back at Maryhill. He had remained in something like a trance since first seeing his brother's face. He had not stopped looking at him. If losing the casino was the cost of seeing Charley again, he was glad to pay it.

"Does she ever speak?" Charley asked.

"Never," Francine answered in the protective, almost irate tone she had used before.

It seemed as if she were arguing the point when Mary Hale suddenly sat up in bed, breathing heavily and looking toward the window nearest her. With her hands she clawed at the blankets to move herself down the bed closer to the window.

"*Chalk-uh-lope,*" she said. Her face was animated. She trembled and grabbed for Charley's shoulder. He stood, and with his enormous arms he gently lifted her up, blankets and all. She stared up into his face and beckoned with her head toward the window. To Francine she seemed to be smiling.

"She has been making that sound for the past thirty-three years, ever since you disappeared into the river," Joe said. "It's just one of the mysteries you left for us."

"I know what she is saying," Francine said defiantly to Joe, and stepped toward the window. Joe looked at her, a new mystery.

"You know about the *jokulhlaup,* then?" Charley said as he turned toward Francine. Mary Hale was nestled in his arms. She looked tiny, like a small bird rescued from a pile of soft leaves.

"Coyote can't free the fishes," Francine said, "so the *jokulhlaup* will." Charley nodded and turned back toward the river.

"It is coming," he said.

"Someone else told me that once," Francine said. "He warned that people would die at the casino, but we found the bomb before it could explode. People died anyway. Now he's gone, vanished like you."

"It is still coming." Charley looked down at Mary. "Nothing can stop it now."

"I would think that you would have gotten tired of bringing death and lies to this world." Francine looked as though she might snatch her mother from Charley's arms.

"Otis said that gathering everyone together to pray for Celilo would stop the killings and bring Smohalla back. Instead it brought you, a father who has known me neither as his child nor as his grown-up daughter, while the man who knew and protected them both and taught me of a father as tall and proud as the sky is now dead. Is that why you came back, to murder Otis, to destroy everything your brother has worked for, and to end any possibility of joy in your daughter's life?" Francine's voice broke. She stepped forward, raising herself to her full height and pointed to the helpless woman who lay so tenderly in Charley's arms. "My mother loved you more than life itself and look what she got for it. Why should I?"

Joe put his hand firmly on Francine's shoulder. "This pain is not your own, Francine. It is not permitted to speak this way to your father. Believe me, if your mother were able to stand, you wouldn't be standing now."

Francine stepped over to the window farthest from the bed. "The Hales did not get your permission when they took your river. I don't need your permission to speak in my mother's house."

Charley walked back over to the bed and set Mary down. He turned to Francine.

"You are my daughter. I would never change that. I would never apologize for what has happened. There is no apology. Each sacrifice is answered with a sacrifice. I cannot give back to you what you have lost; you cannot give back what I have lost. You cannot give to *nusuh* what he has lost. Humans are cursed with the knowledge of all that can never be recovered. All we can do is wager against the chain of sacrifice and when it is interrupted for a moment, declare victory."

"Is that why you came back, to declare victory?"

"No. It is to see the outcome of the game. I made my wager long ago, Francine. You are my victory."

They stayed up into the night and the anger and awkwardness began to wane, drifting like smoke out into the cool desert air that hung over the river. Charley did not leave Mary Hale's side but held her hand and stroked her head, adjusting her blankets effortlessly to make sure she wasn't chilled. Francine had dreamed many times of her father and mother together. This moment of tenderness had been beyond her imagining. Francine thought of the incongruous tenderness she had found with Duke. Their connection was a wager, as her father had described. She wondered where he was. He had known of the bomb. With his father dead now, Duke was a fugitive, trapped upriver in his boat if the authorities knew where to look. She found herself wishing that he could be here with them at that moment, that he could find a way to disappear as Charley had.

Joe and Charley began to speak of old times as though they had only last seen each other the day before. They spoke of their days at Celilo, and soon Mary Hale's room was full of Indian stories and the laughter of brothers. All of the imaginary characters Francine had grown up with, Coyote and Salmon Brother, Bear Woman and Turtle, came alive in the talking of men who joked about them and invoked their names in elaborate curses followed by long, weary peals of infectious laughter. Her family had come alive in the room that had signified death from the time she was a little girl. Francine laughed, smiled, looked over at her mother, and for the first time in her life, believed that her mother smiled back.

They fell asleep together with Mary peacefully watching over the three in the dim light of her bedroom. She had no need for sleep and preferred the delicious pleasure of watching over and dreaming about the three most important people in her life. Charley lay across the foot of her bed while Joe and Francine sat crumpled and wheezing in their chairs. It was Mary who heard the pounding at the front door and tried to wake them.

"*Chalk-uh-lope.*"

Francine opened her eyes and jumped to her feet, suddenly alert.

On her way down the stairs she could see bright lights pouring through the stained glass.

"Is Duke McCurdy in there with you, ma'am?" Madison shouted, and kicked the door open the moment Francine turned the latch. She had last seen Duane at the casino in the moment of relief when McCurdy's bomb was disarmed. There was no relief in his face now.

"No," Francine answered.

"Do you know where he is?"

"No," Francine said, but she climbed into Madison's truck because she knew there was more to it. It was as if every confusing contradiction in her life was resolving itself at that moment, emerging into a pattern of truth she had never had the capacity to understand until now. She listened to him talk and waited for her own mind to tell her what would happen next. It had begun to rain. They drove upriver in Madison's truck with the lights flashing. The oncoming lanes were clogged with traffic. Looking over at the other side of the river, Francine could see even more lights, a traffic jam at midnight. Duane told Francine about the wave moving down from Canada.

"There's no choice except to evacuate. Four hours ago a fifteen kiloton bomb was detonated at Mica. The force of the explosion produced a wave that caused a complete failure of the dam. It was about half again as large as the bomb we found at the casino. We think there is one more out there."

"Duke."

"Do you know where he is now?"

"The last time I saw him was two days ago." Francine paused, not knowing what to say, thinking about the idea of a wave moving down the river, smashing the dams in its path. "Duke is not anything like his father, you know."

"I would agree with that. For one thing, Roy is dead. He couldn't resist the idea of killing. Duke appears to have had a different plan."

"How would I know his plans?"

"Look, we know you and he had a relationship, that he stayed with you at Maryhill on one occasion. We know that if Grand Coulee Dam fails in the next three hours then the wave on the river will triple in size and not stop until it reaches the ocean. You're about all we have to go on right now."

"Who set off the other bomb?"

"A man by the name of Jack Charnock. Have you ever heard of him?"

"I don't know him."

"He sold enough plutonium for perhaps three bombs and his own design for detonating them to Roy and Duke. All we know now is that the design apparently works pretty well. What vehicle was Duke in when you last saw him?"

"He was in a truck hauling his boat upriver."

"Did he say where he was going?"

Francine said nothing. She understood. Tears welled up within her as she felt the lifelong bitterness of being the last to know things. From the time she was a small child, she had been the last to have things explained, as though a curtain was drawn deliberately to keep her in darkness until she found an opening and came into the light.

"Maryhill is on high ground, you know."

"Is that why your granddaddy built it there, to watch the biggest flood in history?"

"There have been bigger *jokulhlaups* than this."

Madison looked over at Francine as he drove. He could see that something had come suddenly to the surface. His head darted back to the road. The traffic was beginning to congest his lane. He drove clumsily around onto the shoulder, honking his horn. He increased his speed at the same time he was thinking that it might already be too late to stop the last bomb.

"Francine, what's a *jokul*—whatever you said?"

"It's a flood that tears open mountains. There hasn't been one since the end of the Ice Age, which was the last time there were giant dammed-up lakes on the Columbia River."

"This has nothing to do with any ice age. This is nuclear terrorism that could kill thousands of people. You have to tell me what you know."

"I know Duke said he was taking his boat upriver because it could do what no other boat could. He said he was entering in some kind of race." Francine paused and put her head in her hands. "And he said for me to stay on high ground and not go near the casino."

"Where upriver?"

"Lake Roosevelt."

Madison recalled the look of the bomb components he had inspected in Roy's truck back at the casino. He imagined them on a boat. It wasn't hard.

"Would you recognize Duke McCurdy's boat if you saw it?"

"Maybe. I remember its name—the *Queequeg*. He told me the first time I met him."

Madison looked at his watch. He was still two hours away from the dam and another hour or so from the main body of Lake Roosevelt. The wave front would reach the lake at about the same time. Madison got on his radio.

"Westcott, this is Madison."

A voice crackled into the radio and was gone.

"Westcott, I think I can locate McCurdy. Have you boys had any luck?"

"Negative, and there are all kinds of traffic problems stalling the evacuation."

"The third bomb is probably on a boat in Lake Roosevelt. We need to begin a search."

"Any ID on the boat?"

"It's a converted Coast Guard surf launch called the *Queequeg*. I would expect it's noisy and very fast. Our only chance will be to take it out from a chopper."

"Lake Roosevelt is pretty big for a nighttime search."

"Westcott, look at it this way. If the bomb goes off there will be plenty of light, okay? If we don't find him by dawn . . . Out." Madison tossed the radio down on the seat. He was disgusted. Westcott was right. He turned to Francine.

"Do you think McCurdy would listen to you?"

"How would he hear me?"

"Maybe we can raise him on marine radio. If he hears you, maybe he'll let you talk some sense into him."

"Maybe." Francine looked out the window as they drove. She wanted Duke to succeed as much as she wanted him to come back to her. "Is there a way to detonate this bomb from off the boat?"

Madison could now clearly see the turmoil on Francine Smohalla's face. "There was a remote-control device at the casino. It's possible, I suppose," he said.

"How soon until we're in radio range?"

"About an hour and a half. Get some rest. I'll get us there."

Francine slumped down in the seat and peered out into the rain and the night. She could not sleep. She thought of the salmon run and how for thousands of years they had worked out the brutal rhythm of their lives. All had to die for any of them to live. Perhaps, she thought as she looked at the lights of cars moving desperately downriver, there were no contradictions in her life.

29

Duke sat in the dark and listened to the quiet, rhythmic sound of the water lapping against the boats. He estimated that there were only about thirty minutes left until dawn broke. The water had begun to rise. It was an inch above where it had been when he first awakened. He peered out the windshield of his boat, which was inside an abandoned, crumbling boathouse about a mile up from the dam. Two boats sat side by side. Duke had hidden them both, the bomb-bearing *Queequeg,* and an outboard-powered decoy.

The boathouse doors were partly open, and Duke could see a narrow slice of the lake all the way to the other side. It was dark except for the lights from the line of evacuating cars. Occasionally one would turn, and the direct beam of a headlight would light up Duke's face and the smiling face of the Indian on his baseball cap. Duke looked at the hardware on deck of the *Queequeg.* Based on what he had been able to learn from the radio in the past few hours, there was something like a fifty-fifty shot it would work. Charnock had finally gotten to see his Hobby Horse demonstration; for some reason, Roy's attempt had ended in failure.

Duke had been listening to the ship-to-shore radio traffic for police activity. There had been nothing, although he had learned plenty about the progress of the flood wave, and that Roy was among the dead at the casino. It caused him great pain to think that at the end of his life, the great Roy McCurdy, the man of destiny with all his bold plans to end civilization, was alone and friendless. Duke had always feared such a fate for his father. It was why Duke had been the one to bail Roy out of all his nasty confrontations. He turned the radio off. He needed quiet to think. The slowly rising water and the lights of the evacuation along the river made him restless.

Protecting Roy from himself had been Duke's single responsibility from the time his mother died. The responsibility was unstated, understood, and he had failed it. Duke wondered if his presence as guardian, throughout his life swooping in to pluck the old man from danger, had the effect of making Roy bolder and more reckless. There was no way of knowing, but he was happy that his father's bomb had failed. There would be only one death at the casino on his conscience. His parents were together now. The thought brought relief even though it brought Duke no closer to them. In a way, they had never been separated. He had always felt more like an intruder than their son: He had certainly never fit into their plans. His story would go on without them, for a little while longer.

He wondered if Francine had heeded his warning and stayed away from the casino. He thought about the destiny his father had spent his life pursuing, when all the time, it seemed to Duke, his own destiny had only been following him around, limiting his options, narrowing his path until he simply vanished, a detail too small to be visible against the horizon. Duke stared across the water. The smallest details were the lightbulbs off in the distance, each only a few inches around, yet they revealed nothing, one was like another. As he watched the current flowing by outside the boathouse, he felt like one of the river's floaters—lifeless, cold, signifying nothing.

He switched on the radio again. There was more ship-to-shore traffic, an edict from the Coast Guard about an orderly departure from the river: Boats were not to be evacuated; trailers would be confiscated. He wondered how far underwater he would be if he simply stayed here and let the wave roll over him. These had always been the choices in his life, to avoid the waves or let them wash him away.

"Duke McCurdy, if you are listening respond, over."

It was the voice of Francine on ship-to-shore. Knowing that she was alive breathed air into his empty lungs. The floater opened his eyes and took a breath.

"Duke, I'm in a truck near Grand Coulee. Please respond."

He looked back at the lights in the distance. She might be one of the lights. He sank into the padded chair on the bridge of the *Queequeg*.

"Duke, please respond. It's Francine, over."

In the darkness he reached over and grabbed the microphone, lovingly pressed the Transmit button and held it down. After a few seconds he released it. The silence gave him away, indicating that he was in radio range and narrowing the search for the bomb on a crazy man's boat. He didn't care.

"Duke, I know you can hear me. You don't have to do this. They're looking for you everywhere. They'll find the bomb before you can explode it. Just let it go. For us."

"So two more wrong people can be together?" he said into the microphone, and looked out at the lights in the distance, imagining that one of them was for him alone. He could see flashing lights of emergency vehicles and hear the sound of helicopters overhead.

"McCurdy, this is Duane Madison. If you indicate the location of the bomb now, we can disarm it, no questions asked."

There was silence. Madison's voice brought back Duke's anger. He felt like a McCurdy. He looked outside to inspect the water level. It had risen noticeably again. It was nearly time to begin. He listened for the sound of the wave, then turned back to the radio.

"Francine, get away from him. When Coyote takes out this dam, you don't want to be anywhere near here."

"Just tell us where the bomb is, McCurdy."

"Madison, was it a jackboot like you who killed my daddy?"

"We made every attempt to bring your father out alive. His death was unavoidable. We made every attempt to save him."

"That's what the Feds say whenever they kill anyone, Francine. Listen to me. You need to get away from him."

"Tell us where the fucking bomb is, McCurdy." Madison was close to shouting. The tone of McCurdy's voice chilled him.

"You're talking to him," Duke laughed into the microphone, and realized that for the first time out of countless hundreds of radio broadcasts, his listening audience at the moment was not the usual crazies he and his father had been speaking to for decades. He looked down at his watch and went on the air for the last time. "It's eleven before the hour. This is *The Tommy Liberty Show* on KGOG radio, voice of the free people of the high-desert country. I'm Duke, the last of the McCurdys, and this is our last show. We'll be taking your calls, for the next few minutes at least."

"Duke, stop this. Listen to me. My father has come home. If you leave the river now, they say you'll be all right. I'm telling you to come home. There is a home for you now." Francine was trying to control herself. She realized that she wanted Duke back as much as she had wanted her father. She squeezed the microphone, holding the Talk button down as though she were holding his hand, until Madison pulled it from her, punched in another frequency, and began to talk.

"Hermiston."

"Why are you calling him?" Francine tumbled out of her trance and looked down at the radio. Madison shouted into the microphone.

"Hermiston. If you can hear me, come in. It's Duane Madison. Hanford Control, over?"

After a pause, Bud Hermiston spoke. He was still perched atop Grand Coulee directly in the path of the flood wave. There was no fear in his voice. To Francine, he sounded as calm as if he were conducting one of his orientation meetings for new employees.

"We're just clearing some loose objects off of our desks and putting on our goddamned bathing suits, Madison. What's the story? Are we going to have to duck and cover?"

"There is another bomb out there."

"Location?"

"Negative."

"Have you found the bomber then?"

"Negative, but we think they're the same. The subject is not using a remote detonator. He's going to pilot the bomb himself. We assume he's on a boat. How close does he need to be to cause dam failure?"

"That's a difficult problem, Mr. Madison. Lots of variables, considering that you can't even tell me how big this bomb is, but I'd say he's got to be right on top of us to do any serious damage."

"Are you evacuating?"

"Not a chance. I'm counting on you Hanford boys to do your job and take him out. How difficult can that be, finding a clear shot at a boat on a smooth stretch of reservoir?"

"We'll get him long before he makes it to the dam," Madison said, although he wasn't as sure as he sounded. "Don't you think you should clear out of there?"

"Negative. You Hanford boys do your job. I'll do mine. Hermiston out."

■

"Hey, Freddie." Bud looked up from his desk and slide rule at the one man who had been at the BPA for as long as he had.

"We're about to pull out." The old man's face was calm, his security uniform pressed and clean although he'd been there through the night. It was as though he were passing by the office to discuss the latest baseball scores. "We've saved a place for you in the van."

Hermiston shook his head. There was silence for a moment. Freddie thought it rude to express the fear he was feeling, so he just looked up at the pictures on the wall, where there was a neatly framed black-and-white picture of every dam on the Columbia, from Grand Coulee down to Bonneville.

"You were at each one of those dedications, weren't you, Freddie?"

"Yes, I was. Just like you." Freddie pointed to both of their faces, younger, smiling, lost in the crowd in one of the pictures.

"I guess we should have taken our retirement a long time ago."

"Or even last week." Freddie chuckled. Bud joined him and then looked back at his papers full of calculations.

"She's hurt pretty bad, isn't she?" Freddie spoke first. "Is she going to make it?"

"I can't say. I think so." Hermiston looked around at the proud artifacts in the office. There was an American flag in the corner; a delicately carved eagle holding an Army Corps of Engineers coat of arms was hung on the wall near the door. "They say that it's terrorists out to bring back the 'real America' who are bombing the dams. Those frontier people from back in the woods who say they want to take America back from the government got their hands on some nukes."

"That's what they say on the news."

"I don't understand, Freddie. This is America right here, in this concrete and steel. This is the American miracle; the American Dream is right here. It's these dams, and we've been giving the miracle away to the people for three quarters of a century now—power, water, everything they need to build their little paradises out in the sticks. Why don't they thank us?"

"The dams were once the biggest thing anyone in America had ever seen. But they were too good, I guess, because people forgot about them."

"I've learned something about our dams this week, Freddie." Hermiston looked down at his calculations. Freddie noticed that Hermiston's voice was tender, serene in a way he'd never heard before.

"What's that, sir?"

"It's much harder to figure what it takes to bring a dam down than figuring out how to put one up. It's funny. All it takes is thousands of men and machines working millions of hours—like ants, building one foot at a time, to defeat a river. It's a sure thing, really. The river doesn't have a chance. But bringing it down, in a matter of seconds, that's a whole different physics problem." Hermiston fiddled with his slide rule, watching the tiny numbers stream past the red hairline marker. "I guess Grand Coulee has a chance. That's about all I can say. I don't think I ever considered anything like this in my fifty-five years of being an engineer. You never think about a dam falling down."

"I guess if she knew we're leaving, it would take the heart right out of her."

"I've got nowhere to go," Hermiston said. "I'll stay. Grand Coulee needs me here."

Freddie paused. "I think I'm going to get on that van, Bud, if that's all right with you."

Hermiston waved him by. "Get out there and start collecting your pension."

"Thank you, Bud. Good luck."

"Engineers hate luck," Hermiston chuckled. "Luck is for when you go fishing. You'll have plenty of time for that now."

"We can go together, bring home a big salmon."

"Sounds good, Freddie. Better buy some good boots. There's going to be some mess here on Monday when you come back to clean out your locker."

"Good advice, Bud." Freddie started down the hall. He turned around to say "see you Monday," but Hermiston was back in his calculations, working his slide rule. He stared at the numbers for a time until his eyes were drawn to the seismograph. The wave was near. Its rumble could be seen in the jagged lines on the paper.

■

Francine's realization that the bomb was with Duke made her desperate. "We have to find him!" she shouted at Madison as she choked back tears.

"Not a chance, Francine. Your boyfriend has already got the pin out of the grenade."

"You don't understand. We have to find him. That part where he said he was the last McCurdy—he's not." Francine looked down at her abdomen. Madison nodded and began to tune the radio back to Duke's frequency.

"I'm sorry to hear that, Francine. But it's too late, the wave will kill him whether his bomb goes off or not."

Madison had pulled the truck off the main road and headed for the high ground at the top of the gorge. "If this isn't some shit for the history books—a black man and an Indian running to escape some crazy white man about to pulverize the earth." The joke fell flat, even to his own ears. He was more scared than in his worst days on the beat in Seattle. If the bomb detonated, they might be shielded from the blast by the dam itself, but they would need some additional protection to escape the burning energy of the first quarter second when the plutonium reached critical mass and the fission reaction began.

When the radio was tuned, Francine grabbed the microphone.

"Duke, you have to listen to me." Her voice was deep and serious. She knew there was only one chance. She thought of her mother, pleading with Charley not to leave, in the early morning hours of a day so long ago.

■

Duke had stepped over onto the decoy boat and started its engine. He let it idle slowly while he opened the doors to the boathouse all the way. He thought about walking away. He could make it to the cliff above Lake Roosevelt and watch the wave hit the dam. It might even take out the span by itself, but Duke knew this was unlikely. He understood what he must do, that the river was changing forever now and that his life was of tiny importance compared to that. He thought of destiny, his father's gift to him. He thought of his mother's river, her gift.

He oriented the decoy boat on a course that would take it to the far end of the dam. He and the *Queequeg* would take a path to the center. He had rigged the remote control to the decoy outboard. He would have partial control of it as they both sped toward the lip of the dam. Duke stepped back onto the *Queequeg* and grabbed the microphone. Francine's voice was on the radio.

"Don't do this. I need you, Duke McCurdy."

"I love you, Francine. But tell me where you are right now. I need you to get to high ground. I need you to live through this and tell your people about me. This is the best way, for the river, for all of us. Where are you?"

Duane spoke next. "McCurdy, we are near the edge of the gorge downstream from the dam. We're on the county road just after the liquor store."

"You're too close."

"Not if you switch off your nuke."

"That's not a smart game to play with me, Madison."

"I'm playing it."

There was silence, then an unfamiliar voice.

"This is Flight One to Madison. We've been listening to everything. When he pops into view, we'll nail him with an air-to-ground missile. We're ready."

"Affirmative. It shouldn't be long now. Can you send me a picture?" Madison looked over at Francine. "It's got to be like this. He's gone too far."

"Sending the picture now. Flight One, out."

"Madison," Duke said, "there's a big rock just a bit down the road from you. It's in a wheat field. Drive out to it now, motherfucker, and put it between your rig and the dam."

"Are you a tour guide or something, McCurdy? I'm not going anywhere until you shut off that bomb." Francine grabbed the microphone and began to scream through sobs.

"He's got a chopper armed with missiles, Duke. You can't win."

"Don't worry, I already thought of that. Just have Madison get you to that rock and promise me you'll stay there until the skies clear."

Madison took the microphone one more time, and as he did, he saw the rock, a boulder about fifteen feet tall in the middle of the wheat field. "McCurdy, what makes you think I'm going to do what you say?"

"I don't know. You just don't seem like a person who would want to be responsible for the death of a pregnant woman."

"How do you know?" Francine asked, almost whispering.

"Destiny," he said. "Promise me you'll tell him about his father. Do that for me, okay, half-breed?"

Francine sat back on the seat and turned to Madison. "Get us out of here."

Duke's last words on the radio were directed at Madison. "Are you ready to place one more bet against a McCurdy? I promise the game is not rigged. You've got one chance now. Over and out."

Madison pulled the truck around to the far side of the rock. "How did he know this was here?" Francine didn't look up. He made one last call on the radio.

"When does the wave hit?"

"Minutes now." It was Bud Hermiston.

"Do you see any boats on the lake?"

"Negative."

■

Duke could hear the sound of the wave echoing down the valley preceded by the ospreys and other raptors, flying together as though emerging from a cave of distant history. He calculated that once he started, he would have three minutes: one minute until he was spotted and one minute for the chopper to choose which boat had the bomb. Then one more minute until the wave took them all out. He would be at five thousand rpm almost immediately, so it would be his call to detonate. His last thought before moving out onto the water was of his rock collection. Remnants of his boat and bones would be found on dry land far downstream thousands of years from this morning. He would become one of the flood-borne erratics he had spent so many years collecting, just like the boulder protecting Francine and his child thousands of years after the flood that had tossed it in a field. He shoved the throttle forward and both boats eased out onto the lake. He looked at his watch. He looked at the sky. It was clearing, a good day to change the world.

The lone chopper above the dam spotted the two boats and radioed to Madison. As they approached the span they separated. The chopper aimed its camera at the wave, which was visible now, tall and black, strewn with tree trunks tossed around like sticks, the liquefaction of earth, resembling no vision of the life-giving water propelling it forward.

"Jesus, there are two fucking boats."

Madison saw the images of the wave and the two boats on a video monitor in his truck. One boat was an inboard, the other had a large outboard motor bolted to its stern. He turned to Francine. "We have one chance. Do you know the one he's on?"

"Yes." She looked up.

"Tell me now, damn it!"

Francine saw that Duke had masked the name *Queequeg* on his boat's stern, but she recognized the inboard, remembering the first time she had seen Duke McCurdy, his silly Indian baseball cap, his sparkling eyes. Francine silently pointed to the screen.

"It's the outboard," Madison barked into the radio. "Take it out." He looked down watching the remaining boat bear directly on the center of the dam. He murmered the words of Hendrix, "And so castles made of sand melt into the sea, eventually."

∎

Duke watched the decoy go up in flames from the single missile fired by the chopper. He shouted, "Well, Jack Charnock, wherever you are, it looks like your concrete tower is finally going to come down!" Duke was at the edge of the dam when the chopper turned toward him. He saw the second missile fire and squeezed the trigger of the microphone saying only the words, "We win." Then he pulled the other trigger.

Miles away, it seemed there was no sound for a long time after those last words on the radio. Francine only saw the shadows from the sheltering granite stone in the intense blue light of the nuclear flash. She looked up at the stone and it seemed as though every shape carved into it by the Indians was glowing. After nine seconds the sound came. It was the sound of a world changing forever.

Resurrection

The creatures of a single mind became aware of the change far out to sea. It was a familiar sound, but they had never before heard it, and it drew them to places that the precious memory in their brains had nearly discarded. But when they became certain they were tasting the breath and soil of their ancient spawning grounds, they were suddenly only a single day away from those times. The river was speaking once again to the sea. They would answer. Slowly they made their way from places far and near on the earth to the mouth of Nch'i-Wana.

For thousands of years the story was told of how Coyote had freed the fishes once more. Early on, the details were sharp. There was old Charley's arrest and trial and how, in the end, there had been too little evidence to put him away in his last few years of life. Charley would never explain to his own people why he had done what he had done, but they did not expect him to have such an answer. His return was simply the signal that prophecy was to be fulfilled. To his daughter on one occasion, Charley expressed regret that his only act as a father had been to awaken her to the voices of nusuh, but she had demanded no explanation. All along, the dead had been a sign for her alone, and the crimes Charley was accused of were nothing compared with the destruction of the dams. Much as people wanted to believe that the Indians were responsible, the circumstances were clear. White men had destroyed their own temples, and chased their own people from Eden. The curious fact remained that the flood had killed almost no one. Its single casualty was a way of life, once so anchored in concrete that no one could imagine it ever changing, suddenly vanished into a dream that, it seemed, had never been.

Over time the story was garbled as time recast characters in the drama and refined it to its essential truth. For a while, the marble castle on the hill reminded everyone of how Smohalla's messenger had returned from the dead, how the electricity from the white man's dams had produced the even more powerful magic that had ended their days, how one man had freed his son from a stone tower and another man had created a son with the winged granddaughter of the dam builders. But all this was eventually lost in the return of the river and the renewed bounty of the salmon, which with the great power of forgetting washed over the hard stones, making smooth what had been rough, making it, once again, impossible to imagine that anything had ever been different. The truth became whatever legend desired.

The single detail that survived the retelling was of the spring morning when the old white woman in the castle was carried to her window on her final day of life. It was said that she looked into the eyes of the newborn baby whose red hair seemed to be on fire, and then down at the river. As she watched the men standing in the spray of Celilo Falls and the salmon jumping, she closed her eyes for the last time. It was always said that the white woman, her Indian daughter, and the child all smiled the same smile that morning, and from that moment the mysterious smile of Tsagaglalal was understood to be a smile of joy.

Acknowledgments

I spent a number of years as a radio reporter in the Pacific Northwest and have largely relied on my memories of those days in writing this story. I have also been guided by the many terrific nonfiction books that chronicle the rich history along the Columbia River. William Dietrich's *Northwest Passage* and Blaine Harden's *River Lost* both capture the tragic contrasts of people and time at odds with each other. Bruce Brown's *Mountain in the Clouds* and Roderick L. Haig-Brown's *Return to the River* are both classic accounts of the salmon's elemental struggle and helped to extend my own appreciation of the powerful (and much diminished) fish I had seen in my own travels. The powerful voice of Mary Brave Bird–Crow Dog in her two-volume memoir was my companion as I struggled to find the voices of Indian characters within these pages.

There are numerous wonderful books by and about the Northwest tribes, and I would mention three in particular from among these: *The Chinook Indians* by Robert Ruby and John Brown, *Nch'i-Wana, "the Big River"* by Eugene S. Hunn, and *The Forgotten Tribes* by Donald Hines. They convey the ghostly Indian presence throughout the Northwest and why tribal culture is alive and available to anyone who wishes to learn from people with far greater experience in these lands than the Europeans who have remade them. There's a fascinating book on Indian gaming published in 1907 by the Smithsonian called *Games of the North American Indians* describing the incredible variety of Indian games of chance and skill collected by nineteenth-century investigators. I relied on the extremely helpful people at the Bonneville Power Administration for information on the Columbia dam system. The definitive book on Hanford is *On the Home Front: The Cold War Legacy of the Hanford Nuclear Site* by Michele Stenehjem Gerber.

I thank my agent, Gloria Loomis, for tireless support and my editor, Pat Mulcahey, for tireless effort. Attorney Skip Rudsenske plowed through the thicket of negotiations required to keep Duane Madison a lyric-quoting fan of Jimi Hendrix. This book could not have been written without a piece of advice the wise and wonderful Bill Maxwell gave me a few years before he died. "Remember," he said, "momentum is your friend." Truer words were never spoken to another writer. Luz Montez and William Blakemore were warm, enthusiastic listeners. Readers Sandy Hockenberry and Tom Keenan gave timely, intelligent suggestions and my wife, Alison, was gripped by the story of Francine Smohalla from the earliest version she read. My last bit of gratitude goes to a Tenino Indian man named Joe whom I tracked down in a nursing home in Richland, Washington, back in 1980. He told me of his years working at Hanford, and as I turned to go, mentioned that he had a real story to tell if I was interested. I sat with him in the waning sun of a summer afternoon in eastern Washington as he told me of Celilo Falls and how it had disappeared. His quiet lament for a vanished river has haunted me for more than twenty years. This book is very much dedicated to Celilo, a nearly forgotten casualty of the Industrial Age, archived in the memories of the dwindling number of living souls who actually witnessed its glory.